the forever contract

A BILLIONAIRE ARRANGED MARRIAGE ROMANCE

LEIGH JAMES

GEMINI PRESS

The Forever Contract

A Billionaire Arranged Marriage Romance

inexperienced

A CRAPPY MOTEL room in the bad part of town was no place for my little brother, but then again, neither was home.

We sat at the chipped little table, contemplating our fate. Actually, *I* was contemplating—Noah, who was eleven, was complaining. "I need something to eat!"

My shoulders slumped. "I told you—we have to wait for dinner."

"But I'm starving." Noah looked at me with wide eyes. "We didn't even have breakfast!"

"Just eat a granola bar," I snapped, then immediately felt bad.

"I finished the box." Noah looked guilty. "Last night."

I sighed, then looked at the clock—it was only four

p.m. "Let's wait one more hour, okay? And then we won't be so hungry when we go to bed."

"Yeah, right." Noah scowled at the ancient clock radio, then at the bed with the ugly, rust-colored comforter, then at me. "When are we going home? I want my X-box."

I groaned. "How many times are you going to ask me that?"

"Home" wasn't much better than the crappy motel room. Dad and Lydia's apartment was dirty, furnished with cast-off items from various East Boston sidewalks. It did, however, contain Noah's X-box.

"I don't know." He scowled. "Have you talked to Lydia?"

I shook my head. "Not yet." Lydia was our step-monster, and she'd thrown us out of the house yesterday. Drunk and yelling, she told us to leave and never come back.

I could just picture her with her feet up, smoking a butt, watching talk shows. She wouldn't be sorry to finally have the tiny apartment, not to mention the television, to herself again.

"Did you try Dad?" my brother asked.

"No." The truth was, I'd called him twice, and he hadn't picked up. Nothing too surprising there.

Noah wrinkled his nose. "Can we even afford to stay here another night?"

"It'll be fine. There's nothing to worry about," I lied. The crappy motel had cost sixty-seven dollars, leaving us with about a hundred and thirty dollars left to our names.

I needed to find some money and soon. But how was I going to work and take care of Noah? Since Mom died, I'd made it my priority to look out for him. I wasn't too keen on leaving him at the ratty Plaza Motel—our next-door neighbor had been outside in his boxer shorts first thing that morning, drinking a Bud, scratching his pale, flabby stomach. The neighbors in the room above us had played loud, banging gangster rap until three a.m., then got into a screaming match. The check-in lady had been vaping behind the desk, scrolling through her phone, and had only grunted when I'd asked where the vending machines were.

What was I supposed to do?

"Earth to Chloe." Noah snapped his fingers. "Your phone just pinged. Maybe it's Dad!"

I checked my cell. "It's an email about a job—I'll be right back." I locked myself in the bathroom so he couldn't read over my shoulder.

The thing about the "job?" It was from an app I'd signed up for—*Sugar Finder*. It was rich men seeking...

companionship...from younger women. A friend from our old neighborhood, Regina Dixon, had told me about it. She'd paid for her room and board at UMass with the money she'd made on the app. Noah and I always needed money, but I'd been too afraid. I'd taken a job at Dunkin' Donuts instead.

But when we'd found ourselves literally on the sidewalk yesterday, I immediately thought of Regina Dixon. She'd been carrying a colossal designer handbag the last time I'd seen her. She'd had her nails done, fancy aviator sunglasses perched atop her head.

I could give a fuck about a bag, but my little brother was another matter.

I'd studied Sugar Finder while Noah slept. The app was gross, but fascinating. The concept was simple: pretty women looking for wealthy men, and vice versa. Women could join for free; men had to pay and fill out an application that included their current income and net worth.

There were a ton of girls on there, all with beautiful, sexy pictures. They mainly were eighteen to twenty-one, young like me. Many listings included the word "innocent." I saw two members that had a ton of likes—both girls described themselves as "inexperienced" and "looking to be taught."

After scrolling through the app some more, I was

pretty sure they weren't looking to be taught which one was the salad fork.

I was inexperienced. In fact, I was a virgin. Were certain men into that? The kind of rich, dirty old men who found their young dates on an app called Sugar Finder? Desperation will drive you to some seriously sick shit, so I made a profile and posted it. I uploaded a picture from the previous summer, right before Mom died. I was wearing a tank top, smiling, with no idea that my world was about to fall apart.

My listing read:

- **Height:** 5'8"
- **Build:** Fit
- **Ethnicity:** Caucasian
- **Lifestyle Expectation:** Moderate
- **Education:** Some college
- **Smokes:** No
- **About Me:** I'm on the quiet side, a little shy, and I love to read. I also love long walks on the beach.
- **What I'm Looking For:** Someone looking to spend quality time. I'm not interested in going to clubs or partying. I prefer sophisticated, intelligent, older men. I'm

young and inexperienced. Show me the
world, and I'm yours!

After I reread it, I felt sick. I'd barely graduated from high school, and I was definitely not interested in being shown the world by some old perv. I was looking to feed Noah his next meal!

My phone pinged again.

Saw your listing. :)

Would love to talk more.

I took a deep breath and hit the reply button. *Great! Let's chat,* I wrote.

The cursor started blinking immediately—my guy was typing a response. *U said u r young and inexperienced,* he wrote. *How young?*

My throat burned like I might throw up. *19.*

How inexperienced? Winking emoji.

I took a deep, shuddery breath. My profile was obviously working. The perv wanted to know if he might have the honor of popping my cherry.

~~Very~~

Totally, I wrote instead. If I was doing this, I might as well...do this.

Blinking cursor. *R u local?*

Yes. My throat started to close up. I was most likely

going to vomit in a minute, not that I had anything much in my stomach.

I want to meet today. I have a proposal for you. An emoji of a bagful of money.

I stared at the emoji. *I'm free,* I typed back.

North End in two hours—the coffee shop on the corner of Harris. I'm wearing a red suit.

A red suit? What sort of weirdo wore a red suit? An image of Santa Claus holding a sackful of money popped into my head, and I almost laughed.

Instead, careful not to drop my phone in the toilet, I threw up.

elena

"ORDER yourself the chicken parm and get a drink," I told Noah as we got in line at a crowded North End restaurant. It wasn't fancy, with its counter service and paper plates, but it was the cheapest on the block.

"Um, Chlo?" Noah looked nervous as he pointed at the chalkboard menu. "The chicken parm is $19.99."

"I know—it's okay." It wasn't okay, but it was his favorite, and I was running late.

I checked the busy restaurant, which was loaded with families. Noah would be safe there while I went to my meeting, safer than at our run-down motel. "Just order, get a barstool at the window, and don't talk to anyone. Okay?" I handed him thirty dollars, mentally tallying what we'd have left.

"Where are you going?" His brows knit together. "I

could come with you." Noah was so much younger than me, still a kid, but he wanted to protect me.

"It's fine, I promise. I'm just going down the street —I'm talking to somebody about a job. Maybe pouring coffee," I babbled.

I could work ten jobs pouring coffee, and it still wouldn't be enough for us to get our own apartment. But he didn't need to know that. He'd been through enough since Mom died. He just needed to eat, a safe place to live. He needed to get away from crazy, drunk Lydia and our useless zombie of a father. Living with them had been hell but being homeless would be worse. I needed to take charge. My brother needed to be a kid.

I was going to make that happen for him, come hell or...Sugar Finder.

After extracting another promise that Noah wouldn't talk to strangers, I hustled down the busy sidewalk toward the cafe. I slapped on some lip gloss and attempted to smooth my hair, but there was little I could do. Early July in Boston was brutal, hot and humid. The heavy, moist air kept my hair perpetually damp and frizzy.

Tourists swarmed the North End. I darted between them, trying to gather my courage. I was no dummy. I knew very well that what I was doing was dangerous and pretty stupid. Meeting a stranger from a dating app named *Sugar Finder*? *Dumb*. Telling him that you're a virgin—and making that a selling point? *Double dumb*.

But...and there *was* a but. Keeping my brother out of a homeless shelter or worse, a foster home? *Priceless*.

I hurried into the cafe, which was relatively quiet compared to the bustle of Hanover Street. I sighed in relief as a blast of air-conditioning hit my face.

But then I stopped dead in my tracks.

Sitting at a small table near the back was a person in a red suit. The fabric was poppy-colored, nothing like I was expecting.

That wasn't the only surprise.

My potential date was a *woman*—long-limbed and elegant, with short hair and thick, black-framed glasses. She appeared to be in her mid-forties, a little older than my step-monster, but much better preserved. The woman looked up from her phone and studied me, arching an immaculately groomed eyebrow. After a moment, she waved.

I felt off-balance and also somewhat relieved. But... Was this actually any better?

I took a deep breath and headed to the table. "I'm Chloe." My voice shook. "Are you—"

"EL1975?" She laughed. "That would be me. Please, Chloe, have a seat."

I slid across from her, taking in her designer bag,

freshly manicured nails, and flawless makeup. *This* woman wanted to know how sexually experienced I was? She looked like someone's mother, like she should be waiting in the school pick-up line in her Range Rover, managing her successful business from her phone.

What sort of freak was she?

"I'm Elena." She extended her hand for a firm handshake. "Thank you for coming on such short notice."

I swallowed hard. "It's nice to meet you."

"Would you like a drink? They make a decent Frappuccino here." She motioned for the server and ordered one, along with several biscotti. When everything arrived, I stared at the biscotti. I'd never tried one.

"Go ahead," Elena said gently. It was as if she was talking to a feral cat.

I took a bite of the biscuit, then another, and another until there was nothing but crumbs. I sucked down the huge, icy drink in about four seconds.

Elena smiled at me patiently. "You're hungry."

I nodded. I wanted to reach for another biscotti and stopped myself.

She pushed the plate closer, then motioned for the server again. She ordered two paninis and more drinks, then looked me over before saying, "You're not just hungry though, are you? You're starving."

"I'm fine." I straightened my shoulders. I hadn't

eaten for two days, but I couldn't tolerate people feeling sorry for me. "What can I do for you, Elena?" I hoped I sounded businesslike.

She leaned forward and kept her voice low. "I saw your listing on *Sugar Finder* and thought we might be able to help each other."

I swallowed hard.

"I run a professional matchmaking service based here in Boston." Elena adjusted her glasses. "I've been in business for a long time. We started out as an escort service—all perfectly above-board, I can assure you—but I've recently branched out."

"Oh!" A *matchmaking* service? I didn't know what I'd been expecting, but it wasn't that. "Okay...? How can we help each other?"

"I'm in the business of finding my high-end clients, mostly millionaires and billionaires, their perfect match."

I gaped at her. Millionaires? *Billionaires?*

"When I saw your listing, I realized that you have something one of my top clients is interested in."

I blinked at her. I literally had *nothing*. I mean, I was good-looking. Despite crappy grades my senior year, I was also pretty smart—smart enough to know that neither of these things added up to anything extraordinary. Pretty and smart? *Pfft.* A girl like me was a dime a dozen, just waiting for the world to chew me up and spit me out.

"You said you were totally inexperienced, Chloe." Elena watched me closely. "Is it true?"

I scowled at her. "Yeah, it's true."

"Are you a virgin?"

"Yes." My cheeks heated. I couldn't believe we were having this conversation. "So what?"

"That sets you apart." Elena arranged her features into a smooth mask as our server reappeared with two glorious-looking paninis. I could see the fresh mozzarella and smell the basil, *omfg*. My mouth watered. Elena might be crazy, but if she was buying, I was eating.

"Go ahead and eat, Chloe. I just want you to hear me out."

I dug into the sandwich, wondering what she would say. She seemed too rich to be totally off her rocker, but what the hell did I know?

"I've been in the business a long time, like I said. I've seen what's starting to happen with these apps. People don't even want to work at an agency anymore—they think they can run their business right from their phones. They want to keep all the money for themselves. And I *get* that, I do. Hell, I'm an entrepreneur. But the dating business can be dangerous. An agency can help. I offer my girls protection that they'd never be able to afford on their own."

My mouth was so full I couldn't respond. Elena continued, "I've been watching the rise of these apps, and I see what's happening to some girls. It's not pretty, Chloe. I'd hate to see something like that happen to you."

I refused to think about what she was saying. Yes, I knew meeting strange men off the internet was dangerous. Yes, I knew I could get hurt—or worse. But what else could I do? I swallowed my food. "It's not like I think this is ideal. I just need money to get my own place."

"I understand. Unfortunately, a lot of young women are in the same position." Elena pursed her lips. "But *you* have an option—I want you to interview for a job with my agency."

I clutched what was left of my sandwich. "To work as an escort?"

"Not exactly," she said, keeping her voice low. "I have a client who is looking for a long-term arrangement. He has very specific tastes, and you happen to fit some of his criteria."

We stared at each other for a beat.

"Because I'm a virgin?"

Elena shrugged. "I'll only share more details if you're serious about interviewing for the position."

"But I need to *know* more details so I can decide." Virgin-shmirgin, there was really only one thing I cared about. "How much money are we talking?"

"A life-changing amount." Elena whipped out her credit card and motioned for the server. "Think about it, okay? There's no guarantee that you'll get the assignment, but you should at least put your hat in the ring. I'll give you my number. Call me if you decide you're interested."

She paid the bill and handed me her card. *Accommo-Dating, Inc. South End, Boston.*

I slipped it into my pocket. Then I started packing the leftover food in the to-go containers the server had left. Elena stood to go.

"Wait," I said. "What are you, like, tracking down every virgin in Boston and interviewing them for the job?"

She laughed. "Something like that."

"Hold on—one more thing. You said the money is life-changing. What does that mean, exactly?"

She watched as I packed up every last crumb of biscotti, her untouched sandwich, and my remaining crust. Some flicker of emotion passed over her face, but I couldn't make it out. Pity? Distaste?

She tilted her head and inspected me. "It means you'll never have to starve again. Call me, Chloe. You won't regret it."

She clicked away in her heels; I watched her poppy-colored suit as she disappeared out into the crowded sidewalk.

And then I unwrapped the second-to-last biscotti and ate it, just fucking *because*.

a match

I'D mulled Elena's words as I tossed and turned in the motel's uncomfortable, squeaky bed. *Never starve again. Won't ever regret it.* Was she telling me the truth? My only qualifications were that I was a virgin and I was desperate. *Those* were the criteria?

What kind of crappy assignment was this?

The first thing that morning, I checked my phone. There were still no messages from Dad. I had two new date offers in the app, but one of them came with a dick pic.

Instead of responding, I called Elena.

"Come right in," she said immediately. "I'll get you set up, and we can start the application process."

We took the T to Back Bay, where I deposited a very annoyed Noah at the Boston Public Library. I parked him with the entire *Harry Potter* series right near the reference desk, so the librarians could keep an eye on him and told him I'd be back when I could.

It was a hot, humid walk to the South End. I barely noticed the classic brownstones and colorful flags as I barreled to my destination. *AccommoDating,* read a small, tasteful bronze sign. The entryway was immaculate, adorned with large flowerpots, the summer annuals in full bloom. I rang the buzzer, uncomfortably aware of my frizzy hair and sweaty armpits.

"Chloe, so glad you could make it." Elena wore a black pantsuit, and despite the heavy humidity, her makeup was perfect. She arched an eyebrow as she took in my rumpled appearance. "Did you *walk* here?"

"Just from Copley." A blessed blast of air-conditioning hit me as I went inside. The office was open and airy, with high ceilings, white walls, and huge windows. I wondered if Elena would let me and Noah sleep there?

"Let's go into the conference room and get started." I followed Elena as she clicked around the corner, leading me to a room with a large table. We sat down across from each other, and she opened her tablet, her long, elegant fingers flying across the screen.

"Okay, Chloe. First of all, you need to sign this." She clicked the tablet and handed it to me. "It's a nondisclosure agreement. It says that if you repeat any of this information to a third party, we can sue you."

"I don't exactly have a lot for you to take." But I signed anyway.

"Good. Now I can tell you more about the client," Elena said. "I can't get into particulars—like his name —but here's the pertinent information: he's from Boston. Thirty years old. Tall and handsome. Well-educated and *very* successful. In fact, he was recently named one of the youngest billionaires in America. He comes from an extremely wealthy family, one you might have heard of. Because of his family connections, he keeps a low profile. He's rarely in Boston these days, and he never does interviews. He works remotely from his island estate."

I sat there, trying to process her words.

thirty

billionaire

island estate

My head spun.

"He's thirty?" I could barely get the words out. "That's a lot older than me."

Elena nodded. "There aren't exactly a lot of women his age who have the qualities he's looking for."

"How much is he willing to pay? Would I get paid by the...hour?" My thoughts zigzagged, trying to imagine different scenarios. I couldn't even guess what a *billionaire* might pay by the hour. Or what he might be paying for. I shivered.

"He won't be paying you by the hour, no. And the amount of money would literally be life-changing, Chloe. Seven figures."

"What?" I almost fell off the couch. *Seven figures...* Wait, if thirty-one dollars—all I had left to my name—was *two* figures, seven was...

"That's a million dollars!"

"Seven figures *start* at a million dollars." The madam pursed her lips. "So... Are you interested?"

I gaped at her. "Are you fucking kidding me? Of *course*, I'm interested!" But icy needles jabbed down my spine. For a million dollars, I was most definitely going to be some sort of virgin sacrifice. I couldn't help my brother if I was dead.

Elena watched me closely. "You don't have to be afraid, Chloe. I understand this is a lot to take in all at once."

"I'm not afr—well, I mean, I don't understand, I guess. Why someone would pay that much."

Elena nodded. "Let me ask you some intake questions, okay? Then I can get more specific about the parameters of the assignment."

"O-Okay." I was jittery, a bundle of nerves and adrenaline. *A million dollars!*

She tapped on her tablet, pursing her lips as she read. "Here we go. Name? Date of Birth? Height and weight?"

"Chloe Burke. November 8, 2002. Five-foot-eight. I don't know how much I weigh."

"Address?"

I gave her my father's address in East Boston.

"Who do you live with?"

"My father, my stepmother, and my younger brother Noah."

Elena tapped away. "Are you still in school?"

"No, I just graduated from EBHS." *Barely.* I left that part out.

"How old is your brother?"

"Eleven."

"And is your mother around?"

I shook my head. "She died last summer. Car accident."

"I'm sorry to hear that." She clicked to the next question. "Any health concerns?" She rattled off a list of different ailments, heart disease, concussions, and cancers.

"No."

"Medications?"

"No."

"What about your family? Any history of any disease?"

I shook my head.

"Any drug or alcohol use?" Elena watched me carefully.

"No. Never."

"Do you smoke or vape?"

"No." I'd inhaled some serious second-hand smoke in the last year courtesy of my step-monster, but again, I left that out.

"Okay, Chloe." Elena clicked on the tablet some more. "Next are some questions specific to my business and this particular assignment. They might make you uncomfortable, but I can assure you this is completely confidential. First of all, the date of your last period."

"Um, two weeks ago?"

"You're going to want to start tracking that more meticulously. There's an app my girls use—I'll show you." She clicked through the next page. "Okay, next: types of sexual activity... Have you ever had sexual inter-course, by which I mean penetration of your vagina with a penis?"

My cheeks burned, but Elena seemed totally casual. "No."

"Anal? Any anal penetration?"

"No."

"Have you ever performed oral sex on someone?"

"No. Elena—let me save you some time. I've never done anything with anybody. *Nothing.*"

Elena looked up from her tablet. "Are you willing to submit to a physical examination to verify that?"

I blinked at her. "What do you mean?"

"By a gynecologist. My client wants proof of your virginity."

We stared at each other for a beat. What sort of freak *was* he?

"Why?" I croaked.

"Because he has very particular taste. He's paying for a virgin. He wants what he's paying for."

"But..." I swallowed hard. "Why does he want a virgin so bad?"

Elena was composed as she answered, "I'm not sure, Chloe. He didn't share that with me."

I drummed my fingers against the table, a nervous habit. "You said that you'd seen some bad things happen to girls on these apps."

She nodded. "This client isn't like *that*. He's just... particular. Maybe a little eccentric."

I licked my lips. "I don't know what that means."

Elena straightened her shoulders. "He has a reason for wanting a virgin, and as I said, he hasn't shared it with me. It's not my business. But what *is* my business is the safety of my girls. I do a thorough vetting on all these clients. Criminal records check, references, the whole nine yards. I also check in with my gut: I don't take on clients who give me a bad feeling."

"*That's* your safety guarantee? Your *gut?*"

She raised her eyebrows. "You're the one posting on *Sugar Finders*, Chloe. Did you think there would be some built-in bodyguard to protect you? No. You'd go and meet your date. Then you'd decide whether or not to run away."

She went quiet for a moment, letting that sink in. "So...are you willing to submit to a physical examination or not?"

"I guess so."

"Good." She nodded, satisfied. "Moving on—okay, these are more personal questions."

More personal than whether I've had anal sex?

"Have you ever been in love, Chloe?"

Oh, shit. That kind of personal.

"No."

"Do you consider yourself close to your parents?"

"I was close to my mom." Despite the adrenaline, my voice sounded dead to my ears.

"What about your father?" Elena didn't look up from her tablet.

"No. My parents divorced when my mom was pregnant with my brother, and I never saw my dad much until this past year."

"So you were, what...seven when they divorced?"

I nodded.

"Did your mother have full custody?"

"My dad was supposed to take us every other weekend, but he never did." He couldn't handle us. He *still* couldn't handle us.

"But you and your brother went to live with him after your mother's death?"

I nodded again.

"And what has that been like for you?"

I shrugged. "Okay."

Elena arched an eyebrow. "I'm going to need you to be a little more specific."

I shifted in my seat. "What does this have to do with the assignment, exactly?"

"I need to present a full profile of the potential matches to the client. He needs to know about your family life, your upbringing, etcetera. He needs to have an idea of who you are before he chooses."

"Well... My mom was great; we were very close. She was an LNA at Boston Medical. She was studying to be an LPN—which is a better job, more pay—because she was always hustling for Noah and me."

"Noah is your brother?" When I nodded, she typed something. "Go on. Why did she and your father divorce?"

"He's a drunk." I shrugged. I didn't remember much from their time together except the yelling. And a pot being thrown at the wall, narrowly missing my mother's pretty face. "She always used to say it was a disease, but it didn't make him any less of an asshole."

Elena kept typing.

"You don't have to put that in there—"

"Trust me, you won't be the only applicant with family problems." She scrolled to the next question. "What about your relationship with your stepmother? What's she like?"

"Not great." I shrugged. "We're not close."

"I see. And how was she about you and Noah moving in with her and your father?"

"It's been an adjustment." *She fucking hates us.* "They were used to doing their own thing."

"Okay, Chloe. Now, let me ask you this: how do you feel about marriage?"

"Huh?"

Elena sat back and regarded me. "How do you feel about *marriage*? The institution of marriage. How do you feel about it?"

"Um... I don't really have feelings about it. Things

didn't work out with my mom and dad, so they got a divorce. I don't have anything to compare it to."

"Do *you* want to get married someday?"

"Me?" I looked at her as though she'd grown three heads. "I'm nineteen. I haven't thought about it." That wasn't exactly true. I'd imagined my wedding since I was a little girl, me in a big white dress, my handsome groom waiting at the altar...

"Are you opposed to it?" Elena's voice was smooth, even.

"No—I mean, not as an institution, I guess."

Elena tapped some more onto her tablet. "How were your grades?"

"I was on the honor roll until this past year." I swallowed hard. "But I started working more once we moved in with my dad and Lydia, and my grades sort of slid."

She nodded. "In your listing, you mentioned that you had some college—"

"I don't. I've been looking into schools, but everything's up in the air."

Elena looked up. "Is that the reason you're wearing the same clothes as yesterday? And that you haven't eaten? Because everything's up in the air?"

I averted my eyes as I answered, "Something like that."

27

Elena blew out a deep breath. "This assignment comes with some major perks. But it could be difficult with respect to your brother. I'm assuming you're his primary caregiver?"

"Yes. Why is that an issue?"

"Because you won't be earning seven figures for a date, Chloe. This client is looking for a *match*."

I blinked at her, not understanding.

"He's looking for a wife," she explained. "Once he chooses one of the candidates I've assembled, he's going to marry her. That's why it's so much money. He wants a bride."

I opened my mouth, but no words came out. I just gaped at her.

Because really, what the fuck could I say to *that*?

dollars

THAT's why it's so much money. He wants a bride.

WTF had I gotten myself into?

"Now, he might be open to some sort of arrange-ment for dependents," Elena continued. "Money isn't an issue, of course. But privacy is. What grade is your brother in?"

I swallowed hard. "He's supposed to start middle school in the fall."

Elena nodded. "I'll make a note of it—we'll see what he thinks."

When she didn't say anything else, I panicked. "That's it? That's the interview?"

The madam smiled at me patiently. "It's not a test you can fail. But I need to know: are you interested?"

I couldn't picture marrying someone. But I also

couldn't imagine walking out of here and telling Noah that we had to beg Lydia to take us back or spend the night in a homeless shelter.

But really, it was Lydia and Dad or nothing. Because if we got processed at the shelter, there was a chance the state would take Noah away from me...

"Of course, I'm interested." As crazy as this was, it was the only lifeline available. When one was drowning, one didn't get fucking picky.

"Great." Elena crossed her legs. "I actually think this is a good fit for someone like you. Much better than working as an escort or that app. You won't have to meet multiple strangers, Chloe. You'll only have the client. It's a big commitment, but like I said, it comes with extraordinary perks.

"First of all, you'll have to sign a contract if he selects you. I'm not going to lie, his lawyers wrote it, and they're the best money can buy. It's airtight—you won't be able to fight it, and if you do, you'll lose. But he's offering to pay a signing bonus of one million dollars, with an additional million dollars per year of marriage."

My heart hammered in my chest as visions of dollar signs danced in my head. Not just a million dollars— more. So much more. *What the fuck would I even do with all that money?*

"Here's the thing." Elena leaned forward. "If you leave the marriage or break any of the contract terms—have an affair, move out of the marital home, there's a whole list—you have to pay it all back. You'd only be able to keep the bonus, but even that gets prorated in accordance with how long the marriage lasts."

"I don't—I don't understand that."

"It's complicated." She nodded. "The client has very generously offered to pay for outside counsel to review the contract with whomever he chooses. The attorney will go through the agreement with you and explain each provision."

My head throbbed. "Why... Why is he doing this? If he's so rich and comes from a big-name family, why is he *buying* a wife? He must be awful."

"No, he's not. Like I said, he's tall, handsome, and a billionaire." Elena pushed her glasses up on her nose, seeming to collect her thoughts. "The thing is, the men who come to me for this particular service—marriage matchmaking—are all rich. They have that in common. But the other thing I've noticed is that they crave *control*. These are successful people, and they want their marriages to be successful. Because let's face it—real life is messy, you know? If you meet someone on Tinder, you don't know what you're getting into. They like the contract aspect. They like that the arrangement is set forth clearly and that they can specify the terms."

"It's a little crazy." That was an understatement. "I can't say no to that amount of money, though."

She nodded. "I'll send this information to the client, and I'll let you know the next steps. Okay?"

"Yes. Thank you." I followed her out to the desk.

"I'm going to need you to keep your phone charged and close. Once I submit the applications to the client, he's going to make a decision quickly. I need you to be ready. Can you come in tomorrow if I need you?"

"I guess so." I longed to ask how many other girls had applied, but I didn't.

"Hold on," Elena said. "I'm texting you something."

My phone pinged. *Elena: one attachment.*

"That's a reservation confirmation from The Stratum Hotel."

"Huh?" The Stratum was a super-fancy hotel over on Newbury Street.

The madam nodded at me. "You have a suite there tonight—you can check in now."

"What? Oh, wow. But my brother—I have to get my brother." My words jumbled out.

"That's fine. The concierge is a friend of mine; I'll tell her to expect the both of you. You can order room service and enjoy all the amenities. I have a corporate account there. There's a car waiting for you out front—the driver will take you wherever you need to go, then to the hotel."

I blinked at her. "Seriously?"

"Seriously. This client is paying me a large sum." She looked me in the eye. "I need to keep his candidates comfortable, don't you think?"

"Thank you, Elena." My voice was hoarse.

"You're welcome. Get a good night's rest—I have a feeling tomorrow might be your lucky day."

Noah didn't believe me when I picked him up in the Town Car. When Kai, the friendly driver, opened the door for him, he almost tripped off the sidewalk.

"What the heck's going on?" My brother's eyes were wide as we circled the Boston Common, the interior of the Town Car cool and sleek.

"I'm up for a job with this agency," I explained. "They offered me a car and a free night for us at a fancy hotel, so I said yes." I kept my tone casual as if this sort of thing happened all the time.

"What type of agency?" Noah wrinkled his nose. "It sounds like someplace a secret agent would work."

"Ha. No, it's nothing like that—it's an employment

agency." That was at least somewhat true. I'd racked my brain to come up with something to tell my brother, but I hadn't gotten very far. "I probably won't get the job. It's working for some rich guy."

"Is this his car?" Noah started pressing buttons, opening and closing the windows, and lowering the privacy screen.

"Don't touch anything—and yeah, it's his car. I think." I shook my head. "Or maybe it's the agency's, and he's paying for it. Anyway, it's something like that. So don't break anything."

"Fine, geez. You're acting like you own the place."

I narrowed my eyes at him. "Just be on your best behavior, okay? We've never been to a nice hotel like this before. I don't want to get in any trouble."

"*I don't wanna get in any trouble,*" Noah mimicked me, scrunching up his face. But when we pulled up outside The Stratum, his eyes almost popped out of his head. The glass-front building soared up to meet the sky, and a doorman wearing a tuxedo waited at the entrance.

"Like I said—*fancy.*" I wished that I had on clean clothes and that Noah was wearing something other than his rumpled Pokemon t-shirt, but there was nothing I could do.

Kai parked out front and opened the door for us,

smiling kindly. "Chloe, Noah—we're here. This is The Stratum. The concierge's name is Gigi, and she's meeting you in the lobby. She's really nice, and she'll show you to your room."

"Thank you." I awkwardly accepted his hand as he helped me out of the car.

"Here, take this." Kai took out a card and handed it to Noah. "If you guys need a ride anywhere, call me. I'm happy to help."

"Thanks." Noah took the card and importantly stuffed it into his shorts pocket.

"Take care, you two. Any friend of Elena's is a friend of mine." Kai nodded as he climbed back inside the Town Car.

"He's nice," Noah mumbled.

As Kai drove away, we both stared up at the hotel. It was so intimidating, all sparkling, fancy glass. Even the sidewalk in front of the entrance was immaculate.

"Are you sure we're at the right place?" Noah croaked.

"Yep." I straightened my shoulders. "Let's go find this Gigi. Then we can hide in our room."

With every step we took, I was certain that someone would spring out and start screaming at us that we didn't belong. If my little brother hadn't been with me, I would've turned on my heel and ran away. The luxurious hotel terrified me.

"Hi there." The doorman bowed and held the door open, smiling as though we were any other guests.

We stopped inside, stunned by the opulence of the lobby. There were marble floors, marble columns, and teak woodwork accents. "Holy shit," my brother said.

"*Noah*. Shh."

A woman, about my height but with fabulous curves, appeared out of nowhere. "Hello—you must be Chloe and Noah. I'm Gigi, the concierge."

I couldn't guess Gigi's age—her dark skin was flawless, without any wrinkles, but there was a streak of gray in her braids. "Nice to meet you, Gigi. Thank you for your help."

"It's my pleasure," she said warmly, obviously trying to put us at ease. "Elena told me to be on the lookout for some very important guests."

Noah and I shifted uncomfortably as a well-dressed family strolled into the lobby. They had an adorable toddler, a little girl, who wore a Louis Vuitton bucket hat. "Can you tell us where our room is?" I asked. My brother and I didn't belong in a lobby like that.

"Absolutely—I'll take you there." We followed Gigi to an elevator and rode up to the fifth floor. The doors opened onto a sleek hallway, softly lit and silent. "Here we are. These are your key cards. Let me show you around real quick."

She opened the door, and I gaped—I'd never seen a beautiful hotel room except in a movie. Floor-to-ceiling windows faced Boston Commons, and there were two queen-sized beds with immaculate, plush white comforters. Vases filled with fresh flowers adorned the elegant space.

"There's a small kitchen through that door," Gigi said, "and two bathrooms. There's a flatscreen television—the remote's in the drawer—and when I heard Noah was eleven, I had them send up a gaming system. Do you play video games, young man?"

Noah nodded, his eyes bright. "Yes, ma'am. That was really nice of you."

No one but me could detect the undercurrent of emotion in his voice. I fought back tears.

"Room service is available twenty-four hours a day. Elena left specific instructions that she wanted you two to eat. The menu's there on the table. Oh, and she's having some clothes sent over. She mentioned something about bathing suits because the indoor pool here is to die for, and no one ever uses it."

Gigi winked at us. "You two call me if you need anything, okay? We want you to enjoy your stay and feel comfortable. Order some food, play video games, and go for a swim. Just call the front desk if you need me. And I recommend the cheeseburgers—they're Boston's best-kept secret. The triple chocolate cake is also a must." She smiled at us on her way out.

As soon as the door closed, Noah jumped on the bed a few times. Then he tore through the rest of the suite, chattering the whole time. "Can you *believe* this? This is as nice as *Ironman's* house! Look at this! Oh my God, Chlo, there's a bathtub big enough to swim in!"

He kept exploring as the doorbell rang and a valet delivered a package. It was from Elena. How did she work so damn fast? Inside was a section with my name and one with Noah's. There were bathing suits for each of us, pajamas, toiletries, clean clothes for the next day, and a note. *Please eat and relax,* she wrote. *I'll text you in the morning.*

I looked around the gorgeous room, only half-listening to my brother freak out about all the video games they'd stacked for him on the console. I sank onto the bed and ran my hands over the plush, pristine comforter.

I did not belong in a hotel room that nice. I felt out of place, a junkyard dog thrust into Best in Show competition. And I *was* in a competition of sorts, wasn't I? I didn't know how many other girls were in the running to be the billionaire's bride. What were they like? Were they wondering what the hell they were doing, just like I was?

Did I even want to be in the running for such a crazy prize—a secretive billionaire who wanted to *buy* a virgin wife? WTF was I *thinking*?

I decided that I wasn't thinking, not really, because I still couldn't wrap my brain around the strange events of that morning. So as Noah snuggled onto the bed and started playing Mario Kart, I pushed all the craziness from my mind. We spent the rest of the day relaxing, ordering room service, and swimming in the fabulous indoor pool. We had the place to ourselves, which Noah took advantage of by doing cannonballs while yelling *"Kowabunga!"* I hadn't seen him smile like that in forever.

At the end of the day, after the kitchen sent us up ice cream sundaes with M-and-M smiley faces, we each collapsed into our queen beds. "This is so comfy." Noah nestled beneath the covers, a smile on his sleepy face. "This was the best day I've had in a long time. Thank you, Chlo. I hope you get the job."

"Yeah?" I tried to keep my voice even.

"Of course I do." He blinked out at the park, the sky above it darkening into cobalt blue. "If you worked for some rich guy, we could live someplace nice. Maybe we could live *here*."

"I don't know about that." I watched his face. "Wouldn't you miss Dad and Lydia?"

He snorted. "You're kidding, right? Dad never talks. Like, *never*. He's always drinking when he's home. And did you know what Lydia said to me right before she kicked us out?"

"No. What'd she say?"

"That they never asked for us to come live with them and eat all their food. She said *good riddance*." He snorted again and rolled over, away from me.

"Lydia's a cunt," I said.

"*Chloe*. I can't believe you just said that." He turned back toward me, eyes wide. "But it's the truth. Even though that's a bad word."

"It *is* the truth, and it *is* a bad word." I got up and tucked him in. "You just remember that you're some-body, Noah Burke. I love you more than anything in the whole world. So don't let Lydia make you feel bad. Like I said, she's a c-word."

He laughed. "Mom would be so mad if she heard you say that."

"Truth." I giggled.

"I wish she was here," he said.

"Me too, buddy. Me too." I turned out the light and stared out at the park, at the beautiful night sky. Just a few stars were beginning to wink. *What should I do, Mom?*

But there was no answer, only silence. And the gentle sound of Noah's breath as he fell into a deep, deep sleep.

the client

WHEN I WOKE up the following day, I immediately texted Elena.

I don't think I was clear enough yesterday, I wrote. *I will only consider this job if my brother can live with me.*

I hadn't spelled it out plainly because I'd been so overwhelmed. But late into the night, I'd wondered what it would be like to live in a mansion. Not so much for me, but for Noah. What if this billionaire had his own indoor pool? What would my brother's life be like if we didn't have to worry about money anymore? If he didn't have to live in a cramped, dirty apartment with people who viewed him as a nuisance, something they barely tolerated?

He deserved better than that. He deserved so much better than that.

My phone pinged. *I've already discussed it with the client,* Elena wrote, *more to come. Can you be at the office by 9?*

My mouth went dry. *Sure.*

I'll send an outfit over, and Kai will pick you up. Talk soon.

I ordered coffee and croissants for me and frosted mini wheats for Noah, his favorite. Then I hustled to the shower, with no idea what the day would bring.

I was surprised by the outfit Elena sent: an elegant but snug-fitting black sundress and thin, strappy high-heeled sandals. It was an outfit for a thirty-year-old, not someone who'd just graduated high school. She'd included a simple gold bangle and what I assumed were cubic-zirconia stud earrings, enormous and sparkling. I applied the lipstick she'd fit in the care package, then swiped on some mascara. When I faced my reflection in the full-length mirror, I almost didn't recognize myself.

"Can you even walk in those crazy shoes?" Noah asked.

I sighed. "Probably not. Do I look okay?"

"You look weird."

"Thanks. Really." I frowned at him. "Are you going to be okay while I'm gone?"

"You're kidding, right?" He hopped onto the bed, stuffed a croissant into his mouth, and grabbed the X-box controller. "This is awesome!" It came out garbled through the pastry, but I still understood him perfectly.

I blew out a deep breath. "Don't leave the room, okay? And you can order lunch, but don't go crazy. *Do* get me another piece of chocolate cake, though."

He saluted me—his mouth was still too stuffed to answer. I ruffled his hair on the way out. "Love you, bud."

He mumbled something which sounded like *love you, too.*

I gathered my courage as I rode the elevator down, praying I didn't trip and fall flat on my face onto the lobby's marble floor. The front desk clerk smiled at me, and I nervously smiled back. With feigned confidence, I strode outside as if I crossed marble floors in opulent lobbies while wearing three-inch heels all the time.

Kai was waiting, standing next to the Town Car, and his pleasant smile reassured me. "Good morning, Ms. Burke. I'll bring you to the South End."

"Thank you." I was so freaking relieved to get into the car and off my feet!

When we reached AccommoDating, Kai helped me onto the sidewalk. "I hope you have a good morning. Take care."

"T-Thank you." My voice and legs wobbled as I headed up the stairs and hit the buzzer. What news did the madam have for me?

What would happen next?

"Chloe, come on in." Elena, who wore a light-gray pantsuit, hustled me through the office. She brought me to the same conference room. "I'm glad you're here— you arrived before the other girls. Please help yourself to water or anything else you might need. I'll be back in a minute."

"Wait! Are they—the other girls—are they coming in *here*?"

"No." Elena shook her head. "We keep the candidates separate; that's better for everyone's nerves. Like I said, I'll be back in a few minutes. With the client."

"*What?*" But she'd already closed the door behind her.

She was going to be back in a minute. With *him*. *The client.*

I longed to get up and pace, but I'd break my neck in the heels. Instead, I sat there, fidgeting, nerves thrumming to an almost unbearable hum.

I didn't have to wait long—before I was prepared,

there was another knock on the door. Elena stuck her head in. "We're ready for you, Chloe. Just be yourself, okay?"

I nodded. My hands were sweaty, clasped tightly in my lap.

Elena strode in, followed by a man in a suit. He was, as she'd described, tall and handsome.

But that description didn't do him justice.

He was big and broad—powerfully built. Even his hands were enormous. His hair was jet-black, thick, and tousled. His suit was also dark and fit perfectly, as though it had been made for him. He wore a white dress shirt beneath, open at the throat. His shoulders were large, hulking. He had the body of a Viking and the face of an angel: a square jaw, aquiline nose, high cheekbones, and pale-blue eyes.

He leaned back against the wall, staring at me. He scowled.

I tried to smile at him and lost courage. "Hi...?"

He turned to Elena. "She's a child," he announced without preamble, crossing his arms against his chest.

"She's nineteen, a legal adult, and *she* has a name: Chloe Burke. Chloe, this is my client, Bryce Windsor. Bryce, this is Chloe Burke."

"Nice to meet you." I sounded like a robot. A scared robot.

He raised his eyebrows, the scowl not leaving his face. "What's your story, Chloe? Where are you from?"

"Here—Boston."

"And you're nineteen—did you just graduate from high school?"

I nodded.

"Jesus, Elena!" he exploded. "Did you go trolling for these girls on a school bus?"

She smiled at him icily. "No, Bryce, I did not. You gave me a set of parameters, and I assembled several candidates who met your criteria. Chloe is only nineteen, but she's mature. She's been caring for her younger brother since their mother died."

"So this is the one with the dependent." He didn't bother to say anything about my mom.

"Yes," Elena continued smoothly, "and I haven't spoken with her yet about your generous offer."

"That's not final. I haven't agreed to anything specific." He turned back to me. "Elena mentioned that you like to read. Is that true?"

I nodded, quite sure my voice would fail me.

"What's your favorite book?"

I cleared my throat. "*Twilight*."

He whipped his head at Elena. "Are you fucking kidding me?"

Bryce Windsor turned and stormed from the office without another word.

Elena gave me a tight smile. "I'll be back in a little bit."

She chased him out, and I just sat there, not knowing whether to laugh or cry.

I'd *thought* that this was my decision to make, my situation to walk away from; I hadn't considered being dismissed so easily. I imagined going back to the hotel, telling Noah that we had to leave. I imagined heading to our crumby apartment in East Boston and begging c-word Lydia and my drunk-ass father to let us live with them again.

What would life be like, then? I was going to work full-time at Dunkin' Donuts, and Noah would sit beneath a cloud of Lydia's second-hand smoke all summer, waiting for his turn with the television, a turn that would never come. The image sickened me. But if we left them, we'd become homeless. If we were home-less, we were vulnerable. Noah could end up in a foster home, and I could end up... I pictured a cold, quiet, dark place. A place where maybe I wouldn't have to worry anymore, ever again, about anything...

"Chloe." Elena stuck her head back into the room. "We have two more interviews to get through. Sit tight, okay? I know that was tough, but don't read too much into it." She closed the door without another word.

Don't read too much into it? Bryce Windsor, douche-billionaire extraordinaire, had outright rejected me. In fact, he'd seemed as though he'd loathed me on sight.

He had the face of an angel, but that was just God playing tricks.

I probably should've lied and said that *War and Peace* was my favorite novel, or at least *Of Mice and Men...*

An hour later, there was another knock on the door. "Good news," Elena said, breezing in blissfully unaccompanied. "It's down to you and one other candidate."

"*What?* He hated me, Elena."

"Not at all. He can be hard to read."

"Please—I might only be nineteen, but I understand what *'are you fucking kidding me'* means."

"So he doesn't like *Twilight*." Elena shrugged. "So what?"

"It's not about that, and you know it." I tugged on the strap of my dress. "There is no way that man is going to ask me to marry him and pay me a fuck-ton of money to do it. *No way.*" I couldn't even picture it; I didn't want to.

Elena looked as though she were going to say something, then stopped herself.

"What?" I snapped. "Just tell me, whatever it is."

She shook her head. "I can't. But I will say you shouldn't count yourself out, not yet." With that, she was gone.

I couldn't sit there any longer—I took off the stupid high heels and paced in my bare feet. I felt like a prisoner. I longed to sneak outside to the cool interior of the Town Car and head back to the quiet, immaculate sanctity of my luxury hotel room. But of course, none of that was mine to return to. Like Cinderella's magic coach and footmen, all my recent upgrades would expire the moment the spell was broken—in other words, as soon as Bryce Windsor chose the other girl.

Another knock on the door. This time, it was a young woman I didn't recognize. She wore a simple navy sheath and a headset. "I'm Anita, the assistant," she said briskly. "I'm going to need your driver's license to process the paperwork."

"I'm sorry?"

"I'm going to need your driver's license," she enunciated slowly, "to finalize the contract. The client made his final decision. He chose you."

I gaped at her, and she sighed. "I need to get moving —he's snappy."

I took out my driver's license and handed it to her

with shaking hands. "Wait—are you *sure* you have the right person?"

She finally smiled, but she looked as though she felt sorry for me. "He made the other girl ugly cry, so she left. I'll just be a little while, okay? We'll send in lunch."

"Great," I said, feeling numb. *Just fucking great, indeed.*

Did this mean that I was the...winner?

Just what on earth had I won?

terms

I SAT in the conference room, which officially felt like a prison cell. Anita brought me a salad, but I couldn't eat it. I called Noah—thank goodness for landlines—he was busy beating some world record on *Fortnite*.

My phone pinged with a text from Elena. *I'm sending the attorney in with the contract—she'll explain everything to you, then we'll talk.*

I immediately responded. *I'm not saying yes to this!*

My phone rang. "Don't say *no* to it until you've heard the contract terms, okay?" Elena asked. "Trust me, Chloe. You'll be glad you stayed."

"I'm the only one left," I hissed. "He drove everybody else away! Don't you see that maybe this is a bad idea?"

"Let's hear what you think after talking to the attorney." Elena hung up before I could argue further.

"Thanks." I glared at my phone. "Thanks a lot."

There was another knock on the door, and a woman with a sleek black bob, a hot-pink dress, and trendy-looking glasses popped her head in. "I'm Akira Zhang. Your lawyer."

I raised my eyebrows. "I have a lawyer?"

"You do now." She smiled at me and set her enormous laptop on the table. "Mr. Windsor's hired my firm as outside counsel to assist you in this contract negotiation. Have you seen it yet?"

"The contract? No. Elena told me a little bit about it, but—"

"It's a complete shit show." Akira typed quickly onto the keypad, then turned the screen toward me. "It says here that you must submit to a physical examination by a gynecologist before the contract is signed. *To make sure your hymen is intact.* Are you aware of that?"

"Yes." My cheeks heated.

"Seriously?" Akira pushed her glasses up on her nose.

"He wants a virgin." I swallowed hard. "He wants to be sure."

She arched an eyebrow.

"I knew I was going to have to do it. Elena already

told me." It was humiliating, but what about this situation wasn't?

"I'm here to represent your interests, Chloe. I'm not passing judgment. If you're okay with it, and you give informed consent..." She sighed. "The doctor's already here; I met her outside. She checks out."

"You googled her?"

"Of course I did." Akira straightened her shoulders. "Like I said, I'm your lawyer, and you're my client. I don't let people fuck with my clients."

"Thank you." Having a lawyer seemed pretty awesome.

"I'm going to send the doctor in, okay? Because apparently, there's zero point in doing anything else if you're not a virgin. You ready?"

"Yes." *No.*

Akira jumped to her feet, shaking her head. "Then I'll send the hymen-checker in."

The gynecologist barely spoke. She was reserved and clinical as she performed the invasive examination. Once she was finished, she snapped off her rubber gloves, washed her hands, and fired off a text. "You can get dressed," she said, and I hustled into my clothes, grateful that it was over.

As soon as she left, Akira came back. "Congratulations! You're a virgin."

"Thanks...?"

"Let's move on. Mr. Windsor's getting antsy, and apparently, His Highness doesn't tolerate waiting." She opened her laptop again and handed it to me. "I want you to read this, each section, then we can talk about it."

I peered at the document, which was thirty-seven pages. "There's no way I'm going to understand it."

"You still have to read it," she insisted. "I'll go through the whole thing with you afterward and explain each provision. Then you can decide what you want to do."

I started reading, but the words swam in front of my eyes. "Why did you call it a shit show?"

She frowned. "Because you only get the money if you stay. Look at Section Fourteen-C. They call it a 'signing bonus' but that's bullshit. You'll barely get anything if you leave the arrangement before a year is up. *Nothing*. And if you leave before two years, you get a pittance. You'd make more working at Starbucks."

"I work at Dunkin' Donuts," I told her, "and I definitely don't make enough to live on."

Akira pursed her lips. "With this, you *do* get room

and board—luxury accommodations—and some other perks. So there's that."

"I'll try to read it."

She nodded. "Just remember that I work for *you*, Chloe. I'll help you any way I can."

"Thank you." She seemed sincere, which was something. It was all I had.

Thirty-seven pages and a throbbing headache later, I turned the laptop around, relinquishing it to Akira. "I don't know if I understood one word. Except that the contract is governed by the laws of Maine, which I don't understand, either."

She nodded. "Mr. Windsor's primary residence is in Maine. But he chose it because it would be more difficult for you to bring suit there. After all, it's not where you live."

"That's a dick move."

Akira nodded. "It's also customary for the party with more leverage to draft the contract that way."

I sat back in my seat, exhausted. "If you were me, what would you do?"

Akira smiled. "I can't tell you that. I don't know your circumstances, but I'm guessing that if you're negotiating an arranged marriage contract at nineteen, things may have been difficult."

I pictured Noah's face, white as a sheet when the

police came to the house after the accident. Then Lydia, smoke curling above her head, grunting at us when we moved in—as though we weren't worthy of the effort of speech. "Yeah... Let's just say I don't have a lot of options."

"I can't substitute my judgment for yours," she said. "You have to decide what's most important to you and *why* you'd actually go through with this. Let's start with that, okay? Your reason."

"My brother—Noah," I said immediately. "We're in a crappy situation, and he's a minor. I need to take care of him, and minimum wage at Dunks isn't cutting it."

"Who has legal custody of Noah?" she asked.

"My father. But he's not happy about it."

"And your living situation...?"

I shook my head. "My mom died last summer. We had to go live with our dad and his wife. They're apartment's filthy, they're both alcoholics, they have friends over and do drugs. It's no place for a kid. Plus, they kicked us out two days ago. I don't even know if we can go back."

Akira nodded. "Mr. Windsor doesn't appear to be offering too much for your brother. There's the money, of course. But you won't get any of it if the marriage doesn't last. That can't help Noah in the short-term."

I read the provision about dependents, but I hadn't understood it. "What *is* he offering?"

"Nothing solid." Akira scrolled through the contract. "It states that Mr. Windsor *may* offer room, board, and financial assistance to any of your dependents. There are no guarantees in here—it's all discretionary. You give up everything, but you may be walking away with nothing. I would absolutely not advise you to sign the contract in its current state."

"Okay." I took a deep breath. "Are we allowed to go back and ask for things?"

"Yes, absolutely. It's a negotiation." Akira got a sparkle in her eyes. "As far as I'm concerned, this is just a starting point. Mr. Windsor appears to be in a hurry, but boo-fucking-hoo. I'm going to help you get some guarantees. If your brother is what's important to you, let's make sure he's taken care of. Let's battle, Chloe—I live for this shit."

Her words gave me hope. "Awesome." Having an attorney was *awesome*.

I got up and started pacing. "I want my brother to be taken care of. I want Mr. Windsor to make sure I get custody of him—*that's* what I want."

"That's a process, though, Chloe. We'd have to go through Massachusetts family court, and it could take a long time," Akira said. "Unless your father willingly waives his rights to Noah."

I stopped pacing and stared at her. "Is that an option?"

"Sure. Suppose Mr. Windsor agrees to make him an offer. In that case, we could prepare documentation substantiating your father's relinquishment of rights and responsibilities." She started typing into her laptop. "It might not hold up in court, but your father won't know that. We could certainly execute a private agreement. Mr. Windsor has enough assets to make it very attractive. Do you think that's something your father would be interested in?"

"You mean—would he trade Noah for money?"

Akira nodded, still typing.

"Absofuckinglutely. He would do it in a heartbeat."

"To use your word—*awesome*," Akira said. "We have a place to start."

Four hours later, we had a signed contract. Bryce Windsor agreed to offer my father money in exchange for my guardianship of Noah. I wasn't going anywhere without my brother. He'd also agreed that the million-dollar signing bonus would be mine, free and clear, after one year. Akira gave me a high-five after we signed.

Bryce Windsor glared at her, then at me.

As soon as Akira left, he turned to his own team of lawyers. "Your firm's fired. I'm hiring Attorney Zhang—send her my files and what's left of my retainer."

They scurried out. Not one of them looked sorry. In fact, they seemed somewhat relieved.

As Bryce Windsor's most recent hire, I didn't blame them. The billionaire hadn't looked at me once as we sat in the larger of AccommoDating's conference rooms, reading the updated contract provisions, initialing each page.

Now that the lawyers had gone, an awkward silence filled the room. Bryce didn't look at me as he gathered his things and checked his phone. He headed for the door.

I'd been high from my win about my brother, but then I crashed back to earth. "Wait—what happens next?"

He paused at the exit, still not looking at me. It was as if he couldn't bear to. "Elena's picking out a dress for you. I'll see you at City Hall in two hours."

"Wait, *what*?" But he was gone, a blur of contemptuous, taut muscle in his expensive dark suit.

Head spinning, I hustled out to the main office.

Anita was the only one there, standing behind the desk with her headset on. "Elena's waiting for you out back."

"Thank you." I headed into the cavernous room at the rear of the building. It was filled with racks of clothes.

"Ah, there you are." Elena put down her phone and smiled at me. "Congratulations, Chloe."

"Um, thank you? I guess?" I twisted my hands together. "So Bryce... He said I was supposed to meet him at City Hall in two hours. But I don't know if I can do that."

"What do you mean?" Elena crossed her arms.

"I'm not going through with it unless my father agrees to sign the paperwork." The words tumbled out in a rush. "I'm not leaving my brother."

"You don't need to worry, Chloe. Attorney Zhang just checked in. She's on her way to meet your father. He already agreed to sign."

My heart sank, even though it was what I wanted. "Already?"

The madam nodded. "It's an awful lot of money, Chloe. Your father's probably never had an opportunity like this before."

"No, of course he hasn't." I shouldn't judge my father so harshly, but then again, he'd always been a deadbeat dad. Maybe somebody *should* judge him.

"So, we need to get you ready. Mr. Windsor said two hours, correct?"

I nodded.

"You need a dress, and then we need to pack some other things for you," Elena said. "There isn't time to go back to your apartment—he wants to leave for his estate right after the ceremony."

Ceremony. Estate. I stood there, reeling, feeling like I was in some dream. "What do you mean? I don't understand what happens next."

Elena came closer and surprised me when she reached out and gently patted my shoulder.

"Next, Chloe, you marry him. And then you start the rest of your life."

white

Elena nudged me in front of the mirror, then smoothed my hair. I didn't want to look at my reflection; it was all wrong. The long, white dress should promise happiness, but it was another lie. It seemed bad luck to wear it—like I was tempting fate by playing dress-up in something that should be sacred.

Everything was happening too fast. I'd be whisked off to city hall to be married in a few minutes. After the ceremony, I would be given one hour to return to the hotel to collect my brother and our things. Then we were flying to Maine on Bryce Windsor's private plane.

I glared at Elena in the mirror. "Why do I have to wear this stupid dress?"

"Don't scrunch your face—you'll ruin your make-up." Elena tried to tame an unruly lock of hair. "And you're wearing the dress because you're getting married, and he needs pictures of the ceremony."

"Why does he need pictures?"

"This needs to appear official." She didn't meet my gaze when she said, "He'll have to share the details with you."

"*He* won't even talk to me. He won't even look at me! You can't just send me to city hall without something! Why is he doing this? Why is he so desperate that he just paid my father off? Seriously Elena—what the *hell*?"

She sighed and gave up on my hair. "I don't know the particulars, but it has something to do with his trust."

"So...money? This is about money?"

"Yes." Elena shook her head. "But I don't think it's something we can begin to understand. Windsor money is a level of wealth that's difficult to conceptualize."

"What am I going to tell Noah?" I asked Elena. My mouth was impossibly dry. "That I married a billionaire so he could keep his membership at the country club?"

"It's a little more complicated than that," she said lightly. "You should probably tell him the truth. Eleven-year-olds know more than we give them credit for."

"I know, but..." I shook my head. "Telling him I married some random guy this afternoon, and by the way, we're moving to Maine in an hour? He's going to freak out." I had zero expectation that the situation was going to last, anyway. But at least Noah could come with me; at least we had someplace to go tonight.

"I understand your concerns, but like I tell all my girls: think about the money." The madam adjusted my dress one final time. "Come on now, it's time. You don't keep Bryce Windsor waiting."

"Elena..." I stopped before we left the dressing room. "I don't want to go."

She sighed. "Then why did you sign the contract?"

"For the same reason I put a profile up on Sugar Finder." My voice rose. "Because I'm *fucking desperate*. You think I want to lose my brother? You think I want to watch what's left of my family be ripped apart?"

"Shh, calm down. You'll get blotchy." She took my hands. Hers were cool; mine were clammy. "I understand that this has been a whirlwind and that you've made an unexpected, life-changing decision in a very short amount of time. But a man like Bryce Windsor only comes around once. This is an incredible opportunity. You're about to enter a world most people only dream about."

"It doesn't feel like an incredible opportunity." My voice was hoarse. The enormity of what I'd agreed to was finally sinking in. "Why won't he look at me? Why did he send a doctor in to make sure my hymen's intact?"

"I don't know," she admitted.

"You told me that this would be better than what happens to some girls on those apps. You said I'd be safe." Our gazes locked. "Is true?"

"I hope so, Chloe. I truly do."

The only thing that kept me from leaping out of the Town Car was the words Elena had left me with. *You don't have to stay,* she said. *And if he hurts you or does something awful, I'll come and get you myself. You aren't alone anymore.* The madam had actually hugged me as I walked out the door.

There was also Kai, who periodically made eye contact with me in the rearview mirror and asked if I was okay.

"Yes," I lied. What on earth did he think of me in this wedding dress as he whisked me off to city hall?

Kai headed for the Back Bay, maneuvering through the light traffic. We arrived at the municipal building's sprawling front steps. "Here we are—I'll help you out. It looks like they're waiting for you."

I peered out the window to find the 'they' he was

referring to—a sour-looking but still incredibly handsome Bryce Windsor, flanked by my attorney, Akira Zhang. "What's she doing here?"

"I don't know, Ms. Burke. But Elena instructed me to wait for you—I'll be outside when you're ready."

I accepted Kai's hand as he carefully helped me out of the car, mindful of my gown. "See you soon."

I felt ridiculous on the sidewalk, vulnerable and on vulgar display in the glare of the afternoon sun. I was all of nineteen, wearing an enormous designer wedding dress and three-inch heels on a Wednesday. The humid heat settled over me, and my stomach roiled.

What the actual fuck was I doing?

I tottered over to Bryce and Akira. "What's going on? Is everything okay?" I half-hoped that my father had reneged on the deal and that the contract had fallen apart.

Bryce glowered. *"She"*—he jerked his thumb at Akira—"insisted that she meet with you before the ceremony."

"Okay?"

"Don't take too long—my plane's waiting. I'll see you in there." Bryce turned on his heel and stalked off, his big shoulders a knot of tense muscle beneath his suit.

Akira waited until he was out of earshot. "You look nice."

"Um...thanks." But she wasn't there to compliment me. I started to sweat, the humidity already breaking down my makeup. "What's up? Did something happen with my father?"

"Not exactly. But Bryce called me on the way to meet with him." Akira adjusted her glasses. "He said to increase my offer from five-hundred thousand to a million. Of course, your father was ecstatic."

I nodded, feeling numb. A million dollars was money my dad could never dream of making on his own. It was a winning lottery ticket, the jackpot of a lifetime. But still...Noah was his *son*.

"I don't really feel like there's any parity with an offer like that," Akira continued. "I don't think it was something your father could say no to."

"Probably not." It would buy an awful lot of whiskey.

"The other thing is that Bryce tried to hire me. He said that I did a great job representing your interests, and I was the type of person he wanted on his team. I said no, of course."

"You did? Why? I bet he pays a lot."

"I said no because it's a conflict of interest." Akira tilted her head. "*You're* my client, Chloe. And I want you to remember that. If there are any issues, I want you to call me. I'm here for you."

I melted a little, and not just because of the humid heat. "Thank you."

"You're welcome. You should get going..." She hesitated. "But there was one other thing he said. I think you should know."

I felt dizzy, the sun too bright. "W-What?"

"I gave him hell about this situation. You're a nineteen-year-old girl. Just because you're legally an adult doesn't mean you don't need protecting."

I swallowed hard.

"I told him I'd be watching—I went up one side of his ass and down the other." Akira frowned. "He said he had zero intention of touching you, and I believe him."

"Really?"

"This is just for show, Chloe, to fulfill an obligation —something to do with his trust. You'll live with him, so it seems real, but he's not planning on anything more. I thought you might want to know that."

I nodded, chin wobbly. *Just for show. Zero intention of touching you.* Relief flooded me. "Thank you, Akira. Thank you for everything."

She smiled, but it didn't reach her eyes. "You know I'm not judging, but this is a fucked-up situation. Call me if you need anything. I mean it."

"I will."

Akira nodded. "Good luck—keep me posted." With that, she turned on her heel and was gone.

I eyed the steps leading up to City Hall. There were so many of them that I felt dizzy. I longed to sit down, crumple the dress and let my tears fall—big, fat drops of black-mascara tears staining my gown.

But I thought of Lydia and my dad, drunk at home, yelling at each other. *Fuck them.* Noah was mine, now. I didn't have to worry—at least, not about that. And if Bryce Windsor had no intention of touching me, that was one less thing to be afraid of.

I lifted my chin and grabbed the hem of my skirt, then climbed the stairs.

I had to go through security, which was almost funny because of my dress. But the guard didn't say a word or crack a joke. I wondered how many nineteen-year-old brides he'd seen.

Bryce Windsor waited in the lobby, leaning against a wall. His arms were crossed against his enormous chest, a dark expression on his face. When he saw me, his features twisted—a momentary flash of relief?—before settling into their customary scowl. "The judge is waiting for us."

"Okay."

He hesitated. "We have to take a picture afterward.

My assistant will do it. Right out there." He motioned toward the plaza outside. "Then the driver will take you to pick up your brother. You'll meet me at the airport after that."

"Then where are we going?" My voice cracked. "Where do you live? I want to tell my brother--this is all going to come as a shock to him."

"Maine. We're flying into Bar Harbor airport."

I nodded, even though that meant nothing to me. "About my brother... I don't think I'm going to tell him the truth. He's only eleven, you know? I think it'd be better if I just say I work for you—"

"You have to tell him the truth." Bryce glowered at me. "You're about to become my wife, and everyone needs to know it."

"But he won't understand—"

"That's not my problem." His icy eyes roamed down my gown, giving me a chill. "*He's* not my problem. You wanted custody; I got you custody. But the negotiations are over now. Please, let's get this over with. I have meetings this afternoon."

He was halfway across the lobby when he abruptly stopped. Shoving a hand into his pocket, he pulled out a black velvet box. "Here's the ring." He placed a heavy platinum band in my palm. "I'm going to need to hold your hand now."

My mouth felt like it was filled with sand. "Why?"

"Because this is a real wedding. It needs to look like it." Looking resigned, he stuck his hand out.

My palms were sweating. I longed to wipe them on the designer dress, but I didn't dare. Instead, clutching the ring in one hand, I reached for him. His palm was dry, rough, and calloused; it surprised me.

Bryce stared straight ahead as he led me to the judge's chambers. I wanted to say *wait*. I wanted to say *stop*.

Instead, I let him drag me to our wedding ceremony.

official

THE JUDGE'S chambers were lined with bookcases filled with heavy-looking textbooks. A woman with caramel-colored skin waited behind a desk. She wore her hair in a bun and glasses on a dainty chain around her neck. "Hi there." She smiled at us warmly. "Congratulations on your happy occasion."

When an awkward silence ensued, her brow furrowed. She eyed my gown. "You *are* the bride and groom, correct?"

"Yes, of course." Bryce sounded all business.

"Ah, it's okay to be nervous. It's normal on the most important day of your lives."

Bryce nodded once. For my part, I swayed on my feet, feeling like I might be sick.

"I'm Judge Patel. You're obviously Bryce Windsor—

I'd recognize Gene's son anywhere. And you must be—" Her gaze flicked to a file open on her desk, then back to us. "Ah yes, *Chloe*. Congratulations, you two."

The muscle in Bryce's jaw bulged. "Thank you for making time for us today, Your Honor."

"Of course. Your father is a good friend." She beamed at him, but Bryce stiffened.

"Let's proceed, shall we? You must be anxious to make it official." She opened a leather planner I hadn't realized she'd been holding. Before I was ready, she said, "You may join hands. Bryce, let's begin with you. Repeat after me: I, Bryce Windsor, take thee, Chloe Burke, to be my lawfully wedded wife."

Bryce took both of my hands, gripping them. He didn't look into my eyes as he recited the words. Instead, he stared at the necklace I was wearing, a platinum cross Elena had secured around my neck.

Icy chills needled my spine as he said his vows.

"...to have and to hold..."

"...for better or for worse..."

"...in sickness and in health..."

"...till death do us part."

I felt like I was outside my body. I heard the judge tell me it was time for Bryce's ring. I obeyed, sliding it onto his finger. He briefly raised his gaze to meet mine, then looked away.

If Judge Patel noticed anything concerning, she didn't let on. I recited my lines like a robot, staring at my handsome groom as he looked anywhere but at me.

Once I completed my vows, he slid the ring onto my finger. It felt wrong against my skin, too heavy. Still, the judge announced: "You are now legally married." To her credit, she didn't mention kissing the bride.

Bryce, however, surprised me by leaning forward. His icy blue eyes narrowed as they met mine—I saw nothing but contempt there. Still, I met him in a chaste kiss. His full lips were unyielding and cold; it felt like I was kissing a very handsome statue.

Disappointment welled inside me.

What...had I been expecting a spark? Did I think a kiss would transform this angry frog into a prince? No such luck. If we were sticking with the fairytale theme, he was fucking Elsa from *Frozen*.

"Congratulations, Bryce and Chloe." The judge's voice broke my thoughts. "May you have a long and happy marriage. Here is your certificate."

"Thank you, Your Honor." Bryce took my hand and led me away, a jailer and his prisoner. *Dead bride walking.*

"Well," I said as we crossed the lobby. I didn't say anything else, and he didn't either.

A young black man in a well-cut suit waited by the exit. "Mr. Windsor, your father called."

"Take the picture and send it to him. And send this to the office." Bryce shoved the certificate at him, then stormed out to the plaza.

"I'm Dale." The man smiled at me, his expression sheepish. "I'm his Bryce's assistant—and no, he doesn't pay me enough. But he pays me a lot."

"Ha." Dale was a breath of fresh air. "I'm Chloe. Bryce's...wife." The word tasted acidic on my lips, some sort of sick joke.

"Congratulations." He ducked his head, making it impossible to read his expression. "We better get out there. He doesn't like to wait."

I longed to ask what Bryce Windsor *did* like. Money? Puppies? Strippers? *Anything?* But Dale hustled me outside before I could find the courage. "You look beautiful, by the way." He smiled at me.

"Thank you." But the happy feeling melted as soon as I stepped outside, facing the glower of my new husband. Even the humidity couldn't soften Bryce Windsor's iciness. Why did he hate me so much?

More importantly...why the hell had I just married him?

Noah, I reminded myself as I took my place by

Bryce's side. He put his arm stiffly around me. *I am taking care of Noah.*

But as I smiled, frozen in front of the camera, I wondered if, in the end, that would be reason enough.

Relief flooded me as the Town Cars pulled up—one was for Bryce and Dale, one was for me. I would be blissfully free of my husband for a little while longer.

Kai's friendly face also put me at ease. "Gigi said she'd meet you in the lobby—you can change before you get your brother." He smiled at me kindly. "When you two are ready, I'll take you to the airport."

"Logan?" I asked. I'd only been on a plane once when we went to my grandmother's funeral.

"Hanscom. You're flying private."

I nodded as though I had any idea what he was talking about. We pulled up at The Stratum, I felt like I might cry. I had the odd sensation that I was being forced to leave home. But that was silly. Our refuge had only been a mirage. Had I actually been afraid of the hotel yesterday?

There was a lot more to fear now.

"What do you mean we're going to Maine?" Noah reluctantly packed his things, but he wasn't moving fast enough. "Who lives in Maine?"

"Um, the Windsor family has a house there."

His scowl deepened. "Who the heck is that?"

"Bryce Windsor is the person we're flying up with. Do you remember going on the plane to Florida?" He'd been little, not even in preschool yet.

"Yes." My brother wasn't really folding his clothes, more like crumpling them and stuffing them into the duffel. "They gave us peanuts in a little blue bag."

"Right. I don't know if they'll have snacks on this flight."

"Why not?" He sounded annoyed.

"Because we're flying private. It's Mr. Windsor's—Bryce's—plane."

Noah's eyes bugged out. "He has his own *plane*? Is this your new boss?"

"Not exactly." I should tell him, I *needed* to tell him, but I couldn't force the words out. "We should get going. Kai's waiting for us outside."

"How long are we staying?" He eyed the X-box with longing.

"A while. Hey, that reminds me—Gigi said you could take it." I nodded toward the console. "Go on." I'd told her I'd pay for it, but when she'd seen what a mess I was, she'd declared the gaming system on the house.

"Seriously?" Noah leaped for it. One thing you could count on with my brother was his enthusiasm over the frickin' X-box. He carefully packed the system up and neatly stacked the games in his bag, unlike his clothes. "Gigi's the best."

"Yeah, she is." I checked my reflection in the mirror. I'd changed into a simple but expensive black mini dress, something Gigi said wouldn't wrinkle. I'd also scrubbed the makeup off my face. Now I looked more like myself, except for the wedding band my brother had failed to notice. Ah, to be eleven.

"Let's get going. Bryce doesn't like to wait."

"How do you even know this guy? Does Dad know we're leaving?"

I took a deep breath. "Yes, he knows. He was fine." *We paid him a million dollars. He's more than fine!*

"You *talked* to him? Why didn't you tell me?" He looked pissed.

"Noah...listen, this is going to sound weird. But we're going to Maine with Bryce Windsor because... I'm sorry I didn't tell you this before... But... But..."

Fuck, I was going to have to be convincing here. "Bryce was my boyfriend, and I didn't tell anybody about it because I thought Dad would get mad."

Noah shook his head. "You have a *boyfriend*?"

"He's not just my boyfriend. The thing is, we just got married."

His face screwed up as though he'd just eaten something shockingly foul. *"What?"*

"That's why we're going to Maine with him. We're moving in with him. You'll love it. He lives in a mansion by the ocean," I babbled, having no idea whether it was true. "Dad said it was okay—he's happy for us. This way, Lydia won't be drunk and yelling at us all the time."

"A...mansion?" Noah's skin was ashen, but at least he looked interested.

"Wait until you see it! It's going to be awesome." I sucked at lying, but when you were trying to protect a child, somehow it was easier.

"Is it just for the summer? What about school? Why didn't you tell me about any of this?"

I waved his very legitimate concerns off. Forcing a smile onto my face, I said, "Let's just take it one day at a time, okay? If you hate it, we don't have to stay. Trust me, this is going to be an adventure."

"You sound crazy," he said as he followed me out the door. He looked upset to leave our room's happy cocoon. I didn't blame him in the least.

"I know. Just trust me, okay?"

In answer, my brother scowled.

The Hanscom airport was busy, but I didn't really pay attention to our surroundings. Noah was not handling the news well. He sat, stone-faced and silent, as Kai sped through traffic on the highway. The friendly driver helped us with our bags when we got to the airport. He nudged my brother. "You still got my card?"

Nodding, Noah patted his pocket.

"I'm just a phone call away." Kai winked at him, then turned to me. "Best of luck to both of you. It's been a pleasure. Take care."

I swallowed over a lump in my throat. "Thanks for everything."

Noah and I watched as he climbed back into the car, leaving us alone. My brother turned to me, glaring. "Do you even have any idea where we're going?"

"No." I masked my nerves with a bright smile. "But don't worry!"

"This is stupid. None of it makes sense—"

"Hey! There they are."

Dale hustled toward us, a worried expression on his face. A thin sheen of sweat glistened on his forehead. It was ninety degrees, and he was still wearing a dark suit, his shirt buttoned all the way up. "Hey, Chloe. Bryce was getting anxious—we're taking off soon. You ready?"

"Yes. We just have a few things." I grabbed Noah and pulled him to my side. "Dale, this is my brother, Noah. Noah, this is Dale, Bryce's assistant."

Dale gave him a firm handshake as Noah stared up at him. "It's an honor to meet you, Noah. You ready for a fun trip? Mr. Windsor's plane is pretty awesome."

Noah shrugged, but Dale had a pleasant energy that was hard to resist. He gave him a friendly smile as he said, "We've got snacks. And juice pouches. And I just downloaded some weird new goose game to my phone. It's supposed to be addictive. You want to try it?"

Noah shrugged again, but his eyes lit up. "The no-name goose game? I'm really good at that."

"I thought you might be." Dale smiled again, then motioned to two nearby men wearing suits. They came and took our luggage.

Noah blinked at them. "Who're those guys?"

"They work for Mr. Windsor, just like me. You ready to go meet him?" Dale gave me a quick look.

"He's as ready as he'll ever be. Right, buddy?"

Noah glared at me again. Goose games and juice pouches were fine, but I was not getting out of this so easily.

"Let's go." Dale led us through the gate and onto a rolling green where a small airplane waited.

Bryce paced beside it, still wearing his suit, a pair of thick black sunglasses shielding his eyes. His cellphone was glued to his ear. "I *told* you, goddammit, to get that contract over to me! I don't care what my father said. I need to review it!" He spotted us. "I have to go."

Glowering, he shoved the phone into his pocket. "You're late."

"Sorry about that. We had to pack." An awkward silence descended. Noah's brow furrowed as he looked from Bryce to me, then back again.

Dale stepped forward. "Bryce, this is Chloe's brother, Noah." The assistant had an almost imperceptible edge to his voice. "I'll get them on board and settled."

Bryce nodded. "Hey, Noah. I'm Bryce, your sister's...husband."

Noah glared. "Yeah, right." With that, he marched up the stairs after Dale.

Bryce stuck his hands in his pockets. "I see he took the news well."

"Please be nice to him." I was surprised by how even my voice was. "He's been through a lot."

He cocked his head. "Haven't we all?"

I inspected the billionaire who'd just paid me to

marry him. He was all big shoulders, tall and handsome in his designer suit, his ebony sunglasses winking in the bright sun.

Was Bryce Windsor fucking kidding me?

It was a rhetorical question—one that I didn't bother to answer as I dutifully followed my new husband up the stairs to his plane.

views

THE RIDE to Bar Harbor was short—just over an hour—and fittingly, it was bumpy. I clutched my armrests, but no one else seemed bothered by the turbulence. Dale and Noah sat together, eating fruit snacks, playing games on Dale's phone, ignoring the rest of us.

As long as Noah was happy, I could bear anything.

But as I glanced back at Bryce Windsor, who'd taken the rear of the plane for himself, I wondered who I was kidding. He'd remained glued to his phone the entire trip. He didn't even look up when we landed. What on earth was Noah going to say about him?

I was relieved to get out of the small plane and back onto solid ground. The Bar Harbor "airport" was unlike anything I'd ever seen: nothing but a rolling lawn as far as the eye could see, with one lone tower adorned by a blinking light. There were a half-dozen small planes parked nearby.

Fir trees and mountains rose in the distance. *Everything* was green. The air was warm but breezy, but not nearly as stifling as Boston. It was the one slight relief the day had to offer. I'd never been to Maine before, but it was exactly how I'd pictured—rustic, lush, and mostly empty. For some reason, this cheered me.

Three large SUVs waited for us in the parking lot. Bryce headed for the first one. "Dale, please take Noah and meet us at the harbor. Chloe and I need to have a word in private."

Noah gave me a quick look. "Is that okay with you?" I asked.

"Whatever." He sounded sullen. The driver opened the door for him, and he climbed up without another word.

"It's not far to the dock." Dale patted my arm. "I'll take care of him."

"Thank you." There was no way Bryce paid him enough.

Bryce motioned for me. "We need to talk."

"Great." But what I meant was, *help!* I was petrified of him. The driver opened the SUV door, and I climbed inside the cool interior. Bryce followed, immediately putting up the privacy screen.

We stiffly sat next to each other as the car rolled out of the airport through the gates. There was no checking out; there was no security. The only sign of life I glimpsed was a dirt parking lot with a few cars. Once we were on the main road, he turned to me. "I read your file, but I need to know more about you."

"Okay."

"Your living situation, for starters. You were in an apartment with your family?"

I nodded. "In East Boston, yes. With my father and stepmother. And Noah."

"Your brother's what—twelve?"

It surprised me that he guessed that close. "Eleven. He's starting fifth grade this year."

Bryce scrubbed a hand over his face. "What about your mother? She died last year?"

I nodded. "She was in a car accident."

He looked at me briefly. "I'm sorry to hear that."

"Thank you." Even though he sounded like a robot, I was flabbergasted that he's said something kind.

"The reason I'm asking these questions," he continued, "is that we've run out of time. We're meeting my father and his wife for dinner, and I'll be in meetings until then."

Panic rose in my chest. "We're meeting your family already?"

"We're meeting my father. I don't consider his wife family." His eyes narrowed. "In any event, he's eager to meet my new bride. I tried putting it off, but he said he needs proof that it's real."

My mind worked furiously to make sense of his words. What had Akira said…something about a trust? "Why does he need proof that you're married?"

A heavy silence descended over us. Finally, Bryce exhaled and leaned back against the seat. "What the hell. You already signed the NDA."

He stared up at the ceiling. "My father has a trust that governs all our business dealings and family money. In order to inherit my share, I needed to be married before I turned thirty-one."

"Why is that a requirement?" I didn't even know if I was using the right words.

"Because my father believes that you need to be stable to be trustworthy. And in his eyes, that means being married."

"Oh." I hesitated, afraid to ask more. I hadn't had much time to stalk the Windsor family online; I knew that Bryce's father was Gene Windsor, and his mother, Celia, had died when he was ten. That seemed to be the only thing we had in common: a dead mother.

"Why didn't you…" How on earth could I put this? "Why didn't you *actually* get married?"

He turned toward me, blue eyes piercing. "We *are* actually married, Chloe."

"I mean—why didn't you marry someone that you knew? Like a girlfriend or something?"

He looked away. "This is business. And I take my business too seriously to risk my future."

I nodded as though *that* made any freaking sense. "What sort of questions will your father ask me?"

"Where you're from, about your family, everything."

I shuddered. "What should I tell him?"

"The truth—about everything except our relationship." Bryce shrugged. "He has more resources than God —he'll find out who you are anyway. We'll tell him about your mother and that your most recent living situation was difficult. I'll have to tell him about your brother, but he won't be happy."

My stomach plummeted. "Why not?"

Bryce raised his eyebrows. "He doesn't like outsiders."

"Noah's eleven, and he's my *brother*."

"We'll tell my father that he can meet him in a few weeks. Noah doesn't seem to be thrilled with this arrangement. It's probably too soon to bring him out."

"Of course he's not thrilled." I winced. "I blindsided him."

"You didn't have much of a choice," he said. "But

back to my father. We need to be prepared. Where was the coffee shop you worked at?"

I was surprised he'd read my file so attentively. "It was the Dunkin' on Bennington, in East Boston."

"What's it near?"

My brow furrowed. "A crappy laundromat and a Peruvian chicken place."

He sighed. "We'll say I met you while you were working, and I was on location scouting real estate. We've been secretly dating for six months."

"Seriously?"

"Seriously." His tone was final.

I shifted uncomfortably. I couldn't picture Bryce in a Dunkin' Donuts in East Boston, let alone flirting with me while I wore a baseball hat and a filthy apron. "Isn't be going to be suspicious? I mean, first of all, there's our age difference. And we're not exactly from the same, er, zip code."

"That doesn't matter. You're a beautiful young woman, Chloe."

He didn't look at me, but my stomach still did a backflip.

Bryce shrugged. "My father doesn't understand much, but he'll understand *that*."

I took a deep breath. "But we're not...together. It's obvious."

"We're going to have to act like we are." He slid his hand over mine, shocking me. "Do you think that you can do that?"

His hand was cool, but for some reason it made me burn. "I guess so."

"For the amount of money I'm paying you, I'm sure you'll figure it out." He released me and whipped out his phone. "I have a call to make. We should be to the dock shortly."

He started barking orders at someone already on the other end of the line.

I rubbed the hand he'd briefly held, feeling as though he'd left a mark.

I barely paid attention to the scenery for the rest of the ride—Bryce stayed on his phone as the mountains and trees swept past. I couldn't seem to focus my swirling thoughts. I was *married*. I was meeting Bryce's father tomorrow night. Noah and I were about to visit our new home. It was impossible, some fever dream I just couldn't wake up from.

Before I knew it, we'd pulled into a large, busy parking lot that faced the ocean. People were unpacking coolers and luggage from their cars—tourist season, families going on vacation. The water was a deep, blue-green, cold, and clear-looking. More majestic mountains rose up in the distance; for a moment, they made my problems seem gloriously small.

"The boat's down on the private dock, Mrs. Windsor," the driver said.

It took me a minute to realize who he was talking to: me. "Of course." Bryce stayed in the car, still on his phone, as I followed the driver down a steep ramp to a dock crowded with families and tourists.

A boat filled with passengers was pulling in. A dad grabbed his young daughter and backed up. "We need to let the people off the mailboat so that we can get on," he explained. "Then it'll take us to the island." The crowd shifted, and I spotted Noah, Dale, and two other employees further down the ramp, checking out the enormous boats.

"Right this way." The driver carried my bag and navigated us past the tourists. Some of them watched me with open curiosity as I headed through a gate to the private dock with all the flashy boats.

"Look at this!" Noah gaped at a bright-red, double-decker fishing boat. It looked brand-new. "Is this Bryce's?"

"Nah, his is bigger than that." Dale jerked his thumb toward the end of the dock where a mammoth white boat—perhaps better characterized as a yacht—beckoned. It had a large open seating area at the rear, furnished with couches, chairs, and what looked like a wet bar, and a tall cabin in the front, replete with tinted windows.

"Woah." My brother's eyeballs almost popped out of his head as we headed toward it. "Is there an *inside*?"

"Of course. It sleeps up to eight. Come on, I'll show you." Dale ushered us down. Up close, the yacht was even more intimidating: bright white, immaculate, and glistening in the late-afternoon sun. *Jules,* read the name in fancy script. "That's Bryce's grandmother's name," Dale explained. "Did you know they always name boats with female names?"

"Of course," Noah lied. We'd never been near a boat before.

"Let's get going." Bryce was suddenly beside us, still on his cellphone, his handsome features twisted in annoyance. "The service sucks here."

We followed him up the ramp and onto the boat. He stopped briefly to check in with the captain while Noah and I gaped at the inside cabin. It was like a living room out of a movie—even nicer than our room at The Stratum—with a flatscreen television bigger than my bedroom back home.

Noah blinked at it, probably imagining the epic

game of Fortnite that could be played on that massive screen. "Holy shit."

"Noah!"

"Sorry, but I mean...holy *shit*."

Dale laughed. "It's a pretty big tv, I know. Bryce likes to watch football—if he's out on the water for some reason on a Sunday, he wants to have the game on. Let me show you two around." We toured the bedrooms below deck, which were compact but luxurious. There was also a kitchen and two bathrooms. It was wild, seeing accommodations like that on a boat.

It started to move. Dale headed up the stairs. "Hey, let's go out on the deck. You'll want to see all the different islands."

Noah peppered him with questions as we headed to the deck. "How many islands are there? Which one are we going to? How many people live there? What's with all the mountains? Where the heck are we, anyway? I've never heard of Bar Harbor."

By the time we got outside, the *Jules* had pulled away from the dock, leaving the mailboat and tourists far behind. Most of them were watching us, probably wondering who the hell owned a boat like that and what they did for work.

At least, that's what I would've been wondering.

"Let's see...the dock is in Northeast Harbor—that's

the main hub for all the islands." Dale motioned behind us, then turned back towards the channel. Our boat sped past tiny motorboats and inflatable rafts; they rocked in our wake, looking like children's toys. "These houses to the right are all part of Northeast, and the ones to the left are Seal Harbor."

Nestled on either side of the channel, ensconced in pine trees, majestic-looking homes rose up. All of them had huge windows to take advantage of the breath-taking views of the harbor.

"Where are we going?" Noah asked.

"Mr. Windsor's island is called the Isle of Skulls."

Noah's eyes grew huge in his face. "Seriously?"

"Nah, just kidding." Dale elbowed him playfully. "It's called Somes Island. There are only two houses on it—Bryce's and his father's."

That caught my attention. "His father lives here, too?"

"Not really." Dale shook his head. "But he built both houses years ago when he bought the island—"

"He owns an *island*?" Noah interrupted.

"Mr. Windsor Senior owns the island. He built two homes there, one for him and one for the rest of the family. He only comes out here occasionally."

"So there aren't any other people who live on Somes?" I asked. "What do you do for groceries? Is there electricity?" I couldn't picture Bryce, who was hiding somewhere below deck, still on his cell phone, without serious creature comforts.

"Ha, it has everything. You kidding me? Mr. Windsor has generators, the best wifi, the best of everything. We get groceries delivered by boat, and sometimes by helicopter."

Even Noah didn't respond to that. He just stared at Dale as though he'd sprouted three heads. Who owned their own island and had their groceries delivered by *helicopter*?

Probably the same billionaire who paid a million dollars for a virgin bride...

The billionaire himself emerged from below. He'd put his sunglasses back on and finally tucked the phone away. The wind ruffled his thick, dark hair, blowing it back from his face. He was so handsome, it was almost uncomfortable to look at him.

"Oh my God—is that the *house*?" Noah practically screamed.

"Yep. That's it." Dale smiled.

I turned away from Bryce and was momentarily blindsided by an enormous mansion rising above the rocky beach. Its stone facade was gray and pristine. It was built on a curve, almost in a semi-circle, with a wall of floor-to-ceiling windows facing the ocean view. It was stunning but also imposing, straight out of a fairytale.

Noah's jaw dropped. "Holy shit!"

I didn't even admonish him this time because...*holy shit*.

the help

WE LANDED at the private dock. More of Bryce's supply of besuited employees met us, carrying our bags and chatting with Dale. Noah and I walked side by side, staring at the "house." I was mesmerized as I looked up at the structure, its gray-stone facade glinting in the sun. I counted eight—*eight*—chimneys.

"Does anybody live here besides him?" my brother whispered.

"I don't know." I didn't think so. "Maybe just his staff."

Noah's eyes bugged out of his head as we reached the landing, the grounds sprawling out before us. The property was unbelievable, the grass so green and manicured it looked fake. The main house soared above us; it had three lower structures adjoined on each side, curving around the circular gravel driveway. A marble fountain bubbled in the center of the drive.

"We're actually going *in* there?" Noah stared up at the house. "I feel like it's too fancy to go inside. Like I'm gonna break something if I breathe wrong."

I patted his shoulder. "You'll be fine."

He gave me a dirty look. "No, I won't be."

The front door opened, and more staff came out. There was a chef—I knew it was a chef because of his hat—and four maids. I knew they were maids because they were wearing legit maids' uniforms, smart black dresses with white aprons, like something out of an old-time movie.

Bryce strode forward. "Good afternoon, everyone. I'd like to introduce you to someone very special." He turned to me and held out his hand. "This is Chloe Windsor. My wife."

I stepped toward him. On instinct, I plastered a smile across my face as I accepted his hand. "It's nice to meet you all." My voice sounded funny, as if it were coming from far away.

"Felicidades!" boomed Chef, his eyes sparkling.

The maids were more subdued, offering their good wishes. Three of them were warm and smiling, but the fourth—who had dyed-black hair, blunt bangs, and the pinched face of a longtime smoker—assessed me coolly.

"Congratulations. You must be delighted," she said eventually.

"Chloe, this is Hazel, our Chief Housekeeper. She's been with my family for over thirty-five years."

Hazel appeared to be in her early fifties, so she must've started really young. "Nice to meet you."

She bowed her head. "You too, Mrs. Windsor."

"Please, call me Chloe."

Her only answer was a smile that somehow looked like a frown.

Bryce motioned to my brother. "This is Chloe's younger brother, Noah. He'll be staying with us, too."

Noah waved meekly at the staff, then hid behind Dale.

"Noah can have the East End suite. Please put Chloe's things in the adjoining master," Bryce instructed.

"Yes, Mr. Windsor." Hazel nodded, then turned to Noah and me. "Please, let us bring you in and get you settled." She started up the stairs, her spindly legs encased in sheer black stockings.

Who wore stockings in July? Better yet, who wore a full-on maid's uniform?

"Please, go and see your rooms. I have a few more calls to make—but I'll join you for dinner." Bryce released my hand. "Welcome home, Chloe."

"T-Thank you." I stumbled away from him, up the stairs after the maid with Resting Bitch Face.

Noah stayed close by my side, and I sensed he was holding his breath as we entered the mansion. The front hall was stunning, with a black-and-white checkered floor, soaring white walls, a giant crystal chandelier, and a grand staircase in the middle. The steps were covered in a crimson Oriental rug. Ferns potted in large, gilded pots dotted the room, as did an ancient grandfather clock.

"Told you so—I'm not breathing in here," Noah whispered.

"I'll just point out some things as I bring you to your rooms," Hazel said, heels clicking across the floor. She gestured to the right, where I glimpsed an enormous sitting room with a fireplace and a piano. "That's the main entertaining space for when Mr. Windsor hosts guests. To your left, down that hall, is the kitchen. We are fully stocked and ready to serve as many as thirty at any time." A note of pride crept into her voice. "Chef is from Barcelona, one of Mr. Windsor's favorite cities. Tonight he'll be serving seafood paella with crawfish— one of his specialties."

Noah silently gagged, and I tried not to laugh.

Hazel started up the stairs, and we followed her. "Your things will be brought up via the staff staircase. It connects the kitchen and our quarters to the rest of the house. We all live here—me, Chef, the other maids, and the various assistants who work for the Windsor estate."

"Does Dale live here?" Noah sounded hopeful.

"Yes, he travels with Mr. Windsor. He doesn't stay in staff quarters, though. Mr. Windsor insisted on him having a regular suite of his own."

I was going to start a new drinking game, even though I didn't drink. It was how many times Hazel would say *Mr. Windsor*.

"Now, Mr. Windsor said that Noah will be staying in the East End suite. That's right this way." We reached the top of the stairs, and she took a right. The hallway seemed to go on forever, with large paintings on the walls and half a dozen closed doors.

"What are all these rooms?" I asked.

"Guest rooms, of course."

Of course. Because Bryce seemed like such a social guy. He definitely needed twenty guest rooms!

"Here we are." Hazel opened a bedroom door at the end of the hall. The suite inside was magnificent; light and airy, and several large windows faced the ocean view. There was a king-sized bed, a sitting area with an overstuffed armchair, a giant television. I glimpsed a pristine-looking bathroom off to the side.

Noah's jaw dropped. "This is *my room*?"

"Yes." Hazel seemed quite pleased with herself. "Your things will be brought up shortly."

"Wow...thanks."

She actually curtsied, and Noah gaped some more. "My pleasure." But when Hazel turned her gaze back to me, her expression hardened. "Now I'll show you to your room, Mrs. Windsor."

"Please call me Chloe—"

She turned on her heel and clacked back into the hall. Noah arched his eyebrow. "Bet your room isn't as nice as mine if she has anything to do with it, *Mrs. Windsor*."

I sighed. "Are you coming?"

He jumped on the bed and started bouncing. "Not on your life. But come back and get me after, okay? Or else I'll get lost!"

I left him to his bouncing and hurried after Hazel. I had a feeling I was already somehow on her bad side, and I wasn't too interested in making it worse.

She was already halfway down the hall, her back ramrod straight. She didn't turn around or say anything until we reached the opposite wing. "This is Mr. Windsor's suite." She motioned to a door. "And this is the adjoining master."

I followed her into the most gorgeous bedroom I'd

ever seen in real life *or* the movies. The bed commanded the far wall: enormous and cozy, it boasted a canopy over the top and a million throw pillows in soft grays and pale pinks. It was a bed fit for a princess...or a billionaire. The walls were white, and the floor-to-ceiling windows faced the ocean; the waves crashed against the rocks, a sound I could never grow tired of.

"The bedroom connects to Mr. Windsor's suite through here." Hazel opened a large white door, and I glimpsed the room beyond. It was the opposite of mine, distinctly masculine—all dark wood, dark walls, and heavy drapes. She closed the door, and I shivered. That was all that would be between Bryce Windsor and me every night?

I immediately thought of his scowl. And his sneer. And his cellphone. *There were plenty of other things between us.*

"I trust that everything is to your liking?" Hazel's lips puckered.

"Um, of course. This is amazing."

She straightened her bony shoulders. "The island is a very special place, and this home is its crown jewel."

I nodded, and she arched an eyebrow.

"We expect that all of our guests, new and return-ing, to treat it with the respect that it commands."

I opened my mouth, but no words came out because *what the fuck was she saying to me?*

"Chloe isn't a guest." Bryce strode into the room, and I was astonished to be relieved to see him. "She's my wife, and she lives here now."

He came next to me and snaked his arm around my waist. "Now, please, have her things sent up. Chloe will let you know if she needs anything further."

Dismissed, Hazel nodded and fled the room.

Bryce immediately released me. "She can be a bit protective of me."

"Is that what you call it?" I listened as her heels clacked away down the hall. "She's a little...intense."

He laughed—just once—then looked surprised, as though the sound was foreign to him. "That's one way of putting it. She's been here from the beginning. I've known her my whole life."

I nodded, then gestured to the room. "This is beautiful. I've never seen a bedroom like this before."

"I'm glad you like it. Is your brother settling in?"

"I should probably go check on him—he's worried he's going to get lost if he tries to find me."

"That can happen pretty easily. I'll walk you down there if you're ready." Bryce headed out of the room, and I followed him, hustling to keep pace with his long strides. "I'll have Dale give you an official tour of the island tomorrow."

He stopped outside Noah's door. "You need to dress for dinner. I'm having something sent over for you this afternoon. You're a size ten, correct?"

"Yes." Was that in my file?

"And shoes?"

"Also a size ten." Why did telling him that make my face turn red?

"Dinner is at seven—don't be late. If you need help with anything, ask Hazel."

"Bryce?" I licked my lips. "Is there anyone I can ask instead?"

He frowned, then whipped out his phone. "I just sent you Dale's number. Call him if you need anything. I'll see you tonight."

He stared down at his phone, furiously texting, and left without another word.

"Bye...?" But he was already gone, big shoulders hulking as he stalked down the hall.

formal

NOAH and I spent the next hour unpacking our few belongings, wandering around upstairs of the house—we were too afraid to explore the whole thing—and praying that we didn't break anything. My phone buzzed with a text from Dale. *Your clothes for dinner have been delivered. I'll send Midge to do your hair.*

What's a Midge? I texted back.

She's one of the maids—she also does hair and makeup. Go get dressed. I'll send her in half an hour. Text me if you need anything.

"Okay buddy," I said to my brother. "Time for you to go back to your room. I have to get ready for dinner."

"What am I going to eat? I'm starved." He frowned. "Am I not allowed to come to dinner or something?"

I sighed. "I'm meeting Bryce's father and his stepmother—trust me, you don't want to be there. I'll make sure you get something to eat, and hopefully not that crawfish stuff."

We both wrinkled our noses. I'd forgotten about the dang crawfish until I said that.

We got back to Noah's room—someone had assembled a brand-new gaming system and attached it to the enormous tv. It sat on his bed, gleaming and full of promise.

"No way!" He leaped for the controller. "This is the newest one, holy crap!" He babbled on about its various capabilities, how fast it was, and how he would be able to crush his competition.

I only listened with one ear—in addition to a pile of new video games stacked up neatly on the table, there was a platter with a silver tray on top. I lifted the handle and was happily surprised to see a plate of chicken tenders, a baked potato, and some steamed broccoli, the one green vegetable my brother would tolerate. "There's food here, too."

"Yum!" Noah grabbed a chicken tender and stuffed it into his mouth. "Mmm, this is good."

"Do you think you could wait until you finish chewing to tell me that?" I laughed as he grabbed the tray and settled himself onto the bed, the video game controller in one hand. "So you're going to be all right?"

"I'm great," Noah said through a mouthful of food. "I still don't believe you're married, but this is the best gaming system *ever*. Plus, there's nuggets." He stuffed another one into his mouth. "This doesn't totally suck."

"I'll come check on you after dinner." As I left him I felt lighter, with at least some hope that my brother didn't totally hate my guts.

But the uptick in my mood landed with a *thud* as soon as I got back to my suite. A spaghetti-strapped gown was hanging on the wardrobe—long, pale lavender, sexy and yet still elegant. Four-inch silver sandals stood beside the dress. How on earth was I supposed to walk down the grand staircase in *those*? I was going to die. Not only that, but the dress looked too expensive to wear. I checked the label; it was a designer name that was so famous, even *I* recognized it. I googled the label —these dresses sold for two-thousand dollars a pop.

I felt like I might throw up.

On the bed, there were two boxes, and an envelope addressed with my name. I opened it with shaking hands.

(1) I noticed your phone's cracked—I replaced it. Same number.
(2) I had the associate at the boutique pick out the appropriate items to accompany this gown. I hope that's okay. I

didn't want you to be offended or think I was insinuating anything.

I am going to try to make you comfortable here, Chloe.

— Bryce

I opened the first box to find a brand-new, top-of-the-line phone, replete with a shiny pink protective case. The contents of the second box made me blush—a pale lavender strapless bra and matching panties, what there was of them. Good thing Bryce had left me that note. If I'd thought he'd picked out underwear for me, I'd hide under the bed and never come out!

It was getting late. I needed to get dressed. I hustled into the shower, amazed and somewhat confounded by the multiple shower heads and all the various gels and shampoos. I managed to wash my hair, condition it, and use soap; it felt like a minor miracle.

I wrapped myself in the fluffiest towel known to mankind and brushed my teeth. For one brief moment, I allowed myself to enjoy the enormous, luxurious bathroom. It was bigger than my room back home and about five million times nicer. There was pale terracotta tile on the floors and a soothing gray paint on the walls. The sink was huge, so immaculate it seemed it had never been used. The toothpaste was the mintiest I'd ever tasted. There was a basket filled with expensive creams and makeup, nicer even than what Elena had stocked at the office.

Living in a billionaire's house did *not* suck.

Someone knocked on the door. I jumped, almost choking on the superior mint toothpaste.

I cautiously headed through the room, wrapping the fluffiest of all towels tightly against me. "Hello?"

"Hey honey—it's Midge," said a sing-song voice. "I'm here to do your hair."

"I'm not dressed yet," I stammered.

"There's a robe on the back of the bathroom door. Hurry up, okay hon? Windsors don't wait."

Shit! I ran for the robe. The last thing I wanted was to offend two generations of Windsors. One was bad enough.

I opened the door, and the shortest of the maids stood outside. Even with her heels on, Midge was all of five-foot-three, with curly brown hair pulled up into a messy bun and a round, very pretty face. She appeared to be in her mid-thirties. Unlike the wiry Hazel, Midge's curves filled out her uniform, making it look cute instead of austere.

"Aw, you're even prettier up close." She bustled past me, and a cloud of perfume followed in her wake. "Let's do your hair first, okay? I don't want it to dry before I get my hands on it."

I followed her into the bathroom. She turned on every light and ushered me into a chair facing a makeup mirror. "Here we go." She whipped out a brush and a blow dryer and started drying before I even knew what had happened. The buzz from the dryer made it impossible to talk, but Midge's touch was gentle. I watched her in the mirror: she looked thoughtful and kind, the fairy godmother of hair and makeup.

She expertly brushed out my long locks, making them silky and smooth for the first time since summer. When she finally turned the blow dryer off, she grinned at me. "You've got good hair, girl."

"Thank you."

She winked. "You're welcome. Now we need to get a move on with your makeup. Like I said, the Windsors don't like to be kept waiting."

My stomach tied itself into a knot—I was dreading dinner. Maybe Midge could help me get prepared. I studied her some more as she rummaged through the basket, selecting different bottles, tubes, and brushes. Her own makeup was perfect, tasteful, with a side of fun pink lipstick. "How long have you worked here?"

"Almost four years. They brought me on to be a ladies' maid, that's what they called it. So I help out around the house, but I do other things, too." She scrutinized a container of something called *Brow Genie*. "I used to be a stylist over in Bar Harbor—but I make *way* more money here. They needed someone to help the female guests, so here I am." She started working on my eyebrows, brushing them with a mascara-like wand.

I fidgeted, unsure of what to make of the information. "Are there a lot of female guests?"

Midge laughed. "No, that's the thing. I think Mr. Windsor was planning on it after you-know-what, but you're actually the first woman he's brought home since I've been here. I didn't even know he was dating someone!"

"What was..." My brow furrowed. "What do you mean by *you-know-what*?"

"Oh." She wrinkled her nose. "Nothing. Sorry hon, I thought you knew."

My mouth went dry. "Knew what?"

"Um..." Midge's phone beeped, and she looked relieved. "Let me check that, okay? They might be looking for you."

She read her screen and nodded. "Okay, Mr. Windsor Senior and his wife are on their way. I need to get you downstairs. Lucky you're gorgeous—you barely need makeup."

"Thank you." I wanted to ask her about *you-know-*

what again, but she asked me to close my mouth and eyes as she applied foundation with a fluffy brush.

Midge chatted on, narrating what products she was using and complimenting my skin. She was kind and reassuring, but all I wanted to know was what she wouldn't tell me—whatever it was she thought I already knew. *I thought Mr. Windsor was planning on it after you-know-what.*

"There you are. You can open your eyes now."

I did and was surprised at my reflection: my hair was smooth and shiny, arranged in bouncy waves over my shoulders, and my makeup was flawless. I looked elegant, pretty, and pulled together, something I rarely achieved. "Wow, Midge. You made me look good."

She laughed. "I didn't do that, hon. God did. You're a beautiful girl. I just enhanced what He gave you. Now let's get that dress on, okay? We don't have much time."

She ushered me back into the bedroom and wolf-whistled when she saw the lingerie. "Mr. Windsor has great taste."

"Ha. Yeah, I guess." I wrung my hands together.

"Don't be nervous, hon. You're the luckiest girl in the world. *Except* for the fact that you have to have dinner with Mr. Windsor Senior and Daphne."

"Daphne? Is that his wife?"

"Ugh, yes." Midge snorted and handed me the bra.

"She's a piece of work. And she's had *all* the work done, too."

Since she didn't seem to be going anywhere, I turned around, snaked the bra under my robe, and somehow managed to fasten it. Without missing a beat, Midge handed me the thong. I shimmied into it while Midge continued.

"She's his third wife, I think. And she's not even *half* his age. That wouldn't be a big deal, but she's totally just into the money. She's always on TikTok, shooting videos from Mr. Windsor's yacht. She thinks she's a lifestyle guru or something. But the truth is, they both drink their faces off. She's totally fake, she's rude to the staff—watch your back, girl. She's not going to like having someone around who's younger and prettier than her."

My stomach sank even further. "Good to know."

"Let's get you into that gown. C'mere, this is going to be awesome." Midge grabbed it from the wardrobe and waited. "Go ahead and take that robe off. Trust me, I've seen it all!"

Blushing, I did as I was told. Midge was mercifully quick—she had me zipped into the lavender dress before I could panic. She grabbed the impossibly high sandals and fastened them. When she stepped back, her eyes were huge in her face. "Mr. Windsor really does have the best taste. You're stunning, Chloe."

She ushered me toward the full-length mirror, and I almost fell over, and not just from the heels. I looked like someone else. Someone rich, someone famous, someone who wore designer dresses and lived in a mansion.

The person looking back from the mirror wasn't me. She couldn't be.

And yet, there I was.

"Are you ready?" Midge asked.

"Sure," I lied. This had been the craziest day of my life. What on earth would happen next?

Taking a deep breath and saying a silent prayer that I wouldn't trip down the stairs and land flat on my face, I left the safety of my room to find out.

forks

"Ah, there she is. My *wife*." Bryce's voice contained a deep satisfaction that made me feel uncomfortably...*his*.

Three figures waited below. I clutched the wide wood railing, knuckles turning white, as I carefully took each step. My ankles wobbled in the heels. I didn't dare look at them, not yet, but I heard them talking.

"You were right—she's certainly lovely," said another man's voice. *Gene Windsor.*

"Did you expect anything less, darling?" cooed a woman. "It's not as though any son of yours is going to bring home a hag." *Daphne Windsor.* These were the first words I'd heard from her, and I could already tell Midge was right. Who used the word *hag*?

Shaking and palms sweating, I finally reached the landing. It was almost too much to take in: two tall, imposing men in suits and a stunning, raven-haired beauty in a floor-length gown. Things sparkled and flashed—a diamond necklace, a heavy-looking watch, glittering eye shadow. They were impossibly glamorous. If money had a smell, they would have reeked.

I don't belong here. If I'm dreaming, can I please please please wake the fuck up?

Before I could make a run for it, Bryce came to my side. He put his big arm around my waist, pulling me close.

His father and stepmother stared.

My new husband palmed my hip. "You look beautiful, Chloe."

"Thank you." My face felt hot. It was uncomfortable enough to be complimented by him; it was almost unbearable to be so close, to feel his powerful chest pressed into my side when I knew he wanted less than nothing to do with me.

"Let me make the introductions," Bryce continued. "Father, this is my wife, Chloe Windsor. Chloe, this is my father, Gene Windsor."

Bryce's father was also tall and handsome, but he was a few inches shorter than his son, with a slimmer build. His gray hair was still thick and full. His blue eyes were piercing, like Bryce's—but they were the watery eyes of a longtime alcoholic.

Gene reached for my hand and kissed it. His lips were cold, papery. "It's a pleasure to meet you, Chloe. I thought this day would never come."

"That makes two of us, dear." Daphne barged in between us, forcing her husband to release me. "Hello, Chloe. I'm Daphne Windsor, Gene's wife. I'm sorry to have to introduce myself, but my stepson likes to pretend I don't exist, and my husband's too busy looking down your dress to bother."

"Hi there." I shakily extended my hand. "It's nice to meet you, Daphne."

I couldn't help but stare. If Gene was in his seventies, his wife was barely thirty. She was also absolutely stunning. Daphne had long, thick, ebony hair pulled over one shoulder. Her skin was porcelain and flawless; her brown eyes were enormous and hypnotizing, framed by unnaturally luxurious, thick dark lashes. She was one of *those* girls, the kind that was so beautiful you wondered if she'd ever had a problem in her life.

But judging from the downward curve of her lips and the way she glared as she inspected me, Daphne definitely had some issues.

Her smile was cool and did not reach her pretty eyes. "The pleasure's all mine, Chloe. So glad you've joined the family—it'll be a relief to finally have someone to talk to."

"You can talk to me, dear." Gene Windsor held out his arm for her, and she reluctantly went to his side, hips swinging. "Let's have a pre-dinner cocktail, shall we? And then we can all get to know the beautiful and mysterious Chloe better."

Gene and Daphne led the way. Her gown was cream-colored silk, and the pale skin of her back was completely exposed. Gene put his hand on her ass, rubbing it, and Bryce stiffened beside me.

He grunted as he leaned down to talk in my ear. "I know you're not twenty-one yet, but you might want to have a drink tonight. You're going to need it."

I shivered as his cool, minty breath wafted over me. *Do billionaires automatically have good breath?* Most likely. They probably patented that shit. I also wanted to ask if his father and stepmother were really that bad —but as Gene proceeded to squeeze Daphne's butt in an insistent, rhythmic manner, I realized I already had my answer.

His back ramrod straight, Bryce kept his arm around me as we entered another room. Bookcases lined the walls, and even though it was July, a fire roared in the fireplace. The windows faced the grounds, the rolling lawn silvery and dim in the fading Maine light.

Gene Windsor headed straight for the bar, where one of Bryce's men poured him an extra-large bourbon.

Daphne's glass of white wine was tame by comparison. Bryce ordered a bourbon and looked at me expectantly, but I couldn't bring myself to do it. "I'd like a water, please." I longed to ask for a Diet Coke, but I worried Daphne might laugh at me.

We gathered in a circle, and Gene Windsor raised his tumbler. "I'd like to make a toast to the bride and groom. I have to say, son, I never thought I'd see the day, especially after..." His voice trailed off, and he shrugged, but there was a ghost of a smile on his face. "I suppose I shouldn't be bringing up the past."

Bryce's lips were set in a grim line, pressed together so hard they turned white. "No, you shouldn't, Father. This is a happy occasion."

"Right—of course it is." But Gene looked smug, his expression mismatching his words. "To the bride and groom. We wish you a lifetime of happiness."

We stiffly clinked our glasses together. Gene chugged his bourbon, and Daphne downed her wine in one sip. *Oh boy.* I'd been to family dinners like this—without the gowns, the mansion, and the roaring fire. But the kind where the booze took over early and did the driving for the rest of the night.

I'd best buckle up.

Gene motioned for another drink. "So tell us, Chloe, how it is that you met my son. How was it you two connected and fell so deeply in love, you just *had* to get married today?"

Bryce's grip tightened around me. "Please don't speak to Chloe like that."

Gene knocked back his next drink. "Like what, son? Like she's an accessory to your fraud?"

"There's no fraud here, Father. I complied with the terms of the trust to the letter." Bryce squeezed me hard, crushing me against him.

"You and your compliance." Gene's smile was cruel. "I raised you to be an independent thinker, and yet, you continue to suck from the family teat."

"Aw, you two! *Behave.* Don't scare the girl off on her very first night." Daphne's eyes were sparkling, indicating that she already had a buzz. Judging from how her form-fitting gown nipped her waist, outlining her flat stomach, the wine was probably hitting her hard. Daphne didn't look like she ate much. She shook her glass at the bartender, indicating she was ready for another round.

This was a Dad-and-Lydia-like drinking pace. *Buckle up, indeed.*

Bryce gripped his tumbler. Unlike his father, he hadn't finished his drink. He kept his hand firmly on my hip, and I suddenly saw myself as an emotional support animal, the kind that people brought to stores and awful family gatherings.

An icy silence descended. The Windsor men glared at each other as Daphne guzzled her wine.

"The story of how we met... It was simple, really," I babbled. Bryce told me this had to seem real. If his father already doubted us, I needed to move quickly.

"Bryce came into the coffee shop where I worked. He was doing business in the area, and he came in every morning for his coffee. We got to talking and, I don't know... I guess one thing led to another." I leaned against him, hoping it looked natural.

"I'd never seen someone so beautiful." He palmed my waist again. "For me, it was love at first sight."

For some stupid reason, my heart fluttered—even though I knew he was lying.

"How optimistic of you." Gene grunted as he had a sip of his fresh bourbon. "Tell me about your family, Chloe. Your background. I need to understand why my son found you so particularly compelling, lovely though you are. It's not unusual for him to keep secrets, but it *is* unusual for him to marry one of them."

Even though Old Gene was a grade-A douche, I forced myself to smile. "When I met Bryce, I was living with my father and stepmother in East Boston. I have a younger brother, Noah—he's eleven. Our mother died last year."

"I'm sorry to hear that. What happened? Cancer?"

I swallowed hard. "Car accident. My mom worked the night shift at Boston Medical Center. She got hit by a drunk driver on her way to her shift."

Even Daphne frowned. "I'm sorry," she said, then held up her glass for yet another refill.

I sighed. It was going to be a long fucking night. "Thank you."

"How old are you, dear?" Gene leaned forward, watery eyes inspecting me. "Barely legal, in my estimation."

"I'm nineteen, Mr. Windsor."

He wolf-whistled, and Daphne looked like she might smash her glass over his head.

"Come now, darling," he chided her, "you're forty years younger than me. Chloe and Bryce are practically the same age compared to us."

"True." She seemed slightly mollified. "Plus, children aren't very interesting. Are they, darling?"

"Not at all." Gene didn't seem to care that his own child was standing across from him. "But tell me more, Chloe. Do you plan to attend college? Did you go to a private academy or public high school? What does your father do for work? Maybe I've heard of him."

"You definitely haven't. My father works at his cousin's landscaping company—they mostly do small jobs." In truth, my father barely worked. His cousin tolerated him because my father sometimes gave him weed. "I graduated from East Boston High. My family's working-class, Sir."

My words hung awkwardly in the air; no one seemed to know what to make of them.

"Chloe's an avid reader," Bryce offered. "She's quite into modern fiction."

"Really?" Gene seemed amused. "What titles do you prefer, Chloe? Pynchon? Vonnegut? Or are you more of a Roth fan?"

"Um." I cleared my throat. "I mostly read Meyer."

He looked confused Fine by me!

"I think it's time for dinner." Bryce came to my rescue, maneuvering me past the bar while leaning down to speak privately. "I told you it was going to be bad. I didn't think he'd go for the jugular right at the beginning, but I shouldn't be surprised."

"It's okay—as long as you think he's buying it," I whispered. I truly hoped we were selling the relationship. If I had to deal with these scary-ass rich people, I better get paid!

"We're doing as well as could be expected. He

doesn't like it when I win." Bryce scowled. "But like I always say, fuck him."

I nodded in agreement as we entered the beautiful dining room. A massive table stretched from one end to the other; I hoped we could be seated far, far away from Gene and Daphne. But as Bryce pulled out my chair, Daphne zoomed in and claimed the spot directly across from mine. Bryce got stuck next to his father.

Ugh. How many courses did rich people eat? Judging by Daphne's jutting collarbones, none. But I had a sinking feeling I wouldn't get off so easily.

Daphne's dark eyes sparkled as she settled into her seat. "Have you ever seen a table this gorgeous before? Look at the settings." She motioned to the multiple forks and other ornately carved silverware, along with what was probably priceless china and cloth napkins that were so soft, they felt like fluffy little clouds.

Fuck me—there were three forks. What the hell was I supposed to do with *three* forks?

I looked up to find Daphne smirking.

"It can be overwhelming at first. Especially if you've never been, like, anywhere." She had another gulp of wine.

"Overwhelming's a good word for it." I fidgeted, wholly uncomfortable. I'd never met someone as fancy as Daphne in my whole life. What the heck was I supposed to say to her?

I remember something my mother used to say: *people love talking about themselves.* "Where are *you* from, Daphne? I feel like I've been answering all the questions."

"And yet, you've said nothing of interest." Her smirk resumed as she had another sip of wine. "But that's probably because you're nineteen. I, on the other hand, had my own life by the time I got married at twenty-six. I'd already built a successful business. That's how I met Gene, of course—I was raising capital for *PV*."

"What's *PV*?"

"*Personal Venue*—it's my company. You've never heard of us? We're all over Insta!" Sounding infinitely more upbeat, Daphne whipped out her phone and started tapping away. "Here's one of my more recent posts. It was a five-minute glute workout from the yacht!"

She shoved her phone at me. In the video, Daphne wore a black thong bikini on the deck of a giant yacht. Her glorious, perfectly round ass was on full display. Blue water sparkled in the distance. She was on all fours on a yoga mat, lifting her legs and making pouty lips at the camera. Her butt was center stage, muscles clenched, thong riding uncomfortably high. "This is how you do it, ladies! Live a life with no excuses!" She kicked her leg into the air.

Once she was done alternating legs, Daphne rolled over and sat cross-legged on the mat. I refused to look at the thong in that position! She smiled at the camera. "After a workout like that, I can take on the world. The best thing I do for myself? Have a PV smoothie, of course!"

She sprung up and stalked to a nearby bar, where she poured a green-colored smoothie from a blender. "Ninety-seven vitamins and antioxidants make the PV smoothie the necessary support for your healthy life-style. There are no excuses, ladies—you *can* reach your goals and live the life you want. Invest in yourself. Invest in a PV-smoothie plan. Link in my bio!"

She grinned as I handed the phone back. "I post four times a day. TikTok has been *huge* for me, too. I'm getting millions of views. Sales are through the roof!"

"Wow." I couldn't think of how else to respond. "What's in your smoothie recipe? That's a lot of vitamins."

"I don't actually know. It's not like I drink it." She waved her hand. "It's all pre-made in China. You don't have to label it because it's not FDA-approved. It's, like, the *thing*. Everybody does it."

Before I could respond, a server appeared with a tray

of salads. Daphne's lip curled as she inspected the plates. "Is my dressing on the side? I've told you a hundred times—I *only* want mine dry!" She suddenly sounded like a small, petulant child right before a temper tantrum.

"Yes, Mrs. Windsor. The dressing is separate." The server set down a small ramekin of dressing and then the salads, elegant arrangements of bright greens, strawberries, and pecans.

"Good thing." Daphne didn't thank her. "I'd like more wine. Bring the bottle—actually, make that two."

"Yes, Mrs. Windsor." The server scurried away.

I stared down at my multiple forks. Daphne didn't touch her salad. Instead, she eyed me gleefully over her glass of wine, waiting for me to flail.

Bryce leaned over. "Sweetheart, have you tried your salad? The strawberries are delicious." Bryce picked up the outermost fork and handed it to me. "See for yourself."

"Thank you."

He smiled at me—a genuine smile. "It's my pleasure, Chloe."

Daphne's gloat morphed into a scowl.

But for the first time that day, I felt the tiniest bit better.

echoes

Dinner was awful, and it had nothing to do with the food—which was excellent, although absolutely above my head. I tried the paella, which was savory, spicy, and delicious, even though I was petrified of the tiny crawfish that stared out at me from the center of the platter.

Alcohol was what ruined the meal. Or rather, what alcohol did to Gene Windsor's already nasty personality.

After more refills than I cared to count, he started harassing Bryce about a business deal. From what I could gather, it was something about a contract. Gene sneered at his son. "You've never understood the power of making them wait. You're always too eager to close— they can smell it. You're an easy mark."

"Being upfront about what I want isn't a weakness,

Father. It's a strength. If I want to close something, I'm not hiding behind playing a game." Bryce straightened his shoulders. "Maybe old men have time for things like that, but *I* don't."

A vein on the side of Gene's forehead bulged out. *Uh oh.* "Maybe I'm old, but at least I know one thing: I'm my *own* man. Everything I have, I built for myself. You and your brothers can't say the same now, can you?"

Bryce has brothers? I filed this information away for later when I could properly ponder whether they were as fucked up as he was.

"Of course not." Bryce took a deep breath, and I had the sense he was counting backward from ten. "How could I ever forget? You remind me every time I see you."

"That's the problem with you." Gene stabbed his dessert spoon in Bryce's direction. "You're angry, you're ungrateful, and yet, you still jump through every hoop. Look at what you did today, eh? Married some public-school girl. It's ridiculous: she doesn't even speak the same language. She's pretty, but you remember the terms of your trust: it's *forever*. Pretty doesn't last forever, son."

I turned away from them and stared at my chocolate mousse, unable to breathe. My cheeks stung with hurt, just as if Gene had slapped me.

"Don't mind him," Daphne slurred. Her eyes were

half-crossed. She'd eaten nothing during the entire meal except for one lettuce leaf with zero dressing. The first two bottles of wine were long gone; she was halfway through a third. "Pretty is important. He likes pretty."

"You don't get a seat at the table unless you're pretty," Gene snapped. "It's the lowest bar there is!"

"Dad, Daphne—thanks so much for dinner." Bryce reached over and grabbed my hand. "But Chloe and I have had a long day. We're going to excuse ourselves now."

"Oh no, you're not." Gene jabbed the spoon again, looking as if he'd like to gouge his son's eyeballs out with it. "You're going to sit here and tell me how it is you think you deserve a stake in *my* company. I'm not going to give in that easily!"

Bryce rose to his formidable height, yanking me up with him. "When have you ever made it easy, Father? And with respect to you giving in, it doesn't matter what you say. I've fulfilled the trust's terms. My interest vested as soon as the ink on my marriage certificate was dry."

"It's fraud!" The vein bulged dangerously. "You can't vest if it's *fraudulent*!"

"*It* is my wife. She's real." Bryce held up my hand.

"Judge Patel legally married us this afternoon—she sends her regards, by the way."

Spittle flew from Gene's lips as he raged. "I don't give a fuck about Judge Patel—"

"If you want to try to contest the terms of your own trust now, after the fact," Bryce interrupted smoothly, "I suggest you go outside and watch for pigs flying first: you might have better luck. Good night, Father. Daphne."

With a firm tug, he hustled me from the room.

I didn't say anything until we were halfway down the hall, our footfalls echoing away from the awful scene.

"That was..." I didn't have words for what it was. And I thought *my* family was bad. I peered up at Bryce. "Are you okay?"

"What?" He looked as if he were surprised to see me and immediately dropped my hand.

"I asked if you were okay."

"I'm fine." He blinked. "Why wouldn't I be?"

"Um..." But he had a blank look on his face, as though he had no idea what I was talking about. "Never mind."

He nodded. "Goodnight, Chloe. I trust you can find your way back to your room."

"Of course." But he'd already stormed off down the hall, leaving me staring after his big shoulders.

Bryce was giving me emotional whiplash. Holding my hand one second, acting as though he didn't recognize me in the next. "Really, I'm fine. Don't worry about me," I whispered. My words ricocheted off the empty walls, making me feel even more desolate.

I wandered through the vast house, which now seemed empty, dark, and cold. I wanted to go and check on Noah, but the clock in the main hall read midnight: he'd have fallen asleep by now. Still reeling from the day, I knew it was best to return to my room and finally be alone. Not wanting to pause long enough to take off my shoes, I crept up the stairs carefully, mindful of my balance.

All the doors in the hallway were closed. Thank fuck mine was easy to locate. I'd be too afraid to accidentally find myself in one of the empty guest rooms late at night. No, thank you!

I stopped outside my room. The door to Bryce's primary suite was closed. Was he already in there? Or was he stalking the grounds, bourbon in hand, wondering what the hell he'd gone and done by getting married to me today?

My head was swimming by the time I got inside and blissfully barricaded myself from the rest of the crazy household. Midge had left the lights on, and she'd turned the corner of the bedsheets down. A glass of water stood on my nightstand, and a silky, lace-trimmed nightgown beckoned from the bed. What did she think I was going to do in a nightgown like *that*?

But then I remembered—it was my wedding night. She probably thought I was going to do all *sorts* of things.

What did the staff think of this arrangement? I hadn't even considered that we had an audience. Mr. Windsor was in his primary suite, the new Mrs. Windsor in a cold bed all her own.

Did we need to be worried about our sleeping arrangements? Was that sort of information something that could be used against us? If Gene Windsor found out we weren't sharing a bed, he'd have a field day...

I shook my head as I stripped out of the dress and unbuckled the blasted sandals, putting everything carefully away. I went into the luxurious bathroom, too tired to enjoy it, and scrubbed the makeup from my face. I slid the silky nightgown over my head, fingering the smooth material. I'd never worn something like it before, another first of many in the strange, long day.

Exhausted, I climbed into bed. *Damn.* Had there ever been a bed this comfortable in the history of all beds? It made my accommodations at The Stratum seem almost sad. I sighed as I snuggled against the pillows and turned off the bedside lamp.

Darkness pooled in the room, but after a moment, the moonlight shone through. My eyes adjusted to my dim surroundings, and I relaxed enough to say my prayers, a habit I'd had since childhood.

Thank you, God, for keeping my brother safe.

Thank you, God, for the money and the chance to turn my life around.

Thank you, God, for my mom.

She was dead, but I would never forget her. She was the reason I got up every morning, the reason I kept going. She would want me to take care of Noah. She would be *appalled* that I'd married a stranger for money, but on some level, I knew she would understand. She'd done anything and everything for us. She made sacrifices—working extra shifts, never getting enough sleep, eating less so that we could have more in our bellies.

I was her daughter, through and through.

I would never let Noah starve. I would never let him rot in Dad and Lydia's smoke-filled apartment, treated as though he were a nuisance. And I would *never* lose him to the labyrinth of social services, applications, court hearings, foster families, and all sorts of things I couldn't begin to navigate. *I've lost enough, and so has my brother.*

No, my mother wouldn't approve of my marriage, but she'd understand what I'd done.

But just in case, I prayed that she would.

I slept like a log. When I woke up, it was in the same position I'd fallen asleep: flat on my back, my hands spread out at my sides.

It wasn't light yet. I glanced at the clock: four a.m. It was rare for me to wake up before six. Usually, I slept through the night no matter what, one of the few positive traits I'd inherited from my dad. The room was still blanketed in semi-darkness, but I could make out the outline of the furniture. I lay still, luxuriating in the insane comfort of the bed and the pillows, the feel of the silk nightgown against my skin. *Mmm.* After such a rough day, and despite the early hour, I felt better, calmer.

But then someone coughed.

I sat bolt upright. "Who's there?"

No one answered. I clutched the blankets around me, heart hammering. I tried to listen over the thudding in my temples.

"Noah?"

No response.

"Is someone in here?" My voice came out small, panicked, as fear gripped my throat.

There was a *click*, the unmistakable sound of a door closing... But the door to my room was already tightly shut.

"Hello?"

No one answered. I had the sense that whoever it was, they'd left. With shaking hands, I turned on my light.

The room was empty, the bathroom door open—no one was hiding in there. I hoped. Just in case, I grabbed a nearby vase—probably priceless—and crept from my bed, ready to break it over the intruder's head.

But there was no one in the bathroom, nothing except for luxurious beauty products. No one crouched in the closet with the fancy wooden hangers, empty shoe racks, and another fluffy robe. After covering every inch of the room, I put down the vase and crawled back into bed, pulling the covers up to my chin. Had I imagined the cough? Was I still half asleep?

Maybe it was a ghost. Possibly the Windsor estate was haunted.

Probably, Chloe! That would just be my freaking luck. Married to a stranger, the grumpiest billionaire *ever*, and held captive in his *haunted island estate.* Trapped for eternity, with endless dinners with my new asshole father-in-law and his starving, crazy, thong-wearing Instagram-star wife. *Way to go, Chlo!*

I prayed to go back to sleep, but there was no escape, no relief.

Way to fucking go, indeed.

brighter

No more ghosts appeared, only Midge. She bustled into my room after one knock, humming, a massive grin on her face, and a pile of clothes in her arms.

"It's your lucky day, girl." She somehow opened the wardrobe with her foot and started hanging up the clothes. "You've got a day date with Mr. Windsor, and he had a *crap*-ton of new clothes delivered for you. What would you like for breakfast, huh? Some bacon? A waffle with Nutella? Berries? I'll have Chef make whatever you want."

"Really?" My mouth pooled with water. The paella had been good, but I was a sucker for an old-fashioned waffle. "I'd love some bacon and waffles."

"You got it." She winked at me. "You sleep okay, hon?"

I nodded. "I woke up early, though. I thought I heard something."

Midge kept arranging the clothes. "It's the ocean. The tide comes rushing in, and it rattles the whole house. You'll get used to it."

I let out a deep breath. "I hope so."

"You will," she said knowingly. "You'll get the best sleep of your life here—it's something about the ocean air. You go and shower, and I'll order your breakfast. You want a latte or something?"

"Just coffee with cream. Thank you, Midge."

"My pleasure. And I'll have your brother join you, so you guys can catch up before you leave for the day." She started arranging an outfit for me on the bed, a dangerously tiny black bikini, a cute coverup, and a pair of designer sunglasses.

I eyed the bikini. "Where exactly am I going?"

"Out with Mr. Windsor, of course. He wants to show off his new bride. Now, go on! You know he doesn't like to wait!" She shooed me out of bed and into the bathroom. If Midge thought anything was strange—like the fact that I'd spent my wedding night in my sexy nightgown all alone in my room—she didn't let on.

Perhaps she'd worked for eccentric billionaires *just* long enough that their shit didn't seem so crazy to her.

I showered, using every delicious-smelling beauty product available, then quickly blew my hair dry. Midge knocked on the bathroom door exactly once before barreling in, and I was grateful for my fluffy robe.

"Let me finish your hair and do your eyes. We can do lips after breakfast." Before I could answer, she stuffed me into the makeup chair and got to work, chattering the whole time.

"I heard the other Mrs. Windsor fell on her ass last night," Midge confided. "Serves her right. She and the old man stayed here pretty late, drinking outside on the deck. She broke a bottle of wine out there, some shit that cost *four-hundred-and-eighty dollars* a pop. No word of a lie! Then she screamed at poor Annette like it was her fault. Bitch got hers, though—she slipped on the last step. The old man had to ask one of the guards to carry her to their house. He's too frail to do it. They're really something, huh? Then the staff said they heard them having *very loud* sex. Like, they didn't even make it to the bedroom. Booze and viagra, I'm telling you!"

I winced, not wanting to picture Daphne and Gene Windsor having loud, drunken sex. Or any sex! *Ew.* "Dinner wasn't fun."

Midge brushed out my hair. "Was Mrs. Windsor a total bitch, or what? Annette said she was yelling about the salad dressing. She doesn't eat a bite of food. I swear to God, I don't know how she's alive."

"She didn't really eat," I agreed. "But she showed me her workout video. She runs some kind of smoothie company?"

She snorted. "Is that what she's calling it? It's a subscription service—*a hundred and sixty dollars* a month for some smoothie packets. All that crap's made in China, probably by little kids who are chained to their workstations. Girl is making *bank* with it. It's true what they say, you know? The rich only get richer. The rest of us just bust our asses and hope for the best."

I blew out a deep breath. "I've never met people this wealthy before."

"There isn't anybody else this wealthy, hon. The Windsors are the one percent of the one percent." She shrugged. "The younger Mr. Windsor's all right, at least most of the time. He was tough when I first started working here, but he's coming around." She finished smoothing my hair, then started on my eyebrows. "Better days are ahead, I can feel it."

"Midge?" I asked. "Why was he difficult when you first started working here? Is it the same thing you mentioned yesterday? His father said something about it last night..."

She frowned as she attempted to tame my brows. "I shouldn't have opened my big mouth."

"Can you tell me what it's about?" I looked up at her hopefully. "I'd like to know. Bryce doesn't say much."

She sighed. "Listen, I shouldn't have said anything. But you should know—the girls and I are rooting for you, okay?"

"You are?" I blinked. "What do you mean?"

Midge furrowed her brow. "My mouth is going to be the death of me, that's what my grandmother always used to say."

"I won't ever tell anyone—you can trust me," I said. "I mean it. Why are you rooting for me?"

She sighed again. "We know that you and Mr. Windsor didn't have an exactly...normal...beginning. It was too quick, and he hasn't left the island much over the past few months. Unless you guys had some hot online romance going or something."

I swallowed over a lump in my throat. "It wasn't anything like that," I admitted.

"I figured." Her eyes softened. "We know about the trust, Chloe. We've known about it for a long time— that Mr. Windsor needed to get married to inherit his share. The thing was, he wasn't dating. At *all*. Not after what happened."

My gut wrenched, a clear signal that "what

happened" was a big-ticket item, the thing I needed to know. "What *did* happen?"

"Close your eyes, okay? I need to do your liner." Midge was quiet for a few minutes as she worked, and I worried she wouldn't say more. But eventually, she cracked. "He had a girlfriend—a fiancé—but things didn't work out. She left him right before I got hired, so I never met her. But girlfriend did a *number* on him. That's all I know. He was alone for a long time—until now."

A fiancé. "What happened?"

She had me open my eyes so she could apply my mascara. "I don't really know. The only one who knows the truth is probably Hazel, but I stay far away from *that* bitch and you should, too."

I shivered. "She doesn't seem very friendly."

"She's crazy as shit. The one good thing I can say about her is that she's loyal to Mr. Windsor. Like an ugly, mangy dog—bitch would bite anyone who hurt him. Funny thing was, she was close to his ex. She used to work for her exclusively."

"Huh." My mind whirred with the information. Hazel was close to his ex... I couldn't picture it.

"What was she like?" I asked. What sort of woman jilted *Bryce Windsor*?

Midge groaned. "Don't be asking questions, Chloe.

And don't even bother trying to find that shit on the internet—these rich people have a way of keeping things quiet. I heard they'd even sent out the wedding invitations, but no one's ever confirmed it. You won't find the story online anywhere. The internet's forever, but when you have as much money as the Windsors do, you can actually erase that shit."

"Why would Bryce hide it?"

Midge swatted me. "Because he's a *man*. He's got his pride, you know? From what I heard, he bawled like a baby when she broke it off."

"Oh." I couldn't picture Bryce *bawling*. Why did that make my stomach hurt?

"No one wants to be jilted, especially not a billionaire like Bryce Windsor. So he kept it quiet," Midge continued. "And like I said, he was alone for a long time. *You're* his trophy now, his prize. He's going to take you out and show you off today—show the world that he's over what happened and that he's got a shiny new life, more responsibilities with the business, and a beautiful wife. A new beginning, Chloe, that's what he needs. You're his proof that he's moved on."

I nodded. "Thank you for telling me. I had no idea. Honestly, I'm surprised someone would do that to him."

Midge shook her head. "Don't ever forget—bitches be crazy, you know? Some people have it all, but it doesn't mean anything to them. You know what I mean?"

I thought of Daphne, who'd sat in front of her gorgeous meal and had eaten exactly one leaf of dry lettuce. "I guess so." But as I'd never said no to food and never jilted a fiancé...

I guess I didn't really know what she meant, not at all.

Noah and I ate breakfast together. He seemed miraculously well-adjusted. Dale and some of the other staff were taking him fishing off the dock; he couldn't stop talking about how excited he was to fish, the awesome video games he'd played, how one of the maids had brought him an ice cream sundae last night. Another had promised to bring over her new puppy for him to play with.

He seemed *happy*. "Are you really okay?" I asked.

He nodded. "Bryce doesn't even seem that bad. He came and gave me a tackle box this morning—he said I could use any lures I wanted."

I nearly dropped my fork. "Bryce came to your *room*?"

"Yeah." Noah shrugged. "He brought me a copy of

the newest Mario game, too, and the tackle box. He said he'd take me jet-skiing one day this week if I wanted."

"*What?*" The man who'd been so rude, glued non-stop to his phone—the man who'd dropped my hand in the hall last night as though I had the plague—was now delivering Mario games and offering to take my little brother *jet-skiing*? "That doesn't sound like him."

"You married him." Noah shrugged. "You can't think he's a total asshole."

"Do not use that word, young man!"

He stuck his tongue out at me. "You're not my mom. Hey, can I finish your bacon?"

I sat, stymied, as Noah took my last piece of bacon and practically skipped from the room. I yelled at him to brush his teeth, and he told me to shut up from the hallway.

My brother seemed back to his usual self. In any event, he was adjusting much faster to all this than I was.

There was another knock on the door. Hazel stuck her haggard face into the room, and I almost screamed.

"Mr. Windsor's ready for you," she announced stiffly.

"O-Okay." I shakily got to my feet and started stacking the breakfast dishes.

"Don't touch those." Her tone was sharp. "That's for

the staff to do. Not you, Mrs. Windsor. It would be considered an insult."

"Sorry." Everything I did was wrong. "I'll just go and grab my things. Is Mr. Windsor downstairs?"

"Yes." Hazel arched her thin, heavily penciled eyebrow. "And Mr. Windsor doesn't like to be kept waiting."

I nodded. "Right, I'm learning that. I'll just be a minute. Thanks for letting me—" But she was already gone, thank goodness.

I shivered, then raced to put on my tiny bikini. I didn't want old Hazel coming back and yelling at me more!

I changed, then scowled at myself in the mirror. When I'd thought the bikini tiny, it had been an understatement. The triangle top barely covered my breasts, and the bottom was low, showing off my ass...ets. Why couldn't I at least have a tan? I cinched the coverup around me, praying that Bryce would approve—or at least be so busy with his phone that he didn't look at me —then slid on the flip-flops. They were *flat*, thank goodness, and comfortable. Maybe things were finally looking up.

But that thought deflated like a day-old balloon when I glimpsed my new husband waiting for me at the bottom of the stairs. He was wearing another expensive-looking suit and texting furiously, the perpetual grim expression on his otherwise handsome face. He didn't even look up when I reached his side.

Citing his cold behavior last night, I didn't say a word—I would wait to speak until spoken to.

"Chloe." He didn't look up.

"Bryce." I couldn't keep the sarcastic tone out of my voice.

That got his attention—he glanced up from his screen, cool blue eyes flicking over me from head to toe. "Good morning."

"Good morning to you."

We eyed each other.

"We're going out on the boat—I'm going to take you to my club and show you around the islands." His gaze skimmed down over my bare, white legs. "There's sunscreen on board."

"Thanks." I cleared my throat, trying to maintain my dignity while standing half-naked next to him. "But why are you wearing a suit if I'm wearing a *bathing* suit?"

He held up his phone, and for a brief moment, a smile ghosted his lips. "I have a video conference."

"Ah."

"Don't worry, it won't take long. Then I'm all

yours, *darling*." He put his arm around my waist and pulled me against him.

Damn. His body was powerful, muscular beneath the suit. I tried to pull away, but he held me tight, leading me through the hall. Various staff members lined our path and wished us good morning. They were clearly eager to catch a glimpse of their master and his brand-new bride. It was our first full day as a married couple, after all.

Bryce clearly intended to give them a show. He kept his arm firmly around me. He actually smiled at his employees and said *good morning* to them. Maybe Chef had spiked his coffee with something to make him more mellow. A girl could hope!

We made it outside and were greeted with a gust of ocean air, the smell of fresh-cut grass, and the sun on our faces. It was warm but not hot. There was zero humidity. Maybe Maine was heaven?

Bryce whipped out his cellphone and started texting with one hand, even as he tightened his grip around my waist with the other. He intended to keep me close— making a show of us for the staff—even though he'd barely spoken to me. *Maybe Maine is hell.*

"Smile, Chloe," Bryce said, not taking his eyes from his phone.

"I am," I lied.

He pulled me tighter still against him. "Don't ever lie to me, Mrs. Windsor. That is the one thing I cannot tolerate."

Geez, he was so serious! "I was just testing to see if you'd look up from your phone. You failed." I held my breath, hoping he'd be okay with me teasing him a little.

"I could feel you frowning." Finally, he did look up. "Was I wrong? Of course not."

"Of course not." I frowned some more. *Was he ever wrong?*

"Now, *smile*. I want the world to see how happy my new bride is." He looked deep into my eyes. "Can you do that for me? Can you act like you're enjoying yourself?"

I felt like he was hypnotizing me with those blue, blue eyes. "Yes." I almost said the word *sir* but stopped myself at the last second.

"Good girl, Chloe." He loomed over me, and my stomach did a somersault. "You see? We're going to get along just fine."

I nodded. And then I smiled.

Because, like everyone else around here, Bryce Windsor was clearly my boss.

pressed

"Sɪʀ?" One of his interchangeable besuited men met us at the dock. "Would you like to do the tour first or head to the club?"

"The tour. I have a couple of calls to take care of." Bryce's brow furrowed as he stared at his screen. "Please bring Mrs. Windsor to see Joren—have him show her around. I'll join them later."

Without another word, he released me. He climbed on board the yacht and disappeared with his phone.

The man in the suit—my new babysitter—smiled. "Ready to meet the captain?"

"Sure." *I'll meet all the king's horses and all the king's men while I'm half-dressed and the king taps away on his cellphone.* I felt annoyed. But really, why was I mad that Bryce had abandoned me again? I should be getting used to it. I reminded myself to keep my expectations low when it came to my husband—I couldn't anticipate any attention or warmth from him. He'd hired me, just like he'd hired my newest friend in the suit. We were all there to do Mr. Windsor's bidding. It was the job.

He helped me climb onboard, then I followed him to a little room with a steering wheel, radios, and other equipment. A young, handsome man with short dreadlocks smiled at me. He wore a white captain's uniform.

"I'm Joren, Mr. Windsor's captain." He was warm and friendly, maybe a few years older than me, with an accent I couldn't place. "It's my pleasure to show you around the beautiful islands today, my lady."

"Thank you. It's nice to meet you, Joren." I wondered how well he knew my new husband, who continued to mystify me. "How long have you worked for the Windsors?"

"Three years," the captain said as he started the motor. "I met Mr. Windsor when he was traveling in the Caribbean. I'm originally from Aruba, in case you couldn't tell from the accent."

"Thank you—I wasn't sure. I'm originally from Boston, in case you couldn't tell from *my* accent."

"Oh, I could tell." He laughed. "Boston and New York, I always know."

I laughed too, relieved to be around someone who would talk to me and seemed nice.

Joren steered the boat away from the dock, the enormous house rising from the rocky coast. It was a beautiful sight, its gray-stone facade a commanding presence above the churning water. I couldn't believe I'd spent the night there. I couldn't believe I *lived* there.

"Congratulations on your marriage," Joren said, interrupting my thoughts. "I wish you and Mr. Windsor every happiness."

"Thank you." There wasn't much else I could say. If he thought it was strange that my brand-new husband had abandoned me for his cellphone, he didn't let on. Lucky for me, Joren was happy to do the talking. He pointed out various landmarks to me, chatting away about the different boats we saw.

"I don't really know anything about boats," I admitted. "This is actually the first time I've ever been to Maine."

"Ah, you will love it. Much better than Boston." He laughed. "Just kidding, my lady. I know you Bostonians take great pride in your city."

"I don't even really like the city. This is so much nicer." It was true. The blue-green water sparkled, dappled with sunlight, and each tiny island we passed was covered with fir trees and rocky beaches. It was so peaceful and beautiful; even the air smelled good. It was heaven compared to the dreary streets back home.

"This is Raven Island, and over there is Caribou Beach." He pointed to a sandy strip of land. "I will take you and Mr. Windsor there sometime, drop you off for a romantic picnic."

I couldn't picture Bryce and me with a blanket spread out, a picnic basket between us, lounging on the gray sand. Actually, I couldn't picture Bryce without his suit and cellphone...

"To your left, that's Spruce Island," Joren continued. "I'll bring you around to see the old lighthouse. It's now owned by a very glamorous couple who've fixed it up. Mr. Windsor knows them, of course."

"Of course." If they were glamorous, they must be interested in the Windsor family. "So you've known Mr. Windsor for three years?"

"Yes, he chartered a boat I worked on. We went from Grand Bahama all the way down to Trinidad. Beautiful trip—I'd never seen all the islands before."

"That sounds amazing."

"These islands here in Maine are beautiful, too. It's just a different sort of beauty, you know? Lots of trees but not many people. And cold, *brr*, the water's freezing even in August." Joren chattered his teeth together for good measure.

"I take it you won't swim here?"

"You crazy?" He laughed. "Only seals swim here. And little kids, because they are insane."

"My brother will definitely go swimming." I shook my head. "He doesn't even wear a coat in the winter. It's like he can't feel the cold."

"Right? I have a little brother, too. He's the same way," Joren said. "He came to visit last summer, and he kept jumping off the dock, over and over, until his lips turned blue."

"How old is your brother?"

"Ten. Ten and crazy." Joren laughed again.

"Mine's eleven, and he's crazy too. So we have that in common."

We rounded Spruce Island, and the lighthouse came into view. It was a beautiful building, tall and pristinely white, with a tower that jutted into the sky. "This cove is great for seeing seals." Joren chatted on about the lighthouse, the seals, and which fishermen owned the various buoys we passed.

We rounded Spruce, and he showed me the island's sole restaurant, which sat over the water on a long dock. "They have the best burgers around. Most of the locals drive their boats over when they want to go for dinner."

"That sounds like fun." I couldn't imagine taking a

boat to go to dinner. "I'll have to bring Noah there—he loves a good burger."

"Let me know when you want to go, and I will take you, my lady. Whenever you wish." Joren smiled at me, and I smiled back.

"You will take Mrs. Windsor and her brother if and when I *instruct* you to do so." Bryce was suddenly in the cabin. He came up behind us and wrapped his arms possessively around me, pulling me back against him. *Shit.* If I'd thought he was muscular when he held me against his side, having him behind me was a whole other ball game. He was an enormous wall of pure muscle. Even his forearms, which enfolded my chest, felt powerful.

I also felt something pressing against my backside. Was he...? No, he *couldn't* be. Not because of me.

But something big poked at me, and inexperienced as I was, I had a funny feeling about it. The pressure made me feel all squirmy inside.

"Of course, Mr. Windsor." Joren's eyes were wide. "I would never take Mrs. Windsor anywhere without explicit directions from you."

"You wouldn't?" The question tumbled out before I could stop myself.

"Of course he wouldn't." Bryce pulled me closer, pressing every inch of himself against me. "He works for *me*, Chloe. And it's essential to me that I take care of *you*. Now please, join me—I've finished my calls for now. Joren."

"Mr. Windsor." Joren didn't say goodbye to me or even look in my direction.

Bryce clamped his big hand over mine and dragged me from the cabin. He looked straight ahead, a somewhat sour expression on his face. He marched to the largest bedroom, depositing me on the bed. "Wait here."

He rummaged through a dresser, grabbed some clothes, then disappeared into the bathroom.

It was an odd sensation, sitting on his bed, waiting for him. I still felt jolted by the feel of him behind me, accompanied by the possessive tone of his words. *You will take Mrs. Windsor and her brother if and when I instruct you to do so.* Damn. Mr. Windsor didn't like anyone else playing with his toys, did he?

I shivered, remembering what it felt like with him pressed against me. Had I imagined it, or had he been...hard?

It was probably all in my head. He'd barely looked at me since I met him—and in any event, I was clueless. I had nothing to compare it to; I hadn't been lying when I'd told Elena that I had zero experience in the sex department.

I'd never even been out on a date, let alone kissed someone. My mother had been pretty strict, and plus, because she worked odd hours, I'd often been in charge of babysitting Noah. I didn't consider it much of a loss —I was never interested in the boys at school. They were all about hooking up, then moving on to snap-chat their next conquest.

I glanced at the bed and its cool-gray comforter. What would it be like to lie there with Bryce? What did he have going on underneath that suit, anyway?

"Are you ready?"

Bryce stood before me in navy swim trunks that showed off his muscular thighs and a tight-fitting T-shirt that showcased his huge shoulders.

"Um."

"Um?" Another smile ghosted his lips. "I'll take that as a yes. Come with me, Chloe." He held out his hand.

As if I were campaigning to be named Employee of the Month, I rose and took it.

We went outside to the deck, the sun bright and blinding after the cool interior of the bedroom. I slid my sunglasses on, relieved that my eyes could roam freely without being seen. He put on his aviators and sauntered to the couch, all the better for me to check out his rock-hard, spectacular body. *Did I already say damn? Damn!* Now that I knew what was going on underneath that suit, I wouldn't ever be able to forget it.

"Come here, Chloe." He patted the seat next to him, his tone commanding.

I went to his side. My body felt like it was acting all on its own, coming when called. It was as if he'd cast some sort of spell over me. The wind whipped the hair back from my face as I settled next to him.

Bryce draped an arm around my shoulders and put his feet up, his muscled calves stretching out before me. "We're going to drive around for a bit. I have lots of acquaintances on the different islands, and I'd like to make our debut."

"We're making our debut by driving around in your boat?" Is that what filthy rich people did for fun?

"I guess we are." He shrugged. "There isn't much to do up here besides take your boat over to the mainland, go shopping or hiking, then drive back. By cruising the harbor, I'll cross at least a dozen names off my list. There will be a lot of smiling and waving—it's my way of letting everyone know you're here. They'll all have heard about our marriage, anyway."

"Already?" It had only been yesterday...

"Yes. Mount Desert Island is a small community, and everyone in my set who summers here keeps track of everyone else. There's been a lot of speculation that I might marry soon. So it's time to show you off." He scooted me closer to him.

That was something I'd noticed about Bryce: he didn't move. He moved *me*.

"After we parade ourselves around for a bit, I'll take you to my club for lunch," he continued. "There will be more smiling and waving, of course. And I'll need us to be close—physically close, I mean. Is that acceptable to you?"

"I guess so," I squeaked. He *was* paying me a million dollars.

"We should start now. We're on our honeymoon, after all. There would be talk if we weren't affectionate." He motioned to an oncoming boat. "Here comes Marty and Hattie Chambers—they live to gossip. Slide onto my lap?"

"Sure." I could barely get the word out. He wanted me on his *lap*?

But he answered my question by grabbing my hips and moving me on top of him. I could feel him—*all* of him—pressed up against the thin material of my bikini bottom.

Bryce wrapped one arm around me, hugging me against his chest, and waved at Marty and Hattie Chambers. Their boat slowed down long enough for them to grin at us and get a long, eager look. Mr. and Mrs.

Chambers were older, with white hair and white teeth, and wore matching fleece jackets. They looked like they'd stepped out of an L.L. Bean catalog.

Joren pulled away before they did, and we waved again as we drove off.

"Are you warm enough?" Bryce asked. He still had his arm around me.

"M-hmm." I couldn't say an actual word while sitting on my boss/husband's lap. Especially not when I felt something stirring beneath me.

Is that...?

"Do you mind removing your cover-up, Chloe? I'm actually looking forward to shaking things up around here a bit." Bryce chuckled.

I opened my mouth and closed it.

"You don't have to do it if you're not comfortable," he snapped.

"No—it's fine." I didn't want to admit that I'd been thrown off by the sounds of him laughing. I pulled the cover-up off over my head, and he took it from me, tucking it below the bench so it wouldn't blow away.

"That's better." Bryce hugged me to his chest, and I wished that I was facing him so I could see his expression. "Nice bikini, Chloe."

I shivered, and it had nothing to do with the wind. "Thank you."

We "paraded" around the bay for some time, waving and smiling at every boat that passed by. Bryce told me the names of his island neighbors, reciting details about each one: Mrs. Kitteridge owned several large commercial real estate properties in Manhattan, and Mateo Hernandez had just sold his Boston-based tech company for fifteen-million dollars.

I was surprised that Bryce was physically capable of staying off his cellphone for so long. I was even more taken aback by the fact that he smiled for such an extended period.

But something else dominated my attention.

The ocean air was brisk, and the wind blew against my exposed skin—and yet, it was mercilessly hot. Bryce kept his arms wrapped around me. At some point, he'd begun stroking my bare skin with his enormous, rough fingertips. For some reason, this made me burn.

I didn't understand what was happening—I'd never felt this way in my life. As my skin grew hotter, I felt him thicken beneath me, pressed against my ass. What was going on? I *didn't* understand it, and yet...

Part of me did. Part of me absofuckinglutely did.

And I couldn't stop myself from wanting more.

first move

SITTING on Bryce's lap was an *event.* I fought the urge to squirm, to rub up against him. His massive chest pressed into my back, a wall of muscle for me to lean against.

For his part, Bryce kept the lower portion of his body rigid, controlled, and completely still. And yet his fingers explored my bare skin, almost as if he couldn't help himself.

"Here are the Mayweathers. Smile and wave," he commanded.

I did as I was told. The Mayweathers smiled and waved back, a pleasant, appropriate exchange. But beneath my accommodating exterior, a rebellion was brewing. Bryce hadn't acknowledged the growing heat between us. Was that because he didn't feel it?

Or for some other reason?

I wondered what would happen if I shifted in his lap. What if I rubbed back against that hardness—what would happen? Would he be angry or pleased? Or was I imagining this whole thing?

"The club's coming up," Bryce said. His voice was controlled, even.

I was probably making all of this up in my head.

"We only have ten more minutes." His grip tightened around me, big fingers trailing down my bare arms.

I could barely breathe. The closer he held me, the more *it* pressed against my ass. At some point, *it* had risen and taken refuge against me, taunting me with its firm, insistent presence. Again, I fought the urge to rub myself back against him.

I would wait for him to make the first move. If he didn't, I obviously imagined the growing heat between us. I could at least save myself a tiny shred of dignity.

"I should probably kiss you, Chloe."

"I'm sorry?" If I hadn't been so intent on staying pressed against him, I would've fallen over.

He put his mouth next to my ear and spoke slowly. "I should kiss you before we get to the club. Because I will be kissing you *at* the club. And at the cocktail party we're going to tonight. People need to know this is real.

And I suppose we should get it out the way, shouldn't we?"

"Get it out of the way?" I shivered as I repeated his words. "What do you mean?"

"Do it now, in private, so it's not awkward," Bryce explained. "Turn around and face me, Chloe."

"Yes..." *Sir. Yes, sir.*

But I didn't need to turn myself around—he did it for me, lifting and positioning my body like I was his doll, his plaything. He scooted out a little so I could wrap my legs around him, then placed my arms around his neck. His *erection*—for that was definitely what it was, I was certain—stayed hard between us, but he didn't acknowledge it.

Bryce took his sunglasses off, then gently removed mine. We locked eyes for a moment. His gaze traveled down my body, openly roaming over my breasts in the tiny bikini top.

"Your file indicated that you have no sexual experience," he said out of nowhere. "Is that true?"

"Yes." Again, I answered as though I were in some sort of trance. I wouldn't have been able to lie to him if I had tried.

"How many boyfriends have you had?" he grunted.

"None." *Sir.*

His eyes snapped back to mine. "Is that the truth?"

I nodded. "I don't lie."

"You lied about smiling this morning," he reminded me.

"I was trying to make a joke."

"It wasn't funny." He ran his hands down my bare sides. "How many men have you kissed?"

"None."

He cocked his head, still looking at me. "How many *boys* have you kissed?"

"None."

"You haven't *ever* been kissed?"

"Only at our ceremony yesterday." I shrugged. "I've never been on a date. I used to babysit a lot because of all the shifts my mom worked. Plus, all the boys at my school were dicks."

Bryce laughed an *actual laugh*. Only for a moment, but still. "I'm glad to hear it. But let's do it now before we have an audience. I'll give you a proper first kiss— even though some people say *I'm* a dick."

I couldn't help it; I laughed.

"Are you ready?"

"Yes." *No. No fucking way.*

He secured his hands around my waist and leaned forward. I watched, fascinated, as his face closed in toward mine.

"Close your eyes, Chloe."

I did as I was told. A moment later, his lips brushed mine. Electricity jolted through me. Unlike our chaste and disappointing wedding kiss, *this* kiss made me feel something—hot chills coursed down my body, and heat pooled in my belly. He pressed his lips against mine again, his mouth slightly open. *Unf.* Why did that feel so good? Bryce's big hands roamed my back, gently but firmly.

His erection moved between us, straining. There was no denying it now.

I leaned in for more kisses. Bryce went slow; I had the sense he was teaching me. His tongue stroked mine, and I couldn't help it—I moaned.

He must've liked that because he pulled me tighter. His bulging swim trunks rubbed against my scrap of a bathing suit bottom. We kissed, then kissed some more, and something else started happening. We were rubbing against each other, heat building.

Holy fuck. I had no idea what I was doing, but it felt incredible.

Bryce's hands continued to roam my back, exploring, as his tongue found mine. We rocked against each other, lost in the moment, and I forgot about everything except the wild sensations running through my body. I could do this all day. I could do this every second for the rest of my life. Who knew I could feel so good?

He pulled me closer and grunted as we ground against each other. I sure hoped old Mr. and Mrs. Mayweather didn't pass by again—they'd get an eyeful!

But perhaps that was the point. I became aware that the boat had slowed down and finally, that it had stopped. But we hadn't.

I realized that the yacht had pulled up to a dock and that an attendant was waiting nearby, scrupulously not looking at us. Bryce kissed me again, his fingers tracing the edge of my bikini bottom. I pulled away. *"Bryce."*

He opened his eyes, looking a bit pissed that I'd interrupted his exploration. "Yes, Chloe?"

"We're *here*," I whispered, mortified.

He blinked at me. "I know."

I opened my mouth and then closed it.

"Do you need something, Chloe?"

"My coverup would be nice." My dignity would be nicer!

The dock attendant appeared to be fascinated by the boats in the harbor, staring out at them as though his life depended on not looking at us.

"Hey, Adam." Bryce didn't take his hands off me. "Can you tell them we're here?"

"Of course, Mr. Windsor. My pleasure." He hustled off, still not looking in our direction.

Another boat headed toward the dock. I scrambled

to cover my bare skin with the dress, but Bryce was unabashed—he sat with his feet up, shirt rumpled, erection straining against his swim trunks, looking as though he were *enjoying* himself. "Everything okay, Chloe?"

"Yes." *No.* "I just don't like to be half-naked in front of people."

"If it's any consolation, you look awfully good."

I stared at him. "Did you just compliment me?"

"No." He shrugged. "I'm just stating a fact. Would you like to go up to the club now?"

Did I have a choice? "Sure."

He stood, adjusted his shorts, then hopped off the boat. "Then let's go."

"Let me help you, Mrs. Windsor." His besuited employee hustled down the boat deck.

"I've got her," Bryce snapped. "Have Joren wait in the bay."

He stopped in his tracks. "Yes, sir."

Bryce held out his hands and helped me out of the boat. As soon as I reached the dock, he tucked me against his side, putting his arm around my shoulder. "I won't be letting go of you for the rest of the afternoon. I hope you understand—I believe one of these old bastards, a friend of my father's, actually put money on me not inheriting my trust."

"Someone bet against you?" I raised my eyebrows. "I can't picture it."

He chuckled. "Some of these people have been rich so long, it's made them stupid."

"Obviously." If he was going to be more lighthearted —if he was going to *chuckle*—I might as well try and join him. It was better than panting and grinding against him in public. How had that even happened? What the hell was going on between us? If it was all for show, why did it feel so *urgent*?

It must've just been me. Bryce seemed calm, cool, and more relaxed than I'd seen him as we climbed the stairs to his club.

But I was anything but chill as we reached the landing. Bryce's "club" was an insanely upscale pool area sprawled out beneath an elegant outdoor dining room. The pool was enormous, all pale-gray stone, the sparkling water a clear aqua. Spiky plants in granite planters discreetly dotted the pool deck. The guests on the loungers wore flowing, intricately patterned caftans, giant sunglasses, and luxe-looking bikinis. Everything was understated and tasteful, a clear sign that this place was intended for guests who were rich AF.

The guests eating at the restaurant—many of whom were staring at Bryce—were dressed as though they were attending some sort of gala. The men wore suits and fedoras, and the women favored trendy jumpsuits or pale-colored, tight-fitting sheaths. In one glance, I counted nine Louis Vuitton totes. Martini and champagne flutes abounded, even though it wasn't yet noon.

A server in a tan linen suit met us and bowed his head. "Mr. Windsor, it's always an honor when you join us. Would you like your regular table, or do you prefer to start with a cabana?"

"I'd like the dais, Serge. I see the Milliken girl over there, but she can move."

"Of course, Mr. Windsor. We'll have it ready shortly." Serge practically bolted down the pool deck, snapping his fingers for some of the other staff to join him. They had a brief conversation during which they looked from one of the young guests—quite possibly the Milliken girl—who lounged on a raised platform right in the center of the action, then back to Bryce.

Perhaps Bryce's expression, which now bordered on impatience, had them moving so quickly. Squaring his shoulders, one of the servers approached the young woman, who looked about sixteen, and motioned to another cabana. Her pretty face puckered. That didn't stop him—he gathered her things, put them neatly into her tote, and set her up across the pool without further ado. She slid her flip-flops on and, with a pouty look in our direction, reluctantly sauntered to her new spot.

Three workers descended on the vacated cabana. They changed out the lounge-chair pillows, put down fresh towels, sprayed the area with some sort of freshener, lit the small fire pit, and filled an ice bucket with several bottles of champagne.

Serge came bustling back. "The dais is ready for you, Mr. Windsor."

"Thank you, Serge. Mrs. Windsor would like some water, as well as an iced tea. She's underage, you see."

Serge didn't hesitate. "Yes, of course. Would Mrs. Windsor like anything else at the moment?"

"Darling?" Bryce wrapped his arms around me. "Are you hungry?"

"I'm fine."

"Bring her some fruit, Serge. She needs to keep her strength up."

I shivered, wondering just what I needed my strength for...

"Yes, Sir." Good old Serge didn't bat an eye. He just led the billionaire and his child-bride to the club's prime real estate. The dais was smack-dab in the center of the action. Our chairs were on a raised platform beneath a sun-chaser, all the better for everyone to ogle us.

"Why is everybody staring at you?" I whispered once Serge left us.

"They're staring at *you*." Bryce dropped down and splayed out on his lounger. He pulled down his sunglasses enough to show his eyes. "My underaged, beautiful new bride." He waggled his eyebrows.

Is that a compliment? And was I insane, or was Bryce in a *good mood*? With my new husband, it was always difficult to tell. I didn't say anything as I sat on my own lounger and primly arranged my coverup.

"Take that thing off," Bryce growled.

"The bikini's pretty small." I shifted uncomfortably, eyeing the other female guests. The Milliken girl was the only one whose suit was as revealing as mine. "And everyone's staring."

"Let them. Take it off and come here, Chloe." He patted his lounger, beckoning me to go and lie with him.

I stripped out of my coverup and went to his side as if I were in a trance. His skin trailed down my bare skin, leaving a trail of icy fire. I shivered beneath his touch, half-wondering if Bryce had a voodoo doll of me hidden somewhere, manipulating my every move.

Maybe it would be better if that were true.

Maybe it would be better if I could pretend that this wasn't exactly what I wanted.

He's making the first move, Chloe. Go for it.

I laid beside him and let him touch me, fingers trailing down my burning skin. He kissed me again, and I felt like I had died inside and gone to heaven.

But heaven didn't charge admission.

Why him?

Why now?

Why do I feel this way, like I'm burning inside?

Like if he stops touching me, I'm going to scream?

I was the employee, the bought bride. The money was flowing *my* way in this arrangement. Still, I had a very bad feeling that eventually, I would pay dearly for this.

I laid back and enjoyed the feeling of his hands roaming over me, consequences be damned.

the job

THE AFTERNOON WAS BLISSFUL. The sun shone as we lounged by the pool, kissing, touching, and being watched by every member of Bryce's club. There was iced tea and fruit for me, water for Bryce.

"Why don't you have champagne?" I asked when he finally stopped kissing me for a moment.

"I want to enjoy this. See that old man over there?" He motioned to an older gentleman sitting at the restaurant. "That's Donald—the one who bet against me. I'd like to be fully present when he cries about losing his fifty k."

"He bet fifty *thousand* dollars?" I glanced at the man, who wore a sour expression as he contemplated his lobster roll.

"That's what I heard." Bryce scowled, but it dissipated as he turned his attention back to me. "I'd like you to resume your position on my lap, Chloe. I'm getting cold."

"It's hot."

"Not hot enough." He playfully grabbed me and positioned me in his new favorite spot—pressed directly against his erection.

If the servers and the other guests thought us inappropriate, they didn't say a word. Similarly, if Bryce found pawing me in public a chore, it didn't show.

Fool that I was, I let myself enjoy.

After introducing me to several club members, including the fool who'd bet against Bryce, we headed back to the boat. This time, he pulled me inside the cabin, dropping my hand as soon as we reached the interior. "I have to work. Please stay indoors for the ride home. It will be better if everyone thinks we're...occupied."

He neither said another word nor looked at me as he entered the boat's study and closed the door behind him.

Whiplash. The man was giving me whiplash.

Without him by my side—more precisely, without

him manhandling me—I felt abandoned and cold. *Eye on the ball, Chloe. Remember, it's the job.*

I would do well to focus on my brother, who was why I was there in the first place. He was what mattered. I grabbed my phone and texted Dale, asking about Noah's day of fishing.

The kid has luck, Dale wrote back immediately. *He was the only one who caught a fish! It was too small—catch and release. Now he's playing with the puppy.* He sent me a picture of my brother sitting cross-legged on the lawn, a tiny puppy sitting on his lap. I stared at the picture, taking in my brother's smile, the new, clean clothes someone had bought for him.

Bryce's office door suddenly opened. He stood at the entrance, phone in hand. "I'm on hold."

I nodded, waiting for him to go on.

"You did well today, Chloe—I expect you'll do even better tonight. Please have the staff arrange another gown for you. We have a cocktail party at eight on Spruce Island." He closed the door before I could respond.

I texted Dale and asked for Midge's number, and once again, he responded instantly. He definitely didn't get paid enough. I texted Midge: *Cocktail party tonight. Dress 9-1-1!*

She also responded right away. *Do you want sexy or*

prim? Please say sexy!

I looked at the closed door. *Sexy,* I wrote back.

There was no way this was going to turn out well. I knew that. Still, I longed to see what Bryce's reaction would be to me in a seductive dress.

Would he enjoy that? Or would it be a wasted effort? I intended to find out.

Midge outdid herself. The dress she'd chosen was black with a plunging neckline, sexy and formfitting but so expensive, it somehow didn't look sleazy. God bless her: the matching sandals she'd chosen were *flat.* "The party's outside," Midge explained. "We can't have you losing a heel in the Nguyen's lawn!"

"Do you know them—the people throwing the party?" I asked while she blew out my hair.

"Kelli and Kenji Nguyen. She's a top executive with some studio, he owns a crap-ton of commercial real estate."

"I'm going to have so much in common with them," I joked.

"You'll be fine, hon." Midge winked at me. "The whole town's already buzzing about you. Old Hazel was having a fit earlier—she had *twelve* phone calls from assistants asking if we would have a coming-out party for you two. Everyone's losing their minds!"

"Really?"

"Absolutely! Mr. Windsor's been the hottest bachelor on the islands for*ever*. The fact that he finally got married, and to someone who can't even drink yet? *Damn.* I heard from my girlfriend who works at the club that you two lit that place *up* today—it's all anyone's been talking about, how he can't keep his hands off you, that he's obsessed, that he's totally over you-know-what..."

"Yeah, well." I stiffened. Why did I feel jealous of his ex? It was silly. "I don't know about that."

"Well, I do." Midge nodded, looking sure of herself. "Mr. Windsor isn't the type to mess around. Everything he does has a reason. If he's showing you off, he's proud of you. Let yourself enjoy it, girl. A man like that only comes around once in a lifetime."

I nodded, nerves thrumming. I was anxious to see him again, anxious to gauge his reaction to my dress. Why I was doing this to myself, I wasn't sure. But a fire had started inside me today. I still felt the heat in my belly, a heat that *he* had awoken. For better or for worse, I wanted to fan the flames. To see what, if anything, would happen. Was this all in my head?

She started applying my makeup, and I held still. "I

saw Noah—he said he had a great day," I said. "The staff here is amazing. Everyone's being so kind to us. Thank you."

"You're welcome. Like I said, we're all rooting for you. Every person on this staff loves a Cinderella story, you know?" Midge gently applied my eyeliner. "Show yourself off in that dress tonight, let him lose his mind over you, and then live happily ever after."

"Ha! You make it sound easy."

"You're making it *look* easy, hon. Have a little faith, okay?"

I swallowed hard. Faith had been in short supply for me lately.

But I couldn't help but feel a spark of hope as Midge zipped me into the dress, and I looked at my reflection.

"Holy fuck." Midge clapped a hand over her heart.

"Ha." But I was stunned at how I looked. The black dress was formfitting up top, the bodice plunging to my waist, the skirt full and gauzy. Midge had fixed my hair so it was silky and wavy, cascading over one shoulder. Diamond studs sparkled on my ears, and my makeup tastefully shimmered. The overall effect was dream-like, a *very* sexy fairy-tale princess.

"Mr. Windsor might have a heart attack. Take it easy on him tonight, okay?" Midge joked.

"I'll do my best." If I was being honest with myself

—which I wasn't—I would admit that I had zero intentions of taking it easy. I wanted something from him; I just wasn't sure what.

Midge glanced at the clock. "We better get going! Mr. Windsor doesn't like—"

"To wait." I smiled at her. "I know, I know."

"Then let's get you downstairs." She waggled her eyebrows. "He will *not* want to waste a second of you in that dress."

"Thank you, Midge."

She winked at me again. "Are you kidding me? I live for this shit!"

She hustled me out the door. I gathered my courage and the hem of the flowing dress as I headed down to where Bryce waited. Tonight he wore another dark suit, his thick hair pushed back from his slightly tanned face and a deep-purple tie that brought out his eyes. He was so handsome it almost hurt to look at him.

"Chloe." His gaze raked over me from head to toe, taking in every inch. "That's quite a dress. Did you pick it out?"

"No." *No, Sir.* "Midge did."

He arched an eyebrow slightly. "Does Midge have some sort of agenda?"

I arched an eyebrow back. "Like what?" I asked innocently.

"Like inciting a riot, which is exactly what that dress will do. You will stay by my side all night, Chloe. You will not leave my arms." His tone was stern, commanding. "Do you understand me?"

"Yes." *Yes, sir.*

Was it wrong that I found his possessiveness *completely fucking hot*?

"You won't have to worry about that because I won't know anyone at this party, anyway." I accepted his outstretched arm as we headed down the hall.

Once again, the staff came out to greet us.

"Have a great time!"

"You look lovely, Mrs. Windsor."

"Gorgeous dress."

"What a beautiful couple."

Hazel said nothing. She watched us, her thin lips pressed together in what I imagined was a show of disapproval.

Bryce leaned closer as we went outside, the ocean air cold against my skin. "Everyone will want to talk to you. But they'll have to understand—you're *mine*."

"Okay," I said, already feeling under his spell.

His hand roamed down my back, dangerously low, even though we were without an audience. And I couldn't help but wonder if I had, indisputably, bitten off more than I could chew.

EIGHTEEN

revealing

JOREN MET us at the boat. He bowed as we approached. "Mr. Windsor. Mrs. Windsor." When he rose, he glanced in my direction. He didn't make eye contact, and his gaze skittered swiftly away.

"Please bring us to the Nguyen's dock. That will be all," Bryce said stiffly. He waited until Joren disappeared to help me aboard.

"The captain seems nice. He told me he's been with you for three years?"

"Did he?" Bryce asked noncommittally. He brought me into the cabin. "It's too cold at night to be outside, especially in *that*." He eyed the dress again.

"Is it..." Insecurity crept up. "Is it too revealing?"

Bryce laughed as he dropped down onto the couch.

"You're asking that now? It's *very* revealing, Chloe. And yet, it doesn't reveal as much as I'd like."

My cheeks heated.

"Come here," he commanded. "Didn't I already tell you that you're not permitted to leave my side all night?"

I went to him. And even though there was no one else there, he put his arm around me. Something bloomed inside my chest—pride, maybe? I'd felt as though I'd won something or passed some sort of test.

"Everyone will be at this party tonight." Bryce arranged me against him, then palmed my hip. "My father, Daphne, Donald—the old man who bet against me—everyone we passed on the Sound, everyone we saw at the club. And everyone else, of course. The hosts are Ginny and Kenji Nguyen. They live on the West Coast and come up for six weeks every summer. Their estate is gorgeous, the biggest on Spruce Island."

"They have an estate they only use for six weeks a year?" Rich AF people were *baffling*.

"Sometimes Ginny only comes for two. She's an entertainment executive. They rarely get a break."

"Wow." I shook my head, unable to imagine a life like that.

"It's pretty common with the people I know. At

least, the ones who're still in the game. What about you, Chloe?"

I blinked at him. "What about me?"

"What do *you* want to do?" Bryce asked. "Do you want to go to college to study something?"

"I don't... I don't know," I admitted. "I couldn't really think about it because of everything that happened."

"Did you have plans before your mom died?"

His directness surprised me. I couldn't answer right away.

Bryce cleared his throat. "Sorry if I shouldn't have brought that up. But no one ever talked about my mother after she died, and I always wished it were different."

I nodded. "I get that. How old were you?"

"About your brother's age."

"I'm sorry."

He shook his head. "It was a long time ago."

"Hey, speaking of my brother... You offered to bring him jet skiing."

Bryce shrugged a big shoulder.

"That was nice of you."

He scrubbed a hand over his face. "Nice isn't really my thing. Anyway, we were talking about *you*. Did you have plans for college?"

"Yeah, I did." It seemed like a lifetime ago. "I wanted to go to school to become a nurse."

"Is that what you'd do if you could do anything?"

"I think so. I was excited about it." I looked at my hands. "My mom worked at the hospital—not as a nurse, but she was going back to get her degree. She always said it made her feel good that she got to help people every day. I think I'd like to do that. She would be proud of me, you know?"

He pulled me closer. "I agree."

One of Bryce's men knocked on the door. "We've arrived, Mr. Windsor. Easy trip, good visibility tonight."

"Thank you." Bryce dismissed him, then rose to his formidable height, pulling me up. "Remember what your orders are for the evening: do not leave my side."

"Your wish is my command," I teased.

"Careful." A small smile ghosted his lips. "I could get used to this."

My heart stuttered in my chest as we left the boat, and it had nothing to do with being nervous about the party. It was the promise of Bryce's words. *I could get used to this.* Did he mean it?

He'd been so cold when I first met him, icy and disdainful. But as he wrapped his arm around my waist and pulled me against his side, he was nothing but warm and attentive. Who was this version of Bryce

Windsor? Was this the man himself—or his carefully orchestrated public face?

But as he possessively palmed my hip, I realized that we hadn't reached the party yet. We were alone on the dock, the stars beginning to wink above us. He had an audience of one: just me.

And I couldn't get enough of his touch.

Tiki torches lit the gravel path from the dock. The Nguyen estate opened up before us, straight out of a luxe fairytale. Their lawn was sprawled out in every direction, running up to the beach. The tall, ancient pine trees lining the forest's edge were bedecked with tiny lights, bathing the party in a twinkly, ephemeral glow. Long tables were set with white tablecloths and laden with platters of food. A fountain of champagne bubbled nearby, surrounded by crystal flutes. The guests—about a hundred of them—were dressed formally in long gowns and dark suits. Everyone chatted beneath the spectacular, darkening sky, a crescent moon watching over us.

"Bryce!" A friendly woman in her forties descended on us. She had long, tawny-colored hair, laugh lines, and a light tan. She wore a tight-fitting, teal-colored dress that showed off her toned figure.

"Kelli." Bryce favored her with a rare smile. "It's always nice to see you."

She air-kissed him on each cheek, then clutched his hands. "I wasn't sure you were going to make it—everyone who was at the club today said you'd be too busy pawing your new bride to make the trip. Speaking of your bride, *there you are*! Let me look at you!"

She dropped Bryce and turned her attention to me, clapping her hands together. "It's true—you're as beautiful as everyone says. Good work, Bryce."

Bryce coughed. "Thank you. Kelli, this is my wife, Chloe Windsor. Chloe, this is our host, Kelli Nguyen."

"It's so nice to meet you. Your property is incredible."

She waved her hand, enormous diamond ring sparkling. "Kenji's the one who picked out the architects—I just moved in after everything was finished." She linked her arm through mine. "You understand that everybody's been waiting for you to show up. You're going to be in demand tonight, Chloe."

"She's not leaving me—don't try and steal her away." Bryce went to my other side and took my arm, preparing to play tug-of-war. "She's mine, Kelli. I know you want to be the one to show her off, but it's not going to happen."

"Fine." Kelli quickly released me, then laughed. "You know I don't care about that crap anyway. But it *would* be fun to watch Daphne lose it because there's a Windsor younger and prettier than her."

"True." Bryce laughed.

Kelli inspected him. "You know what, Bryce? You look happy. It's nice to see you this way." She nudged me. "Nice job, Chloe. I already like you."

Despite her fancy house, enormous ring, big career, and toned biceps, Kelli seemed easygoing and kind. "I like you, too."

She laughed. "Bryce, do me a favor and keep her away from all the assholes here, huh? It's refreshing to be around someone normal—don't let her get tainted. Can I get you two some champagne?"

"We'll stick to water, thanks." Bryce tightened his grip around me.

"Be right back." Kelli went to the bar to fetch our drinks.

"No champagne or bourbon?" I asked.

"I'm rather enjoying myself," Bryce said. "So I don't feel the need." But then we spotted his father and Daphne heading toward us, and he stiffened.

"Oh boy." I leaned against him as though it would lend him support. "Here we go."

Bryce sighed. "Did I say I was enjoying myself? I spoke too soon."

Kelli glanced in our direction, then smartly decided to send a server with our drinks instead.

Gene Windsor's eyes sparkled as he approached, but Daphne looked sour. She wore a tangerine gown that showed off her porcelain skin. Her glossy hair swished as she stalked, but despite her loveliness, the smile she'd plastered onto her face didn't reach her eyes.

I thanked the server and clutched my water as my new in-laws reached us.

"Bryce. Chloe." Gene Windsor nodded his head. "Lovely party, isn't it?"

"We just got here, so we haven't had a chance to settle in. But you already knew that."

Gene shrugged. "I've already been getting an earful. Dr. Milliken said you unceremoniously removed his daughter from her seat at the club today. Is that the case?"

Now it was Bryce's turn to shrug. "She's sixteen without a care in the world. They packed her up and moved her to another cushy lounger. I expect she'll make it."

Gene tipped his glass toward us. "She might, but hoo boy, Donald's having a fit about that bet. He lost two hundred thousand!"

That got Bryce's interest. "I heard it was only fifty." He and Gene kept talking, and perhaps because it was about the down-on-his-luck Donald, they seemed to be okay.

Daphne took the opportunity to get in my face. "What was up with you at the club today? One of my friends said you were *humping* Bryce on the dais."

"Ew, no. We were kissing, but not... Not humping." I shuddered.

"She said it was budget." Daphne sniffed. "I appreciate that you're newlyweds, but we're *Windsors*. We have an image to keep up. And that club hasn't taken new members in over thirty years. You have to marry someone or be reincarnated into a legacy family in order to get in. Please don't make a spectacle of yourself again."

I wanted to ask if showing her ass in a thong on YouTube constituted making a spectacle, but I resisted the urge. "Thanks for the advice. I've definitely never been to a club like that before."

"Of course not, but ignorance is no excuse." She narrowed her eyes at me. "You've been warned."

"Okay. I'm sorry if we were inappropriate—it's the newlywed thing, I guess." I intended to try and keep Daphne on my good side. She was too much of a pain to have as an enemy. "How was *your* day?"

"Fine." She had a sip of her drink, something pink in a martini glass. "I had a headache earlier, but I worked out for three hours then sat in the sauna. Then I saw my acupuncturist. All better now."

"Wow. That sounds productive."

She tossed her hair. "I'm a CEO, Chloe. I'm *always* productive."

"I'm a CEO, and I fucked around all day." Bryce wrapped his arms around me from behind. "I *am* on my honeymoon, though. Even CEOs need a break sometimes."

Daphne scowled; Gene raised an eyebrow as Bryce leaned down and nibbled on my ear. I almost yelped.

He was hard against my backside. *That* made me almost yelp, too. The whole thing was ungodly inappropriate, but what could I do?

"It seems you're relaxing with each other." Gene looked amused. "Better than last night, in any event. Can't say that was the best company or conversation I've ever had at dinner."

"You were being rude," Bryce reminded him. He sounded almost cheerful. "And Chloe was nervous about meeting her new in-laws—especially her mother-in-law."

"Don't you *dare* call me that," Daphne hissed. She shot a warning look at her husband. "You told him he wasn't allowed to use that term!"

"He's a married man now. He does what he wants." Gene had another sip of bourbon.

"I'm too young to be her mother-in-law!"

"Of course you are, dear. Just her older sister."

"Don't you dare say that to me, or it'll be the end of us. Excuse me, Bryce and Chloe. I need some space from my husband." Daphne turned on her heel and stalked away, expertly managing to keep her drink intact.

"Women." Gene snorted. "She taunts me like that as a form of foreplay. Daphne likes to pretend she's hard to get or that she'll divorce me. But four cosmopolitans in, when she sees me talking to another woman, she'll be back. Now that I think about it, I should make a bet about that with Donald."

"Classy, Father. Truly."

"I haven't been worried about being classy in a while." Gene's gaze raked over us, taking in Bryce's arms crossed possessively around my chest. "The thing is, some women *are* difficult to pin down. You know all about that though—right, son?"

"Chloe and I are very happy together, Father." Bryce didn't rise to the taunt. "Some would even say we're ecstatic. Just ask Donald and his missing funds."

"Hmm, maybe someday I will." Gene's watery eyes sparkled, a sure warning sign. "But first, I'd like to know why you and your fresh, nubile young bride aren't sharing a bedroom. The staff told me all about it, of course. Yet, you're parading her around—it makes it seem as though you're putting on a show."

Bryce didn't miss a beat. "I moved Chloe into the adjoining primary suite. Note the word *adjoining*. Not that it's any of your business."

Gene finished his bourbon, then leaned forward. His sharp breath wafted over me, reminding me of my father—although my father's booze came from a plastic bottle instead of a crystal decanter. "If you aren't consummating your marriage, it's absolutely my business—because it can be annulled. Like it never happened."

"Lucky for me, that's not the case. My marriage is real, and it can't be annulled. And that's even luckier for you." Bryce met his father's gaze. "You're going to drink yourself to death one of these days. And I'll be there to clean up the mess."

"Careful, now—don't get nasty and let your true colors show. Chloe might go running off, just like the last one." Gene smiled at his son. His smiles were the *worst*.

"Please excuse us"—Bryce came around to my side and grabbed my hand—"but my wife and I need to circulate. Good luck with Daphne and her four cosmopolitans. Looks like you're going to need it." He nodded in the direction of the bar, where Daphne was doing shots surrounded by a knot of men who were cheering her on.

"Christ." Gene hustled off.

Bryce blew out a deep breath as his father left.

"I was worried he would say something like that," I admitted. "About our rooms."

"It's none of his damn business."

"But... isn't it?" I squeezed his hand. "He needs to think this is real, doesn't he?"

"It is real." Bryce's brow furrowed. "You're my wife, Chloe. It's perfectly legal."

"But is what he said true?" I asked, aware that I was crossing into dangerous territory. "Could our marriage be annulled if we don't consummate it?" I couldn't even believe what was coming out of my mouth. *Annulled. Consummated.* Who TF was I?

"Yes. It's true." Bryce's nostrils flared. "But we don't need to worry about it. What's between us is between *us*. No one will ever know. Now come here, Chloe. You promised to stay by my side. I don't take promises lightly."

He pulled me against him, and I could feel *all* of him. His erection still strained against me. My skin pricked, tingling, alive with heat.

I was so confused. There was definitely something

happening between us. His hardness... That meant he wanted me, right?

So why did I get the feeling that *consummation* was strictly off-limits? If he wanted me, why wouldn't he let himself have me?

I lifted my chin and squared my shoulders. I looked *hot* in this dress. So hot that he was hard for me. If there was ever a time to figure out precisely what Bryce's limits were, tonight was the night.

I intended to find his lines...and cross them.

For better, or more likely, for worse.

touched

BRYCE PARADED me around the party. It was a blur of twinkling lights, champagne flutes, and being ogled.

"Love your dress, darling. Is it a *Leger*?"

"Did you attend East Prep? I have a niece about your age who went there!"

"Bryce, wherever did you find such a charming young creature? I'm guessing Daphne didn't introduce you—she probably doesn't like being the oldest female in the family, ha ha ha!"

Most of the guests were unrelatable. They were older, rich AF, and treated me like a museum exhibit —something to be contemplated, examined from every angle, and commented upon. For his part, Bryce did most of the talking, smoothly lying about our relationship and how long we'd known each other, how happy we were, and how he loved introducing me to Mount Desert Island society. He laid it on thick, keeping his arm firmly around me, holding me close all night.

I wondered why he was making such an effort—it didn't really seem like him—but Gene Windsor kept watch over us from across the party. Bryce was putting on a show for *him*. All the attention gave our new marriage momentum and credibility within their circle. Gene might have his suspicions, but the other guests ate up the love-at-first-sight story Bryce told them. As my new husband's hands roamed my sides, they gave each other knowing looks. *He can't keep his hands off her. Newlyweds!*

Despite the cool ocean breeze and the New England chill blanketing the night island, I was almost unbearably hot by his side. Was this what Gene Windsor had meant by extended foreplay? Bryce had been at this all day—touching me, caressing me, holding me close, teasing me with his hardness.

Then telling me it wasn't necessary for us to consummate our relationship.

It was torture.

I thought I'd be the one to drive *him* crazy in the dress. Instead, he seemed calm and controlled, albeit still aroused. But *I* felt as though if Bryce didn't put his hands on me once we got back on board his yacht, I might scream.

Another hour passed; the party was getting louder. Some of the guests started to slur their words. Bryce whispered to me, "That's our cue—time to go." We took our leave with a wave to Kelli, who was across the lawn.

Joren waited on the dock. "Mr. Windsor. Mrs. Windsor."

"Home, please, Joren." Again, Bryce's tone was clipped. He didn't look at the captain as he helped me on board. Once we were inside the cabin, he sank down onto the couch and pulled me with him. "Did you see my father and Daphne right before we left?"

"Yep." It was an unfortunate sight. Daphne had inserted herself between Gene and a pretty server. She'd been wagging her finger, yelling at the young woman.

"That server was just trying to give my father his drink, and Daphne went after her. The sick thing? The smile on my father's face." Bryce shuddered. "But enough about them—*you* did well at the party, Chloe. A lot of the summer residents are bored, and you gave them life tonight. Especially in that dress."

I adjusted the straps, cheeks heating. It was good if the guests liked it, but the gown hadn't had the effect I'd hoped for.

"Why the long face?"

I shook my head. "It's nothing. I'm tired, I guess."

"Ah. That's too bad. I was hoping you'd have some energy left in case you wanted to practice more."

I looked up at him. "What do you mean?"

"I think you know." He patted his lap. "You're inexperienced, but maybe not so innocent."

I blinked. "I'm innocent."

"Anyone who picks out a neckline like that has an agenda. Now come *here*, Chloe," he growled, pulling me onto his lap. His erection raged against me, but again, he didn't acknowledge it. He did, however, adjust me so that it pressed up against my side, undeniably thick between us.

What am I supposed to do? Ugh, what did he *want* from me?

Feeling his powerful body made me long to see what he had going on underneath his suit. I blew out a deep breath and shifted against him, rubbing against his hard length. *Oof.* Rubbing was bad. It made me want to do it again and again...

The muscle in Bryce's jaw bulged. His pupils were huge. "What are you doing, Chloe?"

"You said you wanted to practice, right?" I asked innocently. I shifted against his erection again, rubbing it against my side through the gauzy skirt of my dress.

He put his hands on my hips, holding tight, then

maneuvered me so that I straddled him. Now his erection raged between my legs, throbbing and dangerously close. *Oh boy.*

My heart stuttered in my chest, zipping around, skipping beats. It was so *hot* in the cabin. Our gazes locked, and Bryce's lips opened slightly. I hesitated, but only for a moment. He'd been the one to pull me onto his lap, to taunt me with his erection.

He'd already made the first move.

I bent to kiss him.

"Mmm." He sank his hands into my hair, his touch forceful, not gentle. Our tongues lashed together, and before I knew what was happening, I was grinding against him. *So good. Oh my God.* The friction of his trousers against my skirts was delicious. It didn't satisfy, but it was at least something.

His hands roamed from my hair, down my back, to my hips once again. He moved me toward him, then back. It took me a moment to realize that he was rubbing me up against his erection, back and forth in a dizzying, electrifying rhythm. The inside of my thighs was slick. I raised up my skirt to feel him better—his pants brushed my skin, chafing. That wasn't what I wanted, but the sensation was at least *something.*

He grabbed my ass, rocked me against him, and thrust his hips forward. His cock pressed against the length of my sex. He was thick, throbbing, and I squeezed my inner thighs around him, all the better to grind.

He laughed, a dark sound. "See what I said? You're not so innocent, are you?" He thrust against me, rubbing up onto my lacy underwear, and I was desperate to strip him of his damn pants.

"Can we... What can we..." I panted, unable to even form a question.

Bryce answered with movement, swiftly pinning me below him on the couch. He kissed me hungrily, and I moaned, relishing the feel of his huge, muscled body above me. *So much power.* Even his tongue was strong, stroking mine and making me quiver beneath him. His hands roamed down my dress, finally finding the hem of my skirt and burrowing below it. His fingertips brushed up my thighs, skin finally touching skin. He roamed higher, thick fingers leaving what felt like a trail of sparks. I writhed beneath him, not knowing what I wanted except that I wanted *more.*

He stroked the outside of my panties, teasing, as I shamelessly ground myself against his hand. I didn't even know who I was anymore or what I was doing—and I didn't care. He slid his fingers beneath the lace and laughed again. "My little virgin's so wet."

I would've been ashamed if I could think straight,

but I couldn't. At first, Bryce's touch was gentle, but his strokes became more intense. His fingers roamed higher, finding my clitoris, and he began to rhythmically circle it. "What are you..." My hips bucked up to meet his touch.

"You know exactly what I'm doing, Chloe. Don't pretend." He was merciless with his touch, circling my clit and then rubbing it repeatedly.

Waves of sensation crashed over me, and I cried out.

"Good girl," he whispered. He stroked my clit with his thumb roughly. He did it again and again until I thought I'd see stars.

"You will come for me, now. I want to hear you." He pressed harder, thick fingers pinching me, making me putty in his expert hands.

I didn't want to go over the edge, but I was already so close. Bryce kissed me deeply as he stroked, circled, and pinched again, his palm rubbing aggressively against the opening of my sex. I couldn't help it: I ground against him. *Oh my God, oh my God—*

An orgasm ripped through me, the most powerful I'd ever experienced. "Oh my *God*!" I yelled, unable to get control of myself.

He kissed me deeply, tongue lashing as my muscles spasmed. I shook beneath him as his touch became more gentle, rocking me through the waves of pleasure. When I resurfaced, he was still hard against me. I reached out and stroked him through his trousers, and he pressed against me. "Another time, Chloe. Tonight was about you."

"But I want—"

"Shh, we'll be back to the house in a minute. We'll practice more, I promise you. We have plenty of time." Bryce sounded so calm that I wanted to smack him.

I sat up and smoothed my dress, but I was fuming. He'd started a fire inside of me, and despite my orgasm, it was raging. "I want to practice *now*."

I eyed the bulge in his trousers. We had unfinished business.

"Eyes off my cock, Chloe." Bryce arched an eyebrow. "For a virgin, you're rather aggressive."

I bit back a curse. "You can't do what you just did to me and not...and not...do *more*," I argued.

"I can do whatever I want, Mrs. Windsor. If I recall correctly, I *own* you. You are legally *mine*. So you will come when I tell you to come, and you will wait when I tell you to wait. Do you understand me?"

I scowled at him and didn't answer.

"I see how it is." Bruce surprised me by smiling. "Chloe has her first orgasm with her husband, and now she's all full of herself."

"Does that mean I get to have another one?" I blurted out.

"If you behave and do exactly what I say, perhaps."

I scowled again. "I don't just want it to be me. And I don't care about the contract, you don't *own* me."

"We'll see about that." His gaze raked down my dress. "But now it's time to get you to bed. You have another busy day tomorrow."

Silence descended over us as we docked. He held my hand as we ascended the stone steps in the darkness, the waves crashing behind us. It was after midnight; the house was dim and silent.

I held my breath, hoping he would come inside my room. But Bryce was cold and quiet as he deposited me outside my door without a goodnight kiss.

"Bryce...?"

He didn't answer.

I stared after him, but it didn't matter: he didn't look at me as he closed the door to his own bedroom.

WTF?

I almost cried when I went into my room. What had I done? Why had he been so cold again and pushed me away? I was miserable as I washed off my makeup. I hung the stupid dress up in the wardrobe, hating myself for wanting to look sexy.

He'd touched me *down there*. He'd acted like he'd

wanted me. He'd pushed me over the edge and seemed so satisfied with himself. And yet, even as he'd had his hands all over me, his tongue in my mouth, he'd kept me at arm's length.

What the hell was Bryce Windsor's deal?

I huffed and I puffed as I went to bed, angrier than I'd been in a long time. *Why would he give me an orgasm, then give me the silent treatment?* I vowed not to think about him anymore.

But of course, I fell asleep thinking about him.

a visitor

THERE WAS A THUD, and I sat bolt upright.

It was dark in my room; the clock read three a.m. I held still, listening, but there was nothing. I must've been dreaming...

I lay back down and pulled the covers up to my chin. The remnants of the dream tugged at me, something about being with Bryce at a fancy restaurant. I couldn't read the menu—it was in a different language. Bryce had been trying to explain it to me when I woke up.

I relaxed, trying to quiet my mind, but I was annoyed. Annoyed that I'd woken up, annoyed that the Bryce in my dreams was trying to be helpful and kind when real-life Bryce had been manipulative and cold. Was I some sort of game to him? Make Chloe Come, Then Deny Chloe?

Play Head Games With Chloe? Give Chloe Emotional Whiplash?

What did he want from me, anyway?

A grunting noise startled me, and I sat upright again. "H-Hello?"

No answer. Was I still dreaming?

I willed my eyes to adjust to the darkness. I listened, but it was silent... Until I heard the sound of heavy breathing. There was another grunt, quieter this time, but I was sure I didn't imagine it.

My eyes focused on a chair on the edge of my room, and I jumped: someone was sitting in it. "Oh my God!"

"Shh. It's just me." Bryce's voice was ragged.

"Bryce? What are you doing? What's the matter?"

I scrambled to climb from the bed, but he commanded, "Stop. Don't come any closer."

A heavy silence descended over the room. I didn't dare move.

"Have you been in here for a while?" I whispered.

"No." His shadowy figure leaned forward. "I was just about to leave."

"Wait, don't go. Why are you here?" Something hot and hopeful bloomed in my chest.

Bryce didn't respond.

"Come here," I said.

He didn't move.

"I said, *come here.*"

"I don't think that's a good idea, Chloe."

"Why? What's the worst thing that could happen?"

He sighed. "I think you know."

"No, I don't." He was so goddamned *frustrating.* Blowing me off, then hiding in my room while I slept. What did he want from me?

What the hell did I want from *him*?

But the throb between my legs told the truth. I knew exactly what it was I wanted from my new husband. If he wasn't going to give it to me... If he was just going to sit there and watch...

Maybe it was time I took matters into my own hands.

It was not at all like me to be bold. I'd never even contemplated a situation like this, but some sort of deep instinct took over. "Fine." My tone was haughty. "Then stay there for all I care." I stripped out of my nightgown and kicked aside the blankets, spreading my legs slightly.

Even though I meant to taunt him, I half prayed that it was so dark he couldn't see me clearly. I'd never been naked in front of someone before!

"What are you doing, Chloe?" His voice was strangled.

"None of your business." I ran my hands over my

breasts, pinching my own nipples. I'd never done that in my life, but it felt *awesome*. I wasn't big into touching myself; honestly, I'd really never thought about sex that much. But Bryce was making me fantasize about all *sorts* of things.

Having him as an audience emboldened me. I prayed that he'd give in and come to the bed.

My hands roamed over my stomach, relishing the cool feel of my own skin. A fire burned me from the inside out, delicious and torturous at the same time, completely out of control. My fingers trailed down to my sex, and Bryce groaned.

"What's the matter?" I started to stroke myself.

"Fuck, Chloe. Stop it."

"Make me," I teased. I sighed as my fingers swirled around my tender, swollen bud. I mimicked the way Bryce had touched me earlier—it was a far cry from the clumsy way I'd experimented with myself in the past. With him watching, I was getting crazy excited. My hips bucked, and I moaned, increasing the pressure on my clit.

Suddenly, Bryce was on the bed. "Let me do that." His voice was commanding, urgent. Even in the dark, I could see his eyes were wild. He wore a T-shirt and boxer briefs, his manhood thick and elongated, poking out toward me.

Yes!

"I got it." I managed to sound haughty, even though I was dying inside.

"I said, *let me.*" He grabbed my wrists and pinned my arms above my head.

I squirmed beneath him, vulnerable, suddenly self-conscious. What had I done? I was naked, entirely at his mercy, and so *turned on.*

He climbed astride me, and I struggled to break free.

"Stop fighting me, Chloe. You're getting exactly what you wanted." He captured my mouth with his, devouring me with a searing kiss. His tongue searched my mouth. My hips bucked against him, and I groaned, relishing the delicious friction his big, strong body provided.

I tried to move my wrists, but he had me pinned. "Not so fast, Mrs. Windsor. I can't have you going rogue again—it felt like you were trying to kill me just now."

I peered up at him. "Why are you here?"

"It seems I hadn't quite gotten enough of you for one day." He kissed me again, slow and deep. Then he moved lower, his lips trailing down my throat. "And I would've gone back to my room like a gentleman, but you toyed with me. Not a good idea, Chloe. You're waking up the beast."

He kissed me again, deeply.

"You started it," I said when we broke apart. "And you said it yourself—practice makes perfect."

"I don't think you need much practice." Without releasing my hands, his mouth explored lower, across my chest, trailing down to my nipples. He suckled them, then pulled back and blew cool air over the tender, elongated buds.

"Ah!" I shuddered in pleasure.

"You like that?"

He sounded so smug, I refused to answer.

"Don't worry—I'll just see for myself." He greedily took my breast back in his mouth, sucking and nibbling and driving me absolutely insane. It didn't help—or maybe it did—that he had me pinned beneath him, his big body covering mine. I felt completely out of control, under his spell. I was *his*—his to conquer, his to claim.

He released my hands so that he could cup my breasts. Something about the way he held me—so possessively, as though he wanted to devour me alive— lit me on fire. I ran my hands down his back as his kisses trailed even lower. Feeling the muscles beneath his T- shirt was *insane*. I scrambled to pull it off over his head, sighing in relief as I finally ran my hands down his exposed skin, relishing the taut feel of every muscle.

But I stopped, petrified, as his kisses reached my sex.

"W-What are you doing?"

"I'm going to take you in my mouth, Chloe. And perhaps my hand, I haven't decided yet."

"Um—" But my half-hearted objection died on my lips as he suddenly ran his tongue up the length of my slit. *Holy fucking hell!*

I almost shrieked, but I was too overtaken by what happened next. Bryce buried his face between my legs. He began lapping at me, his strong tongue stroking my most sensitive, private parts. All thoughts of speech, all thoughts *period*, vanished as the waves of sensation crashed over me.

I thrashed, heart thudding. I felt a wave of panic on the edges of my consciousness—worried if I tasted okay, worried what Bryce was thinking—but then he clamped his mouth around my clit and sucked hard, and nothing else mattered.

"Oh my God... Oh my *God*...!"

He kept up a relentless pace, licking and sucking and palming the base of my sex with his hand. I was no match for him. Never had I ever felt pleasure like what Bryce was giving me. He devoured me, his expert hands and mouth taking over, lighting me on fire. My whole body quivered, moving with his touch, rising and falling to meet him. There was moaning, cries of ecstasy—after a minute, I realized who it was: *me*.

Holy fuck!

The orgasm ripped through me, wild and unexpected, unlike anything I'd ever experienced before. I cried out, writhing against Bryce as he continued to suck me. The sensation was deep, bringing me higher than I'd ever been, to a point where the feeling eclipsed everything else. I was wholly in my body, the pleasure of it, free from all worries, free from doubt.

Small shudders replaced the larger explosion, and as I came back down to earth, a feeling of peace surrounded me.

"So you *do* like it when I touch you." Bryce looked up from between my legs, a satisfied, self-congratulatory expression on his face. "Seeing is believing, but *hearing* is even better. You're loud, Chloe."

So much for peace. "Don't be smug."

"I can't help it. Hearing you scream brings it out in me."

I shivered. Even though he was a smug bastard, he was right—he *had* made me holler. Remembering his mouth on me made me squirm, rubbing up against his big body, getting me all riled up again. He retraced his kisses' path back up, finally landing on my cheek. His erection throbbed against my belly, and I slid my hands down his back, exploring the planes of his muscles. I was knocked out from the depth of my orgasm, but I still wanted...

I still wanted *him*.

I wrapped my arms around him, pulling him closer.

"Not so fast, Mrs. Windsor." Bryce rolled off, leaving me cold.

I groaned. "Where are you going?"

"Over here. We need to stop."

"*Why?*"

"Because I said so."

The billionaire CEO was too accustomed to his word being law. Again, he'd made me see stars. Again, he was right next to me, but just out of reach. It was so frustrating, I wanted to scream. "What are you trying to do to me?"

"I'm not sure," he admitted. "But I'm definitely getting something out of it."

"You won't let me touch you." I turned to him. "So what could you possibly be getting out of it?"

He looked up at the ceiling. "I find your enthusiasm refreshing."

"You mean you find my inexperience refreshing."

"Not at all." He shrugged, then turned to face me. "It's just that you're not jaded, Chloe. I don't think I've ever met anyone like you."

"You've definitely never met anybody like me. Not

only am I a virgin, but I also didn't grow up with a silver spoon shoved up my ass."

He let out a bark of laughter, something I didn't ever expect to hear. "No, you didn't. I do appreciate that about you."

I was about to ask if he appreciated it enough to stay. I longed to do more, to touch him—but he rose from the bed and padded to the door between our rooms, putting distance between us.

"Where are you going?"

"To bed. You need to get your rest." He turned the knob. "You might want to lock this after I leave."

I arched an eyebrow. "So you can't come back in?"

"So it deters you from chasing me." He laughed, and I almost threw something at him.

"Good night, Chloe."

"Good night, Bryce." *You douche.*

But if I was being honest with myself—which I was not—I was sad that he left. At least he'd finally said goodnight to me. And he'd been sitting in my room in the dark, watching me. Then he'd come to my bed, kissed me, and touched me until I hummed with pleasure. That meant something, didn't it?

But...what?

Once he was gone, a heavy wave of drowsiness descended. I wanted to stay awake, to review every moment of the unexpected encounter. But the powerful orgasm had literally knocked me out.

I reached for the T-shirt he'd left behind and inhaled his scent. I pulled it over my head.

Then, strangely comforted, I fell right back to sleep.

glimpses

"YOU'VE OVERSLEPT AGAIN, MRS. WINDSOR." The stern, disapproving voice roused me from my sleep.

"What the huh?" I mumbled, eyes snapping open.

Hazel stood in the middle of my room, holding a breakfast tray. Her eyebrows had been freshly penciled in, and her maroon lipstick bled into the lines around her puckered scowl. "I said, you've overslept again. Mr. Windsor—"

"Doesn't like to be kept waiting. I know, I know." I shouldn't get on her bad side, but couldn't I at least have some coffee before she started harassing me?

"Here's your breakfast," she sniffed, sounding quite put out.

"I'm sorry." I sighed as I sat up. "I didn't mean to be

rude. It's just that everyone says that about Bryce, and I think it's sort of funny."

The maid's sour gaze ran from my face over my shirt. I realized it was Bryce's and wrapped my arms across my chest. For some reason, I felt like I should hide it from her.

But Hazel's sharp eyes missed nothing. Her eyebrow arched. "It seems as though you're settling in."

I cleared my throat. "Everyone's been so kind. Thank you for breakfast, Hazel. I'll make sure I'm downstairs quickly."

"Mr. Windsor is taking you and your brother out on the water. Please dress appropriately." She bowed and, without looking at me, left the room.

Thank fuck! Old Hazel gave me the creeps. Once I heard her heels click down the hallway, I stretched and got out of bed. I poured myself a coffee with cream, greedily sucking it down. Because I was alone, I lifted Bryce's shirt and inhaled its scent. *Mmm.* Memories from the night before flooded me. Seeing him sitting in my chair, watching me in the dark... Him pinning my hands above my head... His hot kisses, trailing lower...

I shivered, remembering what he'd done with his mouth. *Holy hell.* How was I going to look him in the eye today?

More importantly, how was I going to get him to come to my room again?

I hustled to the wardrobe and found a tasteful, modest cover-up and a bright blue, wildly *immodest* bikini, replete with a string-thong bottom. I knew thong bikinis were in style, but I'd never worn one. They looked so freaking *uncomfortable*. But Midge had picked it out and put it in here.

Did that mean Bryce would like it?

There was only one way to find out.

We were hanging out with Noah today, and there was no way in hell I'd wear that suit in front of him. But I could save it for later, hmm...

Feeling as though I had a mission—a naughty one—I skipped off to the shower.

"Give me that! Sheesh, you don't know anything." Noah grabbed the lure out of my hands and secured it to the hook. "See? That's how it's done!"

He expertly cast out the fishing line in a perfect arc. The red bobber landing with a *plop* on the gently rolling waves.

My brother grinned at me. "Told you! I know what I'm doing."

"You learned all that yesterday?" I peered out at the bobber. "Amazing what you can accomplish once you put down the X-box controller."

Noah shrugged. "It's not like I could go out on a boat and go fishing back home. There was nothing better to do."

"Yeah, I know." I studied his profile. He looked rested, slightly tanned, and relaxed. "So... Do you like it up here?'

Noah blinked at me. "Are you kidding? I *love* it. I don't ever want to go back to Boston—it's gross compared to here."

I looked out at the blue, sparkling water and the green mountains beyond. "It doesn't even seem like the same planet."

"Right?" Noah looked back toward the cabin, where Bryce was hiding with his cell phone. "When is he going to come out and take me jet skiing?"

"As soon as he's done with his meeting. Which could be never," I admitted.

Noah turned back toward the water, inspecting his line. "He's not as bad as I thought."

I nodded. "He seems more relaxed now that we're settling in."

"Do *you* like it up here?" My brother didn't look at me.

"You know what? I do. The house isn't exactly hard to live in." I laughed.

"It's so weird having *servants*. And getting room service. Did you know they have a whole game room with darts and everything?"

"No, I didn't. You should show me when we get back to the house."

"Yeah." Noah glanced at me. "Hey, have you talked to Dad? Have you told him about all this? He wouldn't believe it!"

"I haven't talked to him, buddy. But you can call him if you want to."

He shrugged. "Nah. If he wanted to talk to us, he coulda called."

"I'm sure he's just busy with work," I lied.

"Right." Noah didn't sound as though he was falling for it.

Noah didn't catch any fish, but it didn't dampen his enthusiasm. He stood on the dock without complaint— without once saying he was bored, wanted to play a video game, or was tired of waiting to go jet skiing— and fished quietly for another whole hour. I didn't understand the appeal, but my brother seemed wholly engrossed.

Finally, Bryce emerged from the cabin. He wore

swim trunks and a tight-fitting T-shirt, and I tried not to gawk.

He nodded at us. "Sorry about that—I had an issue I had to deal with."

"It's fine," I said. I longed to go to him, but I didn't dare. What did Bryce Windsor want from me in the light of day? I needed to read his mood before I went near him.

But he surprised me by coming over and kissing me on the cheek.

I couldn't help it: I grinned up at him.

"You two having fun?" There was a twinkle in his eye. He seemed like he was...in a good *mood*.

"Yes." I was too flustered to say more.

"Chloe can't fish," Noah informed him. "She couldn't get the lure on."

"Did you show her how?" Bryce asked.

"I tried." Noah shook his head. "I think she might be hopeless."

"Do you think your sister can jet ski?" Bryce asked.

"No way. She doesn't like to go fast! And she hates driving after..." His sentence trailed off, but I knew what he was about to say: I hated driving after what happened to Mom.

"You want to show her how it's done?" Bryce

grinned at Noah, but he sobered when he turned to me. "I won't let him go too fast, I promise."

I twisted my hands together, suddenly nervous. "Okay. Did you hear that, Noah? Nothing crazy out there. And you have to listen and do what Bryce says."

Noah rolled his eyes.

"Be respectful of your sister," Bryce said gently.

"Fine." Noah sighed. "I won't go too fast."

"Thank you." I watched, heart in my throat, as he followed Bryce to the stern of the boat, where two attendants offered them life vests and then started preparing the jet skis, which were sleek and looked brand-new. Noah's whole face lit up as Bryce had him climb up on one and showed him the controls.

Finally, the attendants lowered them into the water, and Bryce and Noah bravely jumped overboard. "It's freezing!" Noah hollered, but he gave me a thumbs-up as he climbed aboard his jet ski. Bryce mounted his and leaned over, explaining more to Noah and pointing out at the water, possibly planning their route.

The engines roared to life. They took off before I was ready, and despite what Noah promised, they looked like they were going *fast*.

"Be careful!" I yelled, but they didn't turn around.

"They'll be fine—jet skis are safe, and Mr. Windsor is a nut about following the rules." Joren was suddenly beside me. His white uniform sparkled in the afternoon sun. "He won't take your brother out for too long, and he'll keep a close eye on him."

"Thank you, Joren." I smiled. "How've you been?"

"Good, thanks." But he froze as he glanced out at the water—Bryce had slowed down and watched us, a deep frown on his face. "Have a nice morning, Mrs. Windsor."

"You too." But the captain had already beat a hasty retreat back to the bow. Bryce watched, scowling, as he disappeared into the cabin. Only then did he rev his engine and rejoin my brother.

After about an hour, during which Noah and Bryce circled the boat, splashed water, laughed, and appeared to be having a blast—they drove the jet skis back. My brother was soaked, grinning, and jubilant. "That was awesome!" He gave Bryce a high five.

"You're a natural." Bryce laughed. "I think you were meant to be a Maine-r—good at fishing, good at jet skiing, you don't seem to get cold even though the water's freezing."

Noah grinned some more as he dried off with a thick, fluffy towel. "That was so much fun. Can we go again tomorrow?"

"Maybe not tomorrow." Bryce secured his own towel around him. "But definitely this weekend."

Noah's eyes were huge in his face. "Thanks, Bryce. That's awesome." He hustled off to change.

Bryce stared after him. "He's a good kid."

I nodded. "He's always been a good boy—even when he was a baby."

Bryce turned toward me, inspecting my face. "What did the captain want? I saw him talking to you."

"Nothing—he just said you'd be good with Noah, that I had nothing to worry about."

The muscle in his jaw tensed. "What else?"

"That was it," I said quickly. "He was just trying to reassure me."

The sunny mood shifted; Bryce was all clouds now. "Are you sure?"

"Of course, Bryce." Why was he so mad? "I only talked to him for a second."

"I'd like you to myself for the rest of the afternoon," he growled. "Is that acceptable?"

"Of course." My cheeks heated. His words held promise, even on the heels of his near-meltdown about the captain. "Noah had so much fun. I'm sure he'd be fine to go back to the house."

"I'll make sure the staff prepares him lunch and that Dale spends time with him this afternoon." Bryce was already on his cellphone, texting away.

"Thank you. That's really nice." I studied him as he

glared at the screen. His thick hair was still damp, the T-shirt was plastered to his muscled chest, and the towel was wrapped snugly around his hips.

I'd like you to myself this afternoon. Hoo boy.

Just what did he intend to do with me?

blue lagoon

NOAH WAS MORE than happy to go back on dry land. Chef had prepared him a triple stack of grilled cheese sandwiches and homemade potato chips. Dale challenged him to a dart tournament. Lilly promised him an ice cream sundae and another visit with her puppy—my brother had it made! If he was upset that Dad hadn't called to check in, he was a master at hiding it.

Much to my surprise, Bryce wanted to spend the rest of the afternoon on the boat. After we dropped Noah on the dock, he called one of the attendants and gave him specific instructions. "Have Joren take us to the private cove near Southwest Harbor. And please have the cook prepare us lunch and bring it out in precisely one hour—we'll be on the deck."

"Of course, Mr. Windsor."

"You have a cook on board?" I asked as Bryce grabbed my hand.

He led me back to the couches at the rear of the boat. "Of course I do." He'd changed into another pair of swim trunks and a dry tee, all the better to show off his muscled thighs and big biceps. "Now sit with me, and smile and wave to everyone we pass. Then we're going someplace private. I trust you have your suit?"

"Yes." My cheeks heated, remembering the tiny thong.

"Good." He squeezed me against him as the boat entered the harbor. "We're going to a spot I like—a place where we can be alone."

"Except for your cook and your staff," I joked.

He shrugged. "They can make themselves scarce if we want." He laced his fingers through mine and pulled me against his massive chest.

Butterflies fluttered in my stomach. *Private cove. We can be alone.* Thong bikini. Massive chest. This was getting good!

His grip remained firm as we smiled and waved at the passengers on the passing boats. I recognized several people from the Nguyen's party and was glad that we couldn't stop to chat. I was anxious to see what this cove was all about...

"Here we are." Bryce's hand roamed my back as the

yacht navigated closer to an island. The water turned a deep aqua color, clear and beckoning. We rounded the corner and found ourselves in another world—the island's beach stretched out in a U-shape, offering a private bay wholly separated from the rest of the harbor. Thick firs bordered the coast, affording us complete privacy. The deep-aqua water beckoned, clean and crystal-clear.

"Wow, this is so beautiful." I'd never been in a such a gorgeous spot.

"I used to come here to swim when I was a kid. Because of how the tide runs, the water's warmer here. Do you want to jump in?" Playful Bryce was back, grinning at me.

"Is it deep?" I peered over the edge.

"Not very. Can you swim?"

I nodded. "I can tread water. I can't do any strokes, though. We didn't belong to a pool or anything growing up." My face flushed, which was silly. Growing up poor was nothing to be ashamed of.

"I can arrange private lessons if you like." Bryce took my chin in his hand, raising my gaze to meet his. "We absolutely don't need to go in if it makes you uncomfortable."

I relaxed at his words. Despite being a smug CEO used to getting his way, I liked that he wasn't pressuring

me. "I'm fine. Let's go." Remembering my blue bikini—
what there was of it—I took a deep breath before
pulling off my coverup.

And then I got up and walked to the boat's edge
with as much feigned confidence as I could muster.

"What the..." Bryce got off the couch and stalked
toward me. He moved slowly, never taking his eyes off
my ass. "That's some suit."

I shrugged as if I wore tiny butt-floss bikinis all the
time. "They're in style, I guess."

"Oh, I know they are." He came up behind and
pressed himself against me—and he was deliciously,
irrevocably hard.

Thong bikinis FTW! I smiled to myself as I leaned
back, relishing the feel of him.

"Do you know why they're so popular, Chloe?" He
leaned down and nibbled on my ear.

I shivered, my whole body breaking out in goosebumps. "No... Why?"

"Sex." He kissed my neck and ground his erection
into my lower back.

Yes! Finally!

"Do you...like it?" I held my breath.

He thrust against me. "I fucking love it. Now jump in
the water before I do something inappropriate."

I hesitated, and not because the water looked cold. I

wanted something inappropriate, and I wanted it *bad*. I pressed back against him.

Bryce grunted, then smacked me on the ass. "There you go again—like I said, you're not that innocent."

"But I am." I wriggled my ass against his erection. "This just feels good."

He treated me to another bark of laughter. For a moment, he just held me as we stared out at the water. With him behind me, holding me, I felt something I hadn't in a long time... Happy.

"You're not budging, are you?" He kissed my cheek again. "Fine—I'll go first." He stripped out his shirt, revealing his gloriously muscled chest and six-pack abs, and dove head-first into the water.

If I'd needed any encouragement, that was it!

I took a deep breath, held my nose, and did what I hoped was a very graceful pencil off the boat's edge. But I spluttered when I broke the surface, my hair in my face, trying to rub the water from my eyes while staying afloat.

"Here, I got you." Bryce swam to my side and held me up while I put myself back together again.

"Thanks." I finally got the hair out of my eyes and could enjoy being in the ocean. "You're right—this is warm. It feels great!"

"Wait until I take you to the Caribbean. You're going to love it."

"What's it like? I've always wanted to go."

"It's gorgeous." He favored me with one of his rare smiles. "I'll have to take you. What about next weekend?"

I blinked at him. "Really? Just like that?"

"We have a house on Exuma. It's a quick flight—you'll love it. The water is crystal clear, and unlike MDI, you won't freeze your ass off. You can swim all day."

"Wow." I couldn't wipe the smile off my face. The fact that he wanted to please me—that he seemed excited to share something with me—lit me up inside. "That would be amazing."

"Then it's a date, Mrs. Windsor." Bryce grinned as he swam close again.

"That's really nice of you."

"Nice? I don't know about that." The sun glinted off his thick, wet hair. "It's selfish. I didn't expect being a newlywed to be so...rewarding."

I laughed. "Me either."

He leaned in for a quick kiss, but I immediately started to sink. "All right, Michael Phelps, let's get you back on board."

We swam to the ladder, and he insisted that I go first. I was more than a little self-conscious as I climbed up, but when he appeared on the deck immediately behind me, I could see that he was rock hard beneath his swim trunks. *Oh boy.*

He looked sheepish. "It's that suit. Actually, it's *you* in that suit."

"Ha." I wrapped my arms around myself.

"Here." He handed me one of his fabulous fluffy towels, grabbed one for himself, and headed back to the couch. "Let's dry off, shall we?"

We spread out, the sun warming our skin. After a few minutes, it was actually warm enough to remove my towel. I sat back and closed my eyes, hoping to get some color on my pale New-England skin.

Bryce sat next to me and put his hand on my thigh. Something about the way he was touching me, how kind he was being—taking my brother jet-skiing, offering to take me on a trip next weekend—was melting my heart. *Oh boy, indeed.* I wanted him badly, but something else was going on beneath the haze of lust.

I was starting to...like him.

As he rubbed my thigh, his touch was gentle and reassuring. Even though it wasn't provocative, it still lit me up. I couldn't get enough of being next to him, of his attention. After a minute, he rolled toward me and put his arm around my midsection, resting his head on my shoulder.

"That feels nice." My voice was shaky.

"It does." He kissed my shoulder. "I didn't plan on...this."

I longed to ask what he meant. But afraid to spoil the moment, I said nothing.

He kissed my shoulder again, and I turned to him, staring up at his handsome face. How was it that Bryce had become *important* to me in the past two days? I felt as though I might die if he pulled away from me.

"When you look at me like that, Chloe..." Instead of finishing his sentence, he came closer. His lips gently grazed mine, making my heart leap. When he tentatively poked his tongue into my mouth, my insides squirmed.

His hands roamed my sides as he deepened the kiss, and almost immediately, that fire was back between us. I couldn't get enough of his touch. He pulled me closer, and I moaned, loving the feel of being wrapped up in his powerful arms.

Even though we were in the secluded cove, we were *still* in public, in broad daylight. His staff was on board, but that didn't stop his big hands from roaming. He fingered the top of the thong, exploring the delicate, thin material. He tugged at it a little, testing, as I moaned.

I didn't object—I couldn't; I was entirely under his spell. Wild horses couldn't pull me away.

Our kissing became urgent, and he pulled me onto his lap. Straddling him in the thong felt fucking *amazing*. I cried out as he thrust in between my legs—even with the swim trunks on, the pressure of his erection rubbing against me made me wild. I started to rock my hips, and he put his hands on my ass, guiding me. *Yes*. Maybe this was almost as good as the real thing. Perhaps this time, he wouldn't stop. I went faster as he kissed my ear, making me shudder in pleasure. His grip tightened around me as his thrusting became more insistent.

"Can you take these off?" I hooked my fingers in the waistband of his swim trunks, but he caught my wrist.

"I don't know if that's a good idea." But Bryce's voice was husky, his pupils huge.

I thrust my hips again, and he moaned. "Why not?"

"Because it's playing with fire." But he didn't stop— he kissed my ear, my throat, his erection massive and straining between us.

"Please," I panted. *"Please."* There I was again, begging him. But I couldn't stop myself.

Bryce pulled back, breathing hard. "Fine, Virgin. But don't complain when you get burned."

He put me to the side and pulled off his swim trunks. His cock sprang out—huge, jutting, and powerful. I was a little afraid of it. But he pulled me back onto his lap so quickly that I didn't have time to freak out.

Bryce put it between my legs against the string of my thong. *Holy fuck.* He looked me in the eyes, grabbed my ass, and rubbed me up against him.

I was so turned on I was wet, so wet. His cock slid against my slit, the thong's fabric the only thing between us. "Oh my God. Oh my God." I pressed my face against his, completely overwhelmed by all the physical sensation, by being so close to him.

He stopped long enough to kiss me slowly, deeply. I felt as though he were devouring me, and I fucking loved it.

His gaze was hooded, determined, as we broke apart. I held my breath as I waited for his next move.

Bryce held my ass cheeks firmly as he thrust against me, again and again, his pace measured but relentless. The friction was *delicious.* He grabbed the top of the thong and wrapped it around his hand, pulling it, all the better for him to have control over me, all the better for him to drive me wild with sensation. The pressure from the fabric mixed with the insistent thrusts of his smooth cock: I almost came right then and there. But I held on because what was most important was paying attention to Bryce. I wanted to stay with him, to please him as he pleased me.

I was on a mission.

I kissed him, and he grunted, tugging at the thong. We slid against each other, bodies entangled in each other's wet heat. I wanted—oh, I didn't know exactly what I wanted, but whatever it was, I wanted it *bad*. "Bryce—Bryce, *please*," I panted. I didn't even know what I was asking for!

Luckily my husband had an idea. He smoothly and gently flipped me onto my back so that I was lying on the couch, and he was somehow expertly above me. His cock sprang out, huge and pale, shining with slickness. He wrenched the bikini bottom to the side and pressed his full length against me, then started to thrust against my slit. The tip of his penis grazed my clit again and again; I arched my back to meet him, moaning every time he grazed the sensitive bud.

My moans seemed to drive Bryce wild. He tore my bikini top to the side as he thrust, greedily taking my breast in his mouth. His hands roamed down, and his thumb found my clit. He circled it, pressing, as his cock rubbed against me, and he clamped his mouth around my nipple. It was too much. He owned me. The orgasm ripped through me, and I saw stars. I cried out, calling his name as I soared. Bryce didn't stop—he suckled on my nipple, thumbed my clit, and thrust his hot, hard cock as I came against him, hard.

"Good girl." His touch became less insistent and more relaxed as I shuddered and returned to earth.

"Bryce." I shifted so that I could reach down and feel him between my legs. My fingertips brushed against his heavy balls, and he involuntarily shivered. "Do you like that?" I whispered.

In answer, he started kissing my other breast, greedily sucking on the nipple. He was getting me all turned on again, but I wanted to make *him* come. More importantly, I wanted to have sex with him, to fill that painful ache between my legs. But I had no idea where to start...

I tried to follow my instinct. I reached down and ran my fingertips over his balls again. They were heavy to the touch. That was a good sign—or so I'd read on the internet, in an article called "How to Drive Your Man Wild." The author said to gently explore his balls. If he seemed to like it, tug on them a little.

Even better, put them in your mouth while you give him a hand job!

I'd read the entire article—twice—along with some others that had some very candid thoughts about How to Make Your Man Come Hard. The authors unanimously recommended a combination of mouth and hands. I'd never done either, but where there was a will, there was a way...

I wriggled against him. "Bryce, let me be on top."

He grunted, never taking his mouth from my nipple, but somehow expertly managing to flip us. Now he was pinned beneath me, mine to play with, mine to conquer. I adjusted my hips so his erection still strained against my sex. I rubbed myself against him shamelessly as he buried his face in my chest. I was wet, so wet. The friction of the thong and his hard, throbbing cock had me close to the edge again...

I ground myself against him, and he moaned, which gave me courage. Now it was my turn to trail kisses from his ear, down his throat, to his massive chest. *Holy fuck.* The man lifted some serious weights. My kisses trailed lower, and I moved off of him, his cock springing out in the daylight.

"Where are you going?" He sat up a little.

"Right here." I scooted down between his legs and kissed the hard muscles at the base of his shaft. *Holy hell.* His cock sprang up, getting even harder, jutting straight into the sky. A tiny bead of moisture stood at the tip. I took the head into my mouth and sucked it, tasting the saltiness.

"Holy *fuck*, Chloe. What are you doing to me?"

I pulled back, appalled. "Did I do something wrong?"

"Babe—*no*. Of course not." He sat up. "C'mere." He pulled me to his chest and kissed the top of my head. "That felt incredible. I just wasn't expecting it."

His cock throbbed between us, but what was even more intense was the sensation of him cradling me in his arms, comforting me.

"Can I try it some more? I've never done anything like this before," I confessed.

"You don't have to—"

"I *want* to." I meant it. He reluctantly released me, watching with a hooded gaze as I trailed my kisses lower again. Once I reached his penis, I remembered what the article said: *easy does it.*

I started slow, licking him from his base all the way up his shaft.

"Holy fuck." He shuddered beneath my touch, and pure female satisfaction bloomed in my chest. Emboldened, I took the head in my mouth, swirling it with my tongue. He moaned and rocked his hips, which I took as an excellent sign.

I gently took more of him in my mouth as I started caressing his balls.

"Oh my God. Chloe..." He thrashed beneath me as I

started to suck him. Good thing the internet was explicit! At least I had a vague idea of what to do. What I hadn't read online I made up as I went along—taking his shaft in my hand, milking him into my mouth, lightly squeezing his balls, and humming so there was a vibration.

Bryce continued to thrash as I continued to suck. The more into it he seemed, the more turned on I got. I took him deeper, all the way to the back of my throat, and he sank his hands into my hair. I didn't have to ask if he liked it—the way he quivered beneath me, the way he thrust to meet my eager sucking, the moans issuing from him—they told me everything I needed to know.

"I'm close, babe. Ah...!" Bryce went rigid, and I gave it everything I had. I sucked him hard, hands working the base of his shaft, cradling his balls—I was everywhere at once. I loved the taste of him, the feeling of being so close, being intimate. He was raw beneath me, as vulnerable as I was.

"Chloe... Chloe... *Chloe!*" He cried out my name as he came. Hot spurts issued into my mouth. I greedily sucked everything down, relishing the feeling of new power I had and how my name sounded on my husband's lips. If I was being honest, I *loved* the way he tasted. I also loved the way he shook, shivering with the depth of his orgasm. When he was spent, he pulled me up and cradled me in his arms.

He kissed the top of my head, and I nestled next to him. His broad, sculpted chest rose and fell rhythmically as he held me close. Again, I had that unfamiliar feeling, something I almost didn't recognize... Happiness.

I clung to Bryce for dear life, not ever wanting to let go.

TWENTY-THREE

falling

THE NEXT FEW days passed in a blur. Noah whupped me at darts and tried to teach me to fish. We started a sea-glass collection, scouring the beach for hours every day. Daphne and Gene had gone off-island for business in Portland—I kept up with their dinner plans and Daphne's workouts on Instagram. Bryce was busy with meetings; we didn't see him much during the day.

But every night, he appeared in my room.

My virginity remained frustratingly intact. He wouldn't make love to me—he never even tried. But we did all other sorts of things, taking turns pleasing each other, exploring each other's bodies with touch. Every time I brought him to orgasm, I felt as if I'd leveled up in a video game: I had new superpowers. I couldn't get enough of him. I couldn't get enough of him wanting me.

Each night, he held me on his chest until I fell asleep.

Each night, he stroked my hair.

Each night, I fell more in love with him.

When I woke up in the mornings, he was gone. And all I could do was wait for night to fall again.

I couldn't explain to myself what was happening. I felt as though my whole life had changed. All I could think about was Bryce—what he was doing, if he was thinking about me, how I missed him.

But it wasn't just missing. I'd begun to *crave* my husband, crave his attention, his touch, his presence. I couldn't think about anything or anyone else. When he wasn't near, I was in a fog. I was *also* on the internet, browsing in private mode, researching how to please him in bed.

Midge must've sensed the difference because she was all over it. She unpacked new lingerie every day— black lace teddies, deep-purple thongs and matching bralettes, a champagne-colored lace romper. When I told her about our upcoming weekend in the Bahamas, she went bananas. "Maybe you'll get pregnant!"

My cheeks heated. "Um...I don't know about that.

But by all means, bring on the lingerie. Ooh, and maybe more thong bikinis!"

Midge laughed. "You got it! He won't be able to resist you!"

I wished I could confide in her. I longed to tell her the truth, to ask her advice. *Mr. Windsor won't have intercourse with me. Even though I'm dying to. Even though there's a sharp pang between my legs every time I think about it.*

What was wrong? Why wouldn't he?

I was too afraid to ask him why. He'd wanted a virgin, and he'd paid for one.

But what if he wanted a virgin forever?

I prayed that wasn't true. I prayed each night that *that* would be the night he would take me, that he would make me *his*. But it didn't happen. Maybe on our special trip to the Bahamas, he would truly make me his wife...

I was sitting outside on the lawn, getting some sun while Noah fished off the dock, when Hazel appeared out of nowhere.

"Mrs. Windsor."

I jumped. "Oh! Hazel, you surprised me."

The reedy maid peered down her nose at me, disapproving. "Are you quite well? You look dazed."

"What? Oh yes—I'm fine." I quickly clicked off my

cell phone. I didn't need Hazel to glimpse the article I'd been reading: *10 Foreplay Tips To Drive Him Wild.*

Her lined lips puckered. "Mr. Windsor has requested you join him for lunch."

"Oh—thanks! Is he ready now?" I eagerly hopped up and brushed the grass from my cutoffs.

"Yes, he is." She arched her penciled brow. In the sun's harsh light, she looked like a walking cadaver wearing caked-on makeup. "Is that what you'll be wearing?"

I glanced down at my jean shorts and loose-fitting tank top. "Are we having company?"

"No."

I raised my chin. "Then yes, this is what I'll be wearing. I think Mr. Windsor would rather have me be on time than in a different outfit, don't you?"

"I suppose." She turned on her heel, which drove a hole into the grass. "Please follow me, Mrs. Windsor. I'll bring you to the patio—he's waiting."

I hustled after her. Maybe Hazel stayed so skinny because of a steady diet of Parliament Lights, or perhaps it was her wicked speed-walk. In either case, I couldn't help but stare at her spindly but surprisingly fast legs, encased in her ever-present black pantyhose, as we headed for the patio.

I sighed in relief when I saw Bryce. Of course, he was

in a suit, but he had his sunglasses on, his tousled hair blowing back in the breeze.

He smiled at me. "There she is—my wife."

I grinned and rushed to kiss him on the cheek. Hazel waited stiffly nearby, observing us.

"You can go, Hazel." Bryce also smiled at her. "Thank you for finding Chloe for me."

"You're welcome." But instead of leaving, she hesitated. "I heard some news today, Mr. Windsor. About the Faber property over on Beale's Island."

Bryce opened up his napkin, set it on his lap, and grabbed my hand. "Yes, what is it?"

Hazel pursed her lips. "The Jones family is renting it for the rest of the summer."

Bryce froze. "Mr. and Mrs. Jones?"

"All of them, Sir. The whole family."

"Are you sure?"

"That's what I heard. I thought you'd want to know." She bowed her head.

"Thank you, Hazel. That'll be all." Bryce sat very still, shoulders tense.

"What's the matter?" I squeezed his hand.

"Nothing." He removed his hand from mine and didn't say another word, not until a server brought our lunch, and he muttered his thanks.

We sat and ate in stony silence. Finally, unable to

stand it anymore, I put down my fork. "Who are the Joneses?"

He shrugged. "No one important."

"Okay..." I had a sip of iced tea, but a gnawing feeling in my stomach made it taste sour. "Could you be a little more specific? You seem upset."

Bryce's phone buzzed. *Saved by the bell.* "I have to take this, Chloe. Are you packed for our trip?"

"Yes." I smiled. Nothing could stop me from being excited about our weekend in the Bahamas. "Noah said he'd be fine with Dale—and the puppy, of course."

Bryce rose. "I'll have a full security detail for him, too. You don't have to worry. The staff is really enjoying him. They'll take great care of him while we're away." He bent down and absentmindedly kissed my cheek. Then he was gone, cell phone already attached to his ear.

"Huh," I said it so myself as I played with my salad. I was no longer interested in eating—I was interested in snooping.

I went off to find Midge. Luckily, she was in my room, packing my things for the trip.

"I don't know who's more excited for this weekend," she joked, "you or me."

I eyed some of the bikinis she'd assembled—all thongs—and laughed. "It might be you."

"No way." Midge grinned at me. "I heard their house is *insane*. They have an infinity pool that faces the *ocean*. And I heard the primary suite is *really* something." She waggled her eyebrows.

I swallowed hard. "What do you mean?"

"Let's just say I heard it's set up so it's the *ultimate* romantic getaway."

"Oh." I had no idea what that meant, but I would be googling the shit out of "ultimate romantic getaway" in private mode as soon as I had a chance.

"Hey, Midge..." I picked a silky coverup with a fun pattern and folded it neatly. "Hazel just mentioned something to Bryce at lunch. About a family renting a house over on Beale's Island—the Joneses?"

"What?"

"I think that's what she said." I shrugged. "He sort of freaked out about it, but then he wouldn't say anything."

"Motherfucker." Midge's face twisted into an angry scowl. "Of course the bitch is back! She probably heard that he's all married and happy now, so she's coming here to blow shit up."

My heart sank. "Who is? Who's coming back?" But I had a bad feeling I already knew.

"The ex. Felicia Jones. Lord, that woman *sucks*. Nothing but trouble."

"I thought you never met her," I said weakly.

"You don't have to meet a bitch to know she's up to no good!" But Midge must've read the pitiful expression on my face because she sighed and softened her tone. "You don't have anything to worry about, Chloe. He married *you*. And all of us can see a difference in him. He's so much happier—happier than he's *ever* been."

"So why did he seem upset?" My voice came out small.

She shrugged. "Because she's drama, and he knows it. There's only one reason she's back up here all of a sudden—she heard he got married, and she wants to stir up trouble."

She kept packing, ensuring that every piece of designer lingerie made it into the suitcase. "You don't need to worry, Chloe. I've seen the way he looks at you. You go and have a sexy weekend in the Caribbean, and you don't worry about a *thing*. She's going to freak when she sees that he's head over heels for you, and that's just what she deserves." With that, Midge packed the last of the thong bikinis and took her leave, promising to check in later.

I thanked her, but my insides were hot with jealousy.

His ex was back for the summer. The woman who'd

broken his heart, who'd left him before their wedding, had returned.

What was worse? Bryce seemed upset.

The things Midge had told me ran through my head, taunting me.

Girlfriend did a number *on him.*

I heard they'd even sent out the wedding invitations, but no one's ever confirmed it.

He bawled like a baby when she broke it off.

There was a knock on my door, and Noah stuck his face into the room. "Hey, want to go into the bay to fish? Nothing's biting near the dock."

"Sure." Anything, even fishing, was a welcome distraction from the news about Bryce's ex being back in town.

I wasn't sure, but I felt as though I might cry.

checked

I FOLLOWED Noah out to the yacht. An attendant was loading his fishing gear on board. "Did you ask Bryce if this was okay?"

"Yeah, Dale did." Noah waved me off. "We're literally just going into the bay—they'll be able to see us. No big deal."

"Okay." We climbed on board, and a moment later, the yacht pulled out into the harbor in front of the house.

"Here we go." Noah cast my line out, then his, and we settled in. The sun was warm on my face as I stared out at my bobber, unseeing. I wasn't sure why hearing about Bryce's ex felt like a terrible blow, but I still felt sick. Maybe it was because of everything Midge had told me—about his tears, about how he was alone for so long after the breakup. It was in the past, but the way he'd acted when he'd heard the news was a red flag.

I was still getting to know my husband, but I could tell when he was in a mood. He'd been upset at lunch.

Noah explained his fishing strategy and everything he'd learned about the different types of fish that favored the cold Maine water. I tried to listen, but my mind wandered. Who was Felicia Jones? What did she look like? Why had she come back? Had she returned to torture Bryce, or did she want to get back with him?

An hour or so passed. Noah caught a fish and released it. I caught nothing, which was fine. I kept thinking about Bryce, wondering what *he* was thinking about, whether it was me or if thoughts of Felicia were already crowding me out...

"Hey, you two." Joren appeared on the deck, his white smile matching his uniform. "I brought you guys some drinks." He put two lemonades down on the table.

"Thanks, Captain!" Noah really loved using people's titles.

I smiled, amused by my brother. "Thanks, Joren."

Joren returned my smile, then bowed. "My pleasure."

The captain stayed out with us for a few minutes, talking to Noah about fishing, asking how he liked Maine so far. Joren was friendly and at ease, a far cry from how he'd been acting around Bryce the last few times I'd seen him. He chatted easily with my brother and was all smiles. After a few minutes, he retreated to the cabin.

"The Captain's nice." Noah cast out again. "Probably a fun job. He seems like he knows a lot about the islands, huh?"

"Yeah." That gave me an idea. I reeled in my line and carefully set the pole down. "I'm going to ask him something, okay? Be right back."

I headed down the deck to the front cabin. Joren was inside, playing a game on his phone. He smiled when I went inside. "What can I do for you, Mrs. Windsor?"

"I was wondering... Do you know where Beale's Island is?"

"Of course." He turned around and pointed toward the stern of the boat. "It's northeast from here, a little further than Spruce Island. Do you need me to bring you there?"

"Um, not today. But thank you, Joren."

"No worries, my lady." His phone rang, and when he looked at it, the smile dropped from his face. He answered immediately. "Yes, Mr. Windsor?"

Joren's face paled as he listened. "She's right here. Of course." The captain handed the phone to me. "He'd like to speak to you."

"Bryce? Is something wrong?"

"What the fuck are you doing alone with him?" he roared. "Get outside where I can see you—*now!*"

I burst through the door onto the deck. "I'm here! What's the matter?"

I could see Bryce standing on the beach in front of the house. "Come home. Right now."

"Of course. What's wrong?" But he'd already hung up. Icy needles jabbed down my spine. "Noah, bring your line in—we're going back."

"But I'm not ready!"

"Doesn't matter—we're leaving." The words were barely out of my mouth when the yacht's motor sprang to life.

"Jeez Louise!" Noah yelled, trying to reel in as the yacht turned toward the house. He scrambled and got everything back on board. "What the heck, Chloe?"

"Bryce needs us back home," I said. I didn't know what was wrong, but it was definitely something. It only took a moment to dock. I hopped out of the boat, then remembered I was still clutching Joren's phone.

"Hey, Joren!" I waved at him through the window, then held up his phone.

His face was ashen as he came out to take it. "I'm sorry, my lady."

I shook my head, confused. "For what?"

But suddenly, Bryce was beside me. "Get away from her," he snarled at the captain. "You're fired!"

Joren's shoulders sagged. "Yes, Mr. Windsor."

"Joren, wait! Bryce, he didn't do anything. I was asking him about an island. Noah said Dale cleared us to go out on the yacht—"

"Then Dale can consider himself fired, too." Bryce's nostrils flared. His eyes were bright with fury. "Come with me, Chloe, *now*." He clamped his hand over my shoulder and marched me up the steps.

I tried to shake Bryce off. "What the hell's the matter with you?"

"Not another word. I'm very close to losing it—you don't want that."

"Where are you taking me?" I spluttered, but he didn't answer as he marched me through the house and into a room I'd never seen before, some sort of an office. Hazel waited inside.

"Tell Dr. Bryan that I need her *now*."

"Of course, Mr. Windsor." Hazel scurried off.

"You—sit here." Bryce deposited me in an armchair. "Do not move."

"Bryce—"

"Do not *speak*." He tapped something furiously on his phone. A moment later, there was a knock on the door.

"It's me, Sir." Hazel led an older woman—presumably Dr. Bryan, by the look of her white coat and the case she carried—inside.

Bryce nodded at the doctor. "You know what to do."

"Of course, Mr. Windsor."

Bryce looked at me. "I'll be waiting outside." He left before I could argue. At least he took Hazel with him...

"Hi, Chloe." Dr. Bryan had ebony skin and short white hair. "I assume you know why I'm here."

I blinked at her. "I have no idea."

She sighed as she set her case down on the table and removed a pair of rubber gloves. "I've been instructed to check your hymen."

I felt as if she'd slapped me. *"What?"*

She smiled at me, and it looked apologetic. "I'm Mr. Windsor's staff physician. One of my duties is to give you regular checkups. Or, in this case, to perform a gynecological examination."

"I'm not letting you do that."

She nodded. "It's absolutely your right to refuse the examination, and I understand. But Mr. Windsor has already informed me that, if at any point you decline an exam, your contract can be voided."

This was so humiliating. My eyes filled with tears. "I didn't do anything."

"Of course not." Dr. Bryan patted my shoulder. "But

Mr. Windsor has set up this system to protect himself, and although I don't understand it, that's not my job. My job is to perform the examination. So will you let me examine you? Or do you want to tell him you've declined?"

I thought of calling Akira so that she could go ballistic and make me feel better. I could break the contract. I could leave.

But the truth was, I didn't *want* to be sent home. Which might be even more humiliating than having my freaking hymen checked because I talked to Joren alone for two-point-five seconds...

I swallowed hard. "Fine. Go ahead."

"Excellent. Just go over and sit on the couch." She took a paper drape from her bag. "Remove everything from the waist down and put this over your lap. This will only take a minute."

Grimacing, I did as I was told. Dr. Bryan was mercifully swift—the whole process took only a few moments. "Everything looks good, Chloe. I'll tell him on my way out."

My cheeks heated with shame as she said goodbye and I got dressed. Why had he done this to me? Why had I *let* him? The whole thing was crazy!

I threw open the door, all the better to yell at Bryce, but he was gone.

Fuming, I locked myself in my room for the rest of the afternoon. The high I'd experienced over the last few days, fueled by happiness, plummeted.

All that was left was me, and I was *pissed*.

"Chloe. *Chloe.*" Bryce's cool breath wafted over my face, and I struggled to open my eyes.

The room was bathed in semi-darkness, the twilight of early summer. Bryce was next to me on the bed. He wore a T-shirt and rumpled-looking sweats, something I'd never seen him in before.

My initial instinct was to bury my face in his chest —but then I remembered everything. "What are you doing here?" My voice was cold, but I could already feel the tears threatening.

"I'm here every night," he reminded me. "When you didn't join us at dinner, I came early."

I rolled onto my back, refusing to look at him.

"What, aren't you speaking to me?"

I didn't say a word.

Bryce cursed under his breath. "I had to have you examined, Chloe. You don't understand. It would be worse if I didn't."

"You're right—I don't understand." Tears sprang to

my eyes. "I didn't do anything wrong. And neither did Joren—he didn't deserve to be fired. Neither did Dale!"

"I didn't fire Dale."

One small blessing. "Good. He didn't do anything wrong. But neither did Joren—all I did was ask him a question."

"He was specifically instructed not to be alone with you," Bryce said quietly. "I will not employ individuals who cannot follow the rules."

"You mean like me?" My voice cracked. "All I did was ask him if he knew where an island was. I was alone with him for *one minute*. Neither of us did anything wrong. You're acting crazy."

A heavy silence descended over us. It was electric with unsaid things.

After a minute, Bryce took my hand in his. "I needed to be certain. You don't understand—you can't."

I *didn't* understand him, and yet, on some level, I had an inkling of what he was feeling. "I would never do that to you. I'm not like that, Bryce."

He squeezed my hand, but he didn't look at me.

And that was how, after a long and heavy silence, we fell asleep.

her

A BRAND-NEW CAPTAIN met us the following day on the dock. He was tall and trim, with thick white hair beneath his cap.

"Mr. Windsor." He saluted Bryce. "Mrs. Windsor."

"Good morning, Johnny. It's nice to have you back."

"Retirement's boring, Sir." Johnny grinned at him. "The wife's got me canning tomatoes. I'm happy to be of service."

"Ha, good. You're hired until she insists you come home."

"Fair enough, Mr. Windsor." The captain's step was jaunty as he returned to the cabin.

"He worked for us for years until he retired," Bryce explained as he helped me on board. "He lives over on Spruce Island. Born and raised there."

"I can't imagine. Is there a school?"

"Yeah, a small one," Bryce said. "But when the kids start ninth grade, they take the mailboat over and go to MDI High."

"Wow, taking a boat to school sounds like fun."

"I've always thought so." Bryce looked out at the water. "But of course, I went to boarding school. Maybe someday, my children will take the mailboat to school…"

I shivered. Hearing him talk about kids made my heart wrench, particularly how he said it: "my children." *His* children. Did he intend to have them with me, his wife? Or was there someone else he was thinking of?

You're starting to read too much into things, Chlo, said the voice in my head. She was right. She was always right.

I sighed, joining Bryce on the couch. The attendants had already put our luggage on board. I was excited and nervous about spending the weekend alone with him. On the heels of everything that had happened over the last twenty-four hours, I was a hot mess, a jumble of mixed emotions.

Earlier that morning, Dale had assured me everything was fine, and that Noah would be well taken care of. Knowing that my brother also had a fleet of maids and bodyguards—not to mention a personal chef and a puppy—looking out for him made leaving a little easier. Still, I had big-sister guilt that I was leaving him with strangers in a new place. Of course, it *was* a mansion. And all of Bryce's employees had been thoroughly vetted, with criminal background checks and references, the whole nine yards. My brother was as safe as he could be with them. Plus, he seemed genuinely happy for the first time since Mom died...

The morning air was chilly, and Bryce wrapped his arm around me as we crossed the Sound. I welcomed his touch even though I was still upset. Last night, he'd fallen asleep holding my hand. But only hours before, he'd gone ballistic, firing his captain and having my freaking *hymen* checked. Once again, he'd given me emotional whiplash.

My husband was an enigma, a complicated puzzle. Part of me yearned to carefully piece him together. But another part, afraid of what I might find, longed to hide from the job.

The route was busy with early morning boat traffic. We drove slowly, navigating the other yachts, and Bryce waved to the people he knew. I saw Kelli and Kenji Nguyen and smiled, but they were the only ones I recognized.

A small boat headed toward us, coming from the dock in Northeast Harbor. Bryce set eyes on it and froze.

"Bryce?"

He didn't respond as the craft came closer. It was a gorgeous, all-wood boat, glossy paint shining in the early morning sun. A tall, handsome older man was driving, a red baseball cap secured to his head. There were three passengers out on the stern's deck, an older, attractive woman in a fleece jacket, a guy in khakis who looked like he was in his early thirties, and a tall, stunning brunette in a *Nantucket* sweatshirt.

Bryce stared at them.

The women said something to each other, then waved as they passed. I couldn't take my eyes off the statuesque woman with the long, brown hair. She wore shorts and a gray sweatshirt, nothing fancy. Still, her body was obviously killer—perfectly round breasts, a tiny waist, and long, tanned, toned legs. Even from a distance, I could tell that she was the most beautiful woman I'd ever seen. Even more so than Daphne because *this* woman looked utterly natural, her blue eyes contrasting with her brown hair, a smattering of freckles across her makeup-free face.

She and Bryce locked gazes as the boats passed, and I fought the urge to throw myself overboard.

He clenched his hands into fists. He turned forward, staring straight ahead.

"W-Who was that?" But I already knew, the same

way you know you're getting the stomach bug that's been going around.

"No one."

I took a deep breath. "Bryce...? It was obviously someone. Was that the Jones family?"

His phone buzzed. *Goddammit, his phone has the worst timing!* "I have to take this." He looked relieved as he attached it to his ear and stormed off to the cabin.

I took the opportunity to open my own phone and browse "Felicia Jones" in private mode, then wished I hadn't. Her picture instantly appeared, and it was worse than I'd thought: she was so pretty, it hurt to look at her face. Blue, blue eyes, and long dark hair made for a stunning contrast. Her complexion sparkled; her freckles were unexpected, making her that much more striking. She was enough of a public figure to have a brief bio right there on the Google search page:

Felicia Tate Jones, American Heiress
Born: March 30, 1994 (Age 28), New York City, New York
Height: 5'8"
Sibling: William Jones
Parents: Mimi Jones, Michael Jones
People also searched for: Bryce Windsor

I clicked to "images" and found dozens of pictures of her online—riding horses, skiing, surfing, and playing golf. *Rich people sports.* There were no pictures of her and Bryce together. A quick but thorough inventory revealed that Felicia had no online profiles, no Instagram, no LinkedIn, nothing. She was apparently too cool for social media, too rich for networking, and too busy living her best life to waste time on the internet.

As I was already so far down the rabbit hole, I ran a search on Bryce's name. The first images that came up were from our recent city-hall wedding: *Billionaire Bryce Windsor Elopes.* He looked handsome, if resigned, in his suit. But I looked petrified, frozen, in the pictures—an amateur, in way over my head. I clearly didn't know how to ride horses or play golf.

I was no American heiress. I had no business marrying a billionaire.

I wondered if Felicia had seen these—but of course, she had. What did she think? She'd probably wondered about me. Who I was, why Bryce married me, if he loved me more than her? If he was still crying about how she'd left him and devastated him...

Maybe she was sorry she'd left him. Maybe now that she saw him with someone else, she wanted him for herself.

Hot waves of jealousy made me shudder. My stomach twisted, making me feel sick. Why was she here for the summer? Why did she have to drive by, her hair blowing in the breeze, in her stupid *Nantucket* sweatshirt? If she'd tossed him aside so coldly, like Midge said, *why* had she come back?

Bryce and I were a transaction, a contract—I knew that. But he'd started to open up to me, at least a little. He'd held me, touched me, and let me touch him: it felt as though something was blossoming between us. But it was delicate, too new to weather a harsh storm. Felicia Jones seemed like fucking Elsa from *Frozen*, blowing in with a Nor'easter, threatening to kill everything I'd hoped might grow.

I shut off my phone and stared out at the water. I'd had high hopes for this trip, but it felt like they'd been dashed again. Honestly, why did I even care? Bryce had fired Joren yesterday and had my *hymen* inspected because I'd talked to the guy alone for *two freaking minutes.* That was not normal. Neither was the fact that he'd *bought me because I was a virgin.*

At that moment, Bryce walked out of the cabin, hands in his pockets, and our eyes locked. It felt like a sucker punch to my gut.

And knew exactly why I fucking cared so much.

The private flight to Exuma was quick and, thankfully, without turbulence. Bryce worked for most of the trip, but he sat next to me and intermittently put his hand on my thigh. It burned where he touched me. For some reason, it made me mad: it was so damn inconvenient.

But thoughts of inconvenience dispersed as we went through customs at the tiny airport. All the locals greeted Bryce warmly. A Range Rover waited for us outside with a driver and an attendant, who swiftly put our bags into the SUV. Before I knew it, we were off, driving with the windows down. I'd seen the water from the plane—it was an incredible, almost unreal turquoise. I'd never seen a color like that before. Palm trees dotted the landscape, swaying in the breeze. We drove through a small downtown and a residential neighborhood, the buildings squat and colorful. The air was so warm, a far cry from Northern Maine, but it wasn't unpleasantly humid like Boston.

We pulled up to a gate, and the driver punched in a code. "The staff will be happy to have you back," he said. "They did exactly as you asked—prepared the house, left meals for you. Everything is perfect. They'll be back tomorrow to clean and prepare more meals."

"I'm looking forward to our visit—it's been a long time." Bryce took my hand. "We're excited to be here."

"Have you traveled to Exuma before, Mrs. Windsor?" The driver politely asked.

"Never—I've never been to the Bahamas." Of course, I'd never been anywhere.

"You will love it. Isn't that right, Mr. Windsor? Your house is the prettiest on the island."

Bryce smiled and squeezed my hand. "Thank you."

The Rover pulled through the gate and down a long private drive surrounded by dense forest. After a few minutes, we reached a clearing. An enormous stucco house, bright and airy, greeted us, with the ocean directly behind it. "Wow." I peered at the estate. "You're right on the beach!"

"Wait until you see the sunset—it's incredible."

"The finest view in all the world," the driver said as he and the attendant hopped out. They grabbed our bags and helped us down. The driver smiled and bowed. "You two have a lovely honeymoon. My wife and I wish you many blessings."

Bryce shook his hand. "Thank you, John. We'll call if we decide to go out."

Bryce led me by the hand into the house, which was open. The windows were all screened, and a fresh breeze cooled the interior. The home was comfortable, elegant, and welcoming—all smooth tiles on the floors and bright Caribbean colors on the walls and furniture. It was a *fun* house, vastly different from the austere beauty of the Maine property.

We stepped through to the living room, which opened into an outdoor living space and rolled right out to an insanely gorgeous infinity pool. The pool overlooked the white-sand beach, the turquoise water lapping at the shore. I gaped at the view: I'd never seen anything like it, except in a movie or on a screensaver. It was too good to be true.

"It's gorgeous!" I turned to find Bryce staring at me, a glimmer in his eye.

"Yes. It is." But he wasn't looking anywhere but at me.

He pulled me to him, and I sighed, burying my face against his chest. He sank his hands into my hair, and I wished he'd take off his damn suit.

"Do you want to go swimming?"

I peered up at him. "Are you kidding? I'm not coming out of the water this whole weekend!" I couldn't keep the excitement out of my voice, even though I knew I'd live to regret it. We'd seen his ex that morning, after all. Compared to her, I was probably nothing to him.

But even though I didn't want to admit it, especially

to myself, Bryce had absolutely become something to me.

He grinned down at me. "Go get your suit. I'll meet you out there." He kissed my nose, and I lit up inside.

For better or more likely, for worse, I skipped as I went to get changed.

TWENTY-SIX

infinity

THROWING CAUTION—AND probably my dignity—to the wind, I selected the tiniest, sexiest thong bikini that Midge had packed. It was dangerously small, with a triangle top and a string bottom. I stopped myself from imagining Felicia Jones in a bathing suit. At least I was ten years younger than her!

I applied some lip gloss and tossed my hair as I checked myself out in the full-length mirror. Youth *was* an advantage. I barely worked out, but my breasts were firm and round, as was my ass. *You look good, Chlo.* The internet had recommended positive self-talk, so I might as well give it a try. *He'll love the G-string. Don't be so self-conscious.*

Sighing and feigning a confidence I most certainly did not feel, I stalked out to the pool deck.

Bryce waited, sprawled out on an armchair overlooking the infinity pool. He'd changed into blue swim trunks and stripped out of his shirt. His enormous pectoral muscles glinted in the sun, and I devoured the lines of his clearly defined six-pack with my eyes. Seeing his powerful body on display made my insides turn to Jell-O. *Unf.* I knew what it felt like to have him above me, to stare up at those big shoulders while he held me down with his bulging biceps. *Double unf.*

Just looking at him made me wet. Forget about Joren, forget about the virginity inspection, forget about the ex. Excitement bubbled inside me. We were alone for three days. His house, which was more of a resort, was utterly private and deserted. We could do whatever we liked...

"Chloe." He lowered his sunglasses and checked out my suit. "Stop right there. Let me look at you."

My cheeks heated as I stood still, all the better for him to take a nice, long look. I was pleased to see his cock stirring, the beginnings of an erection pitching a tent in his suit.

"Turn around." His voice was gruff and commanding, and I did what he said. He moaned when he saw my backside—the black G-string was pretty much the only thing going on back there. I held my breath as he inspected me.

"Are you trying to kill me, Chloe?"

I laughed. "No." *No, Sir.* "I just thought you might like this... You seemed to like the other one."

"I like it. I don't ever want you to wear it in public, though. Do you understand?"

"Yes." *Yes, Sir.*

I turned back to him, and his erection was massive now, almost comical, pointing straight up in the air. I couldn't look away from it.

"Are you staring at my dick, Chloe?"

"No." I tore my eyes away. "Of course not."

"Yes, you were." His tone was forceful, bossy, serious. "Admit it."

"I..." It took me a moment, but I finally met his gaze.

"Tell the truth, Chloe." He took his sunglasses off and watched me, eyes blazing.

"I admit it—I looked." I intended the words to sound teasing, but they came out halting, embarrassed.

"I'll always know if you're lying." He shifted in the chair, leaning back, his cock growing impossibly more immense. "And I told you, lies are not allowed."

"I... I didn't mean to lie. I was embarrassed." Why was he making such a big deal out of this? And why was I so fucking *wet*?

"First of all, you're the one who got me hard. This is all you." He motioned to his erection. "You and that fucking tease of a swimsuit. You're a virgin, and you're walking around in *that*? *Fuck*, Chloe. You're making me want to do all sorts of things to you."

I shivered.

"Second of all, you don't need to be embarrassed with me. I'm your husband." His dick twitched. "Third, you cannot lie to your husband. Do you understand?"

"Yes," I mumbled.

"What was that? I didn't hear you."

"I said *yes*." My face was turning red. Why was he treating me like I'd gotten home after curfew and was about to get grounded...or *spanked*?

"I understand you're embarrassed about staring at my cock," he said, sounding smug. "But I'm going to have to punish you for lying."

"*Punish* me?" I squeaked.

He smiled at me, white teeth flashing in the sun. "Come *here*. On your knees, in front of me. *Now*."

I shivered, then tentatively did as I was told. He was hard, which was a good sign that something delicious was about to happen. But *punishing* me? Um...

"On your knees, Mrs. Windsor." He spread his legs apart and motioned to the ground in front of the chair. Luckily it was grassy, so it was soft as I sank down before him.

I peered up at him from beneath my lashes. "What do you want?"

"For you to do exactly as I say." Bryce's eyes glittered. "It's a game I'm looking forward to playing all weekend. Is that all right with you?"

I was already under Bryce's spell. I immediately shook my head yes.

"I need to hear your consent, Chloe. It matters to me."

"Y-Yes. We can play your game. We can play all weekend." My insides quivered in anticipation of what might await me.

"Good." He favored me with a lopsided smile. "Now, I'd like you to take me in your mouth. Do you understand?"

His dick twitched. My insides shivered. "Yes... Sir."

He arched an eyebrow. "I like it when you call me *Sir*, Chloe. It's very...agreeable of you."

I came closer, putting my hands on his thighs. "May I?"

He chuckled, a dark, low rumbling sound. "You may, Mrs. Windsor. I'm looking forward to it."

I slid down his swim trunks, and his cock sprang out, gloriously, ridiculously hard. Thank goodness we'd been fooling around, and I'd been reading up on the internet; otherwise I would've been petrified of the sight of it in broad daylight. Instead, I was painfully aroused. My inner thighs were slick with wetness, gliding against the thong. My nipples poked against the thin material of the bikini top.

Bryce took my breasts in his big hands, massaging my erect nipples through the fabric.

I licked my palms and started working up and down his hard length. I licked the tip of his cock's huge head —it was already salty, delicious. I swirled the lush tip around in my mouth, licking and sucking on the delicious ridge. Bryce moaned, a guttural sound, and I lit up with pure female satisfaction.

He wanted *me*. It was *my* mouth on him. He was moaning for *me*.

You don't need to be embarrassed in front of me. I'm your husband.

He *was* my husband. And I was going to be damn sure I was his wife after this weekend, his *real* wife...

I trailed kisses down his hard length, chasing my hands. Everything was hot and wet—even my thighs as I bobbed my head up and down, deliriously turned on and drunk on my power over him. His lower abdominal muscles tensed, revealing bulging veins beneath the skin, as he thrust his erection into my eager mouth. I sucked, rubbed, and massaged him, then tentatively took one of his balls in my mouth, testing if he liked me sucking on *that*.

"Fuck, Chloe!" He fisted my hair, and I took that as a *yes*. Emboldened, I ran my tongue over this new area, testing his reaction, working his shaft with my hands as I took his other sac in my mouth. *Mmm.* I sucked him, rubbing my tongue along the surface as he thrashed beneath me.

He was vulnerable beneath my touch...he was under my spell...he was *mine*. I worked my way back up his length, took him all the way into my throat, down to the base of his shaft, and sucked hard. My hands gently massaged his balls, squeezing, tugging, giving a light, consistent pressure that seemed to drive him insane. He thrashed beneath me, straining as he thrust his cock into my eager mouth, his balls retracting as the orgasm started to overtake him.

I sucked harder, swallowing him whole. The head of his cock hit the back of my throat, and he cursed. "Fuck Chloe—yes!" He erupted in hot spurts, and I greedily drank it all down, taking it, sucking him, massaging his balls as the orgasm ripped through him. He thrashed again, big muscles tensing and rippling as he completely lost himself in the moment.

It was so satisfying to see him like that, knowing that *I* was the source of his pleasure, his abandonment. I thoroughly enjoyed sucking down every last drop of him, his delicious saltiness. My husband had come *hard*.

Pride bloomed deep inside as he pulled me up against his chest and kissed the top of my hair. "That was fucking incredible." He laughed, sounding winded. I clung to him—to the compliment, the satisfaction I felt from pleasing him, the feel of his breath rising and falling against mine. I never wanted to let go.

We relaxed in the warmth of the sun for a few minutes. I was lost in him, lost in his touch, and enveloped in happiness because I was in his arms. Eventually, his cock stirred against my skin. He was getting hard again.

"My, my. It seems I'm not done with you." He lifted my chin, so my eyes met his, then he dove in for a deep, slow, sensual kiss. My insides quivered as he ran his hands up and down my skin, fingers skimming the surface, causing me to break out in goosebumps. He was hard again, pressed against my belly, the tip of his cock already beading with moisture.

Bryce kissed me some more, our bodies rubbing against each other. It was heaven on earth to feel his naked skin against mine. This was the only thing in the world that I wanted—to be close to him, be *with* him, and be together like this. He kissed my neck, and I moaned. He must've liked that because he grunted in pleasure and thrust his cock against my stomach.

I kissed him back, hands roaming down his muscled torso. Like I said, this must be heaven. The sun shone down on us, the wind rustled the palm trees, and the infinity pool and amazing ocean sparkled beyond. My hands reached his ass, and emboldened by the orgasm I'd just given him, I squeezed his cheeks and pressed him against me.

Bryce responded by bucking his hips, thrusting against me some more, the salty pre-cum making him slippery against my skin. His kisses trailed lower, and he ripped my bikini top to the side, taking my breast into his mouth and greedily suckling it. I straddled him, moving his cock between my legs, and started to shamelessly rub myself against his hard length. The thong pressed against my sex as I soaked Bryce with my wetness.

We started to move against each other. I was entirely out of my mind, gliding back and forth across his cock. Insane pleasure struck me every time his tip brushed against my clit. He started to grind himself against it, making me whimper. "Bryce, please... Take me." I'd never wanted something so badly in my entire life.

He grabbed my hips in a classic Bryce-Windsor

move, flipping me so I was beneath him. Now *he* was in control. He yanked the G-string over to the side and rubbed his cock against my wet, exposed slit.

"My virgin's so wet for me. As a reward, I'm going to make her come."

"I want you," I panted. "I want..."

But I couldn't finish the sentence. Bryce increased his pace, hips thrusting as he slid his cock back and forth against my slit. His thumb roughly around my clit, making me see stars. I cried out. I wanted him to penetrate me, to take me, but I couldn't argue with his expert touch. He *owned* me. He increased the pace, rubbing my swollen clit in time with his furious thrusts. I was overwhelmed by him, by the sensation of him possessing me, taking control of my body, my pleasure, my goddamned *mind*.

"Bryce—*Bryce*!" I screamed his name as the orgasm tore through me, the pleasure eclipsing everything else. I was one with the sensation, the muscles in my sex spasming, clenching, my clit throbbing beneath his touch. I hit the pinnacle, flying high, my whole body lighting up with pleasure.

"Yes, *fuck yes*, Chloe." Still thrusting, Bryce gripped his cock, milking it, and spent himself all over my sex, rubbing against me, completely out of his mind.

"Oh fuck, what're you doing?" I thrashed underneath him, alive with the pleasure of feeling his seed against me. He kept thrusting as he finished, grunting and cursing, the cords standing out in his neck. I panted, still rubbing furiously against him, desperate for more. He circled my clit with his big fingers, bringing me to the edge again. I screamed, almost unable to tolerate the enormous waves of pleasure. Everything got dark except for the stars swirling in front of my eyes.

Bryce was above me when I came to, a smug look on his face, chuckling. "I guess it's officially a honeymoon."

"I guess so." I laughed too. But inside, I wanted to cry.

It was also official that Bryce Windsor *owned* me.

What the fuck was I supposed to do about that?

TWENTY-SEVEN

dangerous games

I woke up a few hours later, alone in the bedroom. It was still light out, the remains of the sun drifting in through the gauzy curtains. I stretched out, limbs loose, and realized I was naked. *Hmm.* What had we done? I barely remembered Bryce bringing me to the bed, laying me down and kissing me, tucking me in.

What had he whispered? Ah, yes. *"Rest, Mrs. Windsor. I've got more games in store for you later."*

I shivered, nipples prickling. What did my husband mean? Would tonight *finally* be the night he took me, that he made me *his*?

What we'd done out on the patio had been incredible. I got wet again just thinking about him sliding against me, coming all over my sex. *So naughty!* A knot of desire tugged deep in my belly. Surely he wanted me as much as I wanted him...right?

How was he still resisting me?

I jumped into the shower, humming to myself, and decided that he wouldn't be able to stop himself tonight. I was going to *bring it.* I quickly toweled off, put my hair up in a messy, sexy bun, and applied some makeup. I chose a tight-fitting black tank dress that Midge insisted looked great on me. I skipped the bra and wore a black lacy thong, something I knew Bryce would like. I inspected myself in the mirror and almost laughed: I *did* look great, but it wasn't because of the dress—it was because my complexion was sparkling.

I'd read on the internet that orgasms were great for your skin. Hoo boy was that the truth!

I hustled out to find Bryce, eager to be reunited with him. He was outside again, in a white linen shirt open at the throat and a pair of shorts, kicked back on a chair, watching the sunset. He had a half-finished bourbon in his hand. There was a little line between his eyes as if he'd been thinking about something unpleasant.

"Ah, there you are." His expression softened when he saw me. "And don't you look pretty."

"Thank you." I couldn't help but smile.

"C'mere." He patted his lap, and I curled up against him.

This wasn't a sexy touch, though. He seemed as though he needed comfort. "Is something wrong?"

"Not anymore." He kissed the top of my head, snaking one arm around my waist. "Are you hungry? Chef prepared dinner for us. It looks delicious."

"Sure, that sounds great. Was the staff here while I was asleep?" I asked.

"No—they made sure everything was set up for us this morning." He lightly kissed my shoulder. "We're completely alone."

That was precisely what I wanted. I nestled against him and stared out at the beach. "We haven't even made it into the water yet."

"We will tonight. Let's eat, then we can go in before it gets too dark."

"And then?" I asked, pulse quickening.

"And then perhaps we'll play some more." Bryce's voice was a low rumble, and I felt it deep inside my belly. "Sit here and watch the sky. Would you like a glass of wine?"

"No, thank you."

He favored me with a lopsided smile, a smile I was beginning to crave. "Then how about some iced tea? Or a *virgin* daiquiri?"

"Ha ha." I scowled at him as he padded toward the kitchen.

If I had my way—which I planned to—I wouldn't be a virgin by the end of the night.

I listened to the sounds of the gentle surf against the beach, of Bryce rustling around in the refrigerator. *I could get used to this.* The happiness crept back up; I let it. Bryce had told me I looked pretty, which pleased me beyond words. I yearned for his approval, his accep-tance. The fact that he was being complimentary and kind—not to mention how he'd ravaged me earlier—had me all aglow.

Bryce had left his phone on the side table. Its screen lit up with a text message from Dale.

I shared your objections with your father, but he insisted. He said the Joneses are old friends and that there's nothing wrong with having them for dinner. I'm sorry. I tried. But you know how he is.

There was an emoji of a devil after the last sentence.

I stared at the screen. Gene had the Jones family to the house for dinner? As in, *Felicia Jones* and her family?

The hell?

I glanced at Bryce. He was arranging plates at the table, his back turned toward me. I grabbed my own phone, which I'd tossed on one of the couches earlier, and texted Midge.

Who is coming to the house for dinner?

Three dots immediately appeared.

The fucking Jones family. Old Gene and Daphne are cooking up something, IDK what. Want me to poison Felicia's salad?

Ha, I wrote back, *no thank you. But let me know what you hear.*

I tossed my phone down, feeling sick. The thought of Bryce's ex-fiancé having dinner with his father and Daphne made my blood run cold. Not only was she back, but she was *everywhere!*

I glanced at my husband, who was opening a bottle of wine. Now I knew why he'd been lost in his thoughts when I'd found him out on the deck. He'd been thinking about *her.* He knew she would be spending the evening with Gene and Daphne, her family mixing with his once more. What did he feel about it?

And why the hell was she ruining my weekend—if not more?

I went to Bryce and wrapped my arms around him from behind. I put my face against him and inhaled his scent, something masculine, clean, and utterly delicious.

He finished with the wine and poured himself a glass. Its deep-red color perfectly complemented the bright dishes he'd set out. "Dinner looks amazing." In fact, I had no idea what dinner *was* besides pretty.

He arched an eyebrow. "You like ceviche?"

"Sure," I lied. "Love it."

"Chloe Windsor, you have never had ceviche in your life." He inspected me. "Did my virgin just lie to me again?"

I opened my mouth and then closed it. I'd only been trying to be polite, but if a white lie was going to earn me another "game"...

Bryce's eyes glittered. "I'm starting to think you like being punished."

I yearned to distract him from what was going on back at home. I wanted him to think about me and only me. I licked my lips and stuck my bra-less chest out at him. "Maybe I do like it," I said, my voice haughty, challenging.

"Ah." His blue eyes flashed as the tone between us changed, heat gathering. His gaze lowered to my breasts, causing my nipples to pebble painfully. "That doesn't make it okay to lie."

I shrugged, feigning indifference. "It's *ceviche*, Bryce. It's not like it's a big deal."

He gripped my hips with his hands. "The truth is a big deal. It's *always* a big deal. I think your attitude needs adjusting, Mrs. Windsor."

Electricity crackled between us. He tightened his grip.

I shrugged again. "Whatever." Now *I* was the one playing a game.

"Oh, you are asking for it." He clamped a hand around my wrist and dragged me to the living room, to the enormous couch. "Pull up your dress around your waist."

I hesitated, suddenly unsure, even as wetness gathered between my legs.

"Now." Bryce's cock, suddenly hard, strained against his shorts. "Pull the goddamned thing up, Chloe. Don't make me tell you again."

Hands shaking, I hitched the dress up over my ass. Bryce sank down onto the couch and pulled me on top of him, so I lay across him, ass exposed. "Another thong, eh? For a virgin, you're really asking for it." He slid his hands over my bare ass and down the backs of my thighs. Power radiated from him. His erection raged against me, stiff and potent.

Exposed and at his mercy, I fought to regain control. I wanted him to want me, and I wanted him to take me. But now it seemed as though he was in charge again...

I wriggled my ass in the air. His erection jabbed at my stomach. "Maybe I *am* asking for it."

"Doesn't work that way, Chloe. You don't ask—you

get *told*." He rubbed my ass, cupping it, then ran his fingers along the G-string. "And I'm telling you that you are about to be spanked for lying to me *again*."

"Spanked?" I didn't know whether to laugh or cry. My insides went squiggly, completely haywire. Why did the idea of having my husband spank me get me so hot?

His fingers slid along my slit, and he chuckled. "You're already wet. You want me to play with you, don't you? You *want* to be spanked."

"No." My voice was haughty. *Yes. Hell to the yes.*

"That's another lie." He cracked his palm against my ass with a loud *smack*.

"Ow!" But it didn't hurt as much as sting. I wriggled against him, weirdly wanting more.

"I'm going to spank you, and then I'm going to have my way with you." Bryce adjusted me across his screaming erection and grunted. "I am going to enjoy this."

Not as much as I am.

Smack! Smack! His colossal palm whacked one ass cheek, then another. Then he rubbed each cheek tenderly, then slid his hands over my slit. "So wet. My little virgin needs me." He trailed his fingers up to my clit, teasing and rubbing until I mewled against him.

Then he spanked me again—and again—repeating the process. It seemed like it went on forever, but it was also as though I could never have enough. Somewhere between the stinging and the rubbing, I almost lost my mind. Every time he rubbed my clit, I got closer to coming. But then he'd stop and spank me some more, doing it repeatedly until I was a whimpering, wet mess.

"Please... *Please*, Bryce. Take me."

"You want my cock, Chloe?"

Smack, smack, fondle.

Bringing me close, so close, to the edge.

I was so close I thought I might die. I trembled on the edge of something colossal, a physical sensation I couldn't even fathom. "Yes. Please," I whimpered. "I want your cock. Give it to me—*please*." I'd never been so brazen, so bold. I'd also never been so fucking *desperate*.

He pressed his erection into me and continued his assault. *Smack, smack, fondle.* He took his hand away right before I could come. "I'm not sure that's the best idea."

"Yes, it is." I was on the verge of a massive orgasm, the verge of tears. "It's the best idea ever. Please, Bryce. I'm literally begging you."

"Not yet. I'm not ready to give in to you." He spanked me and fondled me more, still teasing, until tears literally ran down my face.

I ground myself against his hands, desperately

seeking release. I angled myself over his cock, rubbing it into my stomach, praying that he'd lose control.

"I know what you're doing, Virgin." His voice was hoarse.

"Please take me—please make me your wife," I babbled. "I'll do anything."

"Anything, eh?" With one final rub to my clit, he somehow flipped me around and stood, lifting me with him. "We'll see about that."

With that, he carried me back to the bedroom.

pierced

DARKNESS WAS FALLING as he deposited me on the bed. "Don't move."

I lay still, heart pounding, as he lit several large candles. He went to the nightstand and removed a box from the drawer. Then he sat down on the bed, holding it on his lap. "Take off that dress, Chloe. Leave the G-string on," he growled.

"Yes..." I swallowed hard, anticipation building. "Yes, *Sir*."

He chuckled darkly. "It's a little late for that, but I appreciate the effort."

I pulled the dress over my head and lay back. My ass cheeks still smarted, but the incessant, keening ache between my legs was even worse. "What's in that box?" I eyed the dark, enameled wood.

"It's tools I'm using for our next game."

I shivered. "What's our next game?"

"I think you know, Chloe. It's the one you've been begging to play."

My hips wriggled of their own volition. "I'm ready."

"Not so fast." Bryce's gaze darkened. "You need to understand the rules."

"Okay…"

He didn't look at me as he said, "Once I take you, you are *mine*. That means you will never lie to me; you will never hide from me. Do you understand?"

"Yes." *Yes, Sir.*

"If I catch you deceiving me, the punishment will be far worse than a visit from Dr. Bryan."

I froze. "What do you mean?"

Bryce opened the box, revealing handcuffs. "You'll be my prisoner, Chloe. I won't ever let you out of my sight again."

"Your prisoner?" I squeaked. I didn't know whether to laugh or cry!

"That's what I said. You need to know what you're getting into."

I eyed him warily as he set about attaching two cuffs to the headboard, two to the footboard. "What are you doing with those?"

"I'm showing you what it means to be *mine*. You

have to give yourself over to me, Chloe. You have to trust me one-hundred percent. You have to let me *possess* you. If I'm going to take you, I'm taking *all* of you."

I shivered again, not really understanding—but deep in my belly, I had an idea what was about to happen. "You're going to tie me up?"

"Yes," he hissed. "And then I'm going to take you. And I'm going to take you *hard*."

I licked my lips, my heart rate jacked. *He was going to take me hard?* I was a little afraid—why did that get me even wetter?

"Then I will own you—after this, there's no going back." Bryce was calm, collected, and dead serious. "Do you understand?"

"Y-Yes."

He knelt before me, his screaming erection already pointing at his target: me. "Are you willing to be cuffed to the bed?"

I nodded. "Yes."

"Are you willing to be penetrated by me?"

A spasm of desire wracked through me. "Yes, Bryce."

He leaned closer. "And do you swear that you will be faithful—to me and only me?"

"Yes. I swear—you're the only one. You'll always be the only one."

We regarded each other.

"That's a big promise, Chloe."

I crossed myself. "I mean it." I'd already married him. But now, naked in front of my husband, I told him what was in my heart: he was the only one I wanted. It shamed me, for some reason, to yearn for him with such intensity. To want so badly to please him and to be pleased by him.

Still, I lifted my chin. "I'll always tell you the truth. And that *is* the truth—I only want you."

He was on top of me suddenly, devouring me with a deep kiss that swept me away. I arched my back, pressing against him, and his hands swept down my sides. He cupped my breasts, his hot kisses trailing down my neck. We were completely lost in each other. He straddled me, and our kisses became more urgent.

He was everywhere at once, intense, on a mission. Bryce took my arms and secured my wrists in the cuffs. The restraints were padded and softer than I expected. Still, I struggled against them as he trailed his kisses down my inner thighs. I wasn't used to being hand-cuffed! I longed to touch him, but it seemed my submission was essential to him, something he needed to take things to the next level.

In that case, I was all for them.

Bryce secured my feet into the other cuffs. Now I

was spread-eagle on the bed, completely vulnerable, my arms above my head, my legs open wide.

I jerked my hands and feet, testing the give of my restraints. There was little. For some reason, this riled me up. I lay there, panting and wild, as Bryce stood. He stripped out of his shirt, then his shorts. I almost passed out from looking at his rock-hard chest and abs, his erection absolutely *massive*. He slid out of his boxer briefs and was finally, gloriously naked.

He came and knelt before me, in between my legs. "Do you trust me, Chloe?"

I shivered. I was so wet already—raw and vulnerable, not to mention restrained—entirely at his mercy. But on a level that went beyond common sense, I understood that Bryce wouldn't hurt me, not in bed, not tonight. "Yes. I trust you."

"Good." He gave me that lopsided smile. So close to taking me, he seemed to be in his element. "Relax, Virgin. It won't be long now."

He didn't make me wait. He ripped the G-string off, tossing it to the side, and buried his face against my sex. I cried out, bucking against him, shocked by the sudden sensation of his tongue stroking me. He slid his hands under my ass, kneading, and lifted me to his mouth. He was voracious, relentlessly lapping me, feasting on his virgin.

Oh my God

Oh my God

Oh my God

He stuck two big fingers inside me and gently stroked, then nibbled on my clit.

An orgasm ripped through me—sudden, wild, and uncontrollable. "Bryce! Oh my God, *Bryce!*" I came hard, all at once.

He continued to suck me, chuckling darkly, his fingers still stroking my insides as I bucked against him. The restraints only added to my heightened sensation. The fact that I was utterly at his mercy stoked something deep and primal in my belly. I was *his* to have and to possess. There was nothing, no one else, that mattered.

He trailed his kisses up my belly and released his grip on my ass, letting the bed buoy me. I shuddered as he climbed higher, his hot kisses finding my breasts. My nipples pebbled, and he took each of them into his mouth, suckling and nuzzling until I mewled against him, wet, empty, and aching once more.

He came even with me, looking into my eyes; my heart soared. Bryce lowered his lips to mine for a long, deep kiss. I moaned, losing myself in his touch, losing myself in *him*. His erection pressed against my slit, and I cried out as he rubbed himself against me. He was deliciously huge and hard. He was everywhere.

I wanted him—badly. And yet, I was a little afraid. Bryce was just so *big*.

As if reading my thoughts, he pulled back. His breath was coming fast, and his pupils were huge. "I'll go as slow as I can. Are you ready for me, Chloe?"

I nodded. I had no words left, only desire.

He kissed me again, slowly at first. He rubbed his enormous erection against me—I was wet, so wet. Soon we were both panting. I was shaking, I wanted him so badly. His kisses became more urgent. He wanted me, too. I arched my back and bucked my hips, creating as much friction as I could. I was *dying*.

He pulsed his hips and notched the head of his cock inside me. I shuddered around him, wishing I could run my hands down his back. I bucked against the restraints, and he grunted, sliding in one more inch. He was so thick that my pussy spasmed around him, trying to draw him in deeper. He obliged, pulsing his hips, his tremendous, hard length entering deeper. *OMFG*. He kissed my ear, my neck, the base of my throat as I lifted my hips, readying myself for him, throbbing for him.

One small thrust, followed by another. He was starting to fill me. His muscled ass pumped as he entered me deeper, slowly opening me up. "You're so fucking tight. And so wet for me. My Virgin. My *wife*."

"Bryce...*please*."

He thrust once more, harder this time, and I cried out as he broke through my maidenhead, finally making me *his*.

Once he was all the way in, I groaned. *This* was what I'd longed for—for him to be inside me, touching me deeper than anyone else ever could. I was *his*.

His thrusts became more insistent, and he grunted, an animal sound of deep satisfaction. *Oh fuck, yes.* He filled me, bucking his hips and stroking a space inside me I didn't even know existed. My eyes rolled back in my head as he thrust all the way in, his huge cock claiming me once and for all.

Because I was tied up and spread-eagle beneath him, he owned every inch of me. He increased the pace, and I realized what we were doing: *fucking*. There was no other word for it. My hips came down hard, meeting him thrust for ragged thrust, as waves of sensation broke over me.

"Fuck, Chloe—*yes*." His thrusts became harder, deeper, and I cried out. He lifted his hips, and his thumb found my clit. He plunged deeper, and I fought my restraints, loving the feel of being completely overpowered inside and out.

I started quaking from deep within. His cock stroked me inside, rough, driving, claiming. His thumb owned my clit. My whole body hummed, and I gave myself over to him—let him claim me, possess me, own me from the inside out. The orgasm built, unlike anything I'd ever experienced. My whole body was singing, humming with the vibration of Bryce. He thrust deeper, and I heard him cursing and grunting as his own orgasm gathered. I stayed with him, my *husband*, my body awake to every sensation, his every touch.

His thrusts got harsher, more urgent, and I could tell he was about to come undone. I bucked my hips, taking him all the way in. His cock hit me at just the right angle, and I cried out.

"Bryce!"

His whole body tensed. *"Chloe! Fuck!"*

He came, his hot seed shooting deep inside. My pussy spasmed as it greedily drank every ounce of him up. My whole body shuddered as I shattered, wholly undone, my orgasm enveloping his.

His thrusts became ragged, then finally slowed and stopped as he clung to me. After a moment, he pulled out. I started to object until he undid my restraints and pulled me tightly against his chest, kissing me, holding me tight. Bryce was breathing hard. "That was incredible."

I shivered and clung to him. I didn't have words for how I felt. I was too overtaken by both the physical sensation and my feelings, which were raw and completely overwhelming.

"You're mine," he whispered, cradling me against his chest. "Forever."

"Forever," I agreed.

I rested against him, wanting to say more. *I love you.* It was the truth—irrevocable, undeniable, and wildly inconvenient. But I felt my love with every cell of my body as I clung to him, never wanting to let go.

Then—with my face pressed tightly against my husband's chest, and happier than I'd ever been in my life—I fell into a deep, dreamless sleep.

reaching

THE NEXT TWO days passed in a blur of lovemaking and intense pleasure. We couldn't seem to get enough of each other; we were constantly touching, always at each other's side. Every time Bryce left me for a moment, I felt cold.

I wanted him, but it was bordering dangerously close to *need*.

After he penetrated me for the first time, Bryce let me sleep. I needed it—I was almost knocked out by the depth of my orgasms. He nudged me awake the following day, and we made slow, intense love. There were no handcuffs this time, just the two of us.

He stared into my eyes and thrust, his big body claiming mine. *I love you.* I couldn't say it to him in words, so I said it with my body, giving myself to him, crying out when he made me come again and again. I relished the new feelings he'd awoken inside of me, pleasure and need and yearning. I felt connected to him, close in a way I hadn't thought myself capable of. What had happened back at the house—with Joren, Dr. Bryan, even Felicia Jones—had slipped away, obfuscated by my happiness.

I recognized that this was dangerous.

Fool that I was, I couldn't stop myself from falling.

After breakfast that morning, we finally went swimming. "It's warm!" I couldn't believe how clear the water was. A school of small fish swam by me, and I yelped. "Oh my God—fish!"

"We *are* in the ocean, Chloe." Bryce swam under and grabbed me, lifting me up. "But don't worry—I'll save you." He grinned and kissed me, and then suddenly, we weren't laughing anymore. He gazed down at me and devoured me with a deep kiss. I wrapped my legs around his waist. He was already hard again, hard for *me*.

We kissed for a minute, his hands on my ass, grinding me against his thick shaft. We were outside, but there was no one around for miles. Turquoise water stretched out as far as the eye could see. The beach's white sand was our only witness; the school of fish was long gone.

The beautiful scenery fell away. It didn't matter where we were—all that mattered was Bryce. My desire for him consumed everything else, set it on fire, until all that was left was ashes. I had to have him again, and it didn't matter how sore I was. It didn't matter that I couldn't control myself or that my desire was taking over and trampling everything in the way. I was burning, out of control, and the only thing that could save me was my husband.

I needed him again. And I felt like it wasn't ever going to stop...

He must've felt the intensity, too, because he carried me out of the water. Bryce didn't bother going back to the bedroom—he deposited me onto an outdoor couch and turned me around, so I was on all fours. "I need you, and I need to be deep. Are you ready for me?"

"Yes. Yes Bryce, *please*..." I squirmed against him, already painfully aroused.

"Hmm, let's see..." Wrenching my thong suit to the side, he immediately put his mouth on me.

"Bryce!" His tongue felt incredible. I cried out, bucking against him, as he sucked on my slit, sliding his mouth up and nibbling on my clit. Before I was ready, I came hard, spasming into his mouth. His laughter vibrated against my clit, and I cried out again, so wet and needy I could barely fucking stand it. "I want you," I panted, "I *need* you inside me."

"I know." I didn't have to see his face to tell how fucking smug he was. Ugh!

But he needed me, too. He notched himself inside me and mounted me from behind, entering me all at once.

My eyes rolled back into my head. "Oh my God!" He was in *so deep* that way. I almost couldn't handle it, but at the same time, it was exactly what I wanted. I was completely filled by him.

"Fuck! You're so fucking *tight*." He stayed still for a moment, letting me adjust to his thickness. Then he grabbed my hips and pulled me against the base of his shaft—so I could feel his power, how huge he was, and understand I was entirely at his mercy.

Holy hell. He was in deep, so deep that way. He put his palms on my lower back and thrust slowly. I held stock still, taking it, his cock already stroking the spot inside me that made me see stars.

"Are you trying to make me come, Virgin?" he growled.

"I'm not a virgin anymore." He wasn't the only one who had power! I reached between our legs and cradled his balls. They were heavy. I rubbed and squeezed them, and he let out a litany of curses, his thrusts getting more ragged.

"What. The. Fuck. *Chloe.*" He fucked me harder, and I loved it.

In response, I lightly tugged on his balls.

"*Now* you're going to get it." He picked up the pace, and I cried out. Bryce fisted my hair, pulling me back against him as he rode me.

Oh fuck

Oh fuck

"*OH FUCK!*" I shattered around him, and he picked up the pace, driving his cock into me while tugging on my hair. I was wholly undone—stars danced in front of my eyes as I flew high, my husband still pumping his delicious body into mine.

I gripped him with my pussy, muscles clenching and twisting. Bryce grunted, tugging my hair, and I knew he was close. "Yes, Chloe, yes—" He slammed himself inside, all the way, as he came into me hard. "Chloe —*fuck!*"

He spent himself, cursing while he pumped his hips, completely lost in the moment. I couldn't help but smile as he emptied himself into me. I felt so full, so satisfied, and admittedly a little smug. *I'd* made him feel this way. He was inside *me*, loving *me*, and it was *me* that had made him come so hard he was out of his goddamned mind.

Bryce stilled and then maneuvered beside me, drawing me to his chest. We both were breathing hard. He cradled me against his enormous muscles, kissing my cheek and the top of my head, holding me close. I never wanted this moment to stop. I wanted to be with him like this forever, our bodies wrapped around each other, safe in his arms.

The rest of our getaway continued in the same vein. I lost count of the number of times we made love. Bryce kept reaching for me. I couldn't get enough of him. I was in a constant state of arousal, incessantly wet, needy, aching.

He must've sensed my mood: he gave me exactly what I wanted, everything I didn't even know I needed, by giving me himself.

He surrounded me—invaded me—and I loved it. Bryce was just so *big*. Not just his penis, although that was freaking huge; it was all of him. He seemed larger than life. To have his full attention was like the sun shining down on me after a long, bitter winter. I felt myself start to unfold, to open up toward his light.

I was his queen for the rest of our romantic weekend. With Bryce holding me, kissing me, my face pressed against his broad chest, I was literally the luckiest girl in the world. I could die of happiness just from looking at him, just from being in his arms. Nothing else mattered.

I'd never felt like this before, but I recognized it for what it was.

I was in love with him.

God help me.

I watched him while he slept. How was it possible that God had made such a perfect man? His full lips were slightly open, his breath coming in adorable little puffs. In his sleep, his handsome face was relaxed, a bit of scruff covering the light tan he'd gotten over the past few days. His thick hair was tousled, unruly from having my hands run through it while we'd made love again. His chest was powerful, the vast muscles rising and falling peacefully.

A yearning unlike anything I'd ever experienced swept through me; tears sprang to my eyes. How had this person, someone I'd just met—someone I didn't even *like* at first—become so important to me?

I knew that sex wasn't love. My mother, a nurse at heart, taught me how your hormones flood you and influence your feelings when you're physically attracted to someone. But she'd always been clear: *sex isn't love.* It was something that you did with *someone* you loved.

I was doing it with Bryce. And although I enjoyed

the sex—immensely, overwhelmingly—in some ways, even though I was inexperienced, it was the easy part. The feelings I was having were much more treacherous to navigate. I wasn't sophisticated, but I knew myself well enough to understand that this was neither a first crush nor a strictly physical connection.

My heart was involved. My whole heart. It was as if he'd taken it, all at once, and I would never be the same. Part of me was attached to him forever, and I hadn't even had a chance to decide whether this was a good idea. It most certainly was not. And yet, it was already decided. It was already done.

I was in love with him, for better or for worse.

It was getting late, and we had an early flight home. I pouted as I headed for the bathroom; I had no desire to leave our secluded island. I missed Noah, of course, and I was excited to be back with him. I *needed* to be with him—that was where I belonged. Still, I'd enjoyed every second of being alone with Bryce. We'd built something between us. It felt like a secret world, a kingdom where only he and I mattered—our touch, our closeness, our love.

Of course, I wasn't kidding myself that he felt the same way about me. Bryce was so much older. Before meeting me, he'd had a whole history, a whole life. I understood that he'd been hurt in the past. I just prayed that, in time, he would come to trust me, to believe that my feelings for him were real. I would prove to him every day that he was my priority, my one true love. Maybe at some point, it would be enough to convince him that I was worthy of *his* love...

I stared at myself in the mirror. I was not the same girl. The weekend of non-stop sex had left little room for eating; my cheeks were hollowed out, my eyes huge in my face. My body even looked different to me—ripe, sexy, touched. I would never be the same. Bryce had taken me and possessed me. I was *his*, and he'd unlocked my body's secrets.

My cheeks heated as I thought about all the different ways he'd made love to me. Even when it had been urgent, every touch and caress had been underscored by something else, something powerful. Was I imagining it, or had Bryce started to have feelings for me? The way he looked at me, the way he cradled me against his chest, the way he came *so hard* inside me, screaming my name...

Maybe he already thought I was worthy. I was afraid to hope for that, but still. My heart squeezed. I climbed back into bed with him, kissed him lightly on the shoulder, and said my prayers. *Let him love me back, God. Please.* I was ashamed to ask God for something like that, but I figured that lying to myself—

pretending that wasn't what I wanted—would be a far worse sin.

I rolled toward him, and in the semi-darkness, the screen of his phone lit up. Someone had texted him an image.

I knew it was wrong, but I leaned over him to look, telling myself it was in case of an emergency at home.

It was a picture of Gene Windsor laughing, his arm thrown around Felicia Jones's shoulders. She was laughing, too. The text read:

See? Some things never change. Red heart emoji.

I recoiled, feeling as if I'd been slapped. Felicia was texting Bryce? His ex-girlfriend was taking selfies with his father—*my* new father-in-law—and sending them to him while we were on our honeymoon?

My heart hammered in my chest. *No, no, no.*

Shaking, I slid out of bed. I grabbed Bryce's phone from the nightstand. I knew it was wrong to look. But what if Bryce had been texting her back? What if I'd been so busy falling in love with him, I'd been too blind to see that he'd been thinking about someone else all weekend?

I'd seen Bryce with his phone—he had the fancy kind that operated with facial recognition. I took the phone, pressed the home button, and held it in front of his sleeping face. It automatically unlocked, revealing his home screen. There were more apps than I knew what to do with, but I quickly found his messages. Feeling like I was about to throw up, I hustled back to the bathroom and locked the door behind me.

I slumped onto the cool tile floor and stared at the screen. It was wrong to snoop through someone else's messages, I knew that. But it would be worse if I assumed anything. Maybe Bryce hadn't texted her back. Perhaps this was the first message Felicia had sent him.

I opened the app with shaking hands.

Felicia Jones was the top thread. I clicked on her name and was stunned to see dozens of text messages from her, mostly pictures—of the island, selfies *on* the island, selfies *in her fucking bikini* on her boat, pictures from the club, from Bryce's father's house, with Bryce's father. Most of her captions were chatty and familiar, trying to remind him of things:

Remember Butler's Cove?
Our favorite seat at the club!
The sunset's not the same without you!

Bryce hadn't replied to her. At least, he hadn't appeared to. I wasn't very tech-savvy, so I didn't know if he could delete his responses. But one of her texts indicated that she hadn't heard back from him:

I know you're "busy" and all, but c'mon. You know you're still thinking about me.

One thing was for sure: Felicia Jones was a fucking cunt. I'd only used that word once before and had assumed that Lydia would be the only one to deserve the label. But nope. Felicia Jones was back from the dead and texting my husband, including pictures of her in a bathing suit, which made her a fucking cunt in my book.

Hands still shaking, I cleared the apps and headed back to the bedroom. I put the phone on the nightstand, then climbed back into bed beside Bryce. His chest still rose and fell rhythmically. He was peacefully asleep.

But I worried I would never feel peaceful again.

THIRTY

catch and release

"CHLOE. *Chloe.* Wake up, sweetheart, we're going to miss our flight."

I blinked my eyes open. Bryce's handsome face stared down at me. "I wanted us to have enough time to jump in the water before we left." He grinned. "You up for it?"

I smiled back, but then memories of the night before came crashing down. I winced.

Bryce's brow furrowed. "What's the matter?"

"Nothing!" I shook my head, forcing myself to stay in the moment—to stay with Bryce. "I'd love to go swimming."

"Good." He kissed the tip of my nose, and my stomach did a somersault. "I'll meet you out there—I just have a few quick emails to do."

My stomach went from somersaulting to lurching as he picked up his phone and ambled out toward the living room. *Fuck.* Would he be able to tell that I'd looked at his messages?

More importantly, was he looking at fucking Felicia Jones's pictures, wishing he was with *her*?

I'd never experienced jealousy before. I had no context for the sick feeling that invaded me, the hot roiling of my stomach. What if he wished he never married me? What if he was going to get back together with her? What if our new marriage was already over before it had even had a chance to begin?

Thoughts swirling, I picked out the sexiest bikini Midge had packed. It was black, strapless, with a tiny scrap of a bottom.

If I was going to have to compete with fucking Felicia Jones, well... I was going to fucking compete!

But I paused before leaving the room. I needed a moment of reckoning. I knew the truth now: I was in love with Bryce. I wanted desperately to go back to last night—to him making love to me, calling my name, cradling me against his chest as he fell into a deep sleep. To the time and space before I'd seen the evil text messages, to the moment when I'd felt safe and protected as he held me. To feeling wildly happy and in love with my new husband.

Steady, girl. I was going to have to watch myself from here on out. Felicia Jones had broken Bryce's heart. She'd been the one to leave *him*—it hadn't been his choice to end their relationship. She might be offering him something he never stopped wanting. I needed to stay wary, on guard. If I stopped myself from falling for him even harder, maybe I could survive whatever was coming.

Maybe.

"Woah." Bryce wolf-whistled when I emerged onto the deck. He pulled his sunglasses halfway down, raking his gaze over me. His penis became erect beneath his swim trunks, tenting them almost immediately.

"You like this?" I pointed to the bikini, what there was of it. The teasing tone of my voice didn't match the hurt I was feeling inside. *Has he been texting her? Was he just looking at her picture from last night?*

"I think you can tell I like it." Mirroring me, he pointed to his dick. "Now, let's get in the water before I bend you over that couch again."

I longed for him to take me, to bend me over and penetrate me, to show me that I was *his*. "Do we have time to do both?"

Bryce grinned. "Yes, because we are going for a *very fucking quick* swim. C'mere." He held out his hand.

Fool that I was, I went to him.

We splashed into the turquoise water, holding hands, laughing. We both went under, enjoying the warm surf as it enveloped us. I pushed my swirling emotions to the side, determined to enjoy the moment.

It was a quick swim, indeed. Bryce pulled me close and kissed me deeply. I moaned, clutching his back. Before I knew it, he'd carried me back to one of the pool deck's chairs and had toweled me off. He sat down, and I knelt before him, sliding off his swim trunks. His thick, elongated cock sprung out at me, glorious in the morning sun.

"What are you doing...?" But he knew exactly what was going to happen. Bryce groaned and threw back his head as I took him in my mouth, licking and sucking on the head. "Fuck, Chloe. Don't make me come like that. I want you."

"You can have me. In a minute." I went to work on him, sucking and swallowing him whole. I cradled his balls, applying the light pressure that made him grunt in pleasure as I ran my tongue along the head of his crown. We'd only been alone for two days, but I'd paid careful attention to what my new husband liked. So I sucked his dick *exactly* the way he liked it—and within a minute, he was fisting my hair, holding my head down as he pumped his hips.

"*Fuck*, Chloe." I could taste his saltiness, and pure

female pride bloomed inside my chest. *I* was the one who was about to make him come. *I* was the one who was giving him pleasure, who was spending the weekend with him at his secluded estate. He'd fallen asleep each night with *my* head pressed against his chest.

Me, not her. ME.

We'd been together every minute. He'd had his arms around me the entire time. Maybe he did feel something for me, maybe my fears were unfounded... In any event, we were together now. I intended to make the most of it.

I knew he was close, so I undid my bikini top, climbed up, and straddled him. I'd only been on top one other time that weekend, and I'd enjoyed it. *I* was in control now. Bryce's pupils were huge, his mouth open as he ran his hands down me, wild with desire. I didn't hesitate—I wrenched my thong to the side, notched his cock inside of me, and slid all the way down.

"Oh fuck!" His voice was strangled. Bryce shuddered, his huge cock twitching inside me, my pussy spasming around him.

I knew what he liked. I'd paid close attention because I wanted badly to please him. Bryce liked to take his time, but sometimes, he wanted it hard and fast. I was going to give it to him. He wasn't going to want anybody but me, not ever again.

I positioned my legs beneath me so that I could pulse up and down, gently at first. Then I increased my speed until I was slamming down on him, his cock filling me, while Bryce's head lolled back and the muscles in his chest flexed like God's greatest gift.

He gripped my hips, and then *he* was in control, moving me up and down, slamming his cock into me, the cords standing out on his neck. He leaned forward and devoured my breast, taking it into his mouth and sucking hard on my nipple.

The sensation drove me wild. And the harder he slammed me on his shaft, the harder my clit rubbed against him. I was going insane. A myriad of sensations exploded inside me, and I saw colored lights. "Yes, Bryce —*yes!*" I shattered, riding him hard. He held my hips and lifted me a little, driving back into me, his gloriously hard cock reaching me deep, so deep inside.

"I'm going to come—ah, fuck Chloe! What are you doing to me?" He came in a torrent, his hot seed filling me, pushing me over the edge again. My body spasmed, my pussy greedily clutching his shaft, sucking up every bit of his seed.

We shuddered against each other, and he clutched

me to his chest. When our spasms subsided, he said, "I wish we didn't have to go back."

I clung to him. "Me, too."

He kissed the top of my head. "But I need to work, and you need to be with your brother."

I nodded, not wanting to speak.

He wrapped his arms more tightly around me. "We can come back, you know. This is our special place now."

Tears sprung to my eyes. Did he mean that? Afraid to speak, I kissed his chest in response.

"We'll come back soon. That bed will always have a special place in my heart." He chuckled, suddenly playful.

"Me too." I peered up at him.

"My little Virgin isn't a virgin anymore." Bryce sounded quite pleased with himself. "And I enjoyed the hell out of the whole process."

"Me too," I said again.

He laughed and held me closer. "This has been a great weekend. I didn't realize how badly I needed it."

"Me either," I said, just to mix things up.

He pulled back and inspected me. "You're not very talkative this morning."

I shrugged, trying to maintain my composure. "I guess I'm sad we're leaving."

He smiled at me, and it was like the sun coming out. "Then we'll have to plan our next trip back. Want to come down next month? I'm sure my company can spare me. Hell, I'm running the place now."

My heart rate kicked up. If he was making future plans with me, maybe there was hope. "I'd love that, Bryce."

He kissed my nose again. "Then it's a date. Mrs. Windsor gets what Mrs. Windsor wants."

He sounded so upbeat, so *sure*. My heart lifted with longing.

"You know what? *Mr.* Windsor gets what he wants, too. And he wants one more turn in the bed." Bryce grinned at me. "Are you up for it?"

"Yes." I threw my arms around his neck, reveling in his attention, his touch, his desire. *I love you, Bryce.*

He picked me up and carried me to our bedroom, where he made me forget my worries again, at least for a little while.

I wasn't sure how I'd feel about returning to the house in Maine. But as we climbed up the dock, the waves crashing against the shore, the majestic home rising above us, the green firs all around—my heart lifted.

It felt, strangely, like coming home.

Noah was out on the front lawn, playing with the puppy. He waved when he saw me. "Chloe—hi!"

I ran to him, even though he would probably mock me for it later. "Hi, buddy!" I hugged my brother, relieved to see his smiling face. "Did you have an okay weekend?" I peered at his face, investigating him for signs of abuse or neglect.

He wrenched himself free. "Of course I did. We went fishing, I caught a *huge* fish—Dale made me release it because he's a big weenie—and Chef made me *fried ice cream*. Did you even know you could fry ice cream? Oh and I reached the new level of Fortnite. I got a victory *royale*, it was so sick!"

"That's awesome, except for the part where you called Dale a weenie. You shouldn't say that."

"Whatever." Noah rolled his eyes. "I said it to his face already and you know what he said? That I was right!" The puppy rolled on its back, and Noah headed for it, dismissing me.

"My trip was awesome. Thanks for asking."

Bryce joined me at my side. "Hey Noah."

"What's up, Bryce?" My brother kept playing with the dog.

It occurred to me that I hadn't really talked to Noah since Bryce yanked us off the boat during his hissy fit. In a show of solidarity, I linked my hand with my husband's. I wanted Noah to know everything was okay —in fact, it was better. I hoped.

"Bryce and I were wondering if you wanted to go fishing one night this week when he gets off work. Does that sound okay?"

Bryce glanced at me, then nodded. "Would you like that, Noah? I have a special cove that's great for fishing at dusk." He leaned closer to me and whispered, "Not *that* cove."

I laughed. "Good."

Noah was busy playing with the puppy but not too busy to pass up an invitation to fish. "Yeah, that would be all right."

"Perfect. I'm looking forward to it." Bryce squeezed my hand.

"Me too. Hey, I gotta take the puppy for a walk. He's supposed to go pee." My brother hopped up.

"Want me to go with you?" I asked.

"Nah I'm fine!" Noah hollered as he ran off, the puppy at his heels.

I sighed, watching him retreat. "He seems really happy."

"I agree. We need to start looking into schools for him for the fall."

I took a deep breath. "Before, back in Boston, you mentioned boarding school—"

"We don't need to do that," Bryce said immediately. "There's a private academy in Ellsworth, a day school, that should be fine for him. I'll have Dale look into it. Or we can get him a tutor if you prefer."

I gaped up at my husband. "You mean he could live here and go to school?"

Bryce nodded. "He's your brother, and he's young. He's been through a lot. He seems happy here. I think it's for the best, don't you?"

My eyes pricked with tears. Bryce had been so cold when I first met him, so *mean*. And now he was wonderful, saying and doing things I hadn't even let myself dream about... "I agree. He'd be so happy living here and going to school every day. I really appreciate it, Bryce. Thank you."

He bent down and kissed my lips. "It's my pleasure. It's never too late to do the right thing—at least, that's what my mother used to say."

"She did? What was she like?"

Bryce stared out at the lawn. "She was very kind. The opposite of my father. She used to keep him grounded, I think. He hasn't been the same since she died."

"I'm sorry to hear that."

He shrugged a big shoulder. "He's made his own choices. At the end of the day, we all do."

He sounded so introspective that I yearned to hear more. But Hazel came bustling out of the house, her spindly stick legs hauling a mile a minute. "Mr. Windsor, Mrs. Windsor." She nodded at both of us, but she only had eyes for Bryce. "I'm so glad you're back, Sir. Do you have a few minutes? I need to catch you up on some of the estate's...activities." She glanced down, taking in our entwined hands. "I trust you had a nice visit to the island?"

"It was wonderful, thank you, Hazel. And yes, I'll be happy to meet with you. Let me get Chloe settled first, okay? I'll come and find you."

She gave a curt nod and headed back inside the house, black stockings flashing.

"What do you think she wants to talk to you about?" I asked. My stomach was already sinking. Of course, it was about the Jones family. What was it Midge had said? That Hazel and Felicia Jones had been close. Hazel probably wanted to tell Bryce all about the dinner, maybe lobby for her former mistress...

"Chloe, is everything all right?" Bryce was watching me.

"Of course," I lied.

"Good. Let me bring you to your room. I think my

father wants to see us for cocktails this evening." Bryce scowled. "So you might want to rest up."

"Okay." But nothing was okay because after bringing me to my suite and kissing me goodbye, Bryce was gone. The happy bubble of our weekend was over, and it was back to the real world.

I had no idea what that might mean for us.

spark

"I'M sorry I didn't text you again, but I wanted you to relax and enjoy yourself. And you *did*, didn't you? That's a complexion only a thousand orgasms can give you." Midge winked at me as she bustled around my room, sorting laundry and unpacking my suitcase.

I sighed. "But what happened with Felicia? She was here for dinner? What did you hear? Please tell me everything."

Midge scowled as she hung up one of my dresses. "It was a cluster. Daphne *hates* Felicia, and the feeling is mutual. But Old Gene loves her—probably because she was nasty to his son, and he gets off on that."

I braced myself, waiting to hear more. "Why does Daphne hate her?"

The maid raised her eyebrows. "Are you kidding me?

Felicia Jones is Daphne's worse fricking nightmare. She has the pedigree, she has the body, she has her own fortune. Felicia doesn't need to marry some old coot to buy a yacht—she already *has* a yacht."

She saw the look on my face and winced. "She's got nothing on you, Chloe. Everyone's talking about how happy Mr. Windsor seems, how they haven't seen him this relaxed in years."

A tiny spark of hope lit my chest. "Really?"

"Really." Midge grinned at me. "A sexy weekend and a thousand orgasms will do that for you! Now, let's pick out a special dress for your drinks with Old Gene and Daphne tonight. I want them to see you shine."

I watched as she dug through the wardrobe, fingering different fabrics. "So...what was Felicia like? What did the staff say? What about Hazel—did she talk to her?"

"I know it probably seems like a big deal that she's back and all," Midge said, not looking at me, "but you shouldn't get obsessed. Like I said, she's got nothing on you. Bitch just doesn't like that she dropped her toy on the floor, and then somebody else came along and picked it up. That's on *her*. She's just looking for trouble, that's all. Don't let her ruin your good thing."

I nodded, taking her words in. "She's beautiful, though, huh? And like you said, she's got the body."

"She's no you." Midge whipped her head around. "*You've* got the body—and don't forget who Bryce married. Not to mention who he whisked away for a sexy weekend. *You.* Don't let that bitch get in your head, I'm telling you. That's exactly what she's trying to do."

I sighed. "So you think she wants Bryce back?"

Midge snorted. "Until she gets him. Then it'll be, like, *huh. Maybe he's not what I wanted.* Again. Mr. Windsor's too smart to fall for that shit. Don't you worry about it."

She dug through the wardrobe, making small talk, picking out flattering dresses, trying to make me feel better.

But I knew that no matter how much she tried to build my shaky confidence, it was already faltering.

"Ah, the Prodigal Son returns!" Gene Windsor shook his already empty rocks glass in our direction. "And his beautiful, nubile bride. You two are looking...refreshed."

Gene's watery blue eyes took in our entwined hands, the way Bryce stood close to me. "I trust you had a good vacation?"

Bryce wrapped his arm around my waist and palmed my hip. "We had an *excellent* vacation, Father.

Chloe and I enjoyed every second of the trip. The house is in great shape—the staff did a wonderful job, as always."

"Yes, well. They get paid to clean an empty house. It's not exactly a demanding task." He didn't thank the server, who appeared out of thin air and refreshed his drink.

"Where's Daphne?" Bryce asked.

"On her way. She had a late workout to film." Gene had a deep sip from his drink. "Would you two like anything?"

"Water," Bryce answered for both of us.

Gene arched an eyebrow. "Trying to avoid whiskey dick, eh? There's a pill for that, you know."

Bryce smiled, a little smug. "I don't need a pill."

"I see." Gene's eyes raked down us again, and I could tell that *he* could tell that our marriage had, in fact, been thoroughly consummated. "Exuma's always been a bit of an aphrodisiac. Something in the water."

Bryce leaned down and whispered, "I think it was more to do with the thong bikinis."

My cheeks heated as Gene watched us, eyebrow still arched. "We had company while you were gone, Son. The Jones family came for dinner."

"I heard." Bryce didn't sound happy about it.

I stiffened.

"Felicia seemed well," Gene continued, eyes sparkling. "She's making some positive changes in her life, it seems."

Bryce shrugged.

"I told her that you'd be sorry you missed her." Gene finished his new drink in one gulp. "Interesting that she's back, don't you think?"

"Not particularly."

Daphne appeared at her husband's side. She didn't look like herself—her skin was pale, dark circles barely concealed by heavy makeup. "Hey Daphne."

"Bryce. Chloe." She faked a smile. "You guys are looking good—must be nice, having a sexy weekend away." She glared at her husband. "I wouldn't know. Your father just wants to keep me on this island, having dinners with old white men in blazers. I think he's trying to do me in."

"I'd be much more direct about it if that was the case." Gene winked at her.

"Anyway, I'm *so* glad you're back." Daphne seemed to perk up a little as a server brought her a glass of wine. "Stupid Mimi Jones talked your father into hosting the Friends of the Museum benefit. It's next week! We've never done an event here. There's going to be at least a hundred people—anyway, I could really use your help, Chloe. It's a logistical fucking nightmare."

"I'd be happy to help out." I'd never even hosted a birthday party for Noah, but whatever.

"You're hosting it *for* Mimi Jones?" Bryce asked his father.

"We're co-hosting." Gene smiled at him, and it was not a nice smile. "I already told Daphne that Mimi and Felicia would be happy to pitch in."

Daphne put her hand on her hip. "Over my dead body. If they wanted to host it, they could've done it themselves. Instead, they put it on us, and I'm not letting them take all the credit. Chloe and I will handle it. It's next Thursday—are you all free?"

"Um..." I glanced at Bryce. His lips were pressed together. "Bryce? Is that okay?"

He stared at his father as he said, "It's fine."

Gene seemed to gloat a little. "The Joneses and the Windsors, together again. It'll be just like old times."

Bryce pulled me closer. "Hardly."

"I'm sure Felicia will be thrilled to see you so... settled." Gene held up his empty glass, and the server scurried to refill it. "Now, let's talk about the Walden deal, Son. Things went to hell this weekend. The survey crew says we have a problem, and I'm ready to cash out."

"Then we'll get a new surveyor—I'm telling you, that parcel's in an up-and-coming neighborhood."

Bryce sighed and turned to me. "Can you excuse me for a moment, sweetheart? I need to talk to my father about this before it blows up."

"Of course." I felt eyes on us as Bryce leaned down and kissed me, gently but firmly, before leaving my side. He and Gene sat down near the fire pit and started discussing the Walden deal. Neither one of them looked happy.

"You are *so* lucky you were away when the Joneses came over." Daphne was already all up in my business. Upon closer inspection, I could see that although she looked lovely as ever, she was definitely wearing a ton of concealer. She didn't appear to have slept well.

"Oh really?" I played dumb. "How come?"

"Ugh, Felicia Jones is the *worst*. You know who she is, right? Bryce's ex?"

I shrugged, hoping I appeared unaffected even though my heart was pounding.

"I've never met someone so self-satisfied, I swear to God." Daphne chugged some wine. "She just sits there and *listens*—silently passing judgment, of course—and then when she finally talks, it's dead silence and everyone hangs on her every word. She's just so fucking *superior*. Like, *I don't have social media because I don't need external validation of my internal goals* and blah fucking blah blah blah. And she quit drinking, so now she's the sobriety guru, too." Daphne rolled her eyes. "Just fucking shoot me."

"But Gene likes her?"

Daphne snorted. "Gene *loves* her. They're old money, and he loves old money. And I think he likes that she blew his son off."

"That's mean," I said.

"He's just jealous of Bryce. He wishes he was still young—that he could do it all again. But he can't. And it makes him nasty." She turned, watching our husbands as they talked. "I don't even care anymore. We have a prenup. If I decide to get a divorce, I'll be fine. I won't have the yacht anymore, but then again, I won't have to deal with *him*."

I studied her face. "You're thinking about it?"

She shrugged. "I hate to admit it, but fucking Felicia Jones got under my skin. She was talking about living her best life and not having any regrets—I'm worried I might be on the wrong path."

"Is that why she's back?" It felt like I'd swallowed a boulder. "She wants to live her best life?"

Daphne glanced at me, and for the first time, I saw something genuine in her expression: she looked truly sorry for me. "She's back because Bryce is married, and she can't stand it. She never thought he'd actually find someone else."

"Oh." I swallowed hard. "Did she talk about him?"

Daphne frowned. "Not directly. It was more like she and Gene were taking a trip down memory lane, laughing and talking about all the vacations they'd gone on."

I didn't exactly trust Daphne, but she was right next to me, and she might be a valuable source of information. "What happened between them, anyway? Bryce hasn't said much."

"It was awful. Felicia got cold feet right after they sent out the wedding invitations. She packed up and left without telling him, then sent him a letter from Paris calling the whole thing off. Very dramatic. He didn't handle it well. And of course, it affected his position in the business."

I nodded, trying to appear calm even though hearing about Bryce hurting over someone else cut me. "And they haven't talked since?"

"I don't think so. He stayed up here for a long time, licking his wounds and working remotely. He didn't date anybody. Next thing you know, he walks in wearing a wedding ring and launches *you* on us." She glanced at me. "But he actually seems happy. I hate Felicia enough to be glad about that."

I took a deep breath. "Thanks, Daphne."

She finished her wine in one gulp. "I wouldn't thank

me yet. She's a tough person to have as an enemy, I'm not going to lie. Watch your back."

I nodded because there was little I could say to *that*.

Later that night, while Bryce slept, I grabbed his phone again. I didn't want to snoop behind his back, but at the same time, I had a sinking feeling I needed to be emotionally prepared for anything.

I held the phone toward his sleeping face and then crept into the bathroom, locking the door behind me.

There were a dozen more texts from Felicia, their tone becoming increasingly demanding.

I know you've gotten these, why don't you respond?

Finally, near the end of the thread, Bryce texted back.

I don't know why you came back now.

Her response gave me chills.

Because of you and me. Remember?

She'd sent it earlier that evening while we'd been with Gene and Daphne. Bryce hadn't texted her back. Yet.

I stared at *his* text, wondering at the emotion behind the words. Was he angry at her or despondent about her timing? I'd give anything to know how he felt.

For Felicia's part, her feelings were pretty straightforward. She wanted Bryce, and she wasn't afraid to put it out there. I remembered Daphne's words: *Watch your back.* I sighed and, putting the phone down, buried my face in my hands.

I would certainly watch my back if I thought it would help. But who was I to battle with Felicia Fucking Jones? She was an heiress. I was a glorified escort. She'd held Bryce's heart in the palm of her hand, and then she'd crushed it. I was a paid transaction to him—a contract. Maybe he'd warmed up to me a little, but he was most likely making the best of a bad situation.

He'd cried over her. He was pretending with me.

I didn't know what would happen to his position in the company if he divorced me. Would he lose everything he'd gained? Or would Old Gene approve of the move, glad that his son had reconciled with American royalty?

I would call Akira in the morning and have her go

over the contract again. If Bryce wanted out, I needed to know what Noah and I would be looking at...

I took a deep breath before returning to bed. It was easier to think about the contract, to focus on the financial and transactional aspects of things. What was going to undo me was my heart.

I was in love with Bryce. I didn't even care about the money anymore. But if he chose Felicia—and why wouldn't he?—it would tear my fucking heart out.

I crept back to the room and gently returned his phone to the nightstand. Bryce threw his arms around me in his sleep, pulling me close. I snuggled against him, feeling his powerful chest rise and fall against me.

I didn't sleep at all that night.

I'd known I was in trouble from the first moment I laid eyes on Bryce. I just didn't know it would be *this* brand of trouble...

The heartbreaking kind.

THIRTY-TWO

charity case

If I'd thought that Daphne was bad before, I quickly discovered that she was worse—much worse—than I'd guessed.

Planning the Friends of the Museum benefit stressed her out so much that she started eating carbohydrates. When she crammed an entire roll slathered with butter into her mouth, I knew we were in trouble. Daphne was awful to the staff, blaming them for her oversights and sniping at them when vendors didn't do what she wanted. Every messenger was shot point blank and also behind the back.

I quickly learned to stay out of her way. I did exactly what she asked, to the letter, and she still complained. But I continued to show up. One thing was for sure:

Mimi and Felicia Jones would be bowled over by this party, come hell or high water. Daphne was determined to show them up.

But after spending several days with her, I learned she had a hidden agenda. There was someone else she wanted to impress.

Multiple times a day, her phone lit up with notifications from an app called Calculator Plus. Confused by why she'd be receiving so many updates from a math app, I hit up my private browser as soon as I could. Turns out, it was an app that was used for cheating—it hid private messages, texts, and videos.

Oh boy. Old Gene wasn't going to like that one bit.

I shuddered, thinking about what would happen when he found out. Because that was the thing about cheating, wasn't it? Eventually, the other person *always* found out. At least, that was what my mom said when her friend from work discovered her husband was having an affair. "The truth always comes out in the end."

I wondered what that meant for Bryce and me.

He hadn't mentioned a word about Felicia. During the days, we'd been busy and apart from each other— I'd been Daphne's right-hand servant; he'd been busy trying to salvage his real estate deal. But every night, he came to my bed. We made love slowly, deeply, our bodies entwined and connected on every level. Afterward, he held me against his chest. I stayed awake as he drifted off to sleep. I stayed awake, thinking *I love you*.

But I never said it, because I was a coward.

I never said it, because I was afraid.

Checking Bryce's phone had become more than a bad habit—it had become an obsession, a compulsion. I scanned his sleeping face each night and then, heart thudding, locked myself in the bathroom while I read his texts.

Felicia continued to write to Bryce multiple times a day, sending selfies from various spots on MDI. She was hiking in the park, she was kayaking across the sound, she was having dinner at the restaurant. She was beautiful in each picture, of course. Her bare skin, sprinkled with freckles, shone brightly as she smiled. I decided, with a ferocity that surprised me, that I hated her fucking guts.

Bryce had texted Felicia back a total of three times. His most recent messages read:

Don't you have anything better to do?

And:

Looks like you've got too much time on your hands.

She sent back a picture blowing him a kiss. Did I mention I hated her fucking guts?

I longed to bring the texts up to Bryce, to talk to him about Felicia's reappearance. But I was too afraid of the truth. What if he admitted he still had feelings for her? Where did that leave me?

It would be a relief to tell Midge or even Daphne about her non-stop messages, just to have someone to talk to. But that would involve me admitting that I'd been breaking into Bryce's phone. I couldn't do that. If things got bad—if Bryce left me, if he wanted a divorce so he could get back together with Bitchface, as I'd taken to calling her—my behavior needed to be impeccable.

If he was going to break my heart, I would at least get the money. I didn't care about it, but I wasn't going to have my brother starve because Felicia Fucking Jones had returned from the dead.

When I crept back to bed each night, I watched him sleep. He hadn't done anything wrong, I told myself. Texting her back and saying that she had too much time on her hands didn't constitute cheating. Getting messages from her wasn't a crime, either, but it still made me uncomfortable.

Still, that he hadn't told me about her texts *was* reason to worry. He was hiding it from me. Hiding something was lying about something. That wasn't what I wanted in my marriage—even in my fake marriage, goddammit. I wanted to be in a relationship where I came first. I didn't know much, but I knew I didn't want to be in love with someone who kept secrets.

I was still in love with him, though. Fucking inconvenient.

I wished, more than anything, that I could call my mother. She would tell me what to do. She would probably advise me to pack my bags, contact Akira Zhang, cash out on my contract and buy a condo in a good school district. I continued to say my prayers and ask for a sign from her, but nothing happened.

Wrapped in Bryce's embrace each night, I felt alone more than ever.

The fundraiser was fast approaching, and I felt like I might be getting an ulcer. Daphne was so stressed out I'd found her eating a doughnut. Not only was she yelling at the staff, but she was also getting about thirty Calculator-Plus messages a day. Her dark circles were purplish, making me wonder if she was sneaking out at night.

Even though I didn't know for sure what she was up

to, I found myself disapproving. *Is it really so hard to do better?* I wondered. But then I'd swipe Bryce's phone again and feel like I was just as guilty as the liars and cheaters all around me.

For her part, Midge was on a mission to find me the perfect dress to wear to the gala. She'd been on the phone with a boutique in Bar Harbor non-stop, barking orders and having samples sent over. "You're going to be the prettiest girl there."

"Thanks, Midge." But I knew it wasn't true: Felicia Jones was the fairest of them all. I couldn't compete with someone like that.

The day of the benefit arrived, and I greeted it with another stomachache. I couldn't believe I would be at a party with Bryce's ex-fiancé that evening. That I would finally be meeting Felicia Jones face-to-face—with Bryce at my side. What the hell was going to happen?

At six-thirty a.m., Daphne was already zipping around the enormous outdoor tent where the party would be held. "Where have you been?" Her hair was up in a messy ponytail, and for the first time that week, she wore zero makeup. Her under-eye circles were on purplish display.

"I was getting coffee. I brought you one." I set down the extra-large mug I'd poured for her. "How're you doing?"

She took a large gulp. "Terrible. The caterer said they're out of the bluefish I wanted for an appetizer, the florist said they're going to be late—"

"I can have Dale pick up the flowers. He already offered. And what about the crab cake appetizer, instead? You were leaning that way to begin with." I smiled, hoping to calm her down.

"Okay...that might work." Her phone buzzed, and she glared at it. "Fuck! It's Mimi Jones—what the hell does she want?"

She clicked the phone and listened. "Yes Mimi, I know. M-hmmm. I won't sit the Prescotts near the Bloomsburys, I *know* they despise each other—"

She went quiet for a full minute. A small vein appeared near her temple and started to throb. "Of course we can take a photo. Yes, all of us. He knows we're co-hosting, you don't need to worry about it. All right Mimi, see you tonight. Looking forward to it!"

She shut off her phone and squeezed it so hard, I worried it might shatter. "That woman is *impossible*! She is literally the worst! She deserves every bad thing that is coming to her!" Daphne proceeded to swear as though a very drunk and irate pirate had momentarily possessed her.

"She wants to take pictures tonight?" I asked once the tirade subsided.

"Of course she fucking does." Daphne chugged her coffee. "She was worried Bryce wouldn't cooperate, but she's worried about the wrong thing. I'll show her," she snarled. She hustled off before I could ask what she meant.

Sighing, I got to work setting up the tables. It was going to be a long fucking day.

"My heart—literally, it's going to burst." Midge fanned herself. "I've never seen someone so beautiful! It's like you're out of a movie."

I peered at myself in the mirror. I was almost unrecognizable. Midge had blown my hair out stick-straight; it hung halfway down my back, smooth and glossy. The dress was stunning—pale pink, beaded, and floor-length. It weighed a ton, but it fit like a glove, showing off my curves. She'd applied my makeup so that it was tasteful and shimmery, and performed some sort of voodoo with eyeshadow so that my blue eyes stood out. "Thank you, Midge. I'm not feeling very optimistic about tonight, but at least I'm wearing a great dress."

"Chloe, *please*." She stopped fanning herself and stepped forward. "You listen to me. You have every reason to be optimistic. Mr. Windsor's been in here every night, all up in your business, and we all know it. He can't stay away from you. You don't have anything to worry about."

"She's been texting him." Tears threatened my spectacular eye makeup. "She's been sending him selfies every day."

"Of course she has—that *bitch*." Midge squared her shoulders. "She left *him*, Chloe. Remember that. Mr. Windsor's a brilliant guy—he sees through what she's doing. He was there when she burnt their house down. Don't let her get under your skin."

"Too late." I shook my head. "I feel like I already lost. I can't compete with *that*, with *her*. They have a whole history together—and like you said, she left *him*. It wasn't his choice to end the relationship."

"True, but it was absolutely his choice to move on." Midge smoothed my hair again, even though it was already perfect. "And he's done that with you. Like I said, none of us have ever seen him this happy. That's not for nothing. Don't let her make it seem like it doesn't mean anything. You won, Chloe. You already won."

I nodded, trying to let her wise words sink in. "Do you think I'm going to make it tonight?"

Midge winked at me. "I don't think it, I know it. Now go get 'em! The rest of the girls and I will be out there, working behind the scenes. I'll keep an eye out—we've got your back, Chloe."

"Thank you."

"You're welcome." She hugged me, careful of the dress. "Now don't start crying—you're going to smudge your mascara!"

I headed downstairs, gripping the railing for dear life. Because the tent had solid flooring, Midge had insisted I wear sky-high heels because, in her words, they made my butt look great.

"Wow Chloe." I'd been so worried about breaking my neck I hadn't even seen Bryce waiting for me at the landing. "You're absolutely stunning."

"Thank you." I smiled up at him. No matter what, I was always grateful to be reunited with my husband.

Bryce was jaw-droppingly handsome in a steel-blue suit that set off his eyes. His shoulders were massive, and his chest was broad beneath his jacket. I suddenly wished that we could just skip the stupid gala and go upstairs, where I could strip him out of his clothes and enjoy being held down by his big muscles. Such a better plan!

"Don't look at me like that, Chloe. I'll throw you

over my shoulder and take you back to your bedroom," he growled.

"Ugh, I wish you would."

"You look too pretty to hide. I guess I'll have to show you off, instead." He bent and kissed my cheek, inhaling my scent. "Have I ever told you that you're the most beautiful woman in the world?"

I blinked at him. "I am?"

He treated me to the rare, lopsided grin that I loved. "To me, you are."

"Thank you." The tears were threatening again. "That means a lot to me, especially tonight."

"Why is that?"

Could he really be so clueless? My mouth went dry, and my heart hammered in my chest as I realized we were about to go to the party and see *her*. "Because your ex is going to be here tonight. I'm dreading it, to be honest."

"Chloe." He took my hand and kissed it. "I didn't realize you were upset. I guess we haven't talked much about it."

"We haven't talked about it at all."

He ran a hand through his hair, making it spike. "That's because there's nothing to say. Felicia and I were together for a while, and then it ended. That's how these things usually go."

I opened my mouth and then closed it, trying to find the right words. "Have you seen her...much...since then? Since you broke up?"

"No. I haven't seen her at all, except when we passed them on the boat."

"Have you...talked to her?" I stammered the words as he took my arm and led me down the hall.

The staff came out and lined the hallway, smiling and complimenting us. I wished I'd waited to ask him about this when we could be alone, but the words had just tumbled out.

"Not really." He shrugged as we stopped at the door. Hazel was waiting nearby.

"You look lovely, Mrs. Windsor," the maid said. "Have a good time tonight."

Surprised, I stood up straighter. "Thank you, Hazel."

She pursed her lips as I clung to Bryce and headed outside. I felt her eyes on us as we crossed the lawn, and I wondered what she thought of her former mistress's return to the estate.

I wondered what she thought about us meeting.

"So... You haven't really talked to her?" I watched Bryce's face. He frowned at the tent, which was enormous and white under the quickly darkening sky.

"There isn't anything to say."

I thought of his text: *I don't know why you came back now.*

"Are you upset that she's here?" I could hear the nagging tone in my voice—he clearly didn't want to talk about it, and I clearly couldn't let it go.

He stopped walking and turned to face me. "I'm glad that *you're* here. Is that a good enough answer?"

I nodded. I wanted to believe that was the only answer, but my mind still raced with questions. Like, *why didn't you tell me she's been texting you so much? Why did you let your father agree to co-host this event with her freaking family?*

But I shoved them away, at least for now.

"Let's get this over with." The lopsided grin was gone, replaced by a look of resignation. "Stay by my side, okay? That will make this more tolerable."

"I will." I linked my arm through his. "I'll stay until you tell me to go."

"That's not going to happen."

I wanted, so badly, to believe him. I held my breath and onto him for dear life as we reached the tent. Daphne and Gene were stationed at the entrance. She looked stressed as she clutched her champagne. "Chloe —*there* you are!"

Daphne yanked me away from Bryce and practically

clawed my arm off. So much for staying by my husband's side! "Where have you been?"

"Walking slow because I'm trying not to die in these heels. But we're here now! And none of the guests have arrived yet." I took a quick look around the tent. The chandeliers were glowing, white tablecloths adorned the tables, and hundreds of candles flickered. The flowers were from a local farm and were gorgeous, bursting with color. "Daphne...it looks *amazing*. You did an incredible job! And you look beautiful, by the way."

To be honest, Daphne *did* look super sexy. Her white dress plunged to her waist, revealing her lithe build and pale skin. Her black hair tumbled over her shoulders, shiny and bouncy. She was dressed to thrill—and I wondered, not for the first time, just who she hoped to impress. Someone who had also downloaded Calculator Plus from the App Store, to be sure.

"Thank you." She lifted her chin, slightly mollified. "These servers are fucking incompetent, but at least it's past five o'clock." She chugged some champagne. "You look beautiful, too. That's a hot dress. I hope Felicia Jones chokes when she sees you."

"Ha."

"I'm not kidding." She drained her flute in one final gulp. "Her mother called me *seven times* today to make sure everything was all set. Can you believe that? She hasn't done one freaking thing to help us! But she had the nerve to pester me all day about whether the party would be a success. That's all right." Daphne straightened her shoulders. "I'll show her."

"Show her what?"

"Ugh, never mind—there they are—the Joneses. Just fucking shoot me, Felicia's wearing white, too."

The Jones family had, in fact, arrived. It was excruciating to look at them: Mimi Jones was toned and lean, with long legs. Her husband Michael was also tall, with white hair and a tanned, handsome face. Their son, William, was strapping and attractive, with a mop of brown hair and big shoulders. But the showstopper, of course, was Felicia Jones herself.

She wore a white column gown that was modest and yet somehow made her look impossibly sexy. Her hair was pulled into an elegant twist; huge diamond studs sparkled on her ears. Tonight she wore minimal makeup, which showed off her already too-pretty-to-look-at face.

She strode across the tent and headed straight for us. Once she got closer, she picked up speed. She didn't look to the left or to the right: she only had eyes for Bryce. She collided with him and wrapped her arms around his back, enveloping him in a huge hug.

"Holy shit, she's got nerve," Daphne whispered.

I just stood there, feeling like my heart was being ripped out.

Felicia Jones continued to hold Bryce tight, rocking him back and forth.

I wasn't sure if I had died in that moment...or if I had passed, and was already in hell.

beast mode

It seemed to take a full minute for Bryce to extricate himself from Felicia's bear hug.

Gene Windsor watched them, amused, a sparkle in his eye.

All I wanted was for the floor to open up and swallow me whole, but as usual, there was no such luck. When Bryce finally ducked out of her embrace, his face was red. He held out his hand for me. "Sweetheart, come here."

I tried to hold my head high as both the Windsor and Jones families stared at me. Felicia was the only one who didn't look in my direction: she still gazed, transfixed, at Bryce's face.

"This is my wife, Chloe Windsor. Chloe, this is Felicia Jones."

I forced myself to smile, but I needn't have bothered. Felicia didn't tear her gaze from Bryce. "Don't I get a title, too?"

I felt like I was invisible. I felt like I might be dead. *Had* the floor swallowed me whole...?

"Felicia, this is *Chloe*. My *wife*. Now if you will excuse us, we have somewhere else to be." He swept me away without another word. Mimi Jones was protesting in the background, claiming we'd snubbed the rest of the family, but Bryce headed straight for the bar. "Unfuck- ingbelievable."

"She's very...determined." That was the nicest way I could say it.

Bryce grunted as he motioned for the bartender. "A double bourbon, please. And a water."

"Is the bourbon for me?" I joked weakly, trying not to notice as Felicia and Mimi Jones sucked up to Gene Windsor while Daphne fumed. I tried not to watch them, to watch *her*. The fact that she'd had her arms around Bryce still had me seeing red.

"You might need one by the end of the night. God, I hate these things." He glared around the tent, avoiding looking in the direction of his ex and his father.

I had a sip of water, trying to steady myself. "Do I need to be worried about her?" I finally asked. My voice came out small. I *felt* small compared to the American

Heiress Felicia Jones, in all her column gown, I-don't-give-a-fuck-about-you splendor.

"You need to worry that she's a pain in the ass. But it'll all be over soon." He pulled me against his side and had a deep sip of his drink. "Once we leave here tonight, we won't have to see her again."

"That's good." I just hoped it was true.

The party started filling with people. We stood guard near the bar while Felicia and her family, flanked by Gene and Daphne, welcomed the incoming guests. I worried that Daphne would be angry that Bryce and I had fled, but she seemed pretty occupied greeting the newcomers.

I also noticed that she'd positioned herself directly next to Mr. Michael Jones and kept brushing up against him. Hmm...

"Chloe! So nice to see you again." Kelli Nguyen air-kissed me on both cheeks. "You look beautiful, of course."

"Thank you, Kelli. So do you." Kelli's biceps were on full display in her black jumpsuit. She wore a diamond choker that probably cost as much as a yacht.

She leaned forward, and I was engulfed by her perfume, something patchouli-esque. "How're you holding up? Felicia's a *nightmare*."

"She's something, all right." I forced a smile. "It was bad at first, but Bryce has me covered."

"Good." She gave me a bright, sincere smile. "Just don't turn your back for a minute. She's a piece of work, that one." Kelli went on to air-kiss Bryce, and my stomach sank to a new low.

Don't turn your back. Ugh. Maybe a hole in the floor could swallow Felicia!

After most of the guests had arrived, the Jones family dispersed into the crowd. Bryce was well into his second drink when Mimi Jones planted herself in front of us. She was tanned, tall, and impossibly smooth-skinned for her age, not a wrinkle in sight.

She put her hands on her hips and gave Bryce a look. "Well? Are you going to hide from me all night?"

"I'm going to try." Bryce's voice was ice. "This is my wife, Chloe Windsor. Chloe, this is Mimi Jones."

"Nice to meet you," I said.

Unlike her daughter, Mimi Jones looked me up and down. Her narrow gaze missed nothing; it lingered on my wedding ring, my collarbone, my pores. "You don't look familiar, dear. I heard you attended public school in Boston?"

"Yes, ma'am." I hoped she disliked being called ma'am.

Mrs. Jones seemed to arch her eyebrow, but there

was so much filler in her face I couldn't be sure. "My Felicia went to Miss Porter's, of course."

I nodded. "Of course."

She turned back to Bryce. "We'd like to do a photo for the foundation website. Family only, of course." Her gaze flicked to me.

"Of course." Bryce pulled me against him and made a big show of running his hand up and down my side. "It will be lovely to have my wife in the picture. I *love* showing her off to the world."

Mrs. Jones looked as if she wanted to respond, but she was thankfully interrupted by a friend—the one and only Kelli Nguyen. "Mimi? So sorry to interrupt, but I haven't seen you in ages!"

God bless Kelli! She swept old Mimi off and plied her with a fresh vodka martini.

I glanced at Bryce, who was finishing his drink and looked as though he wished the floor could swallow him whole, too. "Are you hanging in there?"

"I don't miss that pushy bitch." He sighed. "Here comes Daphne. Why do I have the feeling she's going to take you away?"

Daphne practically sprinted toward us. "Chloe, can I steal you for a minute? We're about to run out of caviar, I am at *my wit's end* with these servers, I've had three complaints about the seating arrangements—"

"Daphne, it's okay." I squeezed her arm. "Let's go talk to the caterers and figure out the caviar thing, I'm sure they can substitute something. Is that okay, Bryce? I'll be right back."

He pulled me to him for a very sexy, lingering kiss that had Daphne raising her eyebrows. "Promise me."

"I promise." I was still grinning, dopey from the kiss, as Daphne pulled me away.

"Okay, we need to see what else they can do for us." Daphne rattled off several other problems as we reached the tent's perimeter. "But also, Chloe? I need a favor. Can you act like we're going back to the house for a few minutes? Just stay out here—I need to take care of something. If Gene's looking for me, tell him you left me in the kitchen, and I'll be right back."

"Sure...?"

"Great!" said Daphne brightly. She immediately disappeared into the shadows, leaving me alone. I caught a glimpse of her white gown heading toward the fire pit.

Um... What the heck was she doing? Had the whole caviar fiasco been an act?

I stood in the shadows, twiddling my thumbs, feeling quite used. Daphne was definitely meeting up with Mr. Calculator Plus for no good. And now I was separated from Bryce. I crept closer to the tent, careful to stay out of view, and peered inside.

What I saw made my blood run cold.

Felicia Jones had made her move as soon as I'd left, THE FUCKING CUNT. She'd joined Bryce at the bar. To my horror, they were laughing about something. She threw her head back, her stupid chic chignon flashing in the candlelight, and howled with laughter.

Rage, unlike anything I'd ever felt, flooded me.

Bryce was laughing, too. What the *fuck*? He shook his head and looked down at her as if he was surprised and delighted that she'd cracked such a funny joke.

I wanted to run into the tent and scratch her eyes out—but that would be leaving Daphne out in the dark, unprotected.

So I did something even worse. A young server walked by—handsome, muscular. He smiled at me.

I smiled back.

"Hey, are you from MDI?" I asked flirtatiously.

"Just for the summer." He was my age with white, even teeth.

"Have you been on any good hikes lately? I wanted to try something new, but I'm not sure where to start." I twisted a lock of hair around my finger. I stuck my chest out at him. No one could see us on the outskirts of the tent. I wasn't sure exactly what I was starting—except trouble.

"Yeah, I actually just did a really cool hike. You start at Jordan Pond and take a trail up..." He was super descriptive about the route. I nodded and smiled, pretending to hang on his every word.

Out of the corner of one eye, I saw Bryce scanning the crowd. Felicia was still talking to him and staring at him adoringly, THAT FUCKING CUNT.

Out of the corner of my *other* eye, I saw a flash of white out on the grounds. *Daphne.* I also thought I saw *another* flash of white—someone's bare, pale ass, moving in a rhythmic motion. *Ugh.* I couldn't believe Daphne was cheating at the party, having sex out by the fire pit! Who *were* these people? All that Calculator-Plus texting must've been some foreplay, all right...

"But you need to watch out because there's two-way traffic, and some of the tourists don't observe the rules of the trail," the handsome dude continued. "I could take you some time if you want."

"I'd love that." I stepped closer to him, into the tent's light where we could clearly be seen.

"Sounds good." He smiled down at me. "Why haven't I seen you around here before?"

"I'm new." I was sticking my chest out so far, my back ached.

Everything happened at once. Bryce's gaze narrowed in on us while Felicia still stared up at him. I moved closer still to the server to brush up against him. In my best Felicia Jones imitation, I threw my head back and laughed—even though he'd started talking about poison oak and looked utterly confused by my response.

Then I moved closer still. My chest pressed against his chest.

Daphne came back to the tent, eyes wild, chest heaving, a triumphant expression on her face. Out of the darkness behind her, I could make out the shadow of a figure. It appeared to be zipping its pants. When it came closer, I realized it was Mr. Michael Jones.

Ew. I'd just seen Felicia's dad's white ass!

"Thanks for waiting for me," Daphne said breathlessly. She peered at me as I rubbed up on the unsuspecting server, who looked just as confused as she did.

"What are you doing?" Bryce was suddenly at my side, white-faced, furious.

"What does it look like?" My head throbbed. My vision tunneled. I was so *fucking mad* it was like I was out of my mind. "I'm making a new friend. I thought you might be too busy to notice," I bit out.

"Not another word." Bryce roughly grabbed me by

the arm, then turned to the server. "You're fired. Get the hell off my property. *Now.*"

"Easy dude, your girl was flirting with *me*—"

Without letting go of me, Bryce punched him in the face. The young man crumpled, going down hard, but Bryce didn't seem to care.

He was too busy dragging me back to the house.

chains

Bryce didn't stop, even as I fought against him. He didn't pause as he threw open the door and stormed past the staff, all of whom jumped out of our way and pretended to be very busy doing something—anything —else.

"Let go of me!" I hollered. "Why don't you go back and let Felicia tell you another fucking *joke*, huh? Why don't you go make a fucking fool out of me?! At least you'll finally make *daddy* happy!"

"Shut up, Chloe." His voice was icy, dangerous.

"Don't tell me to shut up!"

"Send Hazel to my suite," he told one of his men as we passed. "Tell her *now*."

"Yes, Sir." The man disappeared without missing a beat.

I struggled against Bryce, but it was like fighting an angry brick wall. "I said, *let go!*"

"And *I* said, *not another goddamned word.*" He dragged me up the stairs and down the hall, and I was relieved that Noah didn't see us like that.

I thrashed underneath my husband's grip, angry and determined to break free. "What're you going to do, huh? Dr. Bryant doesn't need to check my fucking hymen now, you've taken care of *that*—"

Bryce clamped his massive hand over my mouth and hustled me inside his room. He slammed the door behind him. When he finally released me, he was breathing hard. "Keep your voice down, goddammit. The whole staff doesn't need to know our business."

"The whole staff already saw you out there, falling all over your ex!"

He took a step closer. The muscle in his jaw bulged, and his eyes were wild. "The whole staff saw *you* pawing that college-dropout fuck-hole of a waiter. Your tits were practically in his face! How do you think that makes me feel?"

I didn't back down. I clenched my fists and moved closer. "I know that you've been texting with her. You've hidden it from me for weeks! Do you know what that makes you? A *liar*! A fucking *liar*!"

There was a knock on the door, and Hazel called, "It's me, Mr. Windsor."

Bruce didn't tear his gaze from me. "Come in."

"Don't you dare let her in here right now!"

But Hazel bustled in, carrying a large suitcase.

"Put that on the bed," Bryce ordered. "You're the only one allowed in here until further notice, Hazel."

My gaze flicked from the suitcase to the maid, then back again.

Hazel only had eyes for her master; she completely ignored me. "Of course, Mr. Windsor." She pursed her thin lips. "What explanation shall I give the staff? And the boy?"

Bryce still stared at me as he spoke. "Tell them Mrs. Windsor has the flu and doesn't want to infect anyone else. Tell Noah that she's fine, just tired and that I'll take him fishing tomorrow."

"Yes, Mr. Windsor." Hazel clicked out of the room, happy to follow his orders.

"What do you mean, tell everyone I have the flu?" I eyed the suitcase again. "And where the hell am I going?"

"You're not going anywhere—not anytime soon." Bryce's tone was final. "Sit down, Chloe. Take off your shoes and remove your dress."

"No." I shook my head. "Are you freaking crazy? I'm not staying in here, and I'm not taking off my dress just because you said so. You *lied* to me, Bryce. Why didn't you tell me she'd been texting you so much?"

"Because I didn't ask her to. I didn't initiate it, I didn't respond to it—"

"Yes, you did," I said hotly. "I read your messages!"

"Telling her to stop bothering me isn't exactly a conversation." He removed a pair of handcuffs from the suitcase, holding them up to the light. "Here we are. These should do nicely."

"I'm not playing some sort of game with you!" My voice rose.

"No, you aren't." When Bryce turned back to me, his eyes were glittering. "And that's because I'm not playing, Chloe. I told you that if you became *mine* and you deceived me, you'd be punished. I gave you fair warning."

I stepped back. "You're out of your freaking mind!"

"No, I'm not. I *told* you what would happen if there was someone else, Chloe." He took a step closer.

"There isn't anybody else!" I was close to tears.

"I *saw* you."

"I freaking saw *you!*"

"I didn't do anything—Felicia came up

to *me. You* had your tits pressed up against that guy's chest. He's lucky all I did was punch him." Bryce moved closer still, a hunter stalking his prey.

"I saw the way you were with her." My chest was heaving. I was *so* freaking mad at him, so hurt. "You still want her."

"I want my *wife*, and I want her to remain faithful. You're the one who crossed a line. So now you're staying here, where I can keep an eye on you." He grabbed me by the wrist, and I fought him, but it was futile. Bryce overpowered me. He didn't *hurt* me, but there was no stopping him as he dragged me to the bed and hand-cuffed one of my wrists to the headboard, then the other.

I thrashed, fighting the whole time. I probably ripped my gorgeous dress, but I had zero fucks to give. "I didn't cross a line—you did!"

"I did no such thing." He tested my restraints and then climbed on top of me. Bryce looked smug as he straddled me; he had me now. I was handcuffed to his colossal bed, pinned beneath him.

I felt him getting hard, the fucker.

But as I struggled beneath him, I realized *I* was getting wet. *For fuck's sake, Chloe!* "Get off me!"

"Fine—if that's what you want." He climbed off and

set to work on my feet. I tried kicking him, but he was too quick. Before I knew it, he had each of my strappy sandals off, tossed to the floor, and I was fully restrained.

"Let me *go*! Let me out of here!" I struggled against the cuffs, but it was no use. And goddamnit, I was turned on! My sex throbbed. I wanted him to come back, to feel his weight on me again. But I was *still so fucking mad*!

Bryce stood over the bed, gaze raking down my gown. "You touched that man. You put your *hands* on him—and you did it just to make me jealous. No wife of mine is going to get away with that."

"I didn't do anything! You're the one that was being inappropriate—as soon as I left, Felicia was all up in your business. And you couldn't get enough of it!"

"That's not true. I haven't wanted her for a long time, Chloe. All I want is you, and you betrayed me. So now you're going to pay."

"You can't do this!" I spluttered. "You can't leave me like this!"

"I'm not going to leave you just yet." Bryce undid one of his cufflinks, then another. He set them on his nightstand.

"W-What do you mean?" My muscles clenched,

thighs tight against each other. A deep ache keened between my legs.

He stripped out of his jacket and unbuttoned his shirt, revealing the rock-hard muscles of his massive chest and abdomen. For fuck's sake, the man was hot. "First, I'm going to take that dress off you. Then I'm going to see exactly what else needs to be done."

He came to the bed and fingered the delicate beading of the gown. He was all over me in an instant, kissing my neck, my throat, my ear. My breath started coming fast and hot. Being tied up left me vulnerable and exposed, at his mercy. Why did I fucking love that so much? I was so *angry*, but I couldn't stop responding to his kisses. His tongue lashed against mine, and I moaned, curving my body to his. He was already hard for me, *so* hard...

In one swift motion, Bryce tore my dress. His hot kisses chased the frayed fabric, devouring my exposed skin. *Fuck!* His mouth was everywhere, all at once—my breasts, my stomach, the inside of my thighs. I moaned and writhed beneath him. With the cuffs on, I had no control. I was *his*.

His to punish, if that's what this was. His to possess.

"*No one* crosses me the way you crossed me tonight —especially not my wife. You might not be a virgin anymore, but you obviously have more to learn." His kisses trailed beneath my legs, his hands wrapping around the edges of my panties, taking purchase. He ran his thick fingers underneath the thin fabric and chuckled darkly. "You're so wet for me. See, Chloe? You're still lying. You said you want to be free, but what you really want is my cock."

I thrashed against the bed, in theory trying to get free—but in reality, he was right. I was irrevocably turned on. *Fuck!* This was so not right!

He ripped my thong off, and then his mouth was on me, sucking hard. He pulled back and blew on my clit, his cool breath making me shiver all over.

"Ah!" Wave after wave of sensation crashed through me. My whole body trembled as he again lashed his tongue against my clit, already bringing me to the edge. I didn't *want* to come—I didn't want to give him the satisfaction! But he devoured me greedily, burying his face in between my thighs.

No, no... Bryce took my clit in his mouth, in between his teeth, and nibbled.

"Yes!" I cried. The orgasm ripped through me. I came hard, whole body spasming, and I heard him laugh. I couldn't even get mad—I was too busy rising up, riding the sensation, and then tumbling back down.

By the time I came to, Bryce had already stripped out of his pants. Without preamble, he notched himself inside me and started to thrust. "Fuck Chloe. You're so fucking tight."

"Oh my God, Bryce. *Yes*. Fuck me." I lay back, relishing in the feel of my husband having total control over me. I was still mad, but somewhere deep inside, pure female satisfaction bloomed. He was hard for *me*. He was fucking *me*. He was jealous of *me*. It was me he had tied to his bed, me who had made him so mad that he had to take me prisoner and claim me.

He thrust hard. He drove into me, relentless, deep. After ripping my bra off, Bryce took my breast into his mouth, greedily suckling the nipple as his muscled ass pumped his hard length into me. *Fuck!* I longed to claw at him, to pull him in even deeper, but I was helplessly tied to the bed. He sensed my need, driving hard, hitting at just the right angle. His thrusts stroked the spot inside me that made me see stars. Another orgasm started building, almost too powerful to bear.

Bryce overpowered me. He was everywhere, inside me so deep, claiming me with his cock, his mouth, his enormous body covering mine. Despite the restraints—or perhaps because of them—I felt strangely free. To give myself to him, to let him have control, was the ultimate act of surrender.

"Take me. Fuck me. I'm yours," I whispered. My eyes

rolled back in my head as I met him, thrust for thrust. He was so hard he was about to explode.

"Fuck, Chloe—yes, *yes*!" He thrust hard and deep, then came in a torrent, filling me. My pussy greedily spasmed around him; I felt complete. Pleasure vibrated from deep in my core as my orgasm chased his. I took everything he had to give, my body humming as I flew higher than I ever had before.

"Bryce!" Tears streamed out of my eyes as everything stopped except for the pleasure, except for him and me. "I love you," I heard myself whispering. "I love you."

He collapsed on top of me, spent, breathing hard.

But for a full minute, he didn't look at me, and he didn't say it back.

He pulled himself off me and started getting dressed.

"Bryce? What are you doing?" I'd just told him I loved him—I wanted to ask if he'd heard me. I wanted to ask what was the matter.

"I'm leaving."

Panic rose in my chest. "But...why?"

"You shouldn't have said that." He still wouldn't look at me. "Not unless you mean it."

"I mean it..." But the words died on my lips as he turned away, zipping his pants. He was so cold again, so distant. It seemed he couldn't bear to look in my direction.

Without another word, he fled, leaving me cuffed to the bed. His scent was everywhere, all around me, his seed was still inside me...

But I was very much alone, maybe more so than I'd been in my whole life.

begging

MUCH TO MY HUMILIATION, it was Hazel who finally came in and freed me from the restraints. She covered me with a sheet and undid the cuffs with her eyes averted.

"Mr. Windsor wanted you to know he had a business call to make." She sounded perfectly normal, as if it were a typical day at the office for her to unlock her boss's naked wife from handcuffs.

I clutched the sheet around me. "Where is my brother?" I demanded. "Does he know I'm okay?"

"Of course, Mrs. Windsor. I told him you weren't feeling well and that Mr. Windsor was taking good care of you."

I peered up at her as she busied herself stowing the handcuffs in a drawer, thankfully out of sight. "Is Noah all right?"

"He's playing a video game and eating ice cream in his room. He seemed in good spirits."

"Thank you. Um, Hazel...?" To add insult to an already injurious situation, my eyes filled with tears. This was all so fucking humiliating. "I would like to leave. Can you please get me some clothes?"

"I'm afraid I can't let you out of the suite, Mrs. Windsor." Her thin lips curved into a frown. "I've been instructed to let you take a shower, that's it. But I'll bring you some clothes."

"Thank you." I sat up and wrapped the sheet around me. "Can you give me a minute? I'd like some privacy."

She sighed, and for the first time, she looked as though she might feel a teeny bit sorry for me. "I cannot."

Tears burned my eyes. "That's ridiculous!"

"Mr. Windsor tends to get very particular when he's...upset. It's best to follow his instructions." Hazel pursed her lips. "Just go ahead and get into the shower. It'll make you feel better."

I wanted to say that I doubted it. I wanted to say that Bryce could go die in a hole for all I cared, but I wasn't exactly into the idea of sharing with Hazel. She was Bryce's spindly little lap dog, his rat. Plus, she loved Felicia. She was probably more than happy about all of this!

I wrapped the sheet around me and ran for the safety of the bathroom.

Once the water was running, and the fan was on—once I was sure that Old Hazel couldn't hear me—only then did I let myself cry. I did so briefly, not wanting to get puffy and red, not wanting to have it show on my face how badly he'd hurt me.

In that moment, alone in the shower, tears streaming down my face, I almost hated him. Almost. It was more of a hollowed-out feeling, a sensation of loss. There was an ache in my stomach, a pain in my heart. When I'd seen him with Felicia, laughing, not thinking of me, it had cut me. When he'd dragged me back to his bedroom and tied me up, complaining about how *I'd* wronged *him*, it had infuriated me.

When he'd made love to me and made me come so hard, I'd seen stars...he'd undone me.

And when I'd told him that I loved him and he didn't say it back—and then he'd run away—it had just about killed me.

Nothing. That was how I felt. Like I was nothing, no one. Like I was already dead.

Except dead people didn't hurt like this.

I washed my hair and stayed under the hot water, wishing I never had to leave the safe confines of the bathroom. But I could only shave my legs and slather myself with body wash so many times. I finally dragged myself out, blew my hair dry, and brushed my teeth. I realized it was the first time I'd ever been in my husband's suite: he'd always come to my room. It was just another way he'd pushed me away, a strategy to keep me at arm's length.

I checked my reflection in the steamy mirror. My eyes were only slightly bloodshot. You might not be able to tell I'd been crying...

Good. I swore to myself then that I would never cry over Bryce Windsor again. If he didn't love me, fine. I'd break my contract and be free from him once and for all.

There was a knock on the door, and I jumped. "I have your things," said Hazel. I opened the door a little. She handed me some new underwear—thankfully not a thong—comfy pajamas that I'd never seen before, a big fuzzy bathrobe, and slippers. "I left some hot chocolate out here for you and some food. The remote control is on the nightstand. Please make yourself comfortable. I'll be waiting outside."

"Thanks, Hazel," I mumbled. She *seemed* like she was being sort of human, but I didn't trust her. Still, I was happy to pull on the pajamas and wrap the robe tightly around me. I slid on the slippers, and even if everything else truly sucked, they were comfortable. That was something.

Hazel was in the bedroom, dusting an already immaculate dresser.

I hesitated. "When you said you'd be waiting outside, I thought you meant...not in the room."

She finished her fake dusting and nodded at me. "Mr. Windsor asked me to make sure that you were okay—he wanted eyes on you." Her gaze flicked over me. "*Are* you okay, Mrs. Windsor?"

I couldn't help it: I laughed. "No, Hazel. No I am not. But you don't need to worry about me. Neither does Mr. Windsor." *Not that he would.* I eyed the tray she'd left for me. There was hot chocolate with whipped cream, cupcakes with vanilla frosting, and a large bowl of chips. "Thank you for the snacks."

"You're welcome." She headed for the door. "Midge sends her regards. She wanted to come in and see you, but she's not allowed."

"Of course she's not." *Fucking Bryce.*

"She had a message for you." Hazel faced the door as she spoke. "She said 'Bitchface was disappointed that Mr. Windsor punched that server. She knows he only has eyes for you.'"

I shrugged. "Tell her I said thanks. It isn't true, but tell her I appreciate it, anyway." Midge was the best cheerleader ever, but the game was over. I'd already lost.

Hazel stole one backward glance at me. "I'll be in the hall if you need me. I'll be there all night."

"That's crazy! You don't need to sleep in the freaking *hall*—"

But she was already gone.

I couldn't believe she'd be stationed outside my room all night like some sort of watchman in a maid's uniform. Old Hazel had seen way too much already: Bryce's icy demeanor, his cold request for the suitcase, and his orders for me to be held in his room. Then she'd seen me—*naked*, handcuffed to the bed. She'd seen my bloodshot eyes.

She knew I was his prisoner. What the hell did she think of all this?

Remember—she's his lap dog. She's keeping watch outside your room all night! Maybe she loved it. Perhaps she'd popped some popcorn and was just waiting for the show to continue.

But there would be no more drama. Not tonight, and maybe not ever again. It was over—Bryce was gone, and I had a sinking feeling he wasn't coming back. *Fine by me.*

That was another lie, but I was so done telling the truth that it didn't matter.

Sighing, I climbed into bed. I had no desire to stay at Bryce's estate for another night. I wanted to grab Noah, pack our things and leave. But it was late and dark, and I honestly doubted that Captain Johnny would take us to Northeast Harbor without Bryce's permission.

There were other issues, too. I didn't know if I could leave the house or if his men would stop me. I didn't want to cause a big scene and upset my brother. And I didn't have *any* money—I would have to make arrangements with Akira and Elena to break the contract and get at least some compensation. Enough to get the hell off Bryce's island and bring Noah someplace safe. Bryce owed me that much.

My heart ached when I thought about leaving, but I tried to look on the bright side. At least I had Noah now. My father had already been paid off; he'd signed the agreement. There was nothing he could do, at least that he knew of. And he wouldn't try anything, anyway. He obviously cared more about the money than his own son. He'd been bought so easily; I didn't need to worry about him.

But I would need to worry about the money. I only got the million-dollar signing bonus if I stayed for one year, and there was no way in hell that was going to happen. Not now.

I love you.

And what was his response?

You shouldn't have said that.

Had I truly expected things to turn out any different? He'd been cold to me from the beginning. The ice had thawed a little, probably because of all the sex, but he didn't feel the same way about me that I did about him. I was a naive child, confusing sex with love. He was probably downstairs, scrolling on his phone and texting Felicia. Maybe he'd gone back to the party to find her. *She* was the one he wanted; she always had been. I was just a business transaction with a side of penetration.

But that was the good thing about wrongs, wasn't it? You could eventually make them right...

If I told Bryce I wanted out of the contract, he would probably be relieved. His father seemed genuinely happy that Felicia was back in the picture. Perhaps Gene would be lenient, even encouraging, about Bryce's position in the company. He'd probably be happy if his son divorced me so that he could be free to get back together with Felicia...

Ugh, I hated thinking about her. Was it too much to ask for her to go die in a hole, too?

I sipped the hot chocolate, which was delicious. I ate two cupcakes and all the chips. Stuffing my face didn't make anything better, but at least it was something to do. I clicked on the television, overwhelmed by the number of stations. Then I remembered a trick

Noah had taught me: the remote control operated by voice.

"Twilight," I whispered, hoping Old Hazel couldn't hear me.

All five of the movies appeared as options. God bless rich people's cable packages! If I couldn't have a happily ever after, at least I could watch Edward and Bella gaze into each other's eyes.

I settled in, pulling Bryce's cover up to my chin. I hated that it smelled like him. I hated that he wasn't with me. I hated that I missed him and that I was even thinking about him.

I love you.

You shouldn't have said that.

Heaven was a handsome, muscled, brooding man.

Turns out, so was hell.

closer

THE SUN STREAMED through the windows when I woke up the following day. For a blissful moment, I forgot about everything.

But then I rolled over and faced the other side of the bed. It was empty, still made up neatly. Bryce had never returned.

My stomach ached with that awful, hollow feeling, and my chest followed suit. Ugh, *why* had I told him I loved him? Why had I ever bothered to flirt with that waiter?

I yearned for a do-over of the previous evening. Had I been level-headed and thinking clearly, I would've approached Bryce after seeing him with Felicia. I could have told him that I wanted out of the contract then, before we had a meltdown.

Then we could have skipped the drama, skipped the handcuffs and the resulting hot sex, skipped the *I love you*. It would've been so much more dignified! I could've left the island with my head held high. Instead, I would be going with my tail between my legs, utterly humiliated.

It would've been bad enough. I was already hurt, *so* hurt, just from seeing Bryce with Felicia. It had cut me like a knife. The painful emotions were a wake-up call—I'd let myself fall way too hard, too fast, for my husband. It had been foolish. Why would I ever want to fall in love with somebody? Why would I ever want to care about anyone again when they could so easily be taken away?

I'd already lost my mother. I'd learned the hard way how simple it was to lose someone I loved. *Fool me once, shame on you. Fool me twice, I'm a fucking idiot.*

Why had I told him I loved him? I'd only pushed him away.

But it was for the best. I stared out into space as scenes from the party flooded me. Felicia in her white column gown. Felicia making a beeline to Bryce. Felicia laughing with her head thrown back. Fucking Felicia Jones!

I hope she makes him happy. I truly hoped she was worth it. To me, she was a selfish bitch who had little regard for anyone else. She hadn't even looked at me last night. She'd gone after what she wanted—my husband—and didn't appear to give a flying fuck about either my feelings or my existence.

At the same time, she probably wasn't the real issue if she could wreak so much havoc simply by showing up and sending texts. But that only made me feel a little bit better. I still hoped she would go die in a hole!

Spying my phone on the dresser, I dragged myself out of bed. I was surprised that Bryce hadn't confiscated it. I quickly tapped out a text to Akira and Elena:

Need to talk to you guys.
Please call or text back.

I checked my other messages, alarmed by one Daphne had sent at four a.m.:

Where the hell are you? I need your help. Text me when you get this!

I texted her back, saying I was at the house if she needed me. There were no other messages, nothing from Bryce. Where the hell did *he* spend the night last night? I shuddered as the possibilities ran through my mind. If he'd gone to *her* after being with *me*...

I felt like I might be sick. I ran to the bathroom and splashed cold water on my face. *Don't think about it, Chlo. Just get out of here!*

I straightened my shoulders and went to the door. I opened it a crack. "Hazel?"

But the maid wasn't anywhere to be found. I crept into the hall, planning on grabbing a few belongings from my suite, then waking up Noah and maybe making a run for it.

"Where the hell do you think you're going?"

I whirled around and found Bryce on the floor, slumped against the wall. He was still wearing his suit, which was rumpled. He rubbed his eyes and glared at me. "Get back inside. *Now.*"

"No." I shook my head. "I'm leaving."

"You're not allowed to leave." His voice was flat, unyielding.

"You're not the boss of me." I tried unsuccessfully to match his detached tone—my voice shook. "I don't want to be here anymore."

He pulled himself to his feet. Bryce was a bit of a mess. There were lines around his eyes; he looked as if he hadn't slept. "Get back in the bedroom, Chloe."

"No." I started to back away, but he was suddenly next to me, his hands around my wrists. Being close to him, his smell surrounding me, made my resolve falter. "I don't want to do this—let me go."

"You don't have to do anything. Including leave." He was gentle as he led me back inside the room.

Tears pricked my eyes as soon as he closed the door. It was so humiliating to see him again, to be alone with him. What was even worse? The fact that my heart leaped with hope. *Maybe things will be okay, maybe we can be together, after all...*

"Get back in bed," he ordered.

"Bryce, *stop*." My temper rose. "You're not in charge of me. I don't answer to you anymore!"

"The hell you don't." He started undoing his belt.

"What are you doing?" I shook my head. "We are *not* having sex right now—"

"We're going back to bed, that's all. I've been up all night. I need to get some sleep before work." He stripped out of his shirt and pants, revealing his insanely muscled body. But true to his word, he didn't have an erection.

Bryce climbed into bed and stared up at the ceiling. The muscle in his jaw bulged. "Please come here, Chloe."

I sighed. "Daphne texted me—she needs my help."

"Daphne's passed out in the guest house. She and

my father had a blowout." Bryce paused for a beat. "Are you coming or not?"

I was torn. Part of me wanted nothing more than to be reunited with him, but another part wanted to run away, screaming. But he would just chase me, right? Or maybe he'd let me go, which would feel even worse...

"I don't think I can sleep if we have another fight. Just get in bed, Chloe."

I gingerly climbed onto my side, careful to keep my distance, and pulled the cover up to my chin.

"Hazel said you ate something."

"Yes." *Hazel saw me naked.*

"Good." Bryce grunted his approval.

I turned toward him. His eyes were closed, his arms crossed against his chest. He looked exhausted and as if he'd aged about a year in one night. Why did he care if I ate? Why was he back here—just to torture me?

He opened one eye and squinted at me. "Come here."

When I didn't move, he cursed under his breath. "Are you going to make me beg?"

I arched an eyebrow as I slid closer. Why would he have to resort to begging when he already knew how I felt?

He pulled me to his chest and sighed. "That's better."

"Why?" I held still against him. "I don't understand you."

He was quiet for a minute as he played with my hair. "Do you think that *I* understand me?"

I took a deep breath. "It would be helpful."

"I'm sure it would." Bryce said nothing further. He just held me and stroked my hair. Moments later, he was breathing heavy, already fast asleep.

I so did *not* understand him. I couldn't pretend to. Why had he fled, then spent the night slumped outside in the hall? Why was he back now?

What the hell did he want from me?

He slept like that for an hour, holding onto me tightly. I stayed pressed against his massive chest, listening to his heartbeat. It was exactly what I wanted, and I rationalized that it was okay because Bryce didn't know that I was clinging to him. I could feel ashamed about it later—in that moment, I just let myself enjoy it.

After all, it might be the last time.

When he woke up, Bryce automatically kissed the top of my head. "What time is it?" He sounded groggy.

"Eight-thirty."

"I have to go." He started to sit up, then fell back to the bed. "Ah... Fuck it."

I didn't say anything. I stayed in his embrace,

holding my breath. I had no idea what was going on with him.

"I'm...sorry...about last night." He bit the words out.

I stiffened in his arms. "Which part?"

"All of it. I'm sorry about all of it—except punching that douche waiter, I'm not sorry about that."

I held perfectly still, waiting for him to go on.

"I want to share something with you, Chloe. Something about my past." He kept his arms wrapped tightly around me. "I have some...issues."

No shit! I studied his face. "I'm listening."

"When Felicia and I were together, she..." He went quiet for a moment, never loosening his grip on me. "She cheated on me. It had been going on for some time, and I didn't know about it. We were supposed to get married; the wedding was a few weeks away when she left. Then she called me and broke it off. *Then* I found out about the cheating. It took a while for her to admit to it."

"I'm so sorry." But at least I knew one thing: Felicia *was* a total ass!

"We kept it to ourselves. No one else knows about the affair," Bryce continued, "because we decided to keep that part private. We didn't want our families to know. I was too ashamed, and she knew her parents would have a fit. The guy was someone she'd known since boarding school. He was trouble. Not from a good enough family. Not marriage material."

He stared up at the ceiling. "It took me a long time to get over it. To be honest, I'm still not over it."

My stomach clenched.

"Not *her*," he continued, "so much as what she did. It's an awful feeling when someone lies to you. And I had no idea. It made me doubt myself to my core—which isn't something I'm exactly used to."

I lay there for a moment, processing the information. "That makes sense. It sucks when someone lies to you. But why... Why did she come back?"

"She wanted to say she was sorry." Bryce stared up at the ceiling. "She knows what she did was wrong. She owned it. It's taken her a long time, but Felicia's not someone who apologizes easily."

"So... Do you forgive her?" I didn't know what I wanted to hear.

"I forgive her. I won't forget what happened, but she's fucked up. Her family situation is *not* normal. We've always had that in common."

I didn't move. I didn't want to hear about what they had in common.

"I'm sorry that she acted like that toward you last night."

"You don't need to apologize for her," I mumbled. I didn't want him having anything to *do* with her.

"Fair enough. But I *am* sorry that I talked to her when you weren't around. And that I didn't tell you she'd been texting me."

I nodded against his chest, still very much not over it. Hot jealousy flooded me. I hated hearing that they had things in common, that they had a past. "What were you two laughing about?"

He blew out a deep breath. "She told me that, as usual, I was acting like a fucking asshole. Then she started laughing. And I don't know—maybe it was because she'd said she was sorry, maybe it was because I was tired of being angry for so long—I started laughing, too. It felt good."

I pulled away from him a little bit. "I'm sure it was a relief. She was a big part of your life." It was true; it also made me want to throw up.

He shrugged.

We were quiet for a minute, just lying there. Finally, he said, "I have a meeting—I'm going to have to go."

I sat up. "We need to talk about what I'm doing—"

"You're to stay in the suite." Bryce's tone was final. "I'll have my men on guard outside."

I sat up. "Bryce? You can't lock me up. That's not... normal. And why are there guards? It's not like I'd get very far. We're on a freaking island. It's not like I can swim away!"

He rolled over to face me. He looked more relaxed since he'd slept, but his eyes were still intense. "The guards are for me."

"Huh?" I shook my head. "What do you mean they're for you?"

"I want them guarding you so that *I* feel safe. I can't be worried about you trying to sneak out or that ass-face of a server trying to sneak in. You'll be more secure this way. We both will be."

"You're acting crazy! I don't even know that guy—"

"Not another word, Mrs. Windsor. I just tried to explain why I am the way I am. I can't do much more than that." His eyes glittered. "Now get up and get your ass in the shower. We don't have much time."

Without another word, he stripped out his boxer briefs, revealing a screaming erection. I couldn't help but stare—and *want*, which was very fucking annoying, giving everything that was going on.

Bryce knew precisely what I was thinking. He probably sensed the wetness between my legs, the fucker! He rose and sauntered to the bathroom with a smug look on his face, forcing me to stare at his perfectly round, muscled ass.

Whiplash. The man was giving me emotional whiplash.

"Don't make me wait Chloe," he growled.

Fuck. He was crazy, and he was toying with me. Guards outside of my room. Still not saying he loved me back. Bringing up that waiter as if the poor guy was an actual threat. Saying he forgave Bitchface Felicia. Not letting me leave, and not leaving me the fuck alone. And now he was ordering me to follow him into the bathroom, so he could have his way with me *again*...

"*Now*, Mrs. Windsor. I have something for you. And I happen to know that you like it."

Fuck! He was driving me fucking crazy! What was I supposed to do?

I sighed. Hadn't I just had a serious talk with myself about not falling in love? Even though it was already too late, I might still be able to save myself. That was, if I could stay away from him...

I sighed again.

And then for better—or much more likely, for worse —I got up and followed him inside.

THIRTY-SEVEN
buried

HE WAS INSIDE THE BATHROOM, waiting for me. His hard length sprang out, pointing in my direction with urgency.

Bryce stared at me. "I need you, Chloe. I need *us*."

A deep ache, all too familiar, keened between my legs. *I need us, too.*

He started to stroke himself, which I'd never seen him do before—it was as though he couldn't wait. "Take off those pajamas, then get on your knees. *Now*."

Mesmerized, I did as I was told. I never took my eyes off him as I removed the comfy pajamas—I was way too hot with them on now. I stripped out of the underwear and then went to him, immediately lowering myself onto my knees. I was directly in front of him, eye level with his luscious cock. I couldn't deny the truth: I wanted him.

I craved him.

I would do whatever he asked.

My insides quivered.

I fucking *loved* it when he took control and told me what to do.

When I didn't know what would happen next.

When I knew he wanted me so badly, he was about to burst.

"Good girl." He fisted his cock, stroking it up and down. The tip was wet, and he pointed it at me. "Take me in your mouth."

I greedily licked the moisture from his tip, and he grunted. When I popped the head into my mouth and sucked on it like a lollipop, he threw his head back. Little by little, I took more of him in my mouth. He tasted *so fucking good*. I loved giving him a blowjob! Having control over him, giving him pleasure, was the biggest turn-on.

Bryce started to thrust, gently at first. "*Fuck*, that's good. That's what I want—what I need." His balls were heavy as they slapped against me. I took him all the way in, my tongue gliding up and down along his thick, hard length. I dug my fingertips into his muscled ass and pulled him deeper, sucking hard.

He pulsed into my mouth, totally letting go, totally into it, groaning and throwing his head back. Bryce was free, uninhibited as he fucked my mouth. And I fucking loved it!

"Fuck Chloe. You don't know what you do to me, babe." His thrusts got a little ragged, and I had to take control. I guided him in and out, taking him deep and releasing him. I licked the lush crown of his head and sucked on it, then took him all the way down his shaft again. He cursed as his ass pumped, the cords standing out in his neck. "Yes, Chloe. Fucking *yes*."

I sucked harder, and I could tell that he was close. I wrapped my fingers around his base, stroking, and chased them with my mouth, doubling the sensation. Pure female satisfaction bloomed in my chest as I watched him circle the edge. His eyes were closed, mouth slack in ecstasy. I cradled his balls with my hands, and they contracted; I squeezed more and he thrust into my mouth, cursing.

"Fuck Chloe—yes, *yes!*" Bryce gripped my shoulders and came hard, emptying himself into me. I greedily sucked down every drop, high on the power I wielded over my husband. He continued to thrust, cursing and thrashing, as the powerful orgasm rocked through him.

I licked him and sucked him, greedy, unable to get enough. He shuddered, big muscles rippling as the pleasure peaked and then subsided. He pulled me up and cradled me against his chest. "That was incredible."

"I know." I laughed.

"Now you're getting cocky, eh? My little virgin." He started to stir against me, already getting hard again. He trailed his enormous fingertips down my side and in between my legs. He brushed the wetness there and chuckled. "I knew it—you're wet for me. You need me, too."

I didn't say it out loud, but it was true. I needed him more than I cared to admit. Bryce nudged me against the cool wall and put his knee between my legs, urging them apart. His hand crept between them, and he started to explore, to rub me. *Fuck.* The man knew exactly where to touch me. He trailed hot kisses down my neck to my breasts, then he greedily sucked on my nipples. He was everywhere, all at once, and I was a hot mess, moaning and rubbing up against him, begging him. "Fuck me, Bryce, *please.*"

He maneuvered me from the wall, turning me so I faced away from him. "Bend all the way over—grip your ankles. I need to be deep."

Heart pounding, I did as I was told. I'd just secured my hands around my ankles when he notched himself inside me.

"Are you ready?" His voice was strangled.

"Yes."

He buried his cock in me. I cried out, unused to the position and how deep he was. He slowed, but only for a moment, letting me adjust.

Then he drove harder into me.

Oh, fuck.

I'd never felt him like this. My eyes rolled back into my head as he thrust, stroking the part of me deep inside that only he could reach. He gripped my hips as he relentlessly buried himself in me, driving deep. I saw stars.

"You think you can leave me? You think I'm *ever* going to let you go?" He drove harder, claiming me. "You're *mine*. You're always going to be mine. Don't. Ever. Forget it."

He fucked me so hard, I thought I might pass out.

His hand found my clit, circling it as he drove into me. The combination of sensations pushed me over the edge. "Bryce! Oh my God, *Bryce*!"

"That's right." He thrust savagely while his fingers made my clit sing. "Say my fucking name."

"Bryce, Bryce, Bryce!" I came so hard that everything went black. I came so hard tears streamed down my face while I laughed. Bryce kept thrusting, kept owning my clit, kept fucking me through my earth-shattering orgasm. Then it was his turn. He grasped my hips and drove deep again. I almost couldn't take it, but I fucking loved it!

He exploded inside of me, filling me up. "Fuck yes!" He slapped me on the ass for good measure, gripping my hips as he emptied himself inside of me.

"Oh my God, Oh my God..." Another orgasm built, and I greedily rubbed myself up against his shaft, trying to find another release. He was still buried inside me. Grunting, he thrust and expertly rubbed my clit again.

I came instantly, screaming his name.

By the time we were done, we were both exhausted, shaking. I could barely stand up straight. But it was worth it. He'd given me exactly what I wanted, what I needed: to be claimed by him. The overwhelming physical connection mirrored my emotions. I'd longed for him. When he was inside me, I felt complete.

Bryce pulled me into the shower and washed my hair. He gently washed my body, kissing and nuzzling me and holding me close. I was exhausted. Overwhelmed, I clung to him, relishing the feel of his big body next to mine. He felt like home.

Before I knew what I'd done, I heard myself saying: "I love you, Bryce. I love you." Because I did. I loved him to my core.

He kissed me deeply. "I love you, too."

I almost died from happiness right then and there.

I was so drunk on what he'd said—not to mention the multiple, insanely intense orgasms—that I didn't really remember getting into bed. Bryce tucked me in. He kissed my cheek and promised to return after his meeting.

"Don't try to go anywhere. My men are outside."

He was joking, right? I could barely move. He'd literally fucked me senseless!

I must've fallen back asleep because I was confused when there was a *ping* followed by another *ping ping ping*. Then my phone rang. I hopped up and grabbed it —it was Daphne.

"What are you, still drunk?" She sounded exasperated. "I've been texting you all morning!"

"I fell back asleep." I eyed the clock—ten a.m. "Are you okay? I got your message."

"No I am not okay! Gene saw me with Mike Jones, and he's *so fucking mad*. He threatened to call his wife! He threatened to defund my prenup! What am I supposed to do now?"

Not sleep with someone else's husband when you already have *a husband?* But Daphne didn't sound as though she were in a position to listen to reason. "Did you call your lawyer?"

"Of course I called my lawyer! But I'm not ready to get a divorce. Not yet!"

"Okay...?" I was trying to be supportive, but I wasn't sure how to do that in this situation.

"I need a few more weeks." She sounded out of breath as if she were sprint-pacing. "Mike's not ready to commit just yet, and I'm not leaving until I know I have somewhere to go."

"You think he's going to leave his wife?" I didn't know much about the Jones family, but they seemed pretty traditional.

"He might have to." She laughed. "Let's just say I don't think I should've been drinking last night."

"Okay...?" I sounded like a broken record.

"Can you come over? I don't want to be alone right now."

I hesitated, not wanting to tell her the truth—that Bryce had forbidden me from leaving the room and that there were guards stationed outside my door. "Let me see what I can do."

"I'm at the guesthouse. Bring me some coffee, okay? And a bottle of Advil!"

I threw on some clothes, wincing as I noticed how sore my muscles were. Bryce had really done a number on me! I blushed, remembering the scorching sex we'd had in the bathroom. Then I hugged my arms around myself, remembering how he'd told me he loved me...

He loves me! Oh my God—he'd said it! I couldn't wipe the smile off my face.

I poked my head out of the bedroom, unsurprised to see three men in suits standing guard. "Hey guys. Daphne Windsor wants me to come to the guesthouse and bring her a coffee. Are we allowed to go for a field trip?"

"Let me check in with Mr. Windsor, Mrs. Windsor." The man to my left whipped out his phone.

Just then, my own phone pinged again. It was a message from Elena:

I was in a meeting when you texted. Is everything all right?

I ignored it. I could call her later and explain that Bryce and I had been having issues but that everything was fine now. Better than fine!

The guard nodded at me. "Mr. Windsor approved the visit, but we're going to have to accompany you."

"Of course." I hadn't expected anything else.

My entourage followed me into the kitchen, where I asked Chef to make two coffees to go. He also supplied me with a bottle of Advil. Chef definitely didn't get paid enough!

There was no sign of Midge or Hazel—maybe they actually had the day off. I quickly texted Dale, letting him know that I was feeling much better and was going to visit Daphne, and asked him to check on Noah.

We're playing pinball and then we're in a Fortnite tournament!

Dale included a crying with laughter emoji.

Your husband's going to have to start paying me in v-bucks.

I laughed, even though I felt guilty. Dale had been spending way more time with my brother than I had.

But my spirits lifted again as we headed outside. It was a bright, sunny day, the kind of day that washed away darkness and doubts. *Bryce loves me.* My heart soared again. I couldn't wipe the smile from my face as I headed across the lawn. The guards had told me the guest house was situated privately on the property, away from the main estates. I'd never even glimpsed it before.

Gene Windsor's house came into view on my left. In front of it, the tent was still erected. I shivered, remembering how Bryce had punched that poor server. It was my fault. I should apologize, but he'd surely been fired and sent on his way.

I pictured Bryce with Felicia again but chose to roughly shove the image from my mind. *She doesn't matter anymore. She cheated on him and he loves me!* It gave me a sense of peace. Bryce was much too smart to ever go back to someone who'd treated him so poorly.

"I didn't expect to see you out of your cage today." Gene Windsor was suddenly standing before me in the drive.

"Oh!" I jumped, startled. I'd been so lost in my thoughts I hadn't seen him approach.

He nodded toward Bryce's men. "Take a walk."

"I'm afraid we can't do that, Sir," the lead guard said.

"Just remember who's ultimately writing the checks." Gene pointed to the lawn. "Now take a walk twenty paces that way, to where you can't hear our conversation. Feel free to monitor your charge from there."

They reluctantly followed his orders, leaving us alone.

Gene eyed my coffees. "I'm assuming one of those is for my errant, hungover, unfaithful wife?"

I opened my mouth and then closed it. There was no way in hell I was saying yes to that!

"I know all about Michael Jones." Gene looked tired. His face was drawn, and his gray hair blew in the breeze. It looked thinner in the bright sunlight. "Daphne is a lot of things, but subtle isn't one of them."

"Is there... Is there something I can do for you?" What did he want from me? I longed to get away from him. Even a hungover, cheating Daphne was better than Gene Windsor!

"Actually, there is." He smiled, but it wasn't a nice smile.

I blinked at him. "Yes?"

"You can leave my son."

I opened my mouth to object, but as his smile broadened, the words died on my lips.

"Trust me, when you hear the whole story, you'll want to," Gene said.

second line

"*Trust me, when I tell you the whole story, you'll want to.*"

Gene Windsor eyed me. He was one smug fucker in his linen pants and loafers.

"What do you mean?" I licked my lips, which had suddenly gone dry. "What whole story?"

"The one about my son and why he was desperate enough to marry jail-bait white trash from East Boston."

Tell me how you really feel, Gene. But I had a bad feeling he was about to.

"I'm sure you're aware that he and Felicia were engaged," Gene continued.

I nodded. There was a buzzing in my head—like I was about to short-circuit.

"We were all excited about the marriage. Both families knew that it was an extraordinary union. I had so much confidence in it, in fact, that I amended Bryce's trust. Upon marriage he was to further vest in the company, a sign of my approval."

I swallowed hard.

"When she left, and it fell apart, Bryce took it very hard. Not only because his stake in the company was threatened, but because he truly loved her. They were meant to be." Gene's watery gaze raked over me. "It was the joining of two powerful families, but it was also a love match."

"Until she broke off the engagement and ghosted him," I said, finally finding my voice. "Then they weren't so meant to be."

Gene chuckled. "It's cute when you actually have a personality. I can see why he likes you."

I wanted to say that Bryce *loved* me, but I held my tongue. I didn't owe Gene Windsor anything, not even the truth.

"The thing is, when I executed that clause to Bryce's trust, I intended for him to either take Felicia back, or find someone of a similar stature," Gene said. "He was meant to marry *her*, not *you*. Only people from our world can understand what it's like. Bryce must have that sort of support. That's the only way he'll ever be able to handle running the company when I'm gone.

I've told his brothers the same thing—marry someone from our stratosphere. Everyone else will just drag you down."

He swept the hair back from his face. "Like Daphne, for example. Sure, she's from Greenwich, but she didn't grow up with our sort of money. She has a scarcity mindset—that's why she went after Mike Jones. She has to glom onto someone because she knows she's nothing without me."

I longed to turn and flee. But as I was on an island, Old Gene would catch up with me eventually. "Why are you telling me all this?"

"I need you to do the right thing." He paused for a beat. "Leave my son—get an annulment. I've already made the arrangements. Agree, and I'll make it *very* lucrative for you. I don't know what your pre-nuptial agreement says, but I'll make it look like chump change."

"My marriage isn't your business. It's mine and Bryce's." I lifted my chin, pretending to be brave. But inside I was shaking.

"Leaving *will* be your decision when you hear what I have to say." He took a step closer. "It's not over between them, even now. Felicia shared with me that she and Bryce have been talking ever since she came back to MDI. She said they text multiple times a day."

"I know about that." I swallowed hard. "But *she's* been texting *him*. He's barely responded."

"Are you sure about that?" Gene's watery eyes glittered, hypnotizing me. "Did you know that Bryce has a business phone? It's a second line—separate from the personal one he carries. Felicia sent me screenshots of what he wrote to her. Would you like to see?"

I felt like he was offering me a bite from a poisoned apple. "No thank you." My voice came out small.

"I suppose you don't need to read them—I can give you the highlights." Gene smiled. "He wrote things like, 'I've made a terrible mistake.' And 'There hasn't ever been anybody but you.' Not words that should inspire your confidence, Chloe. That was while you two were in the Bahamas—when you thought you were having a romantic weekend. I'm afraid that wasn't the case. He's wanted to be with Felicia this whole time. He's wanted to be with her since she left."

Tears pricked my eyes. "You're lying."

"There's more! Let me show you—"

"Gene!" Daphne stormed up behind him. Her face was white, except for two small patches of red on her cheeks. "Why the hell did Mimi Jones just call me and threaten me with a lawsuit? What the hell did you do?"

"Hello, dear." Gene turned his icy smile on his wife. "You're looking a bit peaked."

"*What* did you tell Mimi Jones?"

"I told her nothing. Mike's the one who had a lot to say—about you cornering him and being inappropriate. Also, something about you bending yourself over an Adirondack chair...?"

"*What?*" Daphne shrieked. "He's the one who propositioned *me*—"

"Don't they all dear, don't they all." He checked his watch. "Ah, if you'll excuse me, I have a meeting. You two enjoy yourselves. Chloe, don't forget what I said. If you decide to listen to reason, I'll make it worth your while."

He put on his reading glasses and sauntered off, tapping out a text message.

"That fucker!" Daphne stamped her foot, a hungover child about to have a meltdown. "And *where's* my coffee?"

"Here you go." I handed it to her meekly.

"*Fuck!* It's cold." She stomped off toward the guesthouse. "Are you coming, or what? And what the hell did he mean about making it worth your while?"

"Nothing." I could *not* get into that with Daphne.

I followed her down the drive. Bryce's men followed me. I no longer had a smile on my face, and I didn't care that the sun was shining.

What Gene said had entered my thoughts like

poison, and I was feeling the effects. I clutched my stomach. *There hasn't ever been anybody but you.* Was it true—did Bryce write that to Felicia on his private phone? Was he texting her while we were on vacation—when I'd just given him my *virginity*? Or was Gene just fucking with me?

The "guesthouse" came into view, and I gaped at it. It was a mini gray-stone mansion with ivy climbing its facade, straight out of a fairytale. But I couldn't be too enraptured because I felt sick with dread. I knew Gene wanted me gone, but I hadn't realized how motivated he was. He wanted to pay me to get an annulment so that Bryce could marry who he was *supposed* to be with...

"Chloe, are you even listening?" Daphne looked as if she wanted to smack me. "I *said*, can you believe Gene? He told Mimi he would fund a civil suit against me for adultery! Who does that shit?!"

Daphne's woes were the least of my worries, but they were a welcome distraction. "Can you even *be* sued for adultery?"

"Probably in Maine. It's still in the fucking Stone Ages!"

We headed up the staircase and into the living room. The house was impeccably decorated and had soaring ceilings, but I barely noticed. Daphne drank her coffee and began to pace, then eyed the three guards as they took positions around the house. "Why do you have so many babysitters today?"

"Bryce is paranoid." I shrugged.

Her gaze narrowed in on me. "Is that because of the waiter? Bryce hit him *hard*. He had to do a concussion protocol before we sent him home. And then Gene gave him ten grand in cash so he wouldn't come after us and sue. What happened, anyway?"

"Nothing. I was talking to him too much, I guess."

"Because Bryce was talking to Felicia." Daphne sounded sure of herself. "Trust me when I say that she'll get hers!"

I frowned. "What do you mean?"

She looked at the guards. "Don't repeat what I'm about to say, or I'll have you fired. Or worse," she warned.

"Yes, ma'am," the lead guard said.

A small smile crept onto Daphne's lips as she turned back to me. "I don't really care if Mimi Jones sues me. Because if what I think is true, she won't *ever* be able to touch me. I'll be protected for the rest of my life. And then she and Felicia can both suck it!"

I waited to hear more, but I had a bad feeling I already knew what she was about to say.

Her smile widened into a grin. "I'm *pregnant.*

With *Mike Jones's baby*! It's too early to be sure, but I planned it when I slept with him the first time—I was *totally* ovulating. I took one of those early detection tests and it was positive... And I *feel* different." She rubbed her stomach.

"You don't think it's Gene's?"

Daphne snorted. "*He* can't have kids. He waited until after we were married to tell me he'd had a vasectomy, can you imagine that? So I was never protected with him—only a child can do that. And now *my* child is a Jones! They're one of the wealthiest families in America. Felicia is going to be a big sister again. Ha! Serves her right!"

Bryce's stepmother was having Felicia's half-sibling and might become Felicia's *stepmother...* My head swam. "Do you really think you're pregnant?"

"I took the test this morning, right after I threw up." Daphne winced. "Ugh, I should *not* have been drinking last night. I'll be dry from here on out."

"That's good." I nodded. "So...congratulations?" Was that even appropriate in this situation?

"Thank you! I'm *so* excited! Even if Mike refuses to get a divorce, he'll still have to set me up at a property nearby..." She chattered on, talking about the money she'd get from her divorce from Gene, then birthing plans and nursery designs, acting as if the whole whacked situation was the most normal thing in the world.

Sitting there and listening to her at least gave me something to do, something to focus on. But what Gene had told me about Bryce was still working its way through my system.

I've made a terrible mistake.

There hasn't ever been anybody but you.

I prayed it wasn't true. I prayed that Gene had lied to me to get me to leave—that would be bad enough.

But it wouldn't be the worst thing.

After talking non-stop for over an hour straight, Daphne's phone buzzed. "It's Mike Jones!" she screeched.

"Hi babe!" she said brightly. "I had *so* much fun last night. That fire pit will always be my happy place! Top-ten memory..."

But her face turned down, her brows knitting together as Mike took his turn talking. "I understand, yeah. I'm sorry that you feel guilty, babe..."

She listened more. When it was her turn to talk again, she sounded unusually sympathetic. "Your wife of thirty years, I know she's so important to you, truly. I get it! There's so much history."

Daphne looked at me and rolled her eyes.

Then she went in for the kill. "The thing is, Mike?

You actually *can't* break up with me. Because I'm pregnant! With *your* child. Yes, I'm sure! A hundred-percent sure..."

With the phone glued to her ear, Daphne stalked into the bedroom and slammed the door behind her. I took that as my cue to leave. God bless the three guards; they didn't say a word as they followed me back down the stairs to the grounds. I checked my surroundings, careful to ensure that Gene Windsor wasn't hiding in the fir trees, waiting to spring out at me. The coast appeared clear, so I hustled to the house. I needed to talk to Bryce and clear the air. I needed to tell him what his father had said so he could tell me it wasn't true, so I could get the poison out of my veins.

Halfway across the lawn, I stopped dead in my tracks. Hazel, dressed in her full maid's uniform, was ushering someone into the house. Someone with long, dark hair and toned, athletic legs.

It was none other than Felicia Fucking Jones.

once over

IT IS A TRUTH UNIVERSALLY ACKNOWLEDGED, that an American heiress who has tossed aside her billionaire fiancé, must be in want of taking him back AND DRIVING ME FUCKING CRAZY.

What the hell was Felicia doing at the house? Why was Hazel bringing her inside? My blood started to boil as I picked up speed. It was not in my nature to want to fight, but I was going to fuck a bitch up!

Unfortunately, once I got inside, Hazel and Bitchface were long gone. I accosted Chef, who was chopping carrots in the kitchen. "Did you see where Hazel went?"

"No Mrs. Windsor, *lo siento.*"

"Thank you, Chef." I barreled back down the hall, checking the study, checking the sitting room, but they were nowhere to be found.

I ran smack-dab into Midge, nearly bowling her over.

"*There* you are!" She hugged me, pulling me against her ample chest. "I've been looking for you!"

"I've been locked up in Bryce's bedroom."

She gave me a jaunty smile and a once-over. "That's what I heard. Your complexion confirms it!"

"It's not like that. I mean, not exactly... Midge, hey." I leaned closer. "Where's Hazel? She just came in here with You-Know-Who."

Midge, ever loyal, wrinkled her nose. "What's that bitch up to now?"

"I don't know, but I need to find out where they are. C'mon." We searched the rest of the first floor, finding it empty. There was a gnawing in my stomach. Felicia Jones wouldn't be upstairs with Bryce...would she?

"Don't look like that," Midge counseled. "There's got to be an explanation—wait, there they are! On the western patio. See?" She pointed out the window, and I saw Gene, Bryce, and Felicia outside, the wind blowing their hair. Gene was standing, holding up his tablet and talking while Bryce and Felicia sat and watched.

"Let me see if they need some iced tea," Midge offered, "and I'll find out what they're up to. But I wouldn't worry about it—looks like strictly business to me." She hustled off, God bless her.

I crept toward the window, all the better to see what my wicked father-in-law was up to now. Felicia was listening to him and nodding. She looked lovely as ever in wayfarer sunglasses, a simple black sundress, and flip-flops. Her hair sparkled in the sun. She looked at Bryce and smiled, revealing her perfect, even white teeth.

Had I *ever* hated someone so much?

To his credit, Bryce didn't smile back. He stared at his father, a stormy expression on his face.

Midge appeared outside a moment later, bustling to set up a tray of iced tea with lemon. She glanced at Gene Windsor's screen, but no one noticed. In no time, she was back by my side. "It's a business meeting, hon. Mr. Windsor Senior is talking about some real estate deal, that's all. Nothing to worry about."

I shook my head as I watched them, unable to tear my gaze away. "Except that Felicia's invited to the meeting, not me." Gene was looking for any excuse to get Bryce and Felicia together again.

"That's nothing to do with you. Mr. Windsor maybe thinks she can help, is all. Or maybe *she* called the meeting? Don't get your head all messed up." She looked at me with sympathy. "I know you had a rough night. I'm sorry about what happened. That server won't ever work in this town again."

"I didn't mean to get him in trouble," I mumbled.

She sighed. "I know—Mr. Windsor's jealous of you. And that could be a problem, but it's not the problem that's bugging you right now."

I kept staring outside at Bryce and Felicia, the perfect couple.

"Chloe, listen—when a man fires two other men in the span of a week just for looking at his woman? He's invested. I'm not saying it's okay for Mr. Windsor to act like that, but the point is, he's not punching guys out over Felicia. He's doing it over *you*. He's in love with *you*. Not her."

"I'm not sure about that." And as much as it hurt—as much as I hated Felicia—I understood that she might be better for Bryce in many ways that mattered. She was educated, sophisticated, and had a similar background. She was on his level, while there were things about his world I could never understand. What was it Gene had told his sons? *Marry someone from our stratosphere. Everyone else will just drag you down.*

Felicia nodded at something Gene said. Then she started talking, gesturing at the tablet.

"Excuse me. Midge?" Hazel clicked in from the hall. Her gaze swept over us, then trailed to the scene outside. "You're needed in the kitchen. Mrs. Windsor, you were required to return to your room after you visited with the *other* Mrs. Windsor."

I glared at her. Here I'd thought maybe Hazel wasn't so bad when she'd given me hot chocolate and cupcakes, but she was a traitor after all. "Of course, Hazel. I'll just go back to my jail cell while my husband has a good old time with his ex. *Thanks.*"

I stormed off before she could see me cry. I was angry, but I wasn't even sure at who anymore.

I kept thinking about Bryce's second line.

I've made a terrible mistake.

There hasn't ever been anybody but you.

Had he written these words to Felicia? Was it true? They echoed around in my head, sounding more awful every time I replayed them.

I considered the situation. Why *wouldn't* he want her back? I thought about her stupid perfect body, white teeth, and shiny hair. Not to mention that she was intelligent, wealthy, and cultured. And that she'd left *him*. No matter what, it was the fact that it wasn't Bryce's choice to end the relationship that made me feel sick to my stomach.

If she hadn't left, they'd already be married. And now she was back, looking for a second chance.

But in the interim, he'd married me. To use Gene's term, it wasn't a "love match." We'd gotten married through an escort service. The truth was, Bryce had bought a bride so he could vest in his family company. Love had nothing to do with it; it was all about money and power. *I* had nothing to do with it. I was nothing but the hired help. And yet, I'd fallen in love with him, and I'd fallen hard.

I yearned to leave the island, to have some time and space to think. But I knew I wouldn't get far. I planned to confront Bryce that afternoon to tell him about his father's accusations and ask why Felicia Fucking Jones was at the house *again*.

I texted Dale to make sure that Noah was okay. He informed me that my brother was taking a sailing lesson that afternoon. At least *he* was living his best life!

I flopped down on the bed, arguing with myself, mind racing. I'd taken the job to protect my brother, to give him a better life. But I'd completely lost sight of my goal. Wrapped up in my own feelings, I'd become selfish. I only cared about Bryce and if he genuinely cared about *me*.

I wasn't being a very good sister. The fear was

winning—I was scared that what Gene Windsor told me was true. That was eclipsing everything else.

It shouldn't matter; I should stay in the marriage no matter what because that's what would protect Noah. But if Bryce was actually still in love with Felicia, if he'd really sent her those messages? I felt like I might die if I stayed near him. If it was true, I would never be able to be close to him again. It would break me.

But was it bad enough that I could ruin things for my brother?

I pondered my options as I stared at the ceiling. I re-read the text from Elena: *Is everything all right?* I didn't know what to say in response. It seemed as though my circumstances were changing from moment to moment.

Bryce loves me. Bryce's dad is a liar.

Bryce loves me not. Bryce has a second line.

What was the truth?

I heard a boat's motor and looked out the window—Felicia Fucking Jones's yacht was idling at the dock, waiting for her. As soon as I saw it, my pulse started racing. I was *so* angry at her for showing back up here and for texting Bryce.

But maybe that wasn't fair. She didn't owe me anything, did she? It would be nice if she could be a decent human being, but maybe that was too much to ask. What was her deal, anyway? I longed to confront her, to hear what she had to say for herself once and for all...

I peered out the window. She was heading down the dock.

Fuck it. I threw open the door, and the guards looked at me, surprised. "I'm going outside—you can come if you want, but please don't try to stop me."

"Yes, Mrs. Windsor." They followed as I barreled down the back staircase, the one used by the staff.

I flew past Hazel, who gripped the railing and shouted in surprise. "Where do you think you're going, Mrs. Windsor?"

"Out. Don't worry, I have my entourage." I hustled down the stairs, worried I would miss my chance, and then rushed outside.

The wind whipped my hair as I ran down the dock. Felicia Jones was already seated on her boat, facing the sun. She pulled her sunglasses down and watched as I approached. It occurred to me—too late—that I wasn't looking my best. Not only had I sprinted down the stairs, but I hadn't bothered to put on any makeup, and my hair was wild from being with Bryce earlier. I was a mess, inside and out. But...like I said, *fuck it.*

I was out of breath by the time I reached the boat. "Felicia?"

Did I imagine it, or did the bitch look smug? "Can I help you?"

"Yes." I climbed on board without being asked. "I'm Chloe."

She didn't say anything.

"Bryce Windsor's wife."

She pushed her sunglasses up in her head and looked me over. "I assume you know who *I* am."

She didn't say anything else; silence hung between us.

"Anyway, I'm here because I want to ask you something." My heart was pounding so hard it was making my head throb. "What's going on with you and my husband?"

She didn't miss a beat when she asked, "Why don't you ask Bryce? Wouldn't that be more appropriate?"

I took a deep breath. I'd been on her yacht for approximately three-point-five seconds, and bitch had already gotten under my skin. "It might be more appropriate, but I wanted to ask *you*. What's going on with you?"

"We're friends." She met my gaze and didn't say another word.

Felicia was, as Daphne had observed, annoyingly self-assured. And up close, she was so stunningly beautiful it made my eyes sting. It all just made me angrier. "Why won't you stop texting him?"

"Is it really any of your business? If he wants to talk to me, that's between us."

My hands clenched into fists. "There is no *us*—he's with me! He's *my* husband."

"Then I'm not sure why you're here yelling at me." She nodded at the boat's captain. "I'm ready when you are, Jake."

She slid her sunglasses back down, dismissing me. Jake revved the motor, and I hastened off the boat, worried they'd disembark with me still on board—they were acting as though I wasn't even there, like I didn't exist.

As I scrambled onto the dock, I wondered if they were onto something.

effort

"You have to return to the room, Mrs. Windsor—"

"I know, I know." I stomped up the staff staircase. Confronting Felicia had *not* gone how I'd planned. I had hoped she would reveal something or perhaps show some remorse. Instead, she'd dismissed me as though I was the hired help, which was so close to the truth, it hurt. Because the truth fucking hurts.

I paced the bedroom, stewing. I almost texted Bryce fifty different times, but fifty different times I stopped myself. I wanted to confront him in person. I wanted to yell, to get loud, to *matter*. Felicia had made me feel as if I was nothing, no one.

A few minutes later, I burst out of the room again, and one of the guards swore. "You're supposed to stay put, Mrs. Windsor."

"I'm just going to see my brother for a minute. You can follow me." They were going to follow me anyway, so I might as well pretend I had some semblance of control.

Noah was sprawled on his bed playing a video game. "I thought you'd moved to Siberia," he said, not looking up from his screen. "Or were you sick? I didn't pay attention to what Hazel said."

"Nice." I flopped down next to him. "Glad you're so worried about me."

"I've been busy." He took a cheese curl from a nearby bowl and stuffed it into his mouth. "I had sailing lessons, and then I walked the puppy. Now I'm in a tournament. Ugh, stop distracting me, this dude's trying to blow up my build!"

He started yelling at the screen and furiously working his controller. I watched his character rebuild whatever the heck was so important. I grabbed the bowl of cheese curls and listlessly stuffed one into my own mouth. "How was the sailing lesson?"

"Boring." Noah didn't take his eyes from the screen. "The dude taught me how to tie a knot. *Not* exactly exciting—get it?"

"Ha ha." I ate another cheese puff.

"So what's your problem? Why're you down here eating all my snacks?"

I shrugged. "I'm just checking on you. I haven't talked to you in a while."

"It's because you're busy being fancy," Noah said.

I nudged him. "You're the fancy one. Sailing lessons, puppies and cheese curls."

"Ugh, this freaking NPC is *so* annoying!" Noah blasted a character that looked like a huge goldfish with human legs.

"Don't say 'freaking.' And what's an NPC?"

"A Non-Player Character." Noah scoffed. "You seriously don't know anything, do you?"

"What's a Non-Player Character?" I ate more of his food just to annoy him.

"It's a dude that doesn't matter in your video game —he's just there to *exist*. He doesn't mean anything, he just takes up space. You get it?"

"Yeah." I thought of how Felicia Jones had looked at me, as though I was nothing more than a nuisance. "I get it."

We spent another hour together, the sun climbing higher in the sky. Finally, Noah tossed down his controller. "Crap, I gotta go meet Dale—we're having a dart rematch."

"Don't say 'crap.' And doesn't he do any work besides hang out with you?"

Noah shrugged and took the last cheese puff. "He

said Bryce has been preoccupied with you, so he's free to whup me at darts. And lose to me in Fortnite. We've also been eating a lot of ice cream."

"Sounds good. Noah..." I hesitated. "Are you okay—like, really okay?"

He looked at me as if I had three heads. "We live in a mansion on the beach. All I do is fish, play with puppies and eat ice cream. Are you kidding?"

"No, I just..."

He frowned at me. "What's the matter? Did you and Bryce have another fight?"

I shrugged. "Not exactly. I guess I feel like I don't fit in here, you know?" *Like maybe I'm an NPC, caught in someone else's game.*

"Well, you should probably talk to him about it. *Duh.* I gotta go." Noah practically skipped from the room.

"Right Noah. *Duh.*" Even my brother seemed to have a better handle on things than I did. I tried to play stupid Fortnite, but I couldn't figure out how to make the character move, and I just kept walking into a tree trunk. Whatever. I threw down the controller, then noticed a note on Noah's bed.

I didn't forget about night fishing. Want to go Thursday? The weather looks good.

- Bryce

I sighed. It was nice that he'd followed up with Noah; it meant a lot to me. I wished it didn't. I didn't want to have feelings for my for-hire husband. His world wasn't my world. His ex-fiancé sucked, as did his alcoholic, manipulative father. Gene Windsor almost made my father look good, a nearly impossible feat.

But Noah was happy. My brother was thriving on the island.

I sent another quick text to Elena and Akira.

What happens if I break my contract now?

I should at least have all the information I needed. But really, who was I kidding? I knew the truth: I might not want to stay, but I sure as hell didn't want to leave. I didn't want to leave *him*. In a short period of time, Bryce had become my whole world.

I headed listlessly back to his room. It wasn't fun without him in there. I texted Daphne to make sure she was okay—she responded immediately, saying that Mike Jones had agreed to all of her demands, provided she proved paternity. She included a smiley-face emoji. When I asked about Gene, she sent back a shrugging emoji. Then she said she had to get to a hair appointment.

Daphne was something, all right. I could at least get some cold comfort from the fact that Felicia Jones would have to deal with Daphne's crazy ass for the rest of her life. So there!

There were no messages from Bryce, and the big bed seemed cold without him, but I climbed in anyway. I wasn't allowed to go anywhere, and there wasn't anything I wanted to do except talk to my husband. There was nothing to do but wait for him. I was still sore from our lovemaking; I was exhausted from thinking about what Gene had said, not to mention being dissed by Felicia Fucking Jones once again.

There was only one way to escape. I pulled the covers up to my chin and promptly fell asleep.

When I woke up, the light had changed in the room. I rolled over, then yelped, "Oh!"

Bryce was sprawled out next to me, his face in a book. He peered up over the cover. "Hi there."

I gaped at him. "You're reading *Twilight*?"

He waggled his eyebrows. "You were right. She's an excellent writer. Edward's kind of a stiff, though."

I laughed. "Takes one to know one."

"True," he said, "true." Bryce put the book down. "My men said you had a busy day. Daphne, my father, spying on my meeting, hopping onto Felicia's boat, visiting your brother..."

I pulled the covers up to my chin again. "It's been a day, all right."

Bryce slid down next to me. "Why don't you tell me about it, huh?" He pulled me onto his chest and into our favorite position, me curled up against his side.

"Did you already hear about Daphne?" I asked. Crazy though she was, I didn't want to betray her confidence.

He yawned. "Father said they're getting a divorce. Something about Mike Jones?"

"That's what I heard. Is your father upset?"

"No. The only woman I've ever seen him upset about was my mother, and that was because she died on him."

I pressed my face into his chest. "I'm sorry."

"It was a long time ago." Bryce shrugged, making his big muscles move. "But thank you. What did my father want? My men said he intercepted you on the way to see Daphne. I figured I'd ask you instead of him. Much more pleasant."

"Can you tell me what your meeting was about, first? Why... Why was Felicia here?" Ew, I even hated saying her name.

Bryce sighed. "Gene's trying to involve her in one of

our deals. She doesn't know about her father and Daphne yet—I think he's trying to shore up the family relationship before all hell breaks loose."

"And he's also trying to get you two back together," I added.

Bryce sighed again. "He's always viewed their family as an asset. It's not personal, Chloe. Nothing's personal with him—you have to have an actual soul in order to make it personal."

"But he wants you to be with her, not me."

Bryce pulled me closer. "So?"

"He told me that you've been talking to her. More than what I already know about." My head started to pound.

A heavy silence descended. Bryce broke it by cursing. "He's a liar. And an asshole."

"Is he lying, though? He said you had a second phone for work. He said Felicia sent him screenshots—stuff you wrote to her while we were on vacation." The words tumbled out in a rush, and then I held my breath, praying it wasn't true.

"I didn't say *anything* to her. I already told you—I asked her why she was texting and why she was back. That's all." Bryce loosened his grip on me a little.

"That's not what your father said."

He stared up at the ceiling, the muscle in his jaw bulging. "Why would you believe him over me?"

"I didn't. But...think about it. You and Felicia have a history. You told me that she was the one who ended the relationship, not you. And honestly, you and I didn't exactly get together under...normal...circumstances." I swallowed hard. "It was a business deal, remember? So why wouldn't I doubt that you were completely over her? It's not like you owed me anything."

"Except the truth." Bryce shifted away from me. "Jesus, Chloe. I'd thought we'd progressed a little bit from how things started out."

"He told me he had proof. You have to understand how that made me feel."

Bryce scrubbed a hand across his face. "I can't believe you'd fall for his act. He's always looking for an angle with people. You can't let him manipulate you that easily—we'll never have any peace like that."

I pulled away from him. "You don't need to get mad at me because I'm jealous, and your dad used that against me. You have seen your ex, right? *And* she's rich—her family is like your family. She's from your world, and I'm not."

"There's only one world." Bryce sounded tired. "And as far as I'm concerned, what happened between her and me is ancient history. You can't let my father drive a wedge between us. I need to be able to trust that you have my back."

"And I need to be able to trust *you*." I faced him. "Do you understand that I'm the one who's vulnerable here?"

He closed his eyes. "You're not the only one with something to lose."

"It doesn't feel that way."

"Really?" He squinted at me. "Weren't you here this morning?"

"I was. But..." I blew out a deep breath. "Your father got to me. You can understand how I feel, can't you?"

"Come here." He pulled me against him and kissed the top of my head. "What else did he say?"

I hadn't decided whether to tell him about Gene's offer. Things were already so bad between them... "He said you wouldn't have to lose your stake in the company if things didn't work out between us."

He stiffened. *"What?"*

"That if things didn't work out with us, you'd still be protected. He wants you to get back together with Felicia. He doesn't think I'm good enough for you." Fuck, why was I telling him all of this? That had never been my plan, but the words tumbled out. "He said if we got an annulment, he'd give me money to leave. And that you wouldn't lose anything."

"That fucker." Bryce gripped me hard. "I have to give it to him—he's found a new low."

"I didn't want to tell you because I didn't want to make you more upset."

"I don't think I can get any more upset when it comes to him. That's a lot for you to handle, though."

"I'm fine. I haven't been around him for long, but I'm getting a sense of what he's like." Gene had tried to bully me into leaving, and he'd lied about Bryce. It wasn't a great feeling to see the lengths he'd go to in order to get me out of the picture. Still, it was better than what he'd tried to get me to believe.

"I'll deal with my father." Bryce pulled me closer again. "I'm not sure how, but I'll handle it."

"Thank you." I snuggled back against him, relieved. "I'm glad we talked about this—I was upset. I feel better."

He nodded. "And what happened with Felicia?"

I groaned. "She's like the most popular girl in my high school. She had no use for me. I asked her why she'd been texting you, and she said it would be more 'appropriate' for me to talk to you. There was no 'I'm sorry.' If I held my breath waiting for an apology, I'd be dead. She's pretty fucking smug."

Bryce laughed. "That's a good description." He

rubbed my back. "Do you forgive me for having such a dick for a father and a troll for an ex?"

"I guess so." Warmth bloomed in my chest. Bryce had done the impossible: he'd made me feel better about what his father had said and made me feel secure again in the relationship. What did I have to fear from Felicia Jones? Nothing! *She can suck it!*

That brought a big smile to my face.

"Want to kiss and make up?" I grinned at him, running my fingers down his chest.

"Absofuckinglutely, Mrs. Windsor."

proof

WE MADE LOVE AGAIN—SLOWLY. It was different between us this time, intense and passionate. *Love.* I felt the word over and over again, like I was experiencing it in its physical form. When it was over, he didn't pull out. He stayed inside me and rested his face against mine. "I love you, Chloe Windsor."

I shivered. "I love you, too." I'd never felt something so powerful.

This was not how I'd expected the day to turn out. Despite both Gene and Felicia's crap and being imprisoned and "punished" by Bryce—in other words, against all odds—it had been the best day of my life.

Bryce loved me! Had anything ever been so important, so amazing? I felt transformed, reborn into a life happier than I ever could've imagined. *He loves me.* It was a miracle.

We finally broke apart. He kissed the top of my head, snuggled me against him, and fell asleep. *I love you.* I watched his chest rise and fall. I watched his handsome face. *I love you.* Had anyone ever felt this way before?

I glanced at the copy of *Twilight* on the nightstand and bit back a laugh. *Bryce was reading my favorite book.* Wasn't that the cutest thing *ever*? After feeling so stressed and unsure, I was on cloud nine. I snuggled closer and inhaled his delicious, masculine scent. "I love you," I whispered again. I could never grow tired of saying it, of feeling this way.

He squeezed me against his chest in his sleep. OMG, this was heaven.

I couldn't fall back asleep. Instead, I enjoyed experiencing the rise and fall of his chest with my face pressed against it. I almost felt like I might die from happiness. When had lying in bed ever been this much fun? It was the biggest event of my life. I'd pay every cent from my contract for a front-row seat like this...

I heard a *ping* from the dresser. I slipped out of bed and checked my phone, but there were no messages. I heard another *ping* and located the source of the noise —it was coming from the top right drawer.

I glanced back at Bryce; he was in a deep sleep. My

eyes tracked to his nightstand. His phone was on it, sitting next to the book.

Ping!

Curiosity had killed the cat, but Gene's toxic words sprang back into my mind: *he has a second line.*

It was probably nothing. Gene was full of shit, Bryce had said so himself.

Ping!

Almost against my will, I slid the drawer open. On top of some crisply folded white tees was a phone. Its screen was lit up with multiple notifications. I peered down at it.

Felicia Jones

47 Messages

Um...

I grabbed the phone and padded to the bathroom, first checking that Bryce was still asleep. With shaking hands, I locked the door behind me. I tried to use the touch identification, but the phone wouldn't unlock. *Crap!* I hadn't scanned Bryce's face. It was still early; I wasn't sure if he was in a deep enough sleep to risk it. I would never guess the passcode, so what was I going to do?

I stared at the phone. Frustrated, I swiped at the notification.

The lock screen automatically opened, bringing me

straight into the messages app. I was faced with forty-seven messages from Felicia Jones, starting with a text from exactly one minute ago.

When are you going to tell her about us?

I almost feel sorry for her. She's emotionally invested, for Christ's sake! Her voice was shaking.

I'm so glad we're working on this project together. It's the perfect excuse to see each other more!

And then, from earlier in the day:

Yesterday was amazing. It's almost better because we're sneaking around!

That text contained emojis of an eggplant and a peach. I wasn't one-hundred percent sure, but I thought those somehow represented sex.

I ran over to the sink and vomited.

Then I scrolled some more.

Hours later, there was a knock on the door. "Chloe? Are you okay?"

I was sitting on the floor, knees curled against my chest. "I'm not feeling well. I'm going to take a shower, okay?"

"Do you need anything?" Bryce sounded concerned. He should.

"No," I lied. I actually needed a lot of things. A do-over of my life would be a great place to start.

"Okay—let me know if you do." I heard him climb back into bed.

I turned on the shower but didn't get in yet. Instead, I tortured myself with another look at one of the messages. One of the ones from Bryce.

I know we can't be together now, but I'm doing my best. Don't give up on me.

But that wasn't even my favorite. My *favorite* was the one Gene had quoted: *There hasn't ever been anybody but you.*

Bryce had sent that to her. He had actually fucking sent that to her.

For her part, Felicia didn't hold back much. There were lots of pictures, most of her making kissing faces and looking like the fucking bitchface husband-stealing lying cheater douche that she was.

I hadn't let myself cry. I didn't want the evidence of how I was feeling written all over my face. I climbed into the shower and roughly washed my hair. Everything Gene had said was true. Bryce *did* have a secret phone. He *had* been texting with Felicia. He did want her back—of course, he did. I was just the nuisance from East Boston, the child bride who had gotten in the way of true love.

I clutched my stomach as the hot water ran over me. I felt sick, fueled by throbbing jealousy and also, rage. Why had he told me he loved me? Why had he taken my virginity? Why had he acted as though I meant something to him?

Bryce had everything. But was there something inside of him that made it necessary to toy with someone like me, who had nothing?

When I first met him, I thought he was awful. That had been closer to the truth than anything I'd thought about him since.

A plan formed in my mind. I would put the phone back, climb into bed and pretend that everything was alright. Since Bryce had just literally lied to my face, confronting him with the messages would do nothing.

But in the morning, when Bryce went to work, I

would pay a visit to Gene. I would take whatever money he offered and get the hell off this rock.

I dried my hair, brushed my teeth, and climbed back into bed. Bryce was snoring, deep asleep, which was fine with me.

I would never speak to him again.

I looked at the clock: it was after midnight. Had I really thought yesterday was the best day of my life?

I huddled under the covers, wrapping my arms around myself. *You were wrong, Chlo. Today's the best day. Today is the first day of the rest of your life.*

As my husband slept soundly next to me, I vowed to spend it alone.

die in a hole

I HAD plans to sneak out early, but Bryce was already gone when I woke up at five a.m.

I looked around the room—no note.

His phone was missing, as was his second phone. I'd left it on the bathroom floor...he must have grabbed it. *Fuck!*

My phone was also gone. What the hell had he done?

I threw on some leggings and one of his hoodies. I caught his scent, and it made my heart twist. *Easy, girl.* A cheating, lying husband was not worthy of a heart twist. Bryce *sucked.* Felicia *sucked.* Why did people cheat? If they wanted to be together, why couldn't they just be honest? I knew Bryce didn't want to lose his stake in the company, but a conversation with his father would have straightened the entire thing out. No, they were being selfish. They had chosen to blow up my life instead of dealing with their feelings. Bryce had let me fall hard for him. He had a safety net with Felicia, someone to run to. I had nothing.

As far as I was concerned, they could both go die in a hole.

I marched out of the room and groaned when I saw the same three guards outside. "Don't you ever sleep?"

The lead guard blinked at me. "Mr. Windsor said you needed to stay in your room."

"Mr. Windsor can bite me." I straightened my shoulders and headed down the hallway. What were they going to do, use a stun gun on me?

I glanced back over my shoulder just in case. The men were merely following me, grim expressions on their faces. Fine by me!

I decided to wait to tell Noah to get up and start packing. He would be upset, and I didn't blame him one bit. I just hoped Gene would give me enough money to rent an apartment somewhere today. Thinking about it made my head swim. Where would we go? Should I keep Noah in Maine and stay off my father's radar? Did they even *have* apartments in Maine—or just mega-mansions?

I could ask Midge about all that. She was human, normal. She might be able to help me figure it out.

I flew down the staircase and realized I should be prepared to run into Bryce. I turned to the lead guard. "Do you know where Mr. Windsor is?"

"He was going to his father's house."

"Thank you." Gene was literally the last person I wanted to see—he would probably be gloating. But he said he'd pay me to walk away. And since Bryce knew I'd read the secret messages, I needed to deal with the whole thing now. I would face them both.

Game over. This NPC was about to leave the building once and for all.

I hustled across the lawn, the dewy grass soaking my feet in my flip-flops. I had no interest in admitting it, but it was already a gorgeous morning. The sun poked above the horizon. The ocean breeze blew the hair back from my face and stirred the pine trees on the edge of the lush lawn. Gene Windsor's glorious estate came into view, millions of dollars' worth of grey stone.

I hated all of it. Gene Windsor, his house and his green, green lawn could go die in a hole, too.

I'd almost made it to the steps when Bryce stormed out of the house. His face was red, expression thunderous. Gene came and stood in the doorway, wearing his robe open over a white T-shirt and striped pajama bottoms. Unlike his son, he looked happy—surely a bad sign.

"Chloe." Bryce started to walk straight past me.

"Where are you going?"

He wouldn't look at me. "Away from all the people I can't trust."

"What? You're saying that to *me*?"

"Don't. Just—don't." He hurtled away from us.

"Let him go, Chloe." Gene Windsor sounded borderline gleeful. "It'll be better for everyone."

Bryce whirled on him. "Not another word, Old Man!" he snarled. "You've done enough. Stay away from her—and stay the hell away from me, too."

He turned and finally faced me, eyes blazing. "You should get back to the house."

"What's going on?"

But he didn't answer. He just started walking away again.

"Come in, Chloe. I'd love to chat with you." Gene Windsor sounded like a wicked witch, trying to cast a spell on me.

I looked at him, torn. I wanted his money; I wanted to leave.

But I wanted to yell at my husband more.

"Bryce, wait!" I had to hustle to catch up to him. I wanted to ask about my phone, I wanted to yell at him about the text messages, but I was too out of breath to do anything but try and keep up. Bryce didn't look at me. He kept his hands clenched by his sides and stared straight ahead.

When we finally got to the house, he stormed into the kitchen. Chef practically jumped out of his skin.

"Coffee," Bryce said gruffly. "Please."

Chef nodded and pulled out two enormous mugs. Without a word, he poured a black coffee for Bryce and one with cream for me.

Chef didn't need to go die in a hole. Just everyone else.

Bryce grabbed his coffee; I grabbed mine. It occurred to me then that I had no idea what I was doing. "We need to talk," I mumbled.

He snorted. "It's a little late for that."

"You have the nerve to say that to *me*?"

He glanced at the guards and Chef, then shook his head. "Not here."

I followed him back upstairs to his bedroom, chugging my coffee. I needed the caffeine, needed to stay sharp. I eyed the bed, which had somehow been magically made in the ten minutes I'd been gone. Fine by me. I didn't want to see evidence of the rumpled sheets where only hours before, he'd held me in his arms and told me he loved me.

Liar. Motherfucking liar.

Bryce locked the door behind us. I didn't bother asking why—if I wanted to leave, which I definitely would, I'd simply unlock it. The guards hadn't tackled me yet. I'd be okay.

"Do you have my phone?" The question came out sounding angry, which made me happy.

"Did you have mine?" The muscle in his jaw bulged, never a good sign.

"I had both of them, actually." I raised my chin. "Your second phone was the one with the more interesting information, though."

Bryce grunted. "Yours was interesting, too."

"What do you mean?"

He pulled it out of his pocket and held it up. "I saw the message from your lawyer. You didn't need to reach out to her, though. I could've told you that if you break the contract now, you will get nothing except travel expenses."

"What?" I shook my head. I'd totally forgotten I'd messaged Elena and Akira. "That wasn't what you think—"

"Wasn't it?" His face had gone from red to ashen. "It seemed pretty straightforward to me."

He held up my phone to his face. "You said: 'What do I get if I break the contract now?' And Attorney

Zhang responded: 'Nothing.' There's not exactly a lot of room for interpretation, Chloe."

"I asked her that because I was worried what your father had told me was true—and I was right!" My voice was hoarse, dangerously close to tears. "You lied to me, Bryce!"

"*You* lied to *me*." Bryce tossed my phone onto the bed. "You said you loved me—you said you meant it. Instead, you went behind my back. You were planning to leave."

"I wasn't then, but I am now." How *dare* he act hurt? "I saw what you wrote to her! And you had *sex* with her? How could you do that to me?"

"Are you out of your mind?" He looked at me as if I'd slapped him. "If you think I would ever do that to you, this whole thing between us is a joke."

"I *read* the messages—"

"They're fake." He pulled out the phone I'd found in the drawer and held it up. "This was Gene's handi-work. He knew how to manipulate you, and you fell for it."

"How did he have fake messages? That's crazy!"

Bryce shook his head. "It's not crazy. This isn't my phone. I don't know if those texts were actually from Felicia—they might be. But my father did the rest of it, and then he had someone put the phone where you'd find it. Pretty simple. Everything's pretty simple when you have an endless supply of money."

"And if I go ask Gene about it? Or Felicia? What will they say?"

Bryce shrugged. "He'll probably say that I'm lying. And I have no idea what she would say, and I don't care. Because it's not the point. What matters is that you don't trust me."

I threw up my hands. "Why would I trust you when I read all those messages? Why would I doubt what I saw? Seeing is believing!"

"Just like I don't doubt what I saw. You want out of your contract. You were trying to find out what you would get. That's the truth, isn't it?"

"No it's not, and it's the same thing! That isn't fair." I was near tears again. "I asked about my contract before I talked to you—when I was preparing for the worst. If you said you were still involved with Felicia, I wanted to be prepared."

"But even after you *did* talk to me, and I assured you nothing was going on, you fell for *this*." He held up the phone. "You don't trust me, Chloe. You're looking for a reason to leave."

"I wasn't looking for anything! I thought I'd had the best day of my life when I heard the stupid phone beep! And when I saw there were forty-seven fucking messages from your ex-girlfriend, you better believe I read them!"

"Why didn't you just ask me about it, huh? Instead of locking yourself in the bathroom all night?"

"Why didn't you just ask me about the stupid text from Akira?"

We faced each other, both of us breathing hard.

"Because I've been burned before, Chloe." Bryce's eyes were dark. "And it's never going to happen again."

"I wasn't burning you—I was trying to protect myself. And it's not fair of you to punish me for thinking those texts were real. Who wouldn't?"

"Someone who trusts me." Bryce raked a hand through his hair, making the thick waves spike. "And that's the only type of person I can have in my life."

deep

"WHAT ARE YOU SAYING?" Once again, Bryce was giving me emotional whiplash.

His eyes were dark. "I'm saying I can't be in a relationship with someone who believes the worst about me."

"You did the same thing to me!" I cried.

"It's not the same." Bryce shook his head. "You *did* ask about getting out of your contract. You asked about leaving me, Chloe. I *never* sent those messages to Felicia, and I sure as hell never cheated on you. If you knew me at all, you'd know I wouldn't ever do that."

I sank down onto the bed. "You're not being fair. I want to trust you, and when you told me nothing was going on, I believed it. But those messages were awful. Anyone would react the way that I did."

"Maybe that's true." Bryce looked thoughtful. "In fact, I think you're probably right."

When he didn't say more, I asked, "So? What does that mean?"

He sighed. "I don't know. I just know I don't want to talk anymore."

I curled up onto the bed, wrapping my arms around myself. "You really didn't write those messages? When I saw the one where she insinuated you'd had sex, I felt so sick..." I shivered.

"I really didn't write those messages." He sounded sad. "I would never do that to someone I loved."

I peered up at him. Did he say *loved*—as in the past tense—on purpose? "Can you come here?"

"No."

"Please?" Oh my God, I was about to start begging. Hadn't I just been ready to pack my bags and leave? "Please, Bryce?" Who the fuck was I?

He reluctantly sat down on the edge of the bed, and I reached for him. "Please come here, please forgive me..." I started to babble, and then I began to cry.

"Jesus, don't." He finally gave in and wrapped his arms around me, pulling me onto his lap.

"I'm sorry I didn't believe you, I'm sorry I didn't ask

you first..." I clung to him, crying and needy as fuck. I felt desperate. I pressed my face against his chest, linking my arms around his neck, clinging to him. Before I knew it, I was kissing him, begging him with my mouth, shamelessly pressing my tits against his broad chest, doing anything and everything in my power to get him to respond.

"What are you doing?"

In answer, I kissed him, needy and searching. My tongue found his, and he groaned. Bryce stiffened beneath me, growing hard, giving in. His hands roamed my back—and did I imagine it, or were his kisses desperate, too?

We clung to each other, grinding, our tongues lashing in urgency. He pulled the sweatshirt over my head, I took off his shirt, and before I knew what was happening, we were both naked and breathing hard. Still sitting up, he arranged me on his lap, his erection rubbing against my wet slit. We kissed again, deeply and more slowly this time, then he penetrated me.

Fuck. We rocked back and forth, me on his lap, his huge, hard length pulsing inside me. *Yes.* He was in so deep like that. We were so connected. I never wanted to be apart from him. He rocked me back and forth, his cock stroking me deep inside, touching the places only he could ever reach.

He kissed my neck, my shoulder, and I raked my hands down his muscled back. *Yes.* He rocked me again, driving deeper, and I saw stars. Bryce kissed me harder, cords standing out on his neck, and then somehow he'd maneuvered me onto my back.

He drove into me, long, deep thrusts that had us both crying out.

I circled my climax, almost afraid of its intensity. "Oh my God, oh my God..."

"Yes. Give it to me. Come for me." Bryce's ass pumped as he thrust, his heavy balls slapping against me, and that was all it took. We came at the same time, both of us crying out. Tears ran down my face as my whole world went white, then black, the depth of my orgasm overtaking me. I felt Bryce's big body shudder as he emptied himself inside me, making us one, joining us in a way that could never be undone.

His breathing was ragged as he collapsed on top of me, careful not to crush me with his weight. He kissed my cheek, my lips, his touch tender and worshipful. "I love you."

I gazed up at him. "I love you, too." But what I felt for him was more than that. It was beyond words. It was an invisible bond that would tie me to him forever, until death parted us.

He rolled next to me, tucked me against his side, and

we both fell asleep. When I woke up an hour later, Bryce was dressed and sitting on the edge of the bed. His face was in his hands.

I sat up, panicked. "What's the matter?"

He turned to me. His eyes were hollowed out, his mouth set in a grim line.

"Bryce? What's the matter?"

He straightened his shoulders. "I thought about it while you slept."

My stomach plummeted. "Thought about what?"

"I understand why you responded that way to those texts, but I'm afraid I can't risk exposure like that," he said. He sounded businesslike—Billionaire Bryce Windsor, discussing a deal gone wrong. "Don't you remember what I said? I need absolute loyalty to feel safe."

"But that doesn't mean *blind* loyalty! I wasn't wrong to react that way—"

"Of course not." Bryce's voice was smooth, cold. Removed. "Anyone would. And like I said, that's exactly the problem. I made a mistake—I see it now. Marriage was a bad idea. Having a wife makes me vulnerable, and I don't do vulnerable. I'm so sorry, Chloe."

"Sorry about what?" I felt like I was going to be sick.

He rose to go, to leave. To leave *me*. "You're fired. I'll see that you receive something for all the trouble."

Before I could say a word—before I could beg or plead—Bryce was gone.

Leaving me with...nothing.

Note from the Author:

OMG, I know, *I know!* Book two, **THE FOREVER PROMISE**, is available here:

www.amazon.com

Love you guys!

xoxo

Leigh

also by leigh james

Silicon Valley Billionaires

Book 1

Book 2

Book 3

The Liberty Series

about the author

Sign up for Leigh's new release notifications at http://www.leighjamesauthor.com/subscribe!

USA Today and Amazon Top-Ten Bestselling Author Leigh James is currently sitting on a white-sand beach, listening to the waves crash, dreaming up her next billionaire.

Get ready ladies! He's going to be a hot one!

Just kidding! Leigh is actually freezing her butt off in Maine, where she lives with her awesome husband and their beautiful kids.

But she promises that billionaire is really going to be something!

Leigh's books have been translated into German, French, Portuguese, and Italian.

She also writes Young Adult Paranormal Romance as Leigh Walker. Her smash-hit series *Vampire Royals* was previously optioned by Netflix.

She loves to hear from readers! You can reach her at leigh@leighjamesauthor.com.

Lots of love to all of you!

www.leighjamesauthor.com

Made in the USA
Las Vegas, NV
15 September 2024

95297667R00277